"YOU'RE MY SLAVE.
IF I WANT YOU,
I'LL TAKE YOU . . .

Zarabeth saw that he meant it. She scrambled back against the side of the ship. "Please. It isn't right, it isn't—"

"It's what I want!" Magnus insisted. "I've paid dearly for you, Zarabeth."

She was shaking her head wildly. "No. I won't be your whore."

"You're a slave and that is less than a whore, but I'll make do with you. How many men have you had before me?"

Zarabeth stared at him with disbelief. Magnus' eyes were as cold as the North Sea in winter. Could this be the same man who had professed to care for her, the man who had wanted to wed her, the man who had held her so close and kissed her so tenderly? Was the man who had offered to fill the hungers of her heart with love, well and truly gone . . . ?

SEASON OF THE SUN

Catherine Coulter

AN ONYX BOOK

SIGNET
Published by New American Library, a division of
Penguin Putnam Inc., 375 Hudson Street,
New York, New York 10014, U.S.A.
Penguin Books Ltd, 27 Wrights Lane,
London W8 5TZ, England
Penguin Books Australia Ltd, Ringwood,
Victoria, Australia
Penguin Books Canada Ltd, 10 Alcorn Avenue,
Toronto, Ontario, Canada M4V 3B2
Penguin Books (N.Z.) Ltd, 182–190 Wairau Road,
Auckland 10, New Zealand

Penguin Books Ltd, Registered Offices:
Harmondsworth, Middlesex, England

Published by Signet, an imprint of New American Library,
a division of Penguin Putnam Inc. Fourteen previous Onyx printings.

First Signet Printing, April 1999

20   19   18   17   16

To Elizabeth Steffens Youmans

The niece with the beautiful smile,
the dancing knees,
and love of robots

1

York, Capital of the Danelaw

Her name was Zarabeth. She was the stepdaughter of the Dane Olav the Vain, a rich fur merchant of Jorvik, or York, as the local Anglo-Saxons called it. She wasn't the most beautiful woman he'd ever seen. His slave, Cyra, was more enticing, more magnificently endowed, than this woman. Unlike most men and women from his homeland, indeed, unlike many people here in the Danelaw, she didn't have hair so blond it was almost white in the noonday sun. No, her hair was blazing red, a stark vivid red, a red dark as blood when there was no sun to lighten it. She wore it tumbling down her back in loose waves and curls or, when the day grew hot, in two thick braids wound together atop her head. That hair, he thought, had to be the result of a mother from that western island called Ireland. He'd visited the garrison in Dublin several years earlier to buy slaves and trade sea ivory, furs, antlers, and soapstone bowls and ornaments. He'd been told that the Irish bred like dogs, and this bold, rich coloring was many times the result. Her eyes were also an odd color, a strange green, a hue he hadn't noticed in Ireland, a green that reminded him of wet moss. He had but to look at himself in a polished silver plate to know that his eyes, like those of most of his countrymen, were a sky blue when his mood was even, a blue as deep as the Oslo Fjord when he was angry. His mother, Helgi, had told him, much to his embarrassment, that the blue of his eyes was soft and warm as a robin's egg.

Zarabeth was tall, perhaps too tall for a woman, but he was a big man and he still had half a foot above the top of her head, so he didn't care a bit. His first wife, Dalla, had been small, the top of her head reaching only his shoulder, and he'd felt many times holding her that she was a child, not a woman, not a wife.

He had managed to come close to Zarabeth for a few moments, and had seen that her flesh was white and unblemished as a patch of fresh mountain snow, save for those two dimples that deepened in her cheeks when she smiled, a smile that drew him the moment he saw it. Aye, he thought, not at all dissuaded, she wasn't from his Viking stock, and he didn't care a bit.

No, she wasn't the most beautiful woman he'd ever seen, but he wanted her more than he'd ever before wanted a woman. He thought of bedding her, of coming deep into her woman's body and coming to his release, but he also thought of talking to her and sharing his dreams and plans with her. He thought of sailing with her to Hedeby, that southern trading port that lay on an inlet of the river Schlei and gave directly onto the Baltic. And beyond Hedeby, through the small islands, lay the rough bottom toe of Sweden, but two days' sailing away. He thought of sailing through the Great Sound that opened south into the Baltic Sea, and turning inland into the penetrating River Dvina that led to the Upper Dnieper and Kiev. Perhaps he could even take her beyond Kiev to that golden city on the Black Sea known to the Vikings as Miklagard, and to the others as Constantinople. And then, just as suddenly, with just as much clarity, he thought of children with her, of girls with bright red hair and boys with his own thick blond hair. Odd, but he envisioned a boy with eyes as green as wet moss.

He, Magnus Haraldsson, was a twenty-five-year-old karl, the second son of Earl Harald. He held a farm-stead called Malek, passed on to him by his grandfa-ther. The soil was rich, unlike much of the craggy unarable land in southern Norway, and yielded good crops of barley, wheat, and rye. Magnus was also a trader, occasionally a sharp-witted one, his father told him fondly, and he owned his own vessel, the *Sea Wind*. He also owned a dozen slaves as of his last trip, and many jarls now worked for him in return for small parcels of land to raise food for their families. Many of these jarls were his friends, and they not only sailed with him to trading centers but brought their goods to sell as well.

Magnus had been married at the age of seventeen, a marriage arranged by his parents, and he had a son, Egill, who was now nearly eight years old. His wife, Dalla, scarcely more than a child herself, had died two years after the boy's birth. He had mourned her as he might have a lost playmate, and over the years, as he had grown older and taken his pleasure with many different women, decided that he had no need of another wife or of more children. He had come to look upon married men as weak-willed and hearth-bound, even if they were off raiding four months of the year. Now, suddenly, he was beginning to think quite differently. He realized that he was no longer interested in his current mistress, Cyra, though she was even-tempered, at least around him, and could make his body clench with pleasure.

He told himself as he looked at Zarabeth that he had a son who now needed a mother. He was honest enough to admit to himself that considerations for Egill didn't come first in his mind.

Oh, aye, he wanted her and he would have her.

Magnus raised his eyes to her face when he heard her sudden burst of laughter. Sweet and deep, her laugh, and free. He saw the smile, the dimples, the white teeth, and was charmed. Her breasts moved with her laughter. It warmed him, that laugh of hers; it made him hard as a stone, that movement of her breasts; it made him want to haul her over his shoulder and take her deep into the woods and mount her beneath the drooping branches of the thick fir trees.

Since her stepfather, Olav the Vain, was rich, Magnus knew her brideprice would doubtless be high, higher than most men could afford to pay. But he'd pay it, even though he despised Olav the Vain, known to many Viking traders as Olav the Cheat. He made grandiose gestures, dazzling those around him with sudden bursts of generosity, then turned about with no rhyme or reason to cheat those same people on small things. He was difficult, his behavior annoying; he was arrogant yet petty, wide-armed yet mean. Magnus wondered how he treated his stepdaughter.

First, Magnus thought, he had to meet this girl named Zarabeth, a name that was difficult for him to say aloud, a name that was foreign-sounding and exciting and mysterious too, just as she was. He had acted unlike himself since he had first seen her two days before, hanging back, watching her like an infatuated wolf cub, not taking control as was his wont. It surprised and angered him, this sudden fear, this sudden lack of confidence. After all, she was but a woman and would respond to a man's authority, accept a man's commands to keep her on the right path, but he hadn't yet put himself in the middle of that path. The myriad feelings she evoked in him were unnerving. But there was something about her that aroused protectiveness in him, that called forth tenderness. Then, just as quickly, he would see a gleam in her green eyes that made him want to smile, for she was thinking wicked thoughts and he wanted to know what they were. He also knew, deep down, that those thoughts of hers would please him and make him laugh. She confounded him and he was pleased.

And he would tell himself again that she was but a woman and his will would prevail and she would soon belong to him. Her laughter would be only for him. That free movement of her breasts would fill only him with lust. He was Magnus Haraldsson, master of his own farmstead, a trader, owner of a sound trading vessel and twelve slaves. He pictured her at his farmstead, in charge of his household. She would find Malek beautiful, the Gravak Valley beyond compare. She would not feel isolated, for his parents and older brother were nearby and they were only a day's sail from Kaupang, a trading town on the western coast of Norway, just inland from the Oslo Fjord.

He saw that she was leaving and he quickly straightened from the door frame where he'd been standing. He saw her take the hand of a small girl who had been standing silently beside her, lean over to speak quietly to her, using strange hand gestures as she spoke. She straightened, said smiling good-byes to the people she'd been speaking with, and left the local square that held the town well. He watched her walk gracefully about mud puddles and piles of refuse, swat away insects that buzzed about the refuse, that glorious red hair of hers glinting like fire beneath the early-afternoon sun. She was slender, but he knew that beneath that soft wool gown of hers, her buttocks would be soft and white and firm, and his fingers tingled at the thought of kneading her flesh.

Then he frowned. She wasn't a young girl. No, she was at least eighteen years old, older than most females who were already wedded and suckling their own babes at their breasts. But not her, not Zarabeth, stepdaughter of Olav the Vain. Was her stepfather holding out for too high a brideprice for her? Why was she still unwedded? Was she a shrew? Had he completely misjudged her?

Many times a woman was allowed to refuse a suitor. Perhaps Olav the Vain had granted her this right and she simply hadn't yet seen a man she wanted for a husband.

He smiled then. She would want him; he had no doubt about it. He would see to it.

Magnus watched her stop and speak to a local jeweler in Coppergate, the Street of the Woodworkers, a man whose father and grandfather before him had fashioned beautiful arm bracelets and rings of amber from the Baltic and jet from Whitby, intricately set in the finest silver and gold. Again she took her leave, walking more quickly now, and he knew she was going to her own home, a comfortable house with walls of thick oak planking and a roof of finely layered wooden shingles slightly further down Coppergate. All the houses here in York were set close together, the alleys between them malodorous, dark, and often dangerous. Olav's house was larger than most, but still there was darkness in the narrow alleys on either side of it.

Magnus paused a moment, pulling his wolfskin cloak more securely around his shoulders. He unconsciously fingered the carved gold brooch that held the cloak together at his shoulder, a brooch he'd traded three otter skins for in Birka the previous year. It was early April, yet York held a sharp wind today and he was thankful for the wolfskin cloak. The sun, covered by gray clouds, denied its warmth. It wasn't really cold, it was just that he knew uncertainty, a feeling that made him start with surprise and feel shame, for he was, after all, not only a rich farmer and trader but the son of an earl, a leader, a karl trained to control and command.

He'd been brought to uncertainty by a woman with

a strange name, strange coloring, laughter that made him feel warm inside, and breasts that made him feel lusty as a young wolf. He flung off his fur cloak, disgusted with himself, and returned to his ship, the *Sea Wind*.

2

Magnus decided to meet her at the well that lay in the middle of Coppergate, a social place where the men lounged about in the late afternoons, gossiping and telling tall stories that had no more truth now than they'd had a hundred years before. The women drew water and sat near the men, sewing their wool cloth into jerkins and gowns and watching the children. The children played near them, their laughter heard all the way to Micklegate. It was a brief time of ease after a hard day, and a time for talk.

Magnus strode into the wide square, eyeing the small groups of men, an unconscious reaction, for in his experience just two men could attack unwary prey and dispatch that prey easily and quickly. He'd waited until he saw Zarabeth, coming now to the well to draw water in her wooden pail. She was alone; the little girl wasn't with her.

He walked to her, determination in every step, sparing not a word to any of the others, and said, even as she was lowering her pail into the well, "My name is Magnus Haraldsson. I am a farmer merchant and I and my family live near Kaupang in Norway. I am not a poor man, nor am I cruel or vicious, and I wish to wed with you."

Zarabeth dropped the bucket. She stared down in dismay into the darkness of the well, at last hearing the pail thunk into the water. She straightened and turned slowly to the man who'd startled her.

She found herself looking at his throat; then she lifted her face until she met his eyes. That in itself was a surprise, for she was used to staring men straight in the face. "I beg your pardon? You *what*?" She shook her head, wanting to laugh at what she'd thought he had said. "Nay, surely I mistook your words. Forgive me, but I thought you said that . . . But no. What did you say to me, sir?"

Magnus said again, still patient, for he was enchanted with the laughter and sweetness of her voice, "I said I want to wed with you. My name is Magnus Haraldsson. Your name is difficult for me, but I will say it now and come to say it with ease soon enough— Zarabeth."

He accented it charmingly, at least to her ear, and she smiled, despite his outlandish words and his beyond-foolish proposal, if he indeed were serious, which she strongly doubted. He didn't look like a man who'd drunk too much mead or ale. It had been a long, tiring day, and his words cheered her, serious or no. He was a handsome man, rugged and hewn from strong stock, young and tall and well-made, as blond as most other of his countrymen, his hair a thick deep blond, and his eyes were as blue as a summer sky over York, clear and unleached by shades of gray.

She tilted her head to the side, still smiling. He was brazen, this Viking. She peered down the well. "My bucket is lost. What am I to do?"

Magnus looked down at her, fascinated by how that smile of hers lit and warmed her green eyes. "I'll get your bucket for you. My name is Magnus—"

"I know," Zarabeth said. "Magnus Haraldsson, and you are a farmer and a trader and you are not cruel or vicious and you want to wed with me."

He frowned. She was forward, this woman with her foreign name and her laughing smile. She was mocking him, pretending to seriousness, and he didn't like it. "Aye," he said, his voice cool now. "I want to wed with you. Now I'll retrieve your pail for you."

She stepped back and watched whilst he strode like a conqueror to the smithies' forge just to the other side of the square. He returned almost immediately with a long wooden pole, hooked on one end. He leaned over the well, and she heard the water swishing about below. She heard him speak, but it wasn't loud enough for her to make out the words. She imagined that he was cursing. He tried, she gave him that, really tried to retrieve her wooden pail, but it had sunk deeper than the pole would reach. Finally he gave it up and straightened, turning to face her.

"I could not reach it. I will replace your pail since my words made you drop it."

Zarabeth was charmed. "There is no need for you to do that. My own clumsiness caused its loss. You just startled me, 'twas your only fault." She paused a moment, smiling up at him. "You know my name, but you haven't really met me. I am Zarabeth, step-daughter of Olav the fur merchant, and—"

"And you would like to wed with me now that you've met me," he finished for her, his voice utterly matter-of-fact. "You are decisive. That is good in a woman."

"I beg your pardon?"

"It is good that you are a woman with a quick mind and decisive wits. I will speak to Olav the Vain and we will settle on a brideprice and then—"

"I won't wed with you!"

He frowned down at her. "Why not? You just said that you would."

"I said nothing of the sort. I don't know you. I have never seen you before in my life until but minutes ago. You made me lose my pail. Now, what is this all about?"

"I am a farmer merchant. I have come to York to

trade, as I do several times a year. I saw you two days ago and I've been watching you. I have decided you will do nicely as my wife. You will suit me. You will bring me pleasure and bear my children and you will warm my hearth and prepare my meals and sew my tunics."

Zarabeth, once charmed by his brazenness, was off-put by his arrogance, a commodity of which he had aplenty. She was no longer amused by him, for she realized at last that he was utterly serious. And a serious Northman, she'd heard all her life, wasn't to be trifled with. But it made no sense. It sounded as if he needed a slave, after the list he'd made of his expectations of her. She felt a tingling of alarm, for his eyes had narrowed and he no longer had the look of a man of easy nature and ready laugh. Still, she wouldn't back down, she wouldn't show her ill-ease with him.

"And that's all you have to say, Magnus Haraldsson? You believe I would suit you? You make it sound like I would be your drudge. No, no, let me finish. Too, I might be an awful creature for all you know of me, a shrew of loud and vicious tongue perhaps. As for you, perhaps you beat women? Perhaps you don't bathe and smell sour as the rotted innards of a weasel? Perhaps—"

"That is quite enough, Zarabeth." He paused a moment, as if the sound of her name surprised him. Then he grasped her upper arms in his large hands. She froze, then forced herself to relax. They were standing in the middle of the Coppergate square and there were dozens of people she knew around them, some of them even now staring toward her at this moment. She needn't worry. She smiled at him again, but it was a nervous, uncertain smile, and he recognized it.

"I don't mean to frighten you, but when I make up my mind it is done. I bathe often, as is the custom in my country, and I don't smell sour. Sniff me now if you will. I have all my teeth and I don't carry fat on my belly. Men cannot fight to their best ability if they carry fat on their bodies. I never will. I don't beat women." He paused, frowning, then shrugged. "I do have a slave, Cyra, who much enjoys a belt on her thighs and buttocks, but I give it to her sparingly, for I do not wish to spoil her."

Zarabeth could but stare at him, all else forgotten. "You have a slave who likes you to beat her? In those . . . places? That is absurd! I do not believe you. Why?"

Magnus shrugged again. "It is as I said. She is a woman of strong and ardent passions, and the pain on her buttocks adds to her pleasure when I finally take her." His eyes narrowed on her stunned face. "Why would you disbelieve me? I speak the truth, Zarabeth. You will soon learn that I don't lie."

"I don't disbelieve you, but perhaps you should temper this extreme truth of yours with judicious omission. The thought of anyone striking me in those places . . . well, it isn't at all to my liking."

"Then I won't. If you don't wish it, I shan't ever strike you, even if you eventually say you want it."

"I don't desire it," she said, fascinated anew by him despite herself. "I won't ever want that." He was looking down at her, and the look in those blue eyes of his had changed, shifting subtly, and she knew with a knowledge she hadn't realized was already within her that he was thinking of her without her clothing on. "Would you please release me now, Magnus?"

"No. I like the feel of your flesh beneath my fingers. You are warm and soft and I can smell your woman's scent."

"Then will you at least ease your hold? I am easily bruised."

He frowned at that and his fingers quickly became

gentle as sunlight on her upper arms and as warm as the middle-summer sun, though it was still early spring.

He continued to stare down at her, his look thoughtful and intent. "You will tell me what it is that gives you enjoyment. I'm accounted a man who does well with a woman. I am not selfish in the giving of pleasure. And you would be my wife. I should like to please you, to give you the delight of my body and yours. It would be your right to be pleased by me, your husband."

His words were quiet and deep and confident. She continued looking up at him, so absorbed by him that she didn't consider turning away. She said in a small, soft voice, without hesitation, "I don't know what pleases me."

His face changed with the smile that suddenly appeared, and pleasure radiated from him. "Ah, that is good. We shall learn together, then. I will try not to disappoint you." He paused then, and he looked at his long fingers that were even now lightly kneading her upper arms. "I wanted to see you closely. You are as fair as I had thought. Your flesh is very white. I've been watching you now for two days."

"My skin is very fair. More so than yours."

"Aye, 'tis because you're Irish. Am I not right?"

She nodded and he saw the pain flash in her eyes and wondered at it.

"Both your mother and father were Irish? Are they both dead, even your mother?" At her slow nod, he said, "When did she die?"

"Three years ago. Her name was Mara. Olav, my stepfather, met her in Limerick and wedded her when I was only eight years old. My father had died but a year before, and living was not easy for her, a woman alone with a child. We came here."

"The little girl I saw you with yesterday, she is Olav's child?"

Her chin went up and he was pleased at this unconscious arrogance in her, but it also puzzled him. What had he said to put her on guard? "Aye," she said finally, "Lotti is my little sister. Who her father is matters not to me."

"Then Olav is her father."

"Aye, but I love her and she is mine."

"Nay, she is your stepfather's."

Zarabeth simply shrugged and looked away from him. He guessed she wished to say more about the little girl, but his firmness had directed her away from it, and she said only, "It matters not what opinion you hold. I must go now. To find a new pail. I cannot dally."

"I will give you one." Even as she began to shake her head, he added, his voice calm and low, "From this moment forward, my every opinion will count in your life. My every act will touch you, for you will belong to me. You will heed my words and consider them your guidance. Forget it not, Zarabeth. Now, shall I accompany you to your house? To meet your stepfather? Does he ask a large brideprice?"

It was her turn to place her hand on his forearm. She'd gone from amused outrage at his presumptuousness to something like a numb acceptance that scared her to death. Was she losing her wits entirely? She didn't know this man who'd accosted her but minutes before. "Magnus, please, you move swiftly, much too swiftly. I don't know you. You must understand." She stopped, realizing she was wringing her hands. She was so startled by her action that she was silent for many moments. He too remained silent, waiting for her to finish speaking. She drew a deep breath and continued in her usual calm way, "If you wish it, I will meet you on the morrow, here, if you like. We can talk, speak of your life in Norway, of other things too. I must come to know you better. It is all I can agree to now. Can you accept that?"

"You will come to know me well when you are my wife." He saw that she would still argue with him. He looked impatient, frustrated, which he was, yet he smiled down at her then, and it was a smile of sincerity and tenderness and it made something shift inside her, something warm and wondrous strange, something unusual and unknown. "You are a woman of importance to me. I will move more slowly, though it pains me to have to do so, but hear this, Zarabeth: I will have you as my wife and that will happen very soon. I wish to return home in ten days."

"Ten days! Why, 'tis impossible! You ask me to—" She broke off, words for once in her life failing her. She waved her hands wildly around her. "This is my home, where I've spent the past ten years of my life! I know nothing of your Norway, save that all its people are fair and blond and brutal and vicious. They sail into towns in their long boats and they murder and ravish and take everything!"

"I am not vicious."

"Ah, do you not go araiding then? Do you not steal and pillage and rape and destroy?"

"From time to time. One grows bored, and there is always need for coin and for silver and gold. It is the wanderlust too that seems to be bred in all Vikings. Undiscovered places to explore, peoples you cannot imagine living in strange ways and wearing strange clothing and speaking in gibberish tongues. I will take you with me, at least when I am trading, if you would wish to go with me."

"But you are brutal."

"From time to time," he said again, and smiled. "When it is necessary. I am not a needlessly cruel man, Zarabeth. I will protect you with my life, you will see. It is what I would owe you as your husband."

"You seem to claim there is much owed to me, were I to accept you as my husband. But you command me now, when I scarce know you, and you expect me to obey you in all things. I owe you nothing, truly. You must—"

He ignored her words. He clasped her hand and turned it over in his and stared down at her palm. There were calluses on the pads of her fingers, and her hands were reddened from work. "I told you that I am not a poor man. You will have servants to see to the hardest work, and you will direct them. Aye, you will sew my tunics and see that my food is prepared properly, but your hands will be white again, for me, to soothe my temples when my thoughts are harsh, to stroke my back when my muscles are knotted, to caress me when I wish to bed you."

She stared at him, unable to look away. She'd never met his like before. This painful boldness of his. This matter-of-factness that gave no doubts as to his thoughts or intentions. And when he spoke of bedding her, of her hands touching him . . . it was unnerving, and at the same time, she felt excitement pool deep in her belly. She felt suddenly alive, every sense awakened by his words and by his look.

"I will have you, Zarabeth."

"I must speak to my stepfather," she said, desperate now because she'd never seen this man before this afternoon, desperate at what he'd made her feel in only a few moments. He was beyond anything she'd ever before known, and he was beyond her ability to grasp, beyond her ability to deal with in her normally forthright manner. She was indecisive still, she was floundering, and it was obvious to him and to her. She looked away, feeling at once ridiculous and confused. "I must speak to my stepfather," she said again.

He smiled then, for it was his triumph, his victory, and why not savor it for the moment? He had chosen her and she would come to him. He had been clear in his intentions, not mincing matters, and she'd bowed to him. He was certain of it, and quite pleased with himself. "Very well. I will be patient, Zarabeth. I will see you here on the morrow, after your Christian morning matins."

When she only stared up at him, unspeaking, he smiled, lightly touched his fingertips to her chin, and leaned down to swiftly kiss her closed mouth. Then he was gone, striding from Coppergate square as if he were its owner, as if all its minions were his to order.

She stood there silent and wondering until he disappeared from her sight. She saw several of the women coming toward her. She quickly turned and walked away. She wanted none of their sly questions. Doubtless they wanted to ask her what the wicked barbarian had wanted of her.

And he was a barbarian. She'd forgotten that, and she shouldn't have allowed herself to. And wicked, from what he had told her he did to his mistress. She was a Christian, as was Lotti. Ah, her little sister. When she wedded, Zarabeth had always known that Lotti would go with her, for Lotti was hers now and had been since Lotti's second birthday, that day when her mother had died. That day when Olav had told Zarabeth that her mother had run off with another man, taking Lotti with her, and he had caught them and her mother had died from the blow the other man had dealt her. But why would the man have wanted to hurt her mother? Hadn't he run away with her? Hadn't he loved her? Zarabeth hadn't understood, but she'd seen the rage, the boiling violence in her stepfather's eyes, and kept quiet. Her mother was dead, her hair matted and bloody against her head—blood seeping from her nose and mouth, she'd heard some women say. Aye, her mother was dead, long dead. Her beautiful mother, who had supposedly loved her but left her, taking Lotti with her and leaving her behind.

Zarabeth shook away the memories. They lay in the past, dead as summer ashes, and no reason could be made of them, for there were none alive to explain them, none save Olav. And she would never speak of the past to him. Odd that the memories were still painful and frightening. Odd how she still shied away from them.

When she allowed herself to think about her situation as it was now, she realized quite clearly that Olav believed her to have taken her mother's place. Only she wouldn't run away from him as her mother had. She belonged to him as any child belonged to its father.

And now this Viking had come into her life.

3

Olav stared at his stepdaughter as he chewed on the potato cake she'd prepared for supper to go with the broiled beef strips. It was moist and well-baked, yet oddly, it chewed dryly in his mouth, then settled badly in his stomach. He continued to stare at Zarabeth. She was serving her little sister now, that damned little freak that Olav should have thrown into the gutter that day he'd discovered what she'd become and from whose seed she had sprung.

The child was crazy and stupid, but Zarabeth refused to accept it. Aye, he should have killed her then, but he hadn't. And now he couldn't. Zarabeth loved the little idiot and he knew deep down that if he harmed the girl, Zarabeth would turn on him. She might possibly even kill him. He didn't want to be afraid of her.

He wanted to bed her.

She carried none of his blood. She was simply Irish trash, just like her mother had been, trash, but not the whore Mara had been, and he would have her in his bed, soon now. And after he was done with her, why, then he might just sell her back to the slave market in Dublin, or possibly simply take her to be his wife. Her and that little idiot, curse the fates. Perhaps he wouldn't remain in York. Perhaps, if he married her, he would take her back to Hedeby, where he'd been born and which he had left some twenty years before.

He swallowed some of the beef, realizing even as he nearly choked on it that it was quite tasty with the honey and flour coating it. He licked his fingers, pausing a moment before he said deliberately, his voice laden with suspicion, "You seem different tonight, Zarabeth. Did something happen today? Something you're not telling me?"

And because she knew Olav was, unaccountably, jealous of every young man who spoke to her, she looked immediately guilty, even as she quickly shook her head and said no.

"You met a man, didn't you?"

She knew her mistake and said calmly enough, "He is a Viking trader, from Norway, near Kaupang, he told me. He was at the well in Coppergate square. He startled me when he spoke, and that is how I lost the pail."

It sounded plausible, but Olav wasn't satisfied. A man was stupid if he trusted a woman's word. He eyed her closely and decided he couldn't let this pass. "Tell me, what is this Viking's name?"

"I do not know. He didn't tell me, merely spoke to me of the weather, and of you, of course. Aye, he spoke highly of you, for, as I said, he is a trader and interested in doing business with you."

"Perhaps he will come to the shop then," Olav said, and this bite of potato cake tasted quite good in his mouth. Still, she *was* different. It bothered him.

"Why didn't he tell you his name?"

Zarabeth shrugged. She hated this lying, yet the lies had come unbidden and immediately to her tongue. She wasn't certain why. She thought of Magnus, pictured him in her mind, tall and arrogant and sharp-eyed; then she saw that smile of his, that look in his eyes when he had stared down at her. She smiled unconsciously even as she spoke to Lotti and placed her small fingers around a strip of beef and said, "Do eat just a bit more, sweeting. That's right, just another little bite. You must grow up to be a big healthy girl."

Olav watched Zarabeth lean down and kiss the top of the girl's head. Little moron! He felt his loins tighten as his eyes dropped to Zarabeth's breasts. She'd finally grown into a woman's body. She'd been thin and flat as a board until just a year before. Then suddenly she'd become a woman and all the young men had come sniffing around her, lust wetting their lips, all of them wanting her, badly. But, thank the fates, she hadn't seemed at all interested in any of them, so Olav hadn't been forced to name a brideprice that would make their eyes bulge with chagrin and disbelief. And every day she grew to look more and more like her mother, beautiful, gentle, unfaithful Mara. He hadn't controlled Mara well, he'd been too easy with her, too tender, and look what it had gotten him. But Zarabeth, her mother's image, wasn't at all like Mara, except she shared what all women shared, a woman's lying tongue. She would obey him and she would remain faithful to him, for he would bind her firmly to him.

His own son wanted her, and that amused Olav, for Keith was well and firmly married to a girl Olav had selected for him. Keith was always coming around, presumably to see his father, but Olav knew better. He knew that young man was infatuated with Zarabeth. He wouldn't get her. Olav would kill his own son before he let him touch her. He suspected that Toki, Keith's wife, would also kill him were he to stray. He wondered if Toki knew of her husband's infatuation for his stepsister.

Olav stroked his soft golden beard, as was his habit when he was thinking deeply about a problem. There were white strands in the gold now, but not many. He wasn't an old man, not for many a year would he be that. His rod still stiffened easily and his back was still

straight. There was a bit of fat puffing out his belly,
but not enough to repel a woman. His beard was thick
and grew fully, as did the hair on his head. He was
proud of his appearance and stinted nothing in the
jewels and golden brooches he bought for himself.
He'd heard himself called Olav the Vain, and it
amused him. Why shouldn't a man of decent aspect
be a bit vain?

Olav suddenly pushed away his chair and rose.
"There are furs I must inspect before it darkens more.
If your Viking comes to see me on the morrow, I will
tell him that you spoke of him to me."

He paused a moment to see her reaction, but she
merely nodded, saying nothing, her face giving nothing away. That in itself made his suspicions boil, but
he said nothing more, merely left her to go into the
front of the house, which was his store. The way she
was able to make her face blank bothered him, for it
hid her thoughts—be they happy or sad or guilty. He
lit a bear-oil lamp and looked at the piles of beaver,
mink, and otter fur. He dropped to his haunches and
began to methodically separate them according to
their quality and their size, mentally setting a price to
each one. He was good at this, and knew it, and
blessed his long-dead father for teaching him.

In the back living area, Zarabeth went about her
chores automatically, for her thoughts strayed again
and again to the Viking. She spoke to Lotti as she
washed the wooden plates and the knives. She bathed
her little sister and tucked her firmly in soft furs on
the narrow box bed in the small chamber they both
shared.

When finally she herself was lying next to Lotti,
wrapped in a thick wool blanket, she thought again
about Magnus Haraldsson. She would see him on the
morrow, after Christian matins, he'd said. Nay, he
had ordered. She smiled into the darkness. He was

only a man like any other man, she told herself, yet
he had fascinated her. She heard her stepfather enter
the chamber next to this one, a room larger, con-
taining a feather-stuffed mattress on a wide box bed
and a large trunk that held all his clothing. The walls
were thin between the chambers. She heard him pull
off his clothes, knew that he folded them carefully,
heard him carefully remove his golden armlet and the
three rings he wore. She heard him belch, imagined
him rubbing his belly, then crawling into his bed.
Within minutes his loud snores filled both chambers.

She lay there awake for a very long time, wondering
where Magnus was and what he was thinking and
doing.

Magnus was aboard his vessel, the *Sea Wind*. He
was standing between two oar ports near the tiller,
his elbows on the guardrailing, at ease with the slight
movement beneath his feet and the gentle lapping
sound of the water against the sides. The water was
calm, for the inlet was narrow and well-protected with
thick earthen banks. He looked around at the half-
dozen other vessels docked along the lengthened
quayside on the River Ouse. Unlike the Viking war-
ships, all these vessels were used for trading, not for
lightning attacks. They were much broader, the sides
higher to provide more protection from the waves,
their plankings nailed together, not lashed to the
frames. There was a single large square sail of coarse
white wadmal sewn with bright red strips for added
strength attached to the mast and two small covered
areas aft beneath overhanging oak planks to protect
the precious cargo from storms and winds. Further
protection for cargo existed beneath the planked deck.

Magnus had had his vessel built three years before
and had plans this coming year to have another made
by the builder in Kaupang who was known for both
the quality of his work and the speed with which he

completed it. He was also known as a madman, with his black flowing beard and his bright black eyes, and Magnus quite liked him. He was insolent in a completely impersonal way that kept others from taking offense.

Magnus rubbed his hands together. He looked toward the town of York, the largest trading city in Britain and the main Viking trading post in the British Isles. Just off to his left was the old part of the town, which was nothing more than a squalid collection of wattle-and-daub huts. The richer part of the town comprised close-crammed wooden houses, including that of Olav the Vain, low sprawling factories, and a good dozen stone churches. There were also buildings constructed of thick sturdy oak, overlooking the River Ouse and its tributary river, the Fosse. There was a bridge now over the Ouse, built by the Vikings a few years before, to take the increased traffic swerving past the old Roman fort. York had changed over the years since the Vikings had seized power. Now its size had doubled to thirty thousand souls. There were Christian churches next to Viking factories. There were Viking burial grounds next to Christian ones. There were dark-haired Vikings aplenty now, for Viking men had married the Anglo-Saxon women and bred in staggering numbers. And there was peace now, for the most part, but that could change at any time. With every Viking raid into King Alfred's Wessex, there was always the chance of retaliation, even on York itself.

Life, Magnus had discovered, was rarely boring, for it was rarely predictable. Uncertainty always ran high, and Magnus relished it. He frowned then, thinking of Zarabeth, the softness of her upper arms, the smoothness of her cheeks. Uncertainty could mean danger to her, and he didn't care for that thought. But he was strong-limbed and swift-witted. He would protect her and see to her safety, regardless of what threatened, whether it be man or the elements. He didn't doubt that she would meet him in the morning. He'd seen her response to him after she'd recovered from her initial surprise. Most women responded that way to him. He was no stranger to shy, pleased smiles and softened expressions. She would come to him and she would suit him, he was sure of it.

It was early morning, and Zarabeth was at the well before Magnus. She was cold, for the April morning was chill and damp, a wind rising, heralding a coming storm. She was wrapped in a russet woolen cloak, pinned with a finely made bronze brooch over her left shoulder. Her hair, braided and wrapped around her head, was covered with a hood.

When she saw Magnus striding toward her as if he owned the square itself and her, she felt something give inside her. She hadn't dreamed her reaction to him. If anything, she hadn't remembered the sheer power of him, this natural dominance that came so naturally from him, this effortless smiling appeal. He saw her and his face changed from the intent expression of a man on a mission to one of swift approval. She was pleased he had noticed the way she looked.

Zarabeth felt strangely suspended as he approached her, slowing now, as if he wanted to look at her for a very long time before he reached her.

He didn't draw to a halt as she expected him to. He walked up to her, grasped her chin in his palm, and forced her face up. He kissed her, in full sight of anyone who wished to look.

Zarabeth had been kissed before, furtive little forays, but nothing like this. And then he said against her mouth, his breath warm and sweet from honey mead, "Open your mouth to me. I want to taste you."

She did, without hesitation. His arms went around

her and he drew her upward, his hands clasping her firmly at the waist. And he didn't stop kissing her. Deeply, then light nipping bites, followed by soothing licks, and she responded. She didn't seem to have a choice, and when she did respond, he immediately stopped and straightened. He smiled down at her, that triumphant smile that made her want to laugh and punch him in his lean belly at the same time.

"You see how good I make you feel?"

" 'Twas just a simple kiss, nothing more. Any man's mouth could make me respond thus."

He kissed her again, then several more times, each kiss more probing than the preceding one. Once again he didn't stop until she responded fully to him. His look was filled with such pleasure when he released her this time that she did nothing at all, simply stared up at him, wishing he'd kiss her again. She felt his strong hands roving up and down her back, warm hands and big, hands that would give her endless pleasure, hands that would keep her safe.

"Good morning, Zarabeth," he said at last. "You were here waiting for me. That pleases me. I like your taste and the softness of your mouth. In the future you will open your mouth to me without my having to instruct you."

She nodded, words stuck in her throat.

He leaned down and lightly kissed the tip of her nose. He was smiling. He was completely certain of her now. "Did you speak to your stepfather?"

Her foolish besottedness faded and she was once again here with a man she'd never seen in her life before yesterday. She shook her head. "He asked me if something was wrong," she said, looking toward Micklegate, the main great street of York.

"Why?"

"He thought I seemed different; he noticed I was somehow bemused, I suppose."

"Naturally," he said, and his arrogance made her smile. "Why didn't you speak to him of me?"

"I did, finally, but not about what you wanted. I wasn't really certain that it was what you really wanted. Me, that is. You could have changed your mind."

"I have told you I do not lie. I am not pleased with you, Zarabeth. I want to wed with you, and that is that. It should not have been difficult for you to tell him what you wanted and what would happen. I will go to his shop now. I have trading to do and he is as honest as most merchants here. I will deal with both my furs and you."

She grabbed his sleeve, panic filling her. "Wait, Magnus, please. You must understand something about my stepfather. He seems jealous of men who pay attention to me. I don't know why, truly, but 'tis true, and it frightens me." To her chagrin, Zarabeth actually wrung her hands. Again she was shocked at herself. However, that action, so utterly female, touched him as nothing else could have.

He smiled down at her, lightly caressing her cheek with his knuckles. "Don't worry, little one, I will take care of Olav the Vain."

"I'm not at all little."

"You are to me." He paused, looking at her, stopping at her breasts. "I want you naked, Zarabeth, and I want you beneath me. I want to kiss your breasts and fit myself between your legs. It tries me to wait to have you."

She caught her breath. She thought she had come to understand him just a bit; then he would catch her off-guard, shocking her, making her turn red with the explicitness of his words.

She turned away, looking down at the muddy rivulets that ran black near her booted feet. There was refuse everywhere, by the well, from both human and animal. She breathed in deeply. The air was filled with human and animal smells, few of them pleasant. The air itself seemed heavy with the weight of people, always people, too many people. She said suddenly, "This valley where you live, Magnus, it it clean?"

"The air is so pure you will want to suck it into the very depths of you. There are more and more people in the valley each year, for the land is fertile and they want to survive and thus seek to work for me, but there is still enough space for all of us and our boundless fields. There is not the filth of towns like York, Zarabeth."

She was silent.

"I will take you to Kiev someday. There the air is so sharp and pure and cold it hurts you to breathe. Then it rains and snows and you want to die from the endlessness of it all. You see, if you chance to sail into Kiev too late in the fall, why, then you could be forced to remain until spring. The river freezes, you know, and you are a captive for at least six months."

She looked at him then, and there was hunger in her eyes, such hunger that it startled him with its intensity, and he continued, wooing her with the magic of the places he was painting with words. "And the steppes, Zarabeth, nothing but miles and miles of thick dry grass, and then suddenly there's nothing but stretches of barren land for as far as the eye can see. No trees, no bushes, nothing, just that endless savage land. Little survives on the steppes. They are awesome in their primitive beauty. The people who live there are savage and give no quarter. But then again, you would expect none, for they are as they are because they must be to endure."

"You would truly take me to see these places?"

He nodded. "Aye, I'll take you trading with me. But when we reach Miklagard, I will have to take care to protect you, cover your hair and your face with a veil, for the men there would seek to capture you from me. The vivid red of your hair"—he touched his palm to her braids—"and the green of your eyes, aye, they would want you and they would try to take you from me."

"I remember Ireland, the vivid green of the trees and grass. It rained so much there, you see, more than it does here, and the colors were richer, almost lavish, and they blinded the eye. But there was always fighting, endless attacks by the Vikings on the Irish and by the Irish on the Vikings, and so much misery, and it never stopped. My father died in one of the attacks." She stopped, gazing again around the square. "But this is a vastly different place and I have grown to a woman here. There is much here that interests me, mistake me not, and I have many friends, but . . ." She broke off, struggling to explain, but she couldn't find the words to suit her feelings. She shrugged. "I grow foolish."

"Nay, not foolish, merely you have a Viking's longing for other places, the longing to taste the endless variety of the world. Everything I learn about you pleases me. Once you've wedded me, the life you wish will begin."

"You make it sound so very easy, so effortless. I have never found life to be so accommodating."

"It is. You must simply trust me and believe in me. Give yourself to me."

"There is something else, Magnus. There is my little sister, Lotti. She is my responsibility and I would wish her to be with me."

That gave him considerable pause. "What about her father? Olav doesn't want her?"

"Nay, he detests her."

"Very well, then, I will take two females home with me. Now, Zarabeth, I will go speak to Olav."

She looked deep within herself, was content, and said, "You're certain you wish to wed me?"

"Never doubt me, Zarabeth." He kissed her again and was gone.

4

Olav felt his breath hitch in his chest when the Viking strode into his shop. There was no mistake, this man was the one Zarabeth had spoken about. She had lied. This man was formidable, arrogant, and she desired him. He looked like a man who was used to having exactly what he wanted when he wanted it. He looked a proud bastard.

Aye, she wanted this man. She didn't want her step-father. She would leave with this man without a backward look. He felt rage fill him. Zarabeth was just like her whore of a mother, Mara, ready to leave everything important for a handsome face and glib promises. She had probably believed every lying word out of the man's mouth. Aye, she was just like Mara, that witch who'd beguiled him and seduced him into taking her for his wife. He wouldn't allow Zarabeth to leave him, not like Mara had. He drew a deep breath, schooling his features, and prayed his thoughts didn't show on his face. He recognized that this man, young as he was, was nevertheless an enemy to be reckoned with. He had no intention of underestimating him, not for a single moment. He dropped the pelt he was examining and moved forward to greet the Viking courteously. They exchanged names.

Magnus eyed Olav the Vain. A fine-looking man despite his years. He was well-garbed in fine woolen trousers and a soft blue woolen tunic. His soft leather

belt was studded with jet and amber. He wore three
silver rings on his right hand and one heavy gold ring
on his left. There were three armlets of fine silver
inset with amber on his right arm. He was certainly
better clothed than his stepdaughter, Magnus thought,
his jaw tightening. But despite Olav's adornment,
despite his display of wealth, there was a paunch at
his belly that couldn't be hidden by the wide belt,
and a distinct sagging of his jowls beneath that gray-
threaded beard of his. But to be fair, he was nearly
as tall as Magnus and looked reasonably fit for his
years. Magnus disliked him immediately and intensely.
He didn't waste time. He said without preamble, "I
have come for two reasons, Olav. The first and most
important is that I wish to wed with your stepdaughter, Zarabeth. The second is that I wish to trade with
you. I bring fine beaver and otter pelts from the Gravak Valley in Norway. Also I have sea ivory from
walrus tusks, antler, and birds' feathers for pillows,
all from the Lapps who live to the north. When we
reach agreement, I wish to be paid in silver."

"Naturally," Olav said, dazed a moment at the
thought of the birds' feathers. King Guthrum wanted
feather pillows for himself and his new consort,
wanted them badly, and no one had been able to suit
his fancy with the proper kind of feathers. The man
who would bring the desired feathers to him would
doubtless place himself in favor with the Danelaw
king. The young man stood before him—arrogant and
proud and sure of himself. Aye, Olav's initial impres-
sion of him had been quite correct. And he was
comely as a man should be: lean, strong, amazingly
handsome, as most of the Norwegians were, with his
thick blond hair and vivid blue eyes. He was clean-
shaven and possessed of a stubborn square jaw. There
was a small cleft in his chin. A mark of the devil,
some of the more backward Saxons would claim, and

cross themselves. Olav merely wanted to kill him and steal his feathers. Instead, he said easily, "I will willingly trade with you, Magnus Haraldsson, if your goods are of the quality I require. Now that I know your name, I realize I have heard of you from other traders. Your name is respected."

Magnus merely nodded. "Now, I would know the brideprice for Zarabeth."

Olav wished he held a dagger in his hand. He wished he could strangle the life out of this insolent man with his bare hands. At the moment he didn't care about the damned birds' feathers, he didn't care about anything but killing this man. But he didn't have a weapon, nor did he have the strength to kill the Viking with his bare hands. He played for time, saying, "Zarabeth is my only daughter, aye, and even though she carries not my blood, it matters not to me that she doesn't, for I hold her in high esteem. So high is my esteem that I give her free choice to choose her mate. As for her brideprice, it is beyond what most men could pay, for she is valuable, not only to me but also to a man who would wish to take her from me."

"What is her brideprice?"

Olav raised a thick blond eyebrow. "First, Magnus Haraldsson, she would have to tell me that she wished to wed with you. I will not discuss brideprice until I know that I am speaking seriously."

"Zarabeth wants me, doubt it not. I do not lie. What is her brideprice?"

Olav knew that a brideprice quoted to a Viking meant that if the Viking believed the price too high, he would simply steal the woman with no more bargaining, and no warning at all. Thus Olav shook his head. He would take no chances that the Viking would kidnap Zarabeth and sail back to Norway with her. "Not as yet, Magnus Haraldsson. First I must speak with my stepdaughter. If she tells me that she wants you—without your being present to coerce her or in any way influence her—why, then we will discuss the brideprice."

Magnus was impatient to have it done, impatient with this old man and his delaying tactics, but he supposed that Olav was behaving as a parent should. He assumed his father had behaved the same way when young men had asked to wed his younger sister, Ingunn, before she had decided not to wed and to come live with him and take care of his farmstead. He remembered vaguely the discussion between his father and Dalla's father, watching each man preen and strut out his offspring's virtues and ignore the failings. The young people's lust wasn't mentioned, as Magnus remembered.

He smiled then, mostly from that memory, and said, "Very well, Olav. I will return on the morrow to discuss what you will ask for her." Magnus left without another word, strode from the shop without a backward glance. Olav's fingers itched for that dagger. They also itched for the birds' feathers. He would have liked to see the dagger vibrating from the force of his throw between the Viking's shoulder blades. As for the feathers, he would like to see them beneath King Guthrum's head and himself a richer man. He shouldn't have let the Viking leave, for he doubted that on the morrow he would be so eager to sell the feathers to Olav. Others would tell him of their value, curse the fates.

Olav did not immediately go to speak to Zarabeth, for if he found her now he might kill her, so great was his rage, his sense of betrayal.

What to do?

He knew without doubt that she was his and she would remain with him. Ah, but this Viking, this Magnus Haraldsson, he was a man to judge carefully, for

he was no simple merchant's son to be easily manipulated or dangled about. He was a man of determination and strength of purpose as well. Olav worked
steadily, dealing with other traders, showing his wares
to buyers, coming out the victor in most of his negotia-
tions, for he was talented in bargaining, swift in his
wits, and adaptable in his tactics. He waited until the
evening meal.

When he stepped through the back of his shop into
the living area, he saw that Zarabeth looked flushed.
Her eyes looked brilliant. He felt his body harden.
She was the most beautiful creature he'd ever seen,
her mother included. Because it was warm in the
room, tendrils of deep red curled about her face and
forehead. He wanted her now, but he wasn't stupid,
and knew he must bide his time. It was with near-pain
that he watched her, content for the moment to say
nothing.

He watched her bend over to stir a spicy-smelling
stew in the iron cook pot. He watched her scoop a
fresh loaf of bread from its place over the ashes of
the fire and wrap it in a square of coarse wool to keep
it warm. He waited until she had served him, waited
until she was seated beside the idiot child, then said
with the calm of the eye of a storm, "A Viking named
Magnus Haraldsson came to see me today. He wants
to do some trading with me."

She looked up, the peas falling from her spoon.
"Trading?" she said blankly. She paled just a bit. "He
wished to speak to you about *trading*?"

"Aye. It seems he has feathers, exotic feathers he
obtained from the Lapps. King Guthrum seeks feathers for pillows. Perhaps you heard—"

"Feathers? You spoke of *feathers*?"

"Aye, and other things, of course." He saw her lean
forward, her lips parting slightly. "He has otter and
beaver pelts as well."

She stared at him, white now, silent as death itself. He smiled, delighted, took another bite of the beef stew, shrugged with elaborate indifference, and said, "Oh, he did mention that he wished to wed with you."

She drew back and he saw her release a breath of relief. She was nearly standing now, tense and excited. "What did you tell him?"

"I told him that it would be your decision."

"Ah."

"I told him I wouldn't discuss a brideprice with him until you had assured me that you wished to wed with him. Do you wish it, Zarabeth?"

She paused then, a frown furrowing her forehead. "I've known him but two days, Olav. But I feel like I have truly known him for much longer. I suppose it sounds odd, what I've said, but he is a good man, I think, a strong man, and he would make me a fine husband."

"You speak as though you were discussing the merits of a new cloak. He is a man, Zarabeth, a man who is doubtless brutal and cruel, a man who will have what he wants, no matter what he must do it get it." His voice rose to a near-shout. "You foolish girl, don't you understand his kind? Are you so besotted that you can't see the violence in him, the ruthlessness?"

Zarabeth felt Lotti stiffen next to her, afraid at her father's raised voice. She turned and spoke softly to the little girl. "Nay, sweeting, 'tis nothing to concern you. Here, eat the cabbage, 'tis sweet and tasty." Zarabeth cut the cabbage into small pieces as she spoke, and handed Lotti a full spoon. When Lotti had eased next to her, chewing slowly and thoughtfully, as was her wont, her attention back on her dinner, Zarabeth turned to her stepfather.

"You are of his kind, Olav, at least your father was."

"Aye, perhaps, but I've lived my life by my wits,

not my sword and ax. I don't raid King Alfred's shores and kill his people or enslave them."

"I imagine that you've wanted to."

Olav eyed her closely, but her voice remained bland, her face expressionless. "Perhaps, but that isn't the point. Tell me, then, that you wish to wait, Zarabeth. You don't know this man, this Magnus Haraldsson. He could be a raider, he could be as savage as the berserkers."

She shook her head. "Nay, he isn't like that."

"And just what is he like, this Viking of yours you've known for two whole days?"

His sarcasm didn't really touch her. He was worried about her, that was all. But he hadn't worried about Lotti or her mother, beautiful Mara, whom he'd sworn over and over to Zarabeth and everyone else that he hadn't killed, beautiful Mara, who nonetheless had been found with her dead lover, her head smashed. Zarabeth shook away the memories. Olav had had the care of her since her mother's death three years before. He hadn't berated her overly, but neither had he ever shown any kindness to his own daughter, Lotti. "I've told you," she said now. "He is kind. He would be a good husband. He has said that he will take me trading with him, that we will visit faraway places like Miklagard and Kiev."

Olav felt rage twisting and roiling in his belly. He saw the Viking covering Zarabeth as a man would a woman, and taking her, and at the same time he saw Zarabeth welcoming him into her body, smiling at him, urging him into her and moaning with the pleasure of it. She had spoken of how kind the Viking was, how good he was. What puke! What she wanted was to have him corrupt her. Olav turned away for a moment until he had gained control again. The expression he presented to her after but a moment was one of gentle concern. He had learned to shield any vigorous emotions he felt from her, for Zarabeth was unpredictable and he didn't know what she would do if he treated her as he wished to. No, he had come to realize during the last year that she wasn't a woman of a woman's expected parts and pieces. She'd grown in different ways, he could sense it, feel it in the way she spoke of things, in the way she freely expressed her opinions around men. She should have been beaten for that, but Olav had been afraid to touch her. She did keep his home, surely, weaving and sewing and cooking and cleaning, doing all those things women were supposed to do. Aye, she did those things, did them well and willingly, but still there was something in her, something wild and as savage as her ancestors in Ireland; something as wild and savage as in that damned Viking.

She would leave him without a backward glance if she wanted to. She didn't feel the dependence a woman was supposed to feel, even though the world was a capricious place, filled with life one moment and bloody death the next, be it by outlaws, the accursed raiding Vikings, or by nature in a spate of fury. He also guessed she'd leave him if ever he hurt Lotti. He studiously ignored the child as a result, saying nothing to her that would anger Zarabeth. He said finally, chewing on a piece of soft bread, "What if I were to tell you that Magnus Haraldsson is a renegade and nothing more than a barbarian pirate who preys on the traders who ply the Baltic?"

Zarabeth looked at him and smiled. Nothing more; she just smiled.

"Very well, so he isn't a renegade or a pirate." Olav poured himself more ale into the beautiful clouded-blue Rhenish glass. "But he could be something worse, Zarabeth." He sipped it slowly, looking at Zarabeth over the rim to gauge her reaction. There was none, nothing save that superior smile of hers. He had to think, to marshal his arguments. He wouldn't lose Zarabeth.

"I ask that you make no decision this night or tomorrow. You are not a flighty girl to decide her life in a matter of moments. I ask that you wait, that you spend more time with this man, that you be certain he is what you wish." He also wanted to demand that she not give her maidenhead to this man, not yet, but he couldn't find the words.

Zarabeth simply stared at him. She hadn't expected him to be so reasonable, so caring toward her. She'd prepared herself to do battle. She felt herself warming despite the fact that she knew it was a stupid thing to do. Still, it didn't matter now. She would be gone from Olav soon enough. "Thank you, Olav," she said, "thank you. I shall do it. I will make my final decision by the end of the week."

He nodded, content. That gave him three days to determine what to do to stop this marauding bastard from taking her away from him. At that moment Lotti tipped over her wooden cup, filled to the top with goat's milk. It splattered on Olav's fine woolen sleeve before he could jerk his arm away. He felt his face redden with anger at the clumsy little idiot, but he managed to hold his tongue.

Zarabeth patted Lotti's small hand, then rose. "Let me clean it for you, Olav." She rubbed his sleeve, but it was likely the milk would stain the fine pale blue wool. He was foolish to wear such finery, she thought as she leaned down, rubbing at the spot, then gently patting it.

Olav stared at her bowed head, at the rich vivid red of her hair and her smooth white flesh, those long slender fingers of hers. Toward the end there, Mara's flesh hadn't been as smooth or as soft as Zarabeth's. In the candlelight, Zarabeth's red hair was more muted, a deeper autumn-leaf color, and so rich-looking he wanted to bury his face in it. He breathed in the scent of her.

The smell of her was enough to make him hard and ready. To have her so close to him, so close he could hear her breathing, nearly undid him. He looked up to see Lotti staring at him, her small face solemn, her eyes wide and frightened.

The little fool couldn't understand desire, and he knew that was what she saw on his face. Why was she afraid? He'd never struck her since that time before. Zarabeth nodded her head and straightened.

"There won't be a stain," she said, and she blew on the wet wool. He saw her breasts move and he couldn't bear it. He would take her, he had to, and soon. As soon as the Viking was gone, he would make things clear to her.

He looked over at Lotti and suddenly knew exactly what he would do. Even though he had realized for a long time that Lotti was his only power over Zarabeth, he simply hadn't really admitted it to himself. But now he did, and now he knew that he would use the child, without hesitation. The time for turning back had come and gone.

There was a knock on the outer door to his shop and Olav pulled away from Zarabeth, jumping to his feet. "I know not who it is, but have more ale ready," he said over his shoulder, as he walked the length of the room, lifting the thick fur that separated the living quarters from his front shop, and disappeared.

Lotti made a strange sound and Zarabeth whipped about to look at her. The little girl had stuffed her fist in her mouth. Her eyes—a deep golden color—were wide and scared. Her hair was the color of ginger root and wrapped in braids around her small head. Her skin was fair, with a smattering of freckles over her nose.

Zarabeth dropped to her knees beside her sister.

She spoke clearly and firmly. "There is nothing to be afraid of, Lotti. Your father won't ever hurt you, I swear it. You belong to me and I will always take care of you. Do you understand, sweeting?"

The child looked at her, and her look of fear faded. She smiled and patted Zarabeth's hand. At that moment Zarabeth felt something inside her clench and twist at the look of complete trust on her little sister's face. No one should accord another such trust and belief, yet Lotti believed in her unconditionally. Zarabeth knew she was but a woman, not trained in weapons to defend either herself or Lotti. Still, it didn't matter. She would never allow it to matter. She rose slowly, brushing off her gown.

Olav returned to the room, followed by his son, Keith. A man shorter than his father, Keith had dark hair and dark eyes, a sallow complexion, and a thick beard of which he was inordinately proud. He had the habit of stroking his fingers through the coarse strands endlessly. Keith was the image, Olav had always said with just a bit of sarcasm, of his mother. He was well-formed and not unhandsome, despite the slight limp from a broken leg when he had been a boy. There was also a thin scar from his temple to his jaw, but it didn't disfigure him. He wasn't stupid, though he hadn't been able to copy his father's success as a trader. He had not the talent, but Olav wouldn't admit it. He was easily manipulated, Olav would say, shaking his head, though he was the one who usually did the manipulating. Aye, poor Keith was easily swayed, by other traders, by the tanner, by the smithy, by the jeweler—the list was endless.

He was twenty-two, married to a woman who pretended subservience in his presence and was a sharp-tongued bitch when he was gone from her. To his credit, he had, for the most part, simply ignored Zarabeth when his father had brought her and Mara back to York, showing neither like nor dislike for her. But it seemed to her that he had somehow changed during the past few months. He came more often to his father's house, many times without Toki, and she had seen him looking at her while he stroked his beard, pretending to listen to his father's endless stream of advice. She took care never to be alone with him.

She saw him staring at her now, and nodded, her expression remaining passive.

"Where is your wife?" Olav was asking his son.

"Toki is at home, where she belongs. She has her woman's curse and claims she is ailing." Keith shrugged and looked toward the wooden bottle of ale. "You bought her for me, you know her well enough. She has more of her mother's character by the month. I am the only one who knows her sweetness of nature."

Zarabeth wanted to hoot with laughter at Keith's summing-up of his wife's character. Olav chose to ignore his son's whining and the hint of bitterness. By all the gods, he did know Toki's mother, a creature to make a man's rod shrivel. He said only, his voice vague, for his thoughts were still of the damned Viking and Zarabeth, "Excellent. Would you like a cup of ale?"

Keith nodded and seated himself at the table. He said to Zarabeth, "You are well, sister?"

She nodded, saying nothing as she poured him ale.

"And the little one?"

"Lotti is also well.'

Olav shrugged, giving his son a helpless look. "She is useless, but what can I do? She even spilled goat's milk on my sleeve."

"You could have taken her out of the city and left her," Keith said, his voice matter-of-fact. "That is what Toki would have done immediately."

Zarabeth straightened slowly. "You will cease your cruel words, brother, else I will make you very sorry."

Keith spread his hands in front of him. "Acquit me, Zarabeth. It is what Toki would do, not I." He paused, frowning, as if confused. "Nay, that could not be true. Toki is sweet-natured and gentle. She loves children in particular. She would not hurt anyone, certainly not a child, even such as Lotti."

He was weak and blind as a post, Zarabeth thought; despite being a man and being strong, he was still weak. She imagined that Toki managed him very easily. She turned back to Olav when he said, "Don't torment the boy, Zarabeth. Besides, your threat rings hollow." He laughed. "What would you do to him if he displeased you? Hit him with a cooking spoon? Spear him with your dining knife? Perhaps shriek and try to pull out his hair?"

"Nay, I spoke without proper thought. My brother is the kindest of men."

She wished she'd kept her mouth closed and not given him what he immediately saw as encouragement. She added, smiling, "Of course, were he to act a villain, why, I should pour a potion in his ale that would turn his bowels to water."

Keith stared at her, then stared down at the small bit of ale left in his wooden mug.

"No, I did nothing, Keith, not this time. Mind your tongue in the future, for Lotti understands everything. I will not have her hurt."

Keith gave her a helpless look, but she merely went about her work of clearing up the dinner remains. She wasn't afraid of him; oddly enough, she felt somewhat protective of him. He didn't deserve Toki, and she had always believed it a mistake to force a marriage between those two.

Suddenly, like a lightning bolt, Keith said, "I heard

talk from the woodworker's giddy wife that Zarabeth
was kissing a Viking at the well this morning."

There was instant deafening silence. Olav said nothing, but his mouth was tight, the cords in his neck
bulged, and red flushed his cheeks. Keith frowned
uncertaintly toward Zarabeth. "Ah, so 'tis true. I
refused to believe it, for you're known as a cold
woman, Zarabeth, a woman who cares not for beautiful jewels or for a man. This Viking, he's a karl, I
hear, his father a chieftain and a powerful earl. He's
rich and endowed with fine lands in Norway."

"Aye, it's true," Zarabeth said.

"Have you spread your legs for him yet?"

Zarabeth was surprised at Keith's querulous tone,
even more surprised at his words. They were unlike
him. She felt a spurt of fear, then quickly repressed
it. It was jealousy she heard in his voice. But she knew
she shouldn't recognize it as such. She looked toward
the shelf on the far wall, where there was a row of
covered jars. "I wonder how strong I should mix the
potion for you, Keith."

"All right, so you haven't let him take you! What
do you want with him?"

Olav said abruptly, "Enough about the Viking. He
wants to wed with Zarabeth, but she hasn't yet
decided if she wants him. In three days she will give
him an answer."

Actually, Zarabeth thought, as Olav continued
speaking, she'd already decided. The three days were
her concession to him. Odd how it had come clearly
to her in just that instant.

She looked up to see Keith watching her avidly. "I
must wed someone," she said emotionlessly. "Magnus
Haraldsson seems a good choice."

"You will go with him to Norway?"

"Aye, if she weds with him," his father said, his

brow furrowed in his discontent. "We will see. Nothing is settled yet. Nothing."

Zarabeth held her peace. She wanted to see Magnus. She continued her work quietly, then bathed Lotti and tucked her into a thick wool blanket in the box bed. Olav and Keith were drinking steadily. She placed more ale beside her stepfather, then very quietly took her woolen cloak from a peg and pulled it around her shoulders. "I'm going for a short walk," she said, and left before either man realized she was gone.

5

Zarabeth knew it was dangerous to be out alone at night, despite the relative peace York had known for the past few years. There were still villains, beggars, outlaws, any number of ruffians who could sneak into the city at night and prey on the people. Thus she was careful to keep to the shadows of the houses. She walked very quickly, her step nearly soundless. There was a sliver of a moon overhead and the air was heavy with rain that would come before morning. All was shadows and silence. She could hear her own heart but she didn't slow, just kept walking.

She was warm enough wearing her wool cloak. She clutched it to her, remembering her mother telling her that the cloak had belonged to her mother and had been dyed with the finest saffron produced in all of Ireland.

When Zarabeth had left Olav's house on Coppergate, her feet, if not her conscious mind, had known exactly where she was going. Now she accepted what her feet had easily known. She kept her eyes straight ahead, toward the quay on the River Ouse. The earthen fortifications came into view, thick and tall and sturdy, then the snug harbor. There were many vessels along Monk's Pier, tied with stout rope to thick wooden poles that ran the length of the quay. Most of them were Viking trading ships. Her eyes scanned along them. So many of them, and they looked alike.

She stopped then, and nearly laughed aloud. She had come to find Magnus, yet she didn't know if he was here. She didn't even know the name of his vessel. She was appalled at herself. She had met a man and lost her wits as a result. She was a prize fool, and it was disconcerting, because normally she was thoughtful and slow to act either in joy or in anger. But she had simply walked out of her house, walked down Coppergate to Hungate, and directly right to the harbor. Well, she'd done it now, and if there were any outlaws lurking about, she deserved for them to see her. Still, she didn't turn back.

She paused, drew a deep breath, and proceeded to examine each of the vessels. There were at least a dozen, all the great square masts furled, all quiet, all the sailors asleep, the only sound the slap of water against the side of the boats. She hadn't realized it was quite so late. She walked very quietly, from vessel to vessel, the soft leather soles of her shoes nearly silent on the wooden-planked dock. She felt fear now, admitted it to herself. By all the saints, she was a fool. What to do? Then she saw a vessel that was larger than its neighbors, with elegant lines and a look of brutal magnificence. It flew Odin's Raven, carved in black, upon its bow. It was a beautiful vessel and she knew deep down, without question, that it belonged to Magnus.

She smiled then, slowly, threw back her head, and shouted, "Magnus! Magnus Haraldsson!"

There was utter silence, then the low rumbling of men talking.

"Magnus! Magnus Haraldsson!"

She heard a deep laugh. She saw a score of men's heads coming into view over the gunwales, sailors all, weapons in their hands, and then they were leaping lightly off their vessels onto the quay, looking toward her, mouths agape, talking about her, pointing. She heard a blessedly familiar voice say, "Nay, all of you remain here. There is no danger. 'Tis my lady who calls to me. Any of you make a move toward her and I'll slit your fool's throat. If any other man makes a move toward us, come to my aid and we'll slit his throat together."

It was Magnus, and he was striding toward her, his cloak billowing in the heavy air behind him, his head bare. He looked invulnerable and as brutally beautiful as his vessel, and she felt her flesh become warm and her breathing quicken. He was a powerful beast, this man, and she knew in that moment that she would have him and none other. Two days of knowing him was a lifetime. She forced herself to stand quiet, waiting for him to come to her.

Magnus stopped not a foot from her. He said nothing, merely stared down at her, no expression on his face. "I thought I heard a woman's raucous voice shrieking for me, shrill as the caw of a rook. Did you hear anyone like that, Zarabeth?" He looked over her head and to his right and left. "Nay, I see her not. No one is swimming in the water, neither a mermaid nor a sea dragon, and there are naught but hairy sailors yon. All of them were dreaming dreams of plunder and fat casks of silver, no doubt, until her voice came to slice through their dreams, and mine. Ah, behind you. There she is, and she looks the termagant, foul-tempered and sour-mouthed. How very ugly she is—"

Zarabeth whipped around and saw no one. Magnus began to chuckle. She felt his hand fall lightly on her shoulder.

His voice deepened and all humor fell away. "You are impulsive, Zarabeth. It is a dangerous quality, but I shan't chide you for it this time, though it angers me that you would come to me alone. Come here and let me look at you."

She smiled then and turned to find him there, just in front of her, and she leaned forward against his chest and lifted her face to his. She said, "I wanted to see you. It's been too long without the sight of your face."

His hands came up to clasp her upper arms. "Was it, now? So you came here to the quay alone, with no protection, and bellowed out my name? What if another man had come in answer to your call?"

She had no intention of dwelling on that possibility, saying simply, "I knew it was your vessel. It is the most splendid one docked here. It looks like you, Magnus, lean and powerful and savage. I took little risk."

"Your reasoning astounds me and pleases me alike. But do you really see me as being savage?"

"Nay, I meant brutal. It sounds odd, but 'tis true. Your vessel appears brutal in its beauty, as do you, its owner, its master."

"All right, I promised not to chide you, and I won't, for you have made me feel a man above other men. Just know, Zarabeth, any brutality in my nature will never be visited upon you. If you ever annoy me, why, then, I'll simply kiss you." And he did, swooping down, his cloak billowing around the both of them, pulling her up against his chest. His mouth was warm and firm, and when she didn't part her lips to him, he gently eased his tongue along her lower lip, caressing her, nipping her, until she understood what he wanted and opened her mouth just a bit. It was wondrous, feeling his tongue touch hers, feeling the warmth of his body against hers. His large hands were holding her tightly against him. She felt his thighs against hers, felt the hardness of him against her belly.

"Magnus," she said into his mouth, and she felt him

shudder. She wondered at this seeming power she held over him, but only for a moment, for he suddenly swept his hands over her buttocks and lifted her, pressing her hard against him. She stiffened at his assault and he instantly released her, sliding her down the front of his body, slowly, ever so slowly, until her feet once again touched the dock.

He raised his head and looked down at her. "You're breathing hard, sweeting. That pleases me. And you're right. All my men and all the other men in every vessel along this quay are likely watching us behind the gunwales. Their dreams are no longer of plunder but of beautiful females beguiling them and seducing them. I will announce tomorrow that you are mine, and that will be the end to their sniggering and gossip."

She lowered her eyes. "That is kind of you, Magnus. Actually, I have come to become better acquainted with you. I told Olav that I would give him my decision in three days. He cares about me, you see, and doesn't want me to be overly impetuous." She paused; then, to his surprise and fascination, she giggled. "He fears your manliness sways me unduly, though he didn't say that precisely. I should have told him he was quite right." She was serious again. "I wanted to see you, Magnus, to see if you truly were the man who was in my mind all the day long."

"And am I, Zarabeth?"

She smiled at his off-kilter pronunciation of her name as she stepped back, still held in the loose circle of his arms, and looked up at him. The moonlight was scant but she could see his features perfectly. She studied him, cocking her head to one side in serious contemplation.

He held himself perfectly still, not moving, not changing expression, just waiting for her to complete her study.

"You are as you should be, and to me that is all that is perfect." She lightly touched her fingertips to the small notch in his chin. "This is clever."

He raised a thick dark blond brow. " 'Twas not of my doing, though if it pleases you, I will claim full knowledge and the planning of it. One girl told me once that Odin had rejected me, pressing his thumb into my chin to show the world his repugnance."

"This girl who told you that—did you hurt her to make her speak so evilly?"

"Actually, it is so." His voice lightened as he spoke his memories. "She had seduced me, this older girl who was then yet younger than you are now, and I was but an innocent lad of twelve summers when she first took me inside her and I learned the pleasures of a woman's body. Then I discovered that year I preferred hunting walrus to covering her. She cursed me, ranting that my cleft was the sign of Odin's displeasure."

Zarabeth chuckled. "I should have cursed you also. Walrus hunting! 'Twas not well done of you."

"I was but twelve years old, Zarabeth."

"Aye, but were you so beautiful even then, Magnus?"

"When you birth my sons, perhaps one of them will be in my image, and then you will know."

Zarabeth was silent. He continued to do this to her, to speak so bluntly that it robbed her of her wits.

"What bothers you, sweeting?"

"You and the effect you have on me. It's strange and it confuses me and makes me stupid."

He stroked his fingertips over her jaw. "I would make you happy, not stupid."

"Would you bear with both?"

"I will manage to bear with all you ever show me." He leaned down to quickly kiss her. He didn't try to part her lips, just kissed her warmly and lightly.

"I'm afraid," she said, looking up at him, at his

mouth, damp from their touching, firm and gentle. "You come from a land I've only heard about, a land where all the people are strangers to me, a land where the weather is harsh during the winter and there is little sun for many months."

Magnus had considered taking her on board the *Sea Wind*, but he quickly changed his mind. It wasn't at all chilly here in the open, and she felt safe here, with him, a man she'd known for only two days, the man she would marry. He smiled at her and sought to reassure her. "They will be strangers only until you smile at them and tell them hello. My kin will love you, as will Harald Fairhair himself, our king. He comes from the Vestfold, you know, though at present he has no royal residence there. But he is a cousin to my father, and thus of my kin, and he will come to visit and he will approve of you, you will see."

"I have heard of Harald Fairhair. I have heard he is ruthless and he seeks to subdue no matter the cost. It is said he rarely shows mercy."

"Aye, and he is greedy and wants more and then more after that." Magnus shrugged. "He wants every chieftain, every earl in Norway, to bend to his will and obey his every dictum. He is a man and he is a Viking. There is no limit to his appetites, and his power grows by the year, and he falters not, though he is near my father in age. He has conquered an entire country and brought it to heel. He searches for more, as do most men of my country." He grinned then, shaking his head. "The men in my country—if they feel at all crowded by their neighbors or persecuted by their king, then they simply leave to find new lands. We all cherish our freedom and we allow no one to curtail it."

"And does he wish to have your lands and those of your father? Will you wish someday to leave your home?"

"Not as yet, but it would not surprise me to have him levy taxes on us that would break our backs. Then, of course, we would have to fight him, king or no. Distant kin or no. Or we would leave."

She saw that he was perfectly serious. He would enjoy the fighting, she guessed, and he would be as brutal as he had to be and feel no regret. Nor would he flinch at the thought of leaving his home bound for a distant land. He would always do what had to be done. It pleased her, this certain knowledge of him.

"It's also true that during five months of the winter there is little sun and snow covers the ground. We will spend much time in the longhouse, but you won't fret with inactivity. Skalds visit in the winter months and sing songs to amuse everyone. They tell sagas that have been handed down for hundreds of years, and invent new ones to make the master of the farmstead feel like a king with all their flattery. We play games and dance and drink until our heads pound. And when you are not in my bed, or playing, or dancing, you will be sewing, spinning, cooking, directing all the house jarls and the thralls. Do you know how to make butter, Zarabeth? And buttermilk?"

"Butter?" she repeated, bemused yet again with the sudden shift in his talk.

"Aye. I remember my mother lifting and dropping and shaking the churn—such a size it was, but then again, my mother is a woman of great strength—until she had separated out all the yellow butterfat. Ah, but the buttermilk that's left is sweet and wondrous to drink. Children always fight for the first mug fresh from the churn."

"I make butter," she said. "But my churn is small and requires no great strength to shake it."

His fingers were wrapped about her upper arms. "Life isn't easy at home, Zarabeth, but I cannot think you would seek to doze away with boredom. I will protect you and love you and give you as many children as Frey blesses us with. I would like to kiss you again, sweeting. Your mouth is soft and draws me from reason itself."

Without hesitation, she stood on her tiptoes and pursed her lips, her eyes closing.

He looked at her lovely face, a face that was already very dear to him. "After I kiss you, I should like to cup your breasts in my hands, like this." He kissed her, burying her startled cry with his mouth, and his hands opened and he held her breasts in his palms.

"Magnus," she said, and pulled back. "Oh, truly, nay, you cannot."

"Your breathing is harsh," he said, and grinned down at her. "Your words make little sense now. Do you like my hands on you? Ah, 'tis but the beginning, sweeting. Think of me suckling at your breast as will our sons and daughters. And when I part your thighs, I'll come between them and part them wider, and then, Zarabeth, I'll cover you."

She pressed her palm against his mouth. She felt flushed and excited and she knew neither was right, not that she cared overly. "You speak so baldly, I don't know what to do."

"It excites you."

"It makes me stupid and fluttery, for I know not how to answer you."

"Then do not try. You will learn my ways. I will try to remember to speak thus to you whilst I take you. And you will learn to tell me what pleases you even as I tell you how to hold me and touch me."

"Yes," she said, and sighed. She couldn't control him and it occurred to her that he beguiled her so simply because he held the reins of control, firmly, and he wouldn't release them. If he ever did, it would be because he wished to.

It was unbearably exciting to her, his strength, his gentleness, the combination of the two that made him unique, that made him Magnus.

"There is something I would ask you, Magnus." She paused, but he merely continue smiling down at her, waiting. She fretted with the fine silver brooch that held his cloak together at his right shoulder. "Your thrall, Cyra—will you continue . . . that is, will you—?"

"Ah, yes, Cyra who enjoys my hands on her, blending pain and pleasure together—"

"You needn't speak quite so frankly about that! Will you continue with her once I am your wife?"

He looked taken aback. "Certainly not. Do you believe me like those black Arabs in Miklagard? Those men who measure their importance by the number of women they are able to keep for themselves?"

"I don't know. There are those here in York—aye, King Guthrum even—who have several concubines and they are also married."

He shook his head. "You will fill my days and my nights. I want no other woman. Now, do you want to know what we will be doing in exactly four nights from tonight? No, you will listen, Zarabeth—" He broke off at the sound of a man's voice, coming from down the quay, then cursed.

"Magnus!"

"I do believe it's one of my men," Magnus said, and put her away from him, his voice tinged with impatience. "Aye, 'tis Eirik and he's a bit the worse from your York ale, if I mistake it not. The fool, 'tis not safe for a man alone, no matter how many friends he has close by."

Eirik was short, young, built like a Northumbrian bull, his hair nearly white it was so blond. He came to a stop in front of Magnus, and gave him an owlish stare.

"She is the stepdaughter of Olav the Vain, is she not? There are men out searching for her. Olav the Vain is yelling that she is missing, likely kidnapped by you, he is claiming, because you refused to pay the brideprice. He is shrieking like a madman. He has six men with him, all paltry and worth naught in a fight, but still . . . I thought she would be with you, so I came to tell you, Magnus."

"I'll return her," Magnus said. "Get you some sleep now, Eirik. You've done well and I am in your debt."

He turned to Zarabeth. There was humor in his eyes. "I like him not, this stepfather of yours, but I do grant that he could be concerned for your safety."

"I'll leave now. You needn't come back with me. Olav is mayhap foolish now, for he has drunk much ale. I do not want him or you hurt."

"Zarabeth, you are now under my protection. The moment I saw you, you were under my care. You will walk nowhere alone, ever again. You will attend me fully when there is something I wish you to do, or more likely, when there is something I wish you to cease doing. Do you understand?"

She frowned, stiffening at his tone, hard and commanding. But he was right in this one instance. "Very well, then. I am sorry if I disturbed you, Magnus."

"Silly wench," he said, and took her hand in his. He saw that four of his men followed a short distance behind, but held his tongue, and nodded his approval. 'Twas safer thus.

He shortened his step to match hers. "I would have preferred to have carried you to my small cabin, stripped off that gown of yours, and taken you to my bed. It isn't truly a cabin, though, just a covered space on the deck of the *Sea Wind*." He sighed deeply. "But that must wait until we're wedded. Then, Zarabeth, I will keep you in my bed until we are both too exhausted to do naught but sleep."

She looked up at him and grinned, her heart light and bounding in her breast. "Ah, but who will be master of your vessel whilst you are in your bed?"

"I will appoint all my men masters so they will have other duties to occupy them besides listening to our lovemaking."

"I believe I will exhaust you before you exhaust me, my lord."

"Do you think so, sweeting? Even though you have no knowledge of what it is we will do?" At her bemused silence, he laughed and lightly chucked his knuckles against her chin. " 'Tis a contest that will draw me into a frenzy, a contest we will both cherish once you have learned the rules."

Zarabeth was still smiling when she heard her step-father shouting at the top of his lungs in the distance, "There he is! There's that marauding Viking, and he's got my stepdaughter! Kill him! Kill him!"

"He is a very foolish man," Magnus said calmly. "Very foolish."

"What will you do?" She turned and saw Magnus' four men closing behind them, their battle swords drawn. Three of them held both a sword and a battle-ax. They looked ferocious, their faces hard and cold, and utterly without fear. Magnus did not draw his sword from its scabbard. He waited, his arms crossed negligently over his chest.

"I will see what he plans," was all he said. "Don't move, Zarabeth. Stay to my right so that I may see you and know you're safe."

She had no choice but to wait as six men, all friends of her stepfather's, came running toward them, swords in their hands, screaming curses.

Then suddenly Magnus stepped forward and raised both his arms over his head. "Halt!"

The men jerked to a stop. Olav, panting from his

exertion, came around the corner and ran into the back of one of the men.

"Kill him! You cowards, kill the Viking!"

"You, Olav, be quiet or I will cut out your cursed tongue. Zarabeth came to visit me this evening. Beyond foolish, I agree, so I am bringing her to your house. She is unharmed and I suggest that you treat her well and scold her not, for she will soon be my wife, and any chiding will come from me, her husband. Handle her gently or I will make you very sorry."

Olav knew his friends wouldn't attack the Viking. They were all merchants and craftsmen. They knew how to fight, and would die in the fighting if they had to, but they weren't warriors and they would have no chance against this man. He knew that even six of his friends would not try to kill this one man. It would be suicide. He contented himself with the thought that he would beat her when he got her home. He looked at Zarabeth and smiled.

It was as if the Viking read his mind.

"Nay, Olav the Vain, do not what you are thinking. I am a man of my word, an honorable man, and you may trust what I say. You won't harm her, else I will do more than make you very sorry. I will kill you."

There was nothing for it. Olav felt raw hatred churn in his gut, making his belly cramp. "Come," he said shortly to Zarabeth. "You have caused enough worry, girl."

"I know. I am sorry, Olav."

"As for your idiot stepsister, she is writhing about on the floor and trying to cry. It sickens me to watch her and to hear her mewling sounds. Get thee home and see to her before I take her from the city and leave her in the Bentik Mountains, as I should have already done."

Magnus saw Zarabeth stiffen straight as the handle

on his battleax. There was more going on here than she had told him. He didn't understand Olav's venom about his own small daughter. Magnus lightly touched Zarabeth's arm. "Go, sweeting. I will see you on the morrow, by the well at the square."

"Aye. Thank you," she said. She quickly picked up her skirts and walked to her stepfather.

6

Olav fingered his beard as he looked at Zarabeth. He felt now, thank the saints, in full control of himself and of the situation. He felt good knowing he was in charge again, that it was his word, and his alone, that would determine what would happen now. That barbarian merchant Viking was on his vessel, safe from Olav's wrath, and his bitch of a stepdaughter was here, alone with him, at his mercy, at his command. Ah, but he would make her pay for her near-defection. He looked at her in the dim light of the bear-oil lamp. It was very late now, and they were home at last, in the living area, and she knew now that her little sister wasn't here. He enjoyed the fear and confusion on her face. He more than enjoyed it; he relished it.

"You will do exactly as I tell you, Zarabeth," he said at last. She was standing before him now, staring at him.

"Where is Lotti?" Zarabeth asked for the third time, her voice shaking now, her desperation nearer the surface. "What have you done with her? You said she was upset that I wasn't here. You lied to me! Where is she, Olav? What have you done with her?"

"I won't tell you, my girl. At least, not until you have made your promise to me, not until you have sworn to rid me and yourself of this Viking bastard."

Zarabeth shook her head at him. "You told me you

wished me to know my own mind. You told me you would abide by my decision. Where is Lotti?"

Olav waved his hand, clearing away her questions. "Fret not, Zarabeth. Your idiot sister is safe, at least at the moment. You won't see her again until you've done exactly as I tell you."

"I want to marry Magnus Haraldsson. I will go back to Norway with him and I will take Lotti with me."

"Nay, you won't. You will remain here with me, safe in York. Perhaps, if I wish it, I will wed you, for I hold not any of your blood. No one would object, not even King Guthrum. Ha! He himself has three concubines, and one is rumored to be his niece. Nay, he won't object."

He saw the look of revulsion on her face then and lost control. He jumped from his chair and slapped her so hard her head snapped back and she was flung to her side onto the rush-covered floor. He stood over her, hands on his hips. "No more will you act impetuous, Zarabeth. No more will you treat me like a toothless elderly uncle or like a despised old man to be tolerated and nothing more! No more, do you understand me? Nod your head, damn you, else I'll have that idiot sister of yours killed this very night!"

"I understand."

"Good. I wanted to wait, truly I did. I had hoped that in the next three days you would have come to realize that you didn't want to be allied to a savage, to that filthy Norse trader, but you left my house! Alone and unprotected, and you went to the harbor, to him! That you could be so stupid appalls me. Did you let him have your maidenhead? Did you part your legs for him?" His voice was shaking, and he stopped, breathing deeply. "Well, it matters not. You won't have him, Zarabeth, not ever, and there's an end to it."

She tried to think clearly, but she was terrified for

Lotti, and she felt a growing pounding in her head from the blow he'd given her. Lotti. He must have turned her over to Keith. Her blood curdled. Keith and his wife, Toki, had Lotti, there was little doubt. They felt nothing but contempt for the child and scorned her. She felt fear, thick and raw, fill her, slow her thinking, make her react sluggishly.

She had to get back to Magnus. He would get Lotti back. He would know what to do. "Magnus," she said very quietly, but Olav heard her.

"Don't think it, girl. I will kill her the moment you go back to that bastard Viking. Now I will tell you more truths, Zarabeth. Lotti is not of my flesh, did you know that? No, that whore mother of yours, my dear wife, Mara, slept with another man, the same fool man she ran away with, but she left you, choosing herself and her bastard get over you, her only legitimate child. But the whore died and the little bastard is an idiot—"

"She isn't! She was perfect until you struck her that night when you brought her home! And all because she was crying for her mother, you struck her, so hard that she was unconscious for two days! You are the bastard, rotten to your black soul, and you don't deserve to—"

"—and she will also die if you don't do exactly what I tell you to do."

Zarabeth raised her eyes to Olav's face. "I wish I had a dagger. I would kill you."

"Then Lotti would surely be dead by the morning."

Zarabeth rubbed her palm over her cheek. It was still stinging. She said dully now, uncertain, more afraid than she'd ever been in her life, "You want me to wed with you?"

"Perhaps soon. Not now. Now I would simply have you remain in my house. When you are more comfortable with me, I will bed you. Then, if I wish it, you will become my wife."

It was nearly too much to understand. She shook her head, but the pounding only increased, and with it, her despair.

His voice softened and he came down on his haunches beside her. "Listen to me, girl. I don't want to hurt you. Don't force me to. I want you willing and smiling. I want you the way you were before you met the Viking." He frowned at his own words. No, he didn't want her to return to being the way she'd been before the Viking—she'd been unconscious of him, not really seeing him, suffering his presence, actually.

She lay there, balanced up on her elbow, unconsciously pulling back from him. She smelled the sweet violets she had sprinkled into the rushes that covered the packed earthen floor. She looked toward the glowing embers in the fireplace. She looked at her neatly stacked pails and pots and wooden trenchers on the wide shelf in the cooking area. Everything looked so blessedly normal. Yet she was afraid, she felt paralyzed with fear. All the violence in Dublin, all the killing and hatred between the Viking rulers and the petty Irish chieftains, all was but a vague memory. Even the battles between King Alfred and King Guthrum seemed unsubstantial to her now, though the battles had scarred every family she knew, bringing death and tears and torn bodies. No, it was far away, that violence. The true violence was here in this house, and this was real. She stared at Olav, not knowing what to say, not knowing what to do.

Lotti. The child had no one but her, no one to understand her, to care for her. No one but her sister, Zarabeth.

She felt tears spring to her eyes and sniffed them back. Crying was good for naught. Crying was for the helpless, and she wasn't that, at least not yet.

Olav spoke again, his voice more wheedling, more cajoling. "Come, Zarabeth, say you'll bid this Viking farewell. Say you'll tell him you've decided against marriage with him. He'll sail away, and all will become again as it was. It's so easy, Zarabeth. Just promise me you will tell him. You'll see him tomorrow in the square, and you will tell him you don't want him for your husband."

She shook her head. "No, Olav. I won't tell him that. I want him and I think I will come to love him. I won't lie to him for you."

He rose then, with finality, and dusted off his trousers. He said in an emotionless voice, "Then Lotti will be dead by tomorrow morning." She stared up at him. His cross-garters had come down and were bunched at his ankles; his fine woolen hose were wrinkled and bagging at the knees. He looked disheveled and old. Aye, he looked like an old man, a tired old man who wasn't getting his way, and wanted a victim to lash out at.

"Nay, I won't tell him that I don't want him. If you harm Lotti, he will kill you."

Olav shrugged and looked at her with lifeless eyes. "It matters not, then, does it? The idiot child will be dead, I will be dead, and you will have your Viking. You will sail to Norway with him, alone, with nothing but the clothes on your back. And you will know that your selfishness meant death to two people who love you."

"Love! You miserable old liar! You threaten to kill my little sister and you say that you love me? By all the gods, I would that I could kill you right now!"

She rolled over and came up onto her knees. Her face was flushed with anger, with disbelief, and Olav took a quick step backward, for he saw violence in her eyes.

Then he smiled at her, and shrugged. "Believe what

you will. You are a woman and thus your thoughts
are beyond a man's logic. But know this, Zarabeth:
the child will be dead by tomorrow at noon if you do
not do my bidding. 'Tis up to you, girl. I offer you
the child's life for that miserable Viking's lust." He
paused a moment, stared at her, and she fancied she
could see the pounding of his blood in the pulse in his
neck. "Did you let him cover you tonight? Did he
take your maidenhead?"

"Hush your filth! You are much worse than your
son!"

"So 'tis your lust for your little sister's life. You're
just like your whore of a mother, aren't you? You
aren't so much of a loving sister after all. You're nothing but a fake."

" 'Tis enough, Olav. You won't kill Lotti because
you don't want to die. I know you. I know that all
tradesmen here in Coppergate snigger at you behind
your back and call you Olav the Vain. You prance
and strut about, extolling your brilliance at trading—
at cheating the unwary, more's the truth—and you
spend all your gold on finery to adorn your sagging
old body! Look at you, garbed like King Guthrum
himself! Yet even he, an old man like you, doesn't
glitter like a conceited fool!"

"You will be quiet, Zarabeth!" He was shaking with
fury, the life back in him at full strength at her insults.

"Nay, not now, not when I would tell you the truth,
you dirty old man! I won't remain here, wondering if
you will try to crawl into my bed and molest me. I
won't pretend to be your loving stepdaughter when I
know what it is you're really thinking. I won't suffer
your hatred for Lotti anymore, your contempt, your
neglect. I won't listen to your lies about my mother.
You didn't deserve her, damn you! Now, you will tell
me where you've hidden Lotti and I will fetch her and
be gone. I never want to see your ugly face again."

Olav was silent for many moments. Then he raised
his hand in a sort of benediction, and said in a voice
that was certain and cold, "The idiot child will die,
slowly, and I will know pleasure from the knowledge
of it. I swear it on Odin, our All-Father, and I swear
it on the Christian God as well."

She felt the room pitch sideways. In that instant she
believed him. He wasn't lying. He spoke as calmly as
an insane man who would be pushed no further.

Aye, she believed him. This was the point beyond
which he wouldn't retreat. She knew him. He would
have Lotti killed or he would kill her himself. He
wouldn't care. She could see Keith strangling the child
with one hand, lifting her and crushing the life out of
her with but one of his big hands. She could see him
tossing her out as one would refuse. She could see
him whistling even as he finished his murder. No, no,
not Keith, she thought, not gentle weak Keith. Toki,
his wife, it would be she who murdered Lotti.

Zarabeth wasn't overly religious, and thus, in that
instant, she prayed to Odin, to Thor, and finally to
the Christian God for good measure. What to do?

"Go to sleep now, Zarabeth. You have much to
consider. I will know your answer on the morrow. Oh,
think not to kill me during the night, for if you do,
the child will die very quickly after me and you will
have gained naught but death yourself, for all will
know you killed me, and none other."

She moved slowly to behind the thin bearskin that
separated hers and Lotti's sleeping chamber from the
rest of the room. She looked at the box bed. She
slowly unfastened her wide leather belt and stripped
off her soft woolen gown. She remained in her linen
shift and crawled between two wool coverlets. She lay
there, her eyes wide and fixed, staring into the darkness, not knowing what to do.

It was near dawn when she knew that she could not

sacrifice Lotti's life for her own happiness. Even if it meant Olav's death as well. It was then that tears flowed down her cheeks, their salty wetness in her mouth. And it was later still, after the sun had risen over the harbor, that she changed her mind and felt hope build in her.

Zarabeth forced a smile. Her heart was pounding so loudly she thought he would hear it. Aye, a smile, for even in the short time she'd known Magnus, she realized that he knew her very well indeed. She had to persuade him, she had to leave no doubts at all in his mind, so that Olav would be convinced, and then she would act and both she and Lotti would be safe. She prayed to Odin that Magnus would forgive her lie even as he believed it. She prayed to her own Christian God that Magnus would forgive her when he discovered what she'd had to do.

Magnus saw that smile of hers, that ghastly smile, and said without preamble, "What troubles you, Zarabeth? Are you cold? There is rain in the air this morning."

Cold! It was laughable. She turned to stand more closely to the well in Coppergate square. She knew that Olav watched from the tanner's shop just feet away. She knew that he could see her face clearly, her face and Magnus'. She knew he could hear her and Magnus. She knew she had to tread carefully, for Lotti's life, her own future, depended on it.

"I'm not cold. I am glad you are here, Magnus Haraldsson. I would speak to you. I will not mince matters. I am here to tell you that I do not wish to wed with you. I was mistaken in my feelings. I have decided I don't want you. I don't wish to see you again."

Magnus saw her pallor, heard the tension in her voice. He didn't accept her words. He didn't understand her and he was not willing to be patient at her game. He threw back his head and laughed. "This is a show of your wit, sweeting? I like it not. We will jest of many things, but not of this. This is our life, not some sort of joke to be tossed about heedlessly."

"Your conceit is bloated as the rain clouds overhead, Viking. I speak the truth to you. I treat you not to my wit. I don't want you. I bid you good-bye." She turned on her heel to leave him, but he grasped her arm and pulled her back. She felt anger in him now. He would believe her, he would.

He spun her about to face him. He said nothing for a very long time, just looked down at her, studied her face, her expression. She wished she could whisper the truth to him, but she held herself silent. She filled her eyes with contempt, and hoped she did it well. She would take no chance with Lotti's life. She would make it up to him later. There had to be a later. She'd prayed until the full morning light for a later.

"So," he said at last with slow deliberation. "So, at last I find a girl who is all that I wish and she tells me she doesn't want me. I find it passing strange, Zarabeth, this sudden change in you. Why, you would have gone with me to my vessel last night, I think, had I insisted upon it. Do you deny it?"

She probably would have, she thought blankly, pain so sharp her chest ached with it. She looked him up and down and smiled, that same ghastly smile, and filled her voice with insolence. "I admire your manliness, Viking, so perhaps I would have thought to sample your offerings. But to become your wife, to leave York, to journey to a savage land where there are naught but savage people who would look upon me as a foreign oddity? No, Viking, I won't do that. I was temporarily mad, but no more. As for the other, a man is to be enjoyed at a woman's whim. I had nearly decided to enjoy you, 'tis true, but then . . ."

She shrugged, and that one small movement enraged him, and she knew that Olav saw he was enraged. It was enough; she'd won Lotti's life.

She made to leave him then, but Magnus enraged was frightening, and she faltered. She flinched even as his grip on her arm tightened painfully.

"Listen to me, Zarabeth. I don't believe this act of yours. You are under threat from Olav, are you not? Tell me the truth, for I can put a stop to any threats he has made."

She shook her head, afraid to open her mouth for fear of what would come out. She turned her head to the side. "Olav the Vain threaten me? Surely you can't believe that, Viking. I won't be threatened by any man." She spit onto the ground. "Not even by you.

"Call me not a liar, Viking! I think you a conceited fool. Leave me now, for I find your presence tedious and your hold on my arm officious."

He flung her arm away from him and she stumbled. She didn't fall, but she realized that if she had fallen he wouldn't have helped her. He was staring down at her, his face without any emotion at all that she could see. He looked savage and cold and utterly ruthless. He looked as if he would enjoy killing her. He looked like, finally, he believed her utterly.

When he spoke, finally, his voice was as hard and cold as his face. "Perhaps I should take you to my vessel. I can give you a good taste of a Viking man. I won't disappoint you, Zarabeth, but I doubt I would receive any pleasure from our coupling. You've played with me magnificently, pulled me in with gentleness and a candor I had not believed possible in a woman. I have been a conceited fool, aye, 'tis true, but at least I didn't marry you." He shook his head and then threw back his head and laughed.

"To think I considered myself the luckiest of men

to have found you. I saw you and I wanted you. Ah, I thought it so easy, so straightforward, this love business. I thought it was fate intervening to give you to me." He laughed again, deep and harsh. "Aye, and I was so pleased that fate had determined me to be worthy of such a fine creature as you. The irony is beyond reason and beyond pain." Then he turned and strode away. He paused, but didn't turn back as he said over his shoulder. "You are a bitch, Zarabeth, and I devoutly hope you gain what you deserve."

Then he was gone, his cloak billowing behind him, and she watched him, unmoving, and felt such pain that she wanted to scream with it. She got a hold on herself. She'd succeeded, and now Lottie would be safe. Once she had Lotti, she would go to Magnus and explain. All would be well again. He would understand.

She didn't turn when she heard Olav say softly, "You did well, Zarabeth. I wondered if your selfishness would prevent it, but it didn't. Now, my dear girl, let us return home. Soon you will have Lotti back. Then all will be as it was."

She walked away from him.

"Hold, Zarabeth! Where are you going?"

"To Keith and Toki. I will fetch Lotti myself."

"They cannot give her to you. She is not with them, but hidden in another place. Nay, you must wait for me to fetch her."

Zarabeth didn't know what to do. Indeed, she could think of nothing to do, at least at the moment. "Then come with me now, Olav."

He shook his head. "Nay, on the morrow. I will give you a day to settle yourself."

Zarabeth acquiesced, for she had no choice, and she saw that Olav was pleased with her meekness. Then she waited only until he was busy in his shop with several local men who wanted to buy furs, but when she was on the point of slipping from the house, she heard Olav shout, "Stay here, Zarabeth. You must stay or you and the child will regret it."

She stayed and she fretted. That evening she served Olav stew filled with onions and potatoes and small chunks of beef. And in his bowl she poured a sleeping draft. He spoke to her as though she were his wife and all was normal between them. It was chilling, the possessive way he behaved toward her. She held her tongue and waited. Not ten minutes after he'd eaten the stew, his head fell forward onto the wooden table. Zarabeth rose slowly and walked to him. He was soundly asleep, snoring loudly, and would remain so for hours.

Finally.

She quickly left the house and made her way over to Skeldergate, where Keith and Toki lived. Keith was a trader, like his father, and not a very good one. A year before, a visiting Viking trader had nearly killed him, for he had sold him some furs that had moth holes in them. She knew that Olav gave his son gold and furs from time to time. As for what Keith really thought of her, she was afraid to know. If he only knew what it was his father wanted of her, he would surely kill her. She quickened her pace. She and Lotti would be gone and it wouldn't matter what happened between Keith and his father after she had left. It was dark now and there were men of all kind out, many of them bent on mischief. She arrived to the small wooden house, then drew to a stop. There was one window covered with a stretched animal membrane. She could hear through it, at least, and if she pressed her face close, she could make out vague outlines.

"I tell you, you weak bleating fool, that she'll have him yet!"

It was Toki's voice, loud and shrill. Zarabeth leaned closer against the membrane.

"I promised him to hold the child," Keith said, his voice slurred from ale. "I will hold her until he comes for her. My father will be pleased that we have done as he asked. He will reward us for it."

"Ha! 'Tis that miserable little slut Zarabeth he will reward, not you, not his only son! You know 'tis true, Keith, for he was willing to do anything to keep her here in York, to keep her with him. And she told the Viking she didn't want him. She managed to convince him of it. I've heard it from a half-dozen women this day! So pleased they were, to let me hear how she told him at the well in the square that she didn't want him for her husband, that he was naught but a buffoon and a heathen, that she had but played her games with him. Well, now, here she stays, and she'll have Olav, and you're a fool if you don't see it."

Keith mumbled something Zarabeth didn't understand. He was very drunk, yet Toki was still ranting at him, her tongue more virulent with each word she spoke. "Fool, you blessed fool, you have no sense! You are pitiful!"

Well, Toki and Keith would be pleased soon enough, once Zarabeth had taken Lotti to Magnus. Then Olav would have to look to his son.

Zarabeth waited and waited. Her patience was wearing thin and her fear was growing. Still Toki ranted occasionally, her voice a whine now, and Keith seemed to be in an ale-sodden sleep.

Then suddenly Zarabeth smiled. She walked to the front of the house and knocked on the door.

There was a snarl from Toki and the door slitted open.

"You!"

"Aye, 'tis I, Toki. Quickly, let me in. You and I have much to speak about, and you will like my words, I swear it to you."

7

"I shan't listen to you, Zarabeth! You lie to me, and I won't hear you!"

Zarabeth fought for patience against Toki's blatant distrust. "I do not lie. I want Lotti. Give her to me and I will leave York. You will never see me again. Olav will have to treat Keith more kindly. I'm not lying, Toki. For God's sake, why would I?"

Toki was filled with dislike and uncertainty and bone-deep envy, in equal parts. Zarabeth, daughter of that foreign slut who had taken over Olav's affections, stolen them from his only son, aye, she hated the slut's daughter, wished she would leave, wished she would die. Toki shook her head.

"You want this Viking, then? 'Twas all a lie, your meeting with him this morning at the well?"

"Aye, to convince Olav that I was serious. I had to convince Magnus that I didn't want him so that Olav would believe I'd done what he wanted. I succeeded very well, but I must make haste to search out Magnus to tell him the truth. Please, Toki, I must hurry! Give me Lotti!"

Still the woman hesitated. If she gave over the idiot child, she would lose all her leverage. She would have nothing at all with which to bargain. Still, if Zarabeth was telling the truth . . . Toki fretted and drank down the rest of Keith's mug of ale. She wiped the back of her hand across her mouth, feeling the froth from her

upper lip. She looked down at her snoring husband
with contempt.

"Toki, please, think! I have no reason to lie to you,
no reason at all—"

"I don't have a child, you know," Toki said suddenly, and she looked toward her husband, who
belched deeply, his face against the tabletop. "Oh,
Keith comes inside me and humps about and spills his
seed, yet nothing grows in my belly. Soon he'll not
care anymore. Soon I will have nothing to show for
my hours and days with him. But I do have something
now. I have Lotti and I've found that she isn't an idiot
or a freak, not really."

Zarabeth wanted to wrap her fingers around Toki's
neck and squeeze the life out of her. She was breathing hard now, her heart pounding. She tried to keep
her voice pitched low and calm. She didn't want to
risk waking Keith. She couldn't begin to imagine what
he would say to this. "She isn't yours, Toki. Lotti's
mine and will always be mine. You must return her
to me. I have no coin or jewelry to pay you with, or
I would give it to you willingly."

"Why should I give her up? I doubt Olav will let
you escape to your Viking now. He's proud and he's
insufferably vain, but he isn't stupid. If only his son
had but a bit of his trading ability, but he doesn't, and
he won't listen to me even when he knows I am in
the right. And the two of us must look to Olav, else
we'd starve. I grow to hate him, Zarabeth."

Zarabeth wondered if that meant the father or the
son, but she said again, "Give me Lotti, Toki. You
don't want the daughter of a slut, do you? What
makes you think Olav won't come to prefer Lotti over
Keith? He might, you know. She's a beautiful child,
just like her mother. But now, if you give her to me,
when we both leave, perhaps Olav will want both of
you to live with him. He'll provide you with slaves,

Toki, and you'll smile and enjoy yourself. Just think, you'll have fine materials from which to sew beautiful gowns and cloaks and perhaps new jewels."

The avid gleam faded from Toki's eyes as she said, "I don't believe that. You have no slaves. He doesn't adorn you or give you fine materials for new gowns. He fancies only himself and how he appears to the world. Look, even your brooch is merely of pounded bronze. You wear no rings, no armlets. Olav wears only the richest silver and gold. Why would he accord more to me than he accords to you, his beloved Zarabeth?"

"I don't know. He's always told me that there isn't enough money for slaves. He's always told me that he must look successful so foreign traders will notice him and believe he must be good so they will trade with him above all others. I don't care, Toki. But you'll ask him and he'll be grateful that you're there to look after him and his house. Give me Lotti."

"Perhaps I shall," Toki said. She turned away and pulled aside a bearskin that separated the sleeping space from the rest of the house. She came back carrying Lotti in her arms. The child was deeply asleep.

"Don't worry, I just drugged her. She was making too much noise, even with her strange grunts and growls. She kept saying your name as well. I wanted to hit her but I didn't. I drugged her to keep her quiet."

Zarabeth wanted to kill the woman. Fury pounded through her, but she held herself calm. She'd nearly won. She couldn't fail now. She took Lotti, and gently laid her over her shoulder. "I'm leaving now. Forget not what I said, Toki."

"Aye, I'll not forget."

Not ten minutes later, Zarabeth gained York harbor. Dark clouds were strewn over the sky, obscuring the moon. Everyone was sleeping, even the outlaws that lurked in the darkness, even the stray dogs that burrowed about in piles of garbage. There was the gentle sound of lapping water against the wooden piles, nothing more. And there was vessel after vessel moored to the dock. She ran now, wanting only to find Magnus, to explain, to escape with him, and never see York again.

Lotti stirred on her shoulder, and she whispered softly to the child. She quieted again.

Zarabeth wanted to yell out Magnus' name, but something held her back. Something wasn't right, something . . .

She came to a stunned halt and stared at the trading vessel in front of her. She'd never seen it before. There was no carved raven on its bow. She looked frantically to the next vessel and the next, but it was no use. The brutal, magnificent *Sea Wind* was gone.

Magnus had left.

She couldn't take it in. Lotti whimpered, and she gently stroked the child's back. He'd left . . . he was gone, and he believed she had betrayed him. He believed her faithless, a liar. There was no one to tell him otherwise.

Suddenly everything seemed very clear. It was over, all of it. There was nothing more for her. Zarabeth dropped to her knees on the wooden-planked dock. She gathered Lotti into her arms and rocked her, crooning sounds meant to comfort, not the child, but herself.

When Olav found her, it was nearly dawn.

"I've come to a decision," Olav said. Nearly a month had passed since the Viking had sailed away from York, and Olav felt good. Zarabeth was herself again—ah, quieter perhaps, more passive, but he didn't care a whit, for he didn't like a woman's sharp tongue. She was here and she served him and she obeyed him without question. Her submissiveness pleased him completely.

She looked at him now without interest. He didn't like that, and frowned. Perhaps too much passiveness wasn't quite what he wanted from her.

"Aye, I've decided what I will do."

Lotti said her name in that slurred way of hers and Olav looked at the child impatiently. "Can't you teach her to at least say your name clearly?"

Zarabeth gave him a clear, emotionless look. "It is very clear to me." Then she shrugged, saying something that made him rock back in surprise. "Of course, I am young and of clear hearing."

Olav held to his temper.

Zarabeth leaned over and handed Lotti a soft piece of bread she'd just baked an hour before. It was still warm and she'd smeared sweet honey on it.

"What is wrong with you? Why are you acting like this? Don't you care to hear about my decision?"

"You will tell me soon enough, I imagine."

"Very well. I've decided to marry you." She didn't move, she didn't change expressions, but her mind squirreled madly about. Why didn't he simply tell her that he would bed her? Why marriage? Bedding him was obscene; marrying him was even worse. She said nothing now, fearing what would come from her mouth if she did speak. When he had spoken to her a few moments ago, she had given her thoughts words and spoken what was in her mind. It had surprised and angered him, but she hadn't cared. But this decision of his to wed her, it was a travesty, it was mad and pathetic. She kept her head down.

"I've spoken to King Guthrum's counselors, and then to the king himself. You see, I managed to find for him exquisite bird feathers that came from the Lapps. I even traded them with only a narrow profit for myself. He was thus most favorably disposed

toward me when I sought his advice. 'Tis true that
one of his concubines shares his blood; he bows before
the Christian God, but never think any set of gods,
no matter their supposed origin, would distract him
from what he wants. Thus, when I told him I wanted
to wed with you and you carried none of my blood,
he said even the Christian bishops couldn't object."

"Why do you want to wed with me? You know I
despise you. Why?"

"Tread carefully, Zarabeth, for the child hears what
you say. The child could also hear me tell you what I
would do to her were you to resist me and what I
wish."

Zarabeth didn't care. It was really as simple as that.
She simply lived now, endured, for there was naught
else for her to do. She supposed she would have simply lain down and died were it not for Lotti. But Lotti
needed her, and thus she had to continue. She had to
pretend at life. She looked at Olav and said nothing
more, her expression now calm and blank as her
heart.

" 'Tis either bedding me as my wife or as my
whore."

She shrugged. "Aye, your whore, then."

She shouldn't have said that, he thought, eyeing her
with growing irritation. She should be grateful to him,
curse her, on her knees to him that he was willing to
wed with her, a female with no dowry of any sort,
nothing save that damned idiot child. She'd caught
him in a lie of his own weaving and now he must
admit to it. "Nay, I would not have you as my whore,
it would not be good for my business. People would
gossip about me, perhaps question my honor and my
judgment, for you are very young and I, well, I am
not quite so young as I was. No, it wouldn't be good
for me to have you as my whore. You will be my
wife—then none can criticize me. All will believe me

honorable. We will wed soon now. I will have a new gown sewn for you and you will wear it, Zarabeth, and you will look pleased and you will smile and speak gently to me, and you will compliment me to all who ask you."

Zarabeth looked at him. "If I refuse to wed with you, you will kill Lotti?"

"Aye."

He would use Lotti for as long as she lived. Zarabeth looked away and sliced off a piece of the warm bread. She spread butter and honey on it and took a bite. She said nothing, merely ate, one bite after the other.

"Answer me, Zarabeth!"

She took the last bite, then wiped her mouth. "I don't recall your asking me a question. Was there something you wanted, Olav?"

"Damn you, you will wed with me!"

"That isn't a question."

He jumped from his chair and she knew that he meant violence. This time he didn't catch her unawares. She picked up her knife and gripped it firmly. "Don't, Olav, else I'll slice you."

"You wouldn't," he said, watching her hand warily.

"There will be no violence, Olav. You will not hit me, nor will you ever again strike Lotti, or I will kill you. Believe me, for I mean it."

He shrugged, hoping to salvage his pride; when she nodded and put the knife down, he drew a deep breath. "A wife shouldn't threaten her husband."

"But a stepdaughter can."

He frowned at her, at the bitterness of her words. "You act the ill-treated orphan, Zarabeth. In truth, your life is easy and I leave you be to do as you wish. Any woman would wish to fill your place."

"Will you invite your son and his wife to this wedding feast?"

At that Olav smiled. It was a malicious smile, but it didn't touch her. She cared not what happened to Keith. Nothing had really touched her since Magnus had sailed from York. She cared not if Keith ranted and screamed at his father, if Toki shrieked and howled. "Oh, yes," Olav said, rubbing his hands together, "I shall invite everyone."

And he did. He spared no expense. A week later, on a sunny afternoon in May, Olav and Zarabeth were married, first according to the Christian ceremony, the bishop himself officiating to show King Guthrum's favor, then by the vows made before the Viking gods of Odin and Thor and Frey. Olav had garbed Zarabeth in a fine silk gown of soft pink with an overtunic of a darker pink, belted tightly at her waist with a wide band of white leather. She wore two brooches at her shoulders to hold the overtunic in place, both of them of the finest silver, worked by old Crinna himself.

There were banquet tables set up in Coppergate square, covered with trenchers holding cold beef strips and bowls of apples and pears and stewed onions and split baked turnips. There were freshly baked bread and a full bowl of honey and a block of butter. So much food, and Zarabeth saw that the people admired Olav and blessed him for his generosity, and overlooked the fact that he'd wedded his own stepdaughter, who was less than half his age. He'd even given Lotti fine wool for a new gown. The little girl stayed close to Zarabeth even during the ceremony before the Christian bishop, her face pressed against Zarabeth's thigh. Keith and Toki were there, and silent. Even Toki, never one to keep her feelings to herself, remained quiet, for she wasn't stupid and she saw that all the neighbors and townspeople were greatly awed and pleased by Olav's beneficence. King Guthrum himself made an appearance late in the afternoon, and Olav preened and basked in his favor.

Zarabeth accepted the envious glances from the unmarried women and the widows with outward serenity. If only they knew, she thought vaguely, if only they guessed that naught but vast emptiness filled her. She thought then of the coming night, thought of Olav naked, covering her, breaching her maidenhead, and even that didn't overly concern her. It would be done to someone else. It wouldn't really touch her. She felt Lotti press harder against her leg and took the little girl's hand in hers.

She saw her new husband raise a drinking horn of fine Rhenish blue glass and drink yet more sweet honey-mead. She saw him offer the king more of the potent brew. King Guthrum, old and fat and gray-bearded, sat piously beside his wife whilst two of his lemans fluttered in the background, young and charm-ripe and round of arm and breast. Men and women alike were drunk now, and there was much good-natured giving of advice to Olav on bedding his new bride.

It didn't touch Zarabeth. None of it. Even when Toki sidled up to her, a wary eye always trained on Olav, she didn't do more than say calmly, "Yes, Toki? What wish you?"

"You think you've won, don't you, Zarabeth? Well, you haven't. Just look at Olav, so drunk he can scarce keep upright. Just listen to him laughing at the king's inane jests! It's pathetic, and now you will pay, my girl, surely you will pay."

"Probably."

"He'll not give you a brat!"

"I hope not."

Toki fell silent, staring at Zarabeth with drunken concentration. "You don't care," she said at last, and there was a good deal of bewilderment in her voice.

Zarabeth tightened her hold on Lotti's hand. She looked toward Olav and saw that he stumbled from drink. She felt only a mild revulsion, gazing on him.

"Aye, when he pukes, you'll care."

Zarabeth sighed. "I'll probably have to clean it up."

Toki gave a malevolent look at Lotti, then took herself back to her equally drunken husband. Zarabeth held herself apart, but no one noticed, for the drink hadn't yet run out. It was very late before two men approached her, laughing drunkenly, supporting an unconscious Olav between them.

"It will take a woman's gentle care to rouse him!"

"Aye, mayhap 'tis best to let him lie alone. Either he'll die or vow to become a monk on the morrow."

They carried Olav to the house, Zarabeth and Lotti following behind. The king had spoken gracious words to her, as had the queen, and had commended her to her husband's generosity and nobility of spirit. She felt tired after the long day, but little else. She motioned the men to place her husband on his box bed, and after they'd left, giving her leering looks, she pulled a coverlet over him and let him be. She prayed he would sleep through the night.

Olav didn't sleep through the night. He awoke deep in the middle of the night, still more drunk than sick, realized that he was wedded to Zarabeth, and went in search of her.

He found her sleeping by Lotti and grabbed her arm, shaking her and nearly yelling, "Why sleep you here? Why are you with her and not with me? 'Tis your duty to sleep with me! I have paid dearly for you. You're my wife!"

Zarabeth felt Lotti stiffen beside her. She hadn't been asleep; she had heard him stumble across the room. She'd prepared herself, and now she said calmly enough, "Go back to your bed, Olav. The women told me that you would be too drunk to take me this night. I pray that you won't be sick, for I have no wish to clean up after you. Go away now."

Any thoughts Olav had cherished of bedding Zarabeth faded in that moment. His belly cramped and turned in on itself and he moaned, clutching his arms around himself. Zarabeth heard him stumble through to his outer shop, then out into the night. She didn't move, merely said very softly to Lotti, "Go back to sleep, little love. He won't bother us tonight at least."

The next morning Keith found his father huddled against the shop front, sleeping like the dead.

8

Olav's face was gray. His eyes burned and wept. A line of cold sweat threaded above his upper lip. His jowls hung and his clothes looked now like they belonged to another man, a bigger man, a healthy paunchy man.

The pain in his belly had increased, and now he could no longer work in his shop. He sat the whole day now in the living area watching Zarabeth go about her work. Occasionally he would moan softly and run from the room, clutching his belly. His friends came by, but they couldn't drink or eat or jest with him, for he was silent in his pain and withdrawn from their concerns. Thus they left him to go about their own business. Few came around anymore. The women visited Zarabeth, giving her advice, looking sadly toward Olav, and shaking their heads.

Olav looked at Zarabeth now. It was the middle of the day and she was cooking—likely bland soup for him, curse her. Bland soup and bread soft enough for an old man with no teeth and a liquid gut. Damp tendrils of hair framed her face. She was silent, so very silent, never raising her voice even when he screamed at her in his pain and fear and his frustration, for he couldn't bring her to heel as a man should his wife, and he became more afraid by the day. Lotti played near her feet, stacking trenchers, then counting them in that ugly slurred voice of hers, then unstacking them. Repeating and repeating until he wanted to yell. But he didn't; he didn't have the strength.

Every once in a while Zarabeth would bend down and caress the little girl's face, speak to her softly, then smile. Not one of her sweet smiles was ever for him. She was his wife, and yet it meant nothing.

A vicious cramp made him gasp, and he hobbled from the room, bent over like an old man, holding his belly. Zarabeth looked up, frowning after him. He'd been ill since their wedding two weeks before, and now he looked like an old man, frail and gaunt, and he acted like an old man, querulous and spiteful. At first, she knew, Olav had believed his belly pains simple retribution from too much mead and ale consumed at his wedding feast, but the pain in his stomach had continued, and he suffered greatly from bloody bowels.

He wasn't capable of taking her. One night he had ordered her to disrobe in front of him. He'd wanted to see her, to caress her; it was his right as her husband. She hadn't done it. Zarabeth shook away the memory.

Keith and Toki came every day, the son to help his father with his goods and Toki to gloat and ridicule, only in Zarabeth's presence of course, mocking the failing old man and his sweet new bride who hadn't been bedded, his new bride who wouldn't breed a babe.

Zarabeth stirred the soup, mashing the potatoes as she stirred. Olav could eat the soup, and he appeared to enjoy it, even though he cursed under his breath and crabbed and complained. She had asked the ancient old crone Ungarn about Olav's pain, and she had scratched the flaking skin on her arm and muttered that Zarabeth should give him ground-up garlic and smashed onions mixed together inside a bay leaf. The combination sounded nauseating to Zarabeth, but she'd done it. Oddly, it had seemed to make him feel a bit better. But no longer did it have any effect.

She looked up to see Toki saunter into the living area as if she were the mistress. She soon would be, if Olav died, for Zarabeth would have no rights. Surely Olav had willed with the York council to leave all his earthly goods to his son. Zarabeth nodded to Toki, wishing she would simply turn about and leave, and continued her stirring. She felt Lotti move closer to her, leaned down and gave the child a reassuring pat on her head. Lotti had kept her distance from Toki ever since that night so long ago.

"The old man looks ready for a burial. All he needs is a winding sheet."

"I think he does a bit better today," Zarabeth said. "But it is slow and mean, this strange illness he has."

Toki shrugged and looked down at the soup Zarabeth was stirring. "More tasteless pap for the old beggar? What a pity you must eat what he does. Your ribs must be knocking hard against your skin."

Zarabeth said nothing, merely stared into the soup. She mashed another potato to pulp.

"He still hasn't bedded you, has he?"

The long wooden spoon stilled. Slowly Zarabeth turned to face her new daughter-in-law, a woman several years her senior. "Keep your tongue away from things that are none of your business, Toki. I shan't tell you again. You will cease your insults of Olav. Without him, as you once told me, you and Keith would starve."

Zarabeth turned away, fearing her own anger, ignoring Toki's soft hiss of anger.

At times, life was nearly comforting, for it had become so predictable. Zarabeth took care of her husband, endured Toki's ill-humor and Keith's constant questions about his father's health. She thought of Magnus only in the dark of the night when it was still and warm and she couldn't keep him out of her mind. The pain of his leaving didn't lessen. It was sharp and deep and always with her, waiting to flood her with sadness and despair. She supposed that the pain would fade, for pain always did lessen with time. Perhaps by the end of the summer, or perhaps the fall. But for now his face was still clear in her mind, and she could still feel the strength of him when he'd held her, the teasing in his voice, the tenderness, and that bold way he had of saying things that made her dumb with surprise and delight.

She shook him away. It was the middle of another day, not the silence of night. Keith and Toki had come, as usual, for the evening meal. Toki was complaining, as usual. Lotti tugged on Zarabeth's gown, wanting her attention. Zarabeth ignored Toki and came down on her haunches beside her little sister.

It was the wooden trenchers. One of them had a splinter and Lotti had torn the flesh on her middle finger. Zarabeth teased her and petted her and washed the scratch, then kissed the fingertip, all while Toki was sitting in Olav's large carved chair, complaining of her lack of attention, complaining of the miserable meal she would surely have to endure for yet another evening, and telling Zarabeth that the child was stupid and didn't deserve such attention.

Zarabeth rose slowly to her feet. It would never stop, never. Toki's mouth rode on fast and sure wheels, her complaints and her meanness unending. To gain control, she took time to smooth her damp hair back from her face, to smooth down the skirt of her gown. She hated the bickering, the confrontations, but she simply couldn't let it go this time. Then she said to Toki, "Get out of Olav's chair, Toki. Even ill, he fits it better than do you. You will not again speak with malice of either my husband or my sister. Now, do you understand me?"

Toki swung her crossed leg and folded her thin arms over her breasts. She smiled. "You slut! You stand there gloating because all this is yours, but not for long. You won't be the mistress here forever, nay, not even for another month, I'll wager. The old man won't ever bed you. Never. You won't bear a child to take away all that is Keith's. That foolish old beggar won't last, you'll see. He'll soon have ashes in his mouth and worms gnawing at his bones, and you'll starve, you and that brat with you!"

Zarabeth was weary to her bones, her anger now spent. She just shook her head, only to jerk around at the sound of Olav's furious voice.

"You bitch!" He came into the room, his shoulders straighter, his gray face flushed with anger. "Don't you ever again speak to Zarabeth like that! You malignant shrew. By Thor's wounds and Freya's goodness, I never fully realized what my son must endure. Or do you keep your wretched tongue sweet for him? Aye, I wager that you do. How long have you tormented Zarabeth? And she has protected you with silence, you worthless bitch. By Thor, you are the one who should die!"

"Father, it isn't true," Keith said, coming quickly into the room, more quickly to his wife's defense. "Toki only cares that you are well-taken-care-of, nothing more. She distrusts Zarabeth, for she is naught but the daughter of that runaway whore, Mara. She is concerned because Zarabeth is young and heedless and cares naught for you save your wealth. Surely—"

Keith got no further. Zarabeth leapt at him, her fingers going around his throat, and she was screaming, "You aren't worthy to speak her name! My mother wasn't a whore! Say no more, else I'll kill you!"

Zarabeth felt Olav's hands pull hers away from Keith's throat. Toki was yelling, Lotti was cowering in the corner, and Keith simply stood there, his face pale, uncertain what he should say or do.

Olav gently pulled Zarabeth back. He looked first at Toki, then at his son. He said then, his voice low and calm, "Both of you will leave my house. I feel pity for you, Keith, for you are weak and pitiful, letting this woman tell you what thoughts should be in your head, tell you what feelings should fill your heart. I would beat her soundly were I you. Mayhap I would beat her unto death for her viper's tongue. Since I am not you, however, and since you are in the world's eyes a man grown, you will suffer what it is you wish to suffer without my interference. Neither of you is welcome here again. Leave now, both of you."

"Father, no, you can't mean—"

Olav raised a tired hand and merely shook his head. "Leave, Keith, and take this cursed witch with you."

Toki was silent for once in her life. She was trembling with rage, but she held her tongue, knowing that words now would only further endanger her in her husband's eyes. She mustn't allow that to happen. By the saints, he was her only chance, this man who was her husband and thus superior to her, though he was a dolt and couldn't trade a walrus tusk for a rag without losing gold. She would reason with him later; she would convince him to make peace with his father, and quickly. She had no choice but to convince him. Everything depended on it.

Otherwise, Toki wouldn't be able to continue slipping the poison in the old man's nightly food.

Ah, but she couldn't tell Keith that, the squeamish fool, for he was weak of spine. No, she'd spin a tale to turn his head, and he would end up praising her generosity of spirit. She'd been imprudent to attack Zarabeth with the old man in the outer shop. She wouldn't be stupid again. She would play the silly sow, and beg dear Zarabeth's forgiveness.

After Toki and Keith had left, Olav was silent. He remained silent during the evening meal. He ate slowly, as if studying each bite to be certain the soup wouldn't make him immediately ill. But as he ate his second bowl, he began to eat more rapidly. "It is amazingly good," he said, picking up his bowl and drinking the remaining liquid, making loud slurping noises.

Lotti giggled, and Olav, rather than looking at her with ill-disguised loathing, smiled. He said slowly, looking directly at her, "I'm hungry, have been since my wedding day. But not now. Aye, methinks your sister's fine soup will settle without contempt in my belly."

"I pray God it will do so, Olav."

It did. The next day, he was afflicted with bloody bowels but once. The next day not at all. He smiled, he laughed, and he even worked in his shop for an hour. And that night he looked at Zarabeth and she knew what he was thinking. He wanted her and soon he would have the strength to take her. She swallowed. Endure, she would endure. There was no choice. She looked at him whilst he sorted through several otter pelts, here, in the living area, not in his outer shop. He had changed, becoming kinder to her and to Lotti, gentler in his dealings with both of them. This was owing to Toki's vicious attack, and, Zarabeth guessed, it was also the specter of death that had made him judge things differently. Still, the thought of him mounting her, of him touching her, made her recoil.

She could say naught against him. He was her husband, and thus to take her was his right.

The following day he said to her at the noonday meal, "I have met with the council of elders. I have told them that my son is no more a son to me. I have told them that in the case of my death, it is you who will have all my earthly goods."

She stared at him in surprise. "Why, Olav? This cannot be! You still do not hold Toki's silly words against

Keith? Of a certainty, she brings anger with her barbed tongue and her ill-humor, but Keith is your only son and he deserves something from you. He has not your talents and your gifts. He has need of you."

"You are too generous, Zarabeth. The boy became a man, and thus he is responsible for himself. It is done. I will not change it."

"But you arranged for his marriage with Toki. Do you not remember? He was not overly pleased, but he did as you bade him do. How can you turn your back on him now?"

Olav didn't like that reminder, but he said naught to her. It was true that Toki's parents had brought him much gold, but that had been spent in foolish ventures, by Keith, within a year. Still, it gave him pause. Not that it mattered much what he did in the near future regarding his heir, for now his sickness seemed to have abated.

That night Zarabeth lay stiff and silent on the box bed beside Lotti, listening to Olav move about in the living area. She felt her flesh grow cold. He would come to her and ask her to visit him in his bed. She knew it, and she prepared herself for it, yet when it happened, when he pulled aside the animal hide that separated her sleeping area from the living area, she pretended sleep.

"Nay, Zarabeth, 'tis time. I know you're awake. Come with me and I'll teach you things you will enjoy."

She rose, knowing there was naught else she could do. She was wearing her sleep shift, and it came but to her knees. She felt exposed and ashamed and helpless. She had braided her hair and it hung in one thick tail down her back. He took her hand and led her into his sleeping chamber. His box bed was large and made of sturdy oak planking, covered with soft furs and wool blankets.

"I will try to become husband to you, Zarabeth." With those words he leaned forward and kissed her. She forced herself to bear it. She tried not to think of Magnus, but he was there nonetheless, deep in her mind, a part of her that would never be gone. In time, perhaps, she thought frantically, he would be a ghost, a whisper of a smile, and a look, but now he was real and alive and vital within her. And another man was kissing her.

"Unbraid your hair. A woman shouldn't have her hair scraped back from her face. It pleases me not."

She pulled the braid over her shoulder and untied the leather tie. Slowly she pulled the loosely woven hair free of its braid, smoothing her fingers through it until Olav stopped her and freed the tangles himself. "Soft," he said, and brought her hair to his cheek, rubbing it back and forth. "Red as a sunset that tokens a night storm, and so very soft." He sifted his fingers through her hair as she stood still as a stone. When he was done, he stood back.

"I require stimulation even though I have gone a long time without a woman's body. My illness did me no good and dulled my body's appetites. I will sit here and you will disrobe for me. 'Twill make my manhood spring to life again, Zarabeth."

He sat on his box bed, leaned back against the smooth-planed wooden wall, and crossed his arms over his chest. He watched her. His heart pounded in slow, deep strokes. He had left the animal skin pulled back, for he was always cold, it seemed, and he needed the heat from the fire even in the summer. He felt the warmth of it on his flesh now, even as he watched her.

She stood there in the dim light of the dying fire, her hair wild around her face, and wanted to die.

"I cannot, Olav."

He didn't move. "You will not deny me this time, Zarabeth, like you did before. I understood then, for I was unable to become your husband, but now it will be different. You have made me well with your fine care. Now make me a man again."

What could she do? She wished in vain for the numbness, the blankness, that had kept her from feeling much of anything after Magnus had left. But the numbness was only a faint memory now. She felt fear and hideous shame, and she wished wildly that Olav had remained ill.

"Now, Zarabeth."

Her hands went to the narrow straps on her shoulders. Slowly she pulled the straps down until the shift dropped to her breasts. He was staring at her, and she froze. He sat forward suddenly and touched his outstretched hand to her breast. His fingertips were smooth and soft. He jerked the shift down to her waist and stared at her until she was trembling with the strength of her fear. She doubted he saw the revulsion in her eyes, for he wasn't looking above her breasts.

"By Thor's ax, you are beautiful. I hadn't realized . . . so white and soft." He sighed then, and sat forward to press his face against her breasts, his arms wrapped around her back. She didn't move. She closed her eyes and held herself perfectly still. She felt his hot breath against her flesh, felt his tongue lick her cold flesh. His breathing quickened and his arms tightened around her, pulling her more closely against him. His hands went to her buttocks and he was jerking at the shift to have her naked.

"So beautiful," he whispered, then drew back, staring up at her white face. "You don't want this, Zarabeth, but you will learn to accommodate me. Now, I will show you my manhood and you will help me."

He bared himself quickly and she saw how very thin he was, his flesh hanging loosely on him, his man's rod flaccid and small, nestled in the thick gray-gold hair of his groin.

She watched him touch himself, watched as he tried frantically to bring himself to life, but his man's rod remained as it was.

He looked up at her then and saw the disgust on her face, the revulsion she couldn't hide. He felt fury and frustration in equal amounts. "Didn't that damned Viking show you his man's rod? Didn't you touch him, caress him with your hands, take him in your mouth? Was his rod so great, then, Zarabeth? Aye, he is young and vigorous, but I tell you, even he is sometimes like this. Touch me, damn you!"

She took a step back, then another. She was shaking her head, covering her breasts with her hands. "Please, Olav, I cannot. I am a maid. I have never before seen a man's body, nay, not the Viking's. Please, you cannot want me to caress you now . . . not like this."

He stared down at himself and knew it was no good. He was shriveled and dead. Then he looked up at her, saw that she'd covered herself again with her nightshift, and laughed, at himself, at the irony of his life.

"A beautiful young wife . . . just look at you, all that red hair, and your body, so glorious and soft, so very white your flesh, and I can do nothing save gaze upon you. Ah, yes, you're a maid, Zarabeth, and I offend you by showing you my limp manhood. Go to bed. I wish to sleep. I will regain my strength, you will see. I will cover you and come inside you and you won't have to see me like this again. Aye, I'll be a man again and you'll be obedient to my demands."

She fled, dumb with relief.

Magnus stood on the high mound outside his fortified farmstead, Malek, and looked west toward the upper end of the Gravak Valley. It was high summer, and there was much work to do in the fields. Soon would come the harvest and he would join all his men and women and work from dawn until twilight dimmed the night skies and he fell exhausted into his bed. He looked at the steep fir-tree slopes on the far side of the fjord, immensely beautiful land that dropped gradually into water that was in many places over one hundred feet deep at the shore. The green of the tree-thick mountains was vivid against the crystal blue of the water. It was his home and he'd know no other. It was always with joy that he returned here to the valley of his birth, the valley that had belonged to his family for more generations than he could remember. There were many people in the valley now, and soon, like so many other Norwegians, they would be land-hungry, for the earth could not feed their numbers. But for now, the land was fertile and the weather had blessed them with rain aplenty and the wheat and rye and corn grew deep and rich in the soil. It would be another generation, at least, perhaps his son, who would leave the valley to conquer new lands and settle them and rule them.

Upon his return to the valley this time, his wealth had further increased, but it had brought him no joy, for there was the gnawing emptiness and savage fury that mingled in seemingly equal parts within him. He moved, restless now, striding to the edge of the cliff that formed the outward boundary of his farmstead, and felt the pain of it, the sheer rage of it fill him. By Odin's wounds, what was wrong with him that she would scorn him? Was he so repellent of character? So scrawny of body that she didn't like the notion of bedding with him? Perhaps it was just that, in the end, she found she couldn't leave her home to journey to an unknown foreign land. Perhaps she simply hadn't trusted him enough. Perhaps she had lied throughout.

He slammed his fist against his thigh and winced with the pain of his own blow. Damn her! He should have simply taken her and brought her back with him. He'd given her choice, and she'd turned on him. To give a woman choice was foolishness. He hadn't been a man with her, he hadn't taken away her fanciful, capricious choices as his father would have done, as both his brothers would have done. Aye, they would have laughed at her if she had dared to dismiss them so plainly, and carried her away screaming, paying her no heed. Aye, he'd been a fool.

What was wrong with him that she would scorn him? No woman before had scorned him. Why Zarabeth? Why the one woman he'd wanted to wed?

He turned at his sister's voice. "Aye? What is it you want, Ingunn?"

"You brood. It worries me, Magnus. It worries all of us, your men included. You say so little, criticize your men more than is their due, and yell and scowl at your slaves. You don't even take Cyra to your bed as you used to."

"Ha! I did naught but plow her belly when I came home. I took her until she could scarce walk."

"Aye, but then you dismissed her. She feels sorely tried, as if she's failed you in some way."

He shrugged, not looking at Ingunn, but staring fixedly toward the northern side of the fjord. Why in the name of Thor's hammer Ingunn should care a whit about Cyra's feelings was beyond him.

"It's a woman, isn't it? You met a woman on your travels and she gnaws at you."

He laughed at that. "You make me sound like a bone our father's hound would tease."

He felt her fingers on his tunic sleeve. "Nay, brother, jest not, for our father also wonders what eats at you. He said you weren't interested in the men's drinking or the tale-singing at his hall. He said you moped and said aught and acted a morose lovesick boy. But he always says there is a raging anger in you, great anger, and there will be bloodletting before your anger finishes its course."

Again Magnus shrugged. It was true, all of it, yet it was a private matter and he wanted to hold it to himself alone. He supposed he should be pleased that the men who knew of Zarabeth had kept their mouths firmly closed. It concerned none other, not his father, not his brothers, certainly not Ingunn.

Suddenly he smiled, a grim smile, a vicious smile. He turned then with sudden irrevocable decision, and felt that a rock had lifted from his chest. "I am leaving on the morrow. Prepare food enough for a journey of thirty days for twelve men. I will do more trading in Birka. Hurry now, Ingunn."

She didn't want to obey him, but she had no choice. She disbelieved him. Birka was the last place he was going. She left him without another word to do his bidding. She turned once to see him standing in the same spot, staring off at the fjord, but not looking at the clear cold water.

What was he seeing?

9

Olav was dead. He had died early in the morning, just after dawn, whimpering and clutching his belly. All during the night Zarabeth had stayed with him, helpless and frightened, afraid to leave him, yet knowing there was nothing she could really do if she stayed. He hadn't even been able to rise and relieve himself. Toward the end, he hadn't known her. He raved of her mother, how he'd loved her and how she had betrayed him. Zarabeth had held his hand.

It made no sense. He had been well the previous evening, whistling even as he sorted through goods he had traded during the day. And now, only twelve hours later, he was dead.

Zarabeth helped Imara and Lannia, two older women who'd seen their share of death and prepared their share of corpses, ready his body. She was numb, doing the simple tasks Lannia assigned her, not really understanding when Toki came into the living area, sniffed, and said, "By Thor, it stinks in here! Can't you do something, Zarabeth?"

Imara turned on Toki and gave her a malignant frown. "Mind your tongue. 'Tis a place of death, and it will remain so until the morrow."

Zarabeth turned then to face Toki. She was so tired, all she wanted to do was crawl onto her box bed next to Lotti and dream away all the horror. But she couldn't. She had to assume the responsibility of

Olav's burial; she had been his wife. She said, more puzzled than angry, "Why did you hate him so much? He allowed you to come back, he forgave you. You shared our evening meals with us again. Why do you speak so cruelly of him now?"

Toki shrugged. "I didn't hate Olav, 'tis just that I didn't want to marry Keith, but my parents forced me to, and he is not the merchant his father was. Olav owed both of us, and he gave little. No, Zarabeth, Olav cleaved to you—his fancy young slut of a wife. He turned his back upon his only son because you seduced him away from Keith."

Imara straightened now, her shoulders wide as a man's, her upper arms thick with muscle, and walked to Toki, towering over the shorter woman. "Get out, Toki, and do not return until you can control your tongue's venom."

Lannia, bent and scraggle-haired, never looked up from her task. She said, "Toki's mother is a witch, and she birthed a witch. Pay her no attention, Zarabeth."

Actually, Zarabeth had already dismissed Toki from her mind. Her attention was on Lotti, sitting in the far corner, playing with six carved sticks Olav had given her many years before. The child was quiet, too quiet.

She felt the nibblings of fear. Olav was dead. What would become of her and Lotti?

She found out the following day after Olav's funeral. Two of his friends, both on the York council, came to see her. They were old men, gray-haired and toothless, yet they were kind. She gave them sweet mead to drink, then waited respectfully for them to speak.

". . . And so, Zarabeth, Olav has left you all his goods, his shop and his house. He didn't wish his son to have anything."

She hadn't really believed Olav when he told her

he'd done this. She'd known, had been certain, that
he would look after his son, that he would change his
mind, that he would overlook Toki's viciousness and
not strike out at Keith to get back at her. She shook
her head now. "But Keith . . . it isn't right. Surely
Olav—"

"It is as we have said to you." Both of them looked
at her then, closely, as if she were some sort of oddity.
"All wonder at it, yea, 'tis true, but you are young
and comely, and therein lies the answer to all our
questions. Thus it is, and thus it will remain. It is what
your husband wished."

And they left this house of death quickly, for a man
didn't like the thought of a dead spirit leaving with
him and cleaving unbeknownst to him to his own soul.
Still, Zarabeth wondered at their abrupt retreat, their
curtness. She had known but kindness from them until
today. They hadn't disapproved of Olav's marriage to
her before, or if they had, they had hidden it well.
She remembered both of them clearly on her wedding
day, the two graybeards drunk and stumbling and
pinching a female buttock when a woman came near
to them. They'd laughed and clapped Olav on the
back and laughed more when they gave him their old
men's advice in loud whispers. They weren't laughing
now.

For the next two days Zarabeth slept and tried to
regain her strength. Olav's funeral had been the familiar blending of Christian and Viking, and he'd been
laid to rest with a rune stone over his burial mound.
All her neighbors left her alone, as if guessing that
she needed to be alone, to mend, to regain her balance. Two days later, Zarabeth took Lotti outside. It
was high summer and hot, no breeze stirring the still
air. There were the familiar smells of animals and
human sweat and excrement. She saw neighbors and
waved to them, grateful that they'd left her alone.

Then she realized suddenly that they were ignoring her, or turning quickly from her. What was wrong?

As was her wont since Magnus had left, she and Lotti walked to York harbor. She stared over the trading vessels moored there, Viking longboats all, with covered cargo spaces, knowing the *Sea Wind* wasn't there, but looking nonetheless, hunger in her soul. Lotti shook her hand and Zarabeth looked up to see Keith approaching, three men of the York council with him. He pointed to her and yelled, "Don't move!"

Move? Why should she move? She waited patiently for them to reach her, Lotti's hand held firmly in hers.

"It is over and done with, Zarabeth."

"What is, Keith? What do you here? Has something happened? Is Toki all right?"

"Were you going to try to escape on one of the vessels? Has another Viking offered to help you?"

She stared at Keith, wondering at his words, at his pallor, at the strained look in his eyes.

"What is this, Keith? What is wrong?"

One of the council, a man named Old Arnulf, who had danced drunkenly at Olav's wedding feast, strode up to her and said in a voice filled with fury, "We know the truth now, Zarabeth. We know that you murdered your husband, that you fed him poison from the day he wedded with you. You will die now, and justice will be done."

"Poison?" She looked from Keith to each of the three older men. They were serious. "You believe I fed poison to Olav? He was my husband! I cared for him throughout his illness, I didn't try to kill him! This is madness. What goes on here?"

" 'Tis too late for denials, Zarabeth," Keith said, but when she turned on him, he took a quick step backward, as if expecting she would attack him.

"I did nothing to Olav!"

Old Arnulf just shook his head. "Both Keith and Toki are witnesses to your deed. That a wife would seek to kill her husband—'tis something we won't tolerate, and thus you will die."

"No!" Without thought, without conscious decision, Zarabeth grabbed Lotti up into her arms and ran down the long wooden quay. Two rough-garbed sailors stopped her, laughing, holding her, looking at her as if she were a feast and they starving men.

"Hold her! She's a murderess!"

The sailors dropped their hands as if touching her would taint them or she would turn on them with a knife. This time, though, Zarabeth didn't move. She waited for them to approach her again, then said, "You say that Keith and his wife say I poisoned Olav. How do they know this?"

Arnulf took her arm, saying briskly, "You will have a chance to ask your questions and make your pleas before the king, for he was Olav's friend and has said he will pass judgment on you. Come along."

And it was done. Zarabeth made no more protest until she realized they were taking her to the slaves' compound. It stood on a barren moor just outside the city fortifications, a place of misery and filth. It was surrounded by its own earthen wall, three feet thick, and there was one great longhouse that was covered with a thatched roof. Around the longhouse were separate huts for the guards. There was a central well but nothing else.

Still she didn't give in to the awful fear. She would tell King Guthrum the truth of the matter. It was soon clear to her: Toki had poisoned Olav and had convinced Keith to blame Zarabeth. No wonder Olav had gotten well once he had forbidden Toki and Keith to come back to the house. And then, because of her pleas, Olav had forgiven his son and allowed him and Toki back. And he had signed his own death warrant

with his generosity. It was too much. She couldn't at
first take it in. There was no hope for it. She would
tell the king what had happened and then she and
Lotti would be left in peace.

Old Arnulf handed her over to the single guard, a
huge man with a flattened nose and thick black brows
that met, forming a single line. "Guard her well, for
she is a murderess. She will see King Guthrum on the
morrow. See that none abuse her or ravish her. See
that her clothes aren't stolen."

The guard grunted and took her arm. Suddenly
Arnulf said loudly, "Nay, the child cannot enter into
the compound! Keith come and take your sister. She
is your responsibility now."

It was then that Zarabeth lost all control. Panic
filled her and she whirled around, screaming, "Nay!
You cannot take her, no! Keith despises her . . . Toki
will beat her and kill her!" But they pulled Lotti from
her arms, looking at the child with contempt as she
cried softly, strangled, ugly sounds that sounded terrified and lost.

"Take her, Keith, and see to her. The child will
come to no harm in your care." Lotti struggled as
Keith lifted her high in his arms to avoid her flailing
hands.

"No!" Zarabeth went wild. She grabbed for Lotti,
only to feel her arms pulled back and held painfully.
The guard eased his hold, but still held her firmly.
Tears streamed down her face and choked in her
throat as she watched Keith try to hold Lotti still. The
child reared back, trying to get free of him, but it was
no good. Zarabeth felt a helplessness so deep that she
wanted to die with it. But she couldn't. Somehow she
had to save Lotti. But first she had to save herself.
She managed to say very softly, "Nay, Lotti, hold still,
love. Keith won't hurt you, nor will Toki. Arnulf of
the council said that he will take good care of you.

Go now with him, and I will come for you when this
is over."

To everyone's surprise, Lotti looked at her sister,
then smiled, a beautiful smile that held faith and complete trust. She then lay against Keith's shoulder,
small hiccups coming from her mouth.

"Come," the guard said, and his voice was rough
and ugly as his face. He wouldn't let her walk, no, he
had to drag her toward the longhouse. She turned and
saw the council leave, Keith holding a now-silent Lotti
behind them.

The guard shoved her inside the longhouse. It was
so dark within that at first she could see nothing. Then
she saw the people. They were a sorry lot, filthy, some
of the men manacled, the women slovenly and uncaring, their eyes empty of hope. Each one, she knew,
had a home, a story to tell, and both would become
garbled and vague in future years. It was sad, perhaps,
but it was the way things were. Slaves were property,
nothing more.

Zarabeth gave her attention to the guard as he said,
"You won't be harmed." He raised his head and
looked at all the men and boys who had stirred at
their entrance. "Any of you beasts touch her, and the
flesh will be flayed from your backs and your cocks
severed clean off."

He turned to her then, and shoved her toward the
end of the long dark room. "Keep your tongue in
your mouth and you will be all right." And he left her
there in the middle of the thatched longhouse, and it
was dark within, for there were no windows, and the
stench of the people was raw and ugly in her nostrils.
She walked slowly toward a bare place against the far
wall and sank down. No one said anything to her. No
one even paid heed to her now. There was silence.

She was numb, but not so numb that she wasn't
aware of the awful silence. There were some twenty

men and women waiting here, waiting for someone to buy them and remove them. Then they began talking amongst themselves, and she recognized the accents of her homeland, Ireland. She wondered what they been before the Vikings had capture them and brought them here to York. She wondered if they'd been so ragged and scraggly then, or if their captivity had made them look like filthy animals.

The day passed, as did the night. Zarabeth ate a thin stew from a rough wooden bowl. She didn't have to worry that any of the men would try to ravish her. They were too locked into themselves and their own fates to concern themselves with her. She was cold during the night, but it didn't matter. No one cared. She thought about Lotti and felt sweat trickle down her back and sides. The dirt was in her nostrils, covered her gown, and when she awoke the following morning, the ugly guard was standing over her and in his hand he held the beautiful brooch Olav had given her. He had pulled it off her gown, and the soft linen was ripped off her shoulder.

She said nothing. It didn't matter. She said to the guard, "I will see the king soon. I am dirty and need to bathe myself."

He looked at her as if she'd sprouted a pheasant's wings. Then he laughed, throwing his shaggy head back, and soon he was shouting his mirth. She tried to comb her fingers through her hair but knew how she must look. She felt cramped and dirty and wrinkled.

It was nearly noon before Old Arnulf arrived to take her to see the king. He looked at her and just shook his head. Zarabeth again pleaded for a bath, but he wouldn't hear of it.

"There is no place for you to bathe or change your gown. Keith and Toki have moved into Olav's house.

Come now, for we don't wish to keep the king waiting."

King Guthrum's palace stood on high ground above York harbor, stone walls surrounding it, and its white stone, quarried nearby at Helleby, gleamed in the summer sunlight. She had visited the palace once before in the company of Olav when he'd delivered a magnificent otter pelt to the king as a birthday present. She had waited in an outer chamber and been awed by her surroundings. She wasn't awed now, she was too frightened. Exquisite tapestries in bright colors still covered the stone walls. Those walls that were wooden rather than stone had been smoothed down and covered with more hangings of vivid red silks and blue wools. The king, Olav had told her then, was fond of red silk. He wore little else. And jewelry. He loved finger rings and neck chains and arm bracelets of thick, heavy gold and silver.

But today she wasn't in Olav's company. She was no longer a girl to gawk and admire. She was a prisoner. She straightened her shoulders, waiting.

Old Arnulf's hand stayed flat on her back. He pushed her forward as if she hadn't the ability to walk herself without his direction. It angered her. She wanted to turn on him and scream that he was a fool, and more than that, he was blind to the truth. No, no, she must wait, she would tell the king the truth and he would at least have to consider her words.

King Guthrum was no longer the handsome young Viking who had held all the Danelaw in his hands for nearly three decades. He was old and gnarly and white-haired and his face was deeply creased from the sun. He was seated in a magnificently carved throne chair of oak with finely ornamented arms. He believed them magic. Whenever he fought, the chair arms went with him. He was garbed splendidly in red silk, as was his wont, and he wore many arm bracelets and rings.

Around his neck was a thick gold neckband, polished and inset with rubies and diamonds. At least a dozen men stood around him. None sat save the king. Arnulf shoved Zarabeth forward and she stumbled to her knees.

"Stay there," he hissed behind her.

She looked up into the king's eyes.

"You are Zarabeth, widow of Olav."

"Aye, sire."

"Before, you were his stepdaughter, and then he condescended to wed with you. At your wedding I believed Olav had made a fine choice."

She jerked back at the cold words and the wrong conclusion. She shook her head. "Nay, sire, 'twas not like that. He wished to protect me and Lotti, my younger stepsister. Thus he insisted that I wed him."

King Guthrum turned to Keith, and she followed his gaze and saw Keith shake his head. She saw Toki standing behind him. She looked around frantically for Lotti, but the child wasn't there.

She felt fear and rage pound through her, choking her, but she managed to hold herself silent.

The king turned back to her. "Arnulf tells us that you wish to speak in your own defense. Do it now. There are more important matters that await my attention."

Slowly Zarabeth got to her feet. She straightened her gown and pulled back her shoulders. Her chin went up. She knew her life hung on her words.

"I will say the truth, sire. I did not kill Olav. I tended him faithfully during his illness. He was kind to me. You were there at our wedding and you saw that he was pleased. That night he was drunk, as were all the guests. The next day, he became ill and his illness remained for weeks and each day he worsened. I did all I could for him. Then there was an evening when Keith's wife, Toki, was more than passing cruel to me and Olav ordered both his son and his wife from his house. They were not to come back. Almost immediately Olav began to improve. He was nearly well when he forgave Keith his wife's ill-temper and they returned yet again to share our evening meals. He became ill and died that same night. I did not poison him, sire, but I imagine that Toki did, and now she has convinced her husband to have me blamed."

The king said naught, sat there stroking his gnarled fingers over his chin.

"We have heard speech from both Keith and Toki and now we have heard your words. A young wife seeks to have her husband's wealth but she doesn't want him, for he is old and no longer comely. She wishes to free herself of him and his demands on her."

At least part of it was the truth, and Zarabeth felt herself paling under the king's gaze. Then she shook her head. "You will ask Arnulf about my husband's wishes. He wanted to leave to me all his earthly goods, not to his son, for he felt no more kinship for him. This is why Keith and Toki blame me for it. They are responsible, there is no one else! They want what is mine, what is my sister's!"

The king raised his voice then, and it was stern and cold, cutting her off. "I have heard how you wished to leave Olav's house to travel away with a Viking, a man young and comely and finely hewn, but then you changed your mind, for Olav had offered to wed with you. You decided to stay and have your wealth, for you saw it there and did not wish to take a chance on offerings in a faraway land."

"That is not true! Where did you hear this, sire?"

Arnulf poked her in her ribs. "Watch your tongue, stupid wench!"

"Hold," the king said, lifting a beringed hand. "Leave her be, our good Arnulf. She deserves to know all the proof against her, then perhaps she will beg and plead for forgiveness. Now, girl, I heard it from the man you encouraged, then scorned, for you could not be certain that he would give you all that you wanted. Aye, I have it from Magnus Haraldsson that you are a perfidious, faithless wench who, in our view, decided to make Olav jealous, and thus prodded him until he promised to wed with you. And then you dismissed the man who wanted you and promised you all his loyalty and his wealth. And thus there will be no consideration for you. Olav's son deserves his father's possessions, not a young wife who wedded him only to gain his wealth, a young woman who eagerly turned away another man, a young man with true honor, and taunted him with her decision in full view of York's citizens so his humiliation would be all the greater."

Zarabeth stopped thinking, nearly stopped breathing, for as the king spoke, the deep crimson silk curtain behind his chair parted, and Magnus came through to stand beside Guthrum. He stared at Zarabeth and she saw the coldness in his eyes, the loathing for her in his heart. She felt shock at the sight of him, an instant of wild hope, then despair. Only he could have told the king these things.

"It isn't true," she heard herself say in a low whisper.

"Well, girl, speak if you would, for I would have this done and punishment meted out!"

"Olav made me dismiss Magnus! He forced me to do it!"

"And how did he do this?"

"He threatened to kill Lotti, I swear it!"

Keith yelled, " 'Tis a lie, a damnable lie! My father loved the little girl, gave her all that she wished to have. He favored her and played with her. Zarabeth killed him and now she lies! My father was a sainted man. Never would he threaten a child!"

The king said aught for several minutes. Then he turned slowly to Magnus and said something in a low voice. Zarabeth waited, so terrified that she couldn't have moved in any case. She saw Magnus lean down and reply to a question.

Then slowly Magnus straightened and looked directly at her. He said nothing. Then he smiled as the king rose and said, pointing a finger at Zarabeth, "Your punishment for murder should be death, but Magnus Haraldsson, a young man of good faith and fine family, has convinced me otherwise. You, Zarabeth, who could have once been his wife and lived a life of honor, are now his slave to do with as he pleases. If he pleases to kill you, then so be it. If he pleases to beat you until you are senseless, then so be it. Go with your master and never again return to the Danelaw, for death awaits you here if ever you return."

"No," Zarabeth said, "no."

She stood still as Magnus strode toward her, his face set and cold, nothing but contempt in his eyes.

10

Magnus stared at her from behind the crimson curtain. He felt such pain he thought he'd choke on it. As he watched her, his pain cleansed itself into pure anger. Even though she was dirty, her hair straggling down about her face, her gown torn at the shoulder where someone had ripped off a brooch, still, she looked proud and unbending.

By Odin, he had missed her, had dreamed of her more nights than he could remember now, for she always seemed to be there with him, in his mind, soft beneath his hands and whispering his name only the way she could; and yet she was naught but a fraud, the woman who had played him for a fool, the woman who had betrayed him.

He listened to her speak, so impassioned she was, and felt the pain return in full measure, but not with pity or longing for her, but with building rage. She had wronged him. She deserved to suffer for it, and she would.

When he came out to stand beside King Guthrum, when she saw him, he thought she would faint. For an instant he thought he saw joy in her expressive eyes, and hope . . . nay, it was surprise and chagrin he saw, for he was here now, to face her. It was guilt too, he realized, for what she'd done to him, perhaps even a moment of remorse.

Had she killed Olav?

He hadn't wished to believe it, had initially dismissed it as absurd, but the witnesses were many and their words rang true to his ears and to the king's ears as well. They reported how Olav had told all of his love for the little girl, how Olav had wanted Zarabeth and the little girl to be protected and thus he wedded with her, how Olav had planned to give Zarabeth all upon his death because of her hold on him. Did that make her guilty of murdering him? Did that mean she had turned Olav away from his own son? Evidently most believed so.

But then, many witnesses also spoke of Zarabeth's kindness, her care of Olav during his illness, and her love for her little sister. Still, he found himself looking again and again at Keith and Toki. Again he found himself going over Zarabeth's story in his mind, and he looked toward Toki. The woman's eyes were lowered now, modestly, her mouth a tight line, but he felt something malignant about her, something that was cold and unwholesome.

Not that it really mattered to him. He was glad Olav was dead, truth be told. The man was no longer Zarabeth's husband and she was free now to be whatever he, Magnus, wished her to be. He had come in time to save her, and that should have amused him. He, the man she'd betrayed, saving her. Aye, there was humor in that. But when he tried to find the humor, he failed. The thought that if he had been just several days later she would have been dead made him nearly double over at the empty blackness her death would bring him. But he refused to dwell on that. No, what would happen now would give him pleasure, great pleasure. She would get the punishment she deserved.

He realized in a moment of truth that what he blamed her for, what enraged him to the point of near-senselessness, what he wanted to punish her for until she was pleading with him, was not the poisoning

of her husband, but her betrayal of him, her humiliation of him, her freely given pain to him.

He nearly rubbed his hands together at the pleasure
of his revenge on her. She was alive and the king
had agreed he could have her. He had paid Keith the
danegeld for Olav's life, an amount of gold that wasn't
all that great after all, for, strangely enough, Keith
had seemed anxious that Zarabeth not be killed for
her act. His wife, Toki, had carped and yelled and
screamed at him, but he'd stood firm.

Now Zarabeth was his slave. He could do with her
whatever he wished to. He thanked Guthrum once
again, then turned to walk toward her. He wanted to
see the fear in her eyes, see her shrink back from him
because of the lies she'd told him, because now she
was whatever he dictated that she would be. He
wanted to see her pale; he wanted to see her cower.
Instead, to his surprise, her shoulders straightened
even more and that damned pride of hers radiated
outward like a shield.

He met her then, halting but inches from her, and
he said low, "Justice has been served. You are mine
now, completely mine. We are leaving on the morrow."

Zarabeth felt the room darkening, felt the floor tilt
toward her. She was going to faint, she realized,
astounded, and the knowledge made her blink and
shake herself. She looked up into his face, the beloved
face that she had held close in her mind since the first
morning he had come to her. She would make him
understand. She had to.

"There is no justice in this instance, but there seems
to be nothing I can say to change that. Very well, I'll
come with you." She would not thank him for saving
her life, for it seemed to her that his words to King
Guthrum had made her look all the more guilty.

Magnus frowned. Somehow he hadn't expected her
to bend to his demands so quickly.

"I need my clothes."

"You look like a witch, and your smell sickens me."

She merely nodded. "Very well, then, clothes and a bath and a comb for my hair."

"No."

She found nothing strange at his show of perversity. She'd lived too long with Olav. Again she nodded, saying nothing more.

Actually Magnus had already had her clothing fetched from Olav's house, over Toki's loud and shrill objections. She had wanted to sell the clothing. The vicious bitch would die, so who cared what would happen to her clothing? But Horkel, a man of few words and frightening aspect, had merely taken Zarabeth's things without heeding the shrieking woman. In fact, he had smiled as he'd left Olav's house, Toki running behind him, yelling her head off.

"Come. We will go to my vessel now."

She turned to walk with him from the presence of King Guthrum. She saw Old Arnulf standing there, displeasure weighing heavy on his face. Toki and Keith hung back, Toki looking furious and Keith looking, strangely, somehow relieved. And Zarabeth knew why. She wished she could place her hands around Toki's throat; she wanted to kill her, for it was she who was the murderess. No, there was no justice. Zarabeth didn't believe that Toki would ever be punished for her deed. As for being eaten with remorse, she doubted Toki had ever had a twinge of remorse in her life. She had won, but still she was furious because Zarabeth wasn't to die. At least by King Guthrum's order.

Zarabeth waited until they were outside the palace compound before saying, "Magnus, please, I will explain everything to you. But first we must fetch Lotti. She is frightened of Toki and she will hurt her, I know it. Please, we must get her."

Magnus felt equal portions of rage and pain, and all

because of this damned woman who stood disheveled and dirty in front of him, still so proud, so certain of her ability to charm him that she gave him no real notice. He said, his voice as cold as the viksfjord in winter, "No. The child stays here with her brother. I do not wish to have her on the journey home."

Zarabeth reeled back from his words. She'd never believed Magnus to be cruel; it hadn't occurred to her that he would refuse her in this, no matter what he felt about her. By the saints, what a fool she was. If ever she'd thought that he could be so quick to hurt a defenseless child, she wouldn't have come to care for him so quickly. She felt that pain, not elusive now, but full and deep, grind inside her. She wanted to scream at him that it was all a lie, that she loved him, but she knew that now, at this moment, he was set against her.

But she had to get Lotti. She shivered at the thought of the child with Toki for even another hour, let alone another day. But she was now Magnus' slave. His *slave*. A creature with no rights, no choices, no freedom. She would have to figure out something. She had to. She would not leave Lotti here at Toki's mercy.

She walked in silence now beside Magnus, trying to gather the proper words together to speak to him. She had to explain, to make him believe her. It was a goodly distance to the quay, but neither spoke. She was tired, so weary she was trembling, unable to find words to beg him to stop, just for a moment. She realized she was hungry, for she had been given nothing to eat since the previous evening. It was hot, the sun brutal on her head, and she felt herself becoming light-headed. She tried to shake it away, to keep control of herself and her body. She couldn't afford to show weakness. Not to Magnus, never to Magnus. She would die first.

Magnus was fully aware that she was slowing beside him, but he didn't shorten his step. He saw her weave, then get control of herself again, and against his will he admired her. He quashed it. He saw her swipe her hand over her forehead and rub her eyes. He said nothing. He knew that if he did, he would want to strike her, and a blow from him could kill her. He didn't want her dead.

He remained silent. When she fell behind, he stopped and turned to face her. "Quicken your step. I have matters to see to and have not the time to waste in coddling you."

The sun shone so brightly in her eyes that for a moment he blurred before her, his hair glistening nearly white in the shimmering heat. She raised her hand, then dropped it. She was so very thirsty. Her tongue felt swollen in her mouth. Slowly she shook her head and forced one foot in front of the other. One more step, she told herself, just one more step, and then perhaps another.

She smelled the water, the sharp salty smell, and the odor of fish. So very close now to the *Sea Wind*. She would make it; she wouldn't shame herself in front of him. And she would find the words to convince him of her innocence, soon, soon now.

It was the stone in her path that did her in. She didn't see it. She stumbled and went down to her knees, flinging out her hands at the last minute to protect herself. She felt the pain sear through her, felt the tearing of the pebbles and dirt into her palms. She remained as she was, on her hands and knees, her head lowered, her hair straggling to the ground on either side of her face.

"Get up."

She thought about it, hard, and told herself to rise. But her body didn't obey her.

"Get up, else I'll tether you and drag you."

She raised her head then, and her eyes were on line with his boots. She looked upward. He was bare-legged, his tunic coming to his knees, belted at his waist. A long knife hung from the belt. His forearms were bare save for a thick gold arm bracelet. Then she saw his face, saw the emotionless coldness, and felt herself shrink inside.

"Get up," he said again, impatient now, and she forced herself back onto her knees, drew her breath, and tried to rise. There were people gathering around them, people who knew her, and they were murmuring words she could hear:

"Aye, 'tis a slave she is now, but what she deserves is to have her bowels cut out."

"Nay, 'tis our sweet Zarabeth, and she couldn't have killed Olav."

"A sweeting she was when she was small . . . but now she is a woman grown, and greedy and evil, ah . . ."

It was suddenly too much. Zarabeth looked around at the faces of men and women she'd known since her mother had wedded Olav and brought her to York. She saw anger and contempt; she saw uncertainty and pity. She looked up at Magnus' face and saw nothing but coldness. Then she saw nothing. She fell sideways, unconscious.

He felt his heart lurch. Quickly he leaned down and drew her up into his arms. She felt lifeless, her head lolling backward, her hair wrapped around his arm and in thick tangles to the ground.

He said not a word to any of the people, but strode to the *Sea Wind*. He crossed the narrow gangplank.

Horkel greeted him. "This is the woman?"

"Aye, she fainted. From the heat, from her guilt, I know not."

"I wonder when she last ate. She was in the slaves' compound, you know. 'Tis not a place for such as she."

Magnus hadn't known. He'd assumed she was being kept in Olav's house, with Keith . . . but no, that couldn't be, else Horkel would have told him. He hadn't asked her whereabouts and no one had said anything. He swallowed, then hardened himself. "I will take her into the cargo hold. It's covered and there is privacy and protection from the sun."

"I will bring water and some food for her."

Magnus nodded, then strode carefully over the planking to the bow of the vessel, where there was a good-size space aft, enclosed for cargo. There was also room enough for three or four men to be protected from the weather when it was foul. He heard Ragnar, another of his men and a cousin, say to Horkel, "Will he kill her, I wonder."

Magnus could practically hear Horkel shrug. If the man felt deeply about anything, he never let on. He was always so calm, so matter-of-fact, that it was a challenge to get him to bend, to yell, to jest even.

"Do you think her guilty of murdering her husband? All of York speaks of it. They call her young and greedy and evil. They say she betrayed Magnus."

"I know not. Magnus believes it is so. He will bend her to his will."

"I cannot believe she would not have him," Ragnar said, his voice now more distant, for he'd moved away. "I thought he had forgotten her, for he bedded Cyra until she was sprawl-legged from his plowings. But now we are returned and he has taken her."

Magnus smiled grimly at that, then pushed aside the otter skins that partitioned off the cargo hold.

It was hot in here, but he couldn't help that. He laid her on the woven mats that covered the bare planking. He paused, then pulled a woolen blanket from a trunk, spreading it out, and placed her on it. She was so pale. It brought him pain to look at her. By Odin, she'd nearly broken him with her lies and her deceit. But now that he had her, she could do no more to hurt him, for she was completely in his power.

The otter skins were suddenly shoved aside and Horkel entered, bending, for the wooden ceiling of the hold was low, and offered Magnus a wooden cup of water.

Magnus slapped Zarabeth's cheeks. She stirred and moaned softly.

"Zarabeth, wake up!" He took the cup of water from Horkel and put it to her lips. She didn't open her eyes, but her lips parted and she tried to gulp at the water.

"Slowly. Nay, go easy, else you'll choke." He withdrew the cup and she cried out. "All right, but slowly." After she'd drunk all the water, she regained some of her color. She opened her eyes and looked up at Magnus.

Without thought, she smiled and raised her hand to touch her fingers to his face. "Magnus," she said. "I thought I would never see you again." He jerked back, fury darkening his eyes, and he saw the truth of her situation come back to her.

"You give me much trouble already. Here, Horkel has brought you some food. Are you hungry?"

She wanted to cry, but she didn't. For a brief instant he had been there with her and all had been as it was; now was now, though, and he was distant from her, so she merely nodded. She tried to sit up, but was too weak.

Magnus cursed softly. He helped her up so she could lean back against the ship side. He gave her a wooden bowl filled with stewed potatoes and chunks of mutton. She felt her mouth begin to water. When she swallowed the first bite, she closed her eyes, savoring the food.

It angered Magnus, this weakness in her. Had they starved her? By Thor, the slave compound! "Eat your fill, then you will rest here. Do not come out into the ship, else you will be sorry."

He rose then, still bent, for the roof of the tented space was low, and followed Horkel from the cargo space.

"Her hair is like flame," Horkel said matter-of-factly, with no undue sign of interest.

"Aye, as red as the flames in the Christian hell."

"You saved her life."

"She won't thank me for it, however, for I intend to break her."

Horkel said nothing more, but he wondered silently at his friend's depth of hatred of the woman. Every man had been rejected by a woman; surely Magnus wasn't above a woman's scorn, a woman's perfidy. He went about his tasks, leaving Magnus alone to brood. There was always activity aboard a vessel, always some job to be seen to. But each of the twenty men were good and experienced and they knew what had to be done without instruction from Magnus.

The woman wanted her little sister. Magnus shook his head even as he recalled her request, her only plea to him. No, the little girl would be safer here; Zarabeth was wrong that Toki or Keith would try to harm her. Besides, he could not give in to her. Not on anything.

And so the evening fell and he did not go into the cargo hold to see to his slave. He left orders that Ragnar, handsome, brash, arrogant as a cock, and filled with boundless energy, guard her, and left to visit with a trader who had messages and goods to send to his father, Harald Erlingsson, earl and chieftain of the Gravak Valley. A powerful man, his father, a man who was beginning to feel cramped and crabbed about by King Harald Fairhair. He wondered what his sire would say about his bringing Zarabeth home with him. He would say something, for his father always spoke his mind, regardless.

Zarabeth finished the stew and felt strength seep back into her body. She moved slowly at first, waiting until she was certain she wouldn't faint again. She rose. She didn't have to bend over, for the stout wadmal covering was a good two inches above her head. She had to regain her strength and her wits. She had to rescue Lotti. She felt a numbing pain but ignored it. Magnus wouldn't help her. She must help herself, and then she

would escape from Magnus, from York. She would journey with Lotti south, to Wessex, to the land of the
Saxons ruled by the great King Alfred. Her mind made
up, she began to plan. Any pain she felt at leaving
Magnus, she ignored. He'd left her no choice when he'd
refused to get Lotti.

Ragnar was leaning against his oar when he saw the
young woman pull back the otter pelts and emerge into
the open vessel. She looked weary and dirty and afraid,
and he felt stirrings of pity for her. Then he remembered
that she had scorned Magnus and was naught but a
murderess and now a slave. He called out to her, his
voice rough, "Go back inside and come not out again.
Those are your master's orders."

Zarabeth ignored his words and came toward him,
saying as she made her way carefully along the center
plank, "I have need to relieve myself. Please help me."

Ragnar was on the point of telling her to relieve herself and be done with it when it occurred to him that
Magnus might not be pleased. She was in a miserable
state. There was no need, surely, to make her relieve
herself in front of him and the other men. Such humiliation wasn't necessary. Thus, he rose and motioned for
her to follow him. Zarabeth ignored the ten other men
who lounged about in the vessel, and went after Ragnar.
In the folds of her skirt she held an ivory-handled knife
that she had found in one of the trunks in the cargo
hold. She had no intention of hurting this man, merely
disabling him so she could escape. The knife represented
freedom, and she would die before she gave it up.

Ah, Magnus, she thought, you will but hate me more,
but I have no choice. She walked silently beside Ragnar.

He took her but a few steps from the *Sea Wind* and
motioned her into the small dirty alley. "I will wait here
and see that no one comes. Hurry, for Magnus would
not be pleased to see you out of the cargo hold."

She nodded, her head down, the picture of meekness,

and made to walk past him. Then suddenly she stumbled, crying out as if she had fallen into the alley. Ragnar, without thought, jumped after her, and when he did, he felt the sharp pain of the knife handle on his temple. He crumpled where he stood, his last thought that Magnus would kill him for his stupidity.

Zarabeth stood over him, panting, staring at the knife handle and shivering with reaction at what she'd done. She pulled him deeper into the alley, then quickly, silently, she moved swift as a shadow along the quay away from Ragnar, away from the *Sea Wind*. She'd struck a man, knocked him unconscious. The thought that he could even be dead terrified her. No, she wouldn't worry about him. She had to get to Lotti and rescue her and then escape from York. She firmly rejected any thoughts of ever seeing Magnus again, for if she did, she doubted not that he would kill her for escaping him and striking Ragnar.

It was twilight when she reached Olav's house, and no one that knew her had seen her. She eased up to the single window in the living area and looked within. She sucked in her breath, thanking Odin for her luck. Keith wasn't there, only Toki, and by all the gods, she could handle Toki. Where was Lotti? Then she saw the child curled up in a corner, her face silent and still, her eyes wary, fastened on Toki, who was shuffling about preparing a meal. Zarabeth felt pain and anger twist in her belly. Had Toki already hurt Lotti? At the very least she'd terrified the child. Zarabeth firmly intended to gain revenge on Toki herself.

She entered Olav's shop, flipping the latch in the secret way Olav had taught her, and walked quietly to the living area. When she opened the skins that separated the two areas, she saw Toki look up, a frown on her face, for she expected Keith. When she saw Zarabeth, she paled. Her mouth opened to scream, but Zarabeth was faster. She was on her in an instant, her arm around her throat, squeezing hard as she felt her rage flow through her.

"Listen to me, you lying slut, you damnable lying bitch. You keep your tongue still, do you understand me?" Zarabeth squeezed harder, heard a weak croaking sound, squeezed again for good measure, and hissed in Toki's ear, "You miserable witch, I know you killed Olav. I know that you managed to keep Keith quiet about it. And you go free from punishment. However, you won't keep Lotti. Now, let me look at you one last time. I wish to remember a face of treachery."

Zarabeth turned Toki in her arms, saw the terror in the woman's eyes. She smiled down at her. With great pleasure Zarabeth struck Toki hard on the head with the knife handle. She watched the woman slide to the floor, and she was pleased. Her heart pounded. It would be the only punishment Toki would receive for murdering Olav. At least it was something. Lotti was already running across the room, crying softly, calling out Zarabeth's name, her arms raised. Zarabeth crooned softly to her as she lifted her in her arms. "You're safe now, little love, safe. You and I are leaving here now, and I won't let anyone harm you."

She remembered her clothing but knew there wasn't time. Both she and Lotti would simply have to make do with what they wore on their backs. She knew she looked a beggar, but there was naught she could do about it. It wasn't important. Getting away from York unseen was important.

She slipped out of Olav's shop—no, Keith's—and blended with the shadows and the near-darkness. She heard people talking, heard neighbors laughing, but saw no one. She hurried toward Coppergate square, wanting a last drink of water before she escaped from York. She knew she couldn't carry Lotti much further. When she reached the square, there were people, people who knew her. Well, it wasn't to be helped. She turned away, hiding in the shadow of the line of houses along Coppergate, and made her way swiftly toward the southern fortification of the city. There was a gate there, to keep out enemies, not to keep in the inhabitants of York. She would slip away easily.

She felt a stitch in her side and lifted Lotti to her other shoulder. She slowed. Her breath was coming harsh and raw now. Her hair, sweaty and tangled, slapped her face.

She saw the gate ahead of her, saw that only a half-dozen people lolled around the gate, thankfully, and she didn't recognize any of them.

Her eyes fastened on that gate; she saw nothing else. When she heard a deep voice say behind her, "Your stupidity passes all bounds," she felt as if she'd been struck. She whirled about to see Magnus standing directly behind her, tall and powerful, raising his hands to capture her even as he spoke.

She cried out, turned on her heel, and ran toward the gate, shuffling and bowed like an old woman from the stitch in her side.

11

Magnus stared at her, laughed at the appalled horror in her eyes when she saw him, then read the desperation, and frowned. He caught her quickly enough.

"You've run your race, Zarabeth," he said, and twisted her around to face him. So relieved was he to have found her so quickly, he hesitated at her obvious fear, only to have her jerk her arm free of his hold, back away from him, snarling even as she drew the knife from the folds of her gown, "You stay away from me, Magnus! Don't make me hurt you. I must leave York and you, surely you understand that—you refused to fetch Lotti. I couldn't leave her there with Toki. Now I'm going, and you have no choice in the matter. No, no, stay back!"

To her fury, he laughed. He was laughing at her! She felt the blood pounding at her temples, felt herself begin to tremble with rage and fear and uncertainty. She cried out softly, wheeled about, and fled from him. It was foolish and useless. When he grabbed her arm again to jerk her back, she turned on him this time, so panicked she couldn't think, her right arm lifted, the knife poised in her hand, ready to strike.

He was so astonished to see her raise that knife on him that once again she managed to free herself, but the child dragged her down, pulling her off-balance. Zarabeth had but a moment to react, and she dropped

Lotti, feinting to the side when Magnus lunged for her. He wasn't laughing now, and she felt an instant of victory. But just an instant, for he looked at her as he would someone of no account at all, as if it couldn't possibly matter what she tried to do.

"Stay away from me!"

He moved slowly now, assessing her calmly, and she drew away, knowing she would use the knife if he forced her to it. Then she heard Lotti crying softly, her voice slurred and terrified, and she looked down at the child. In that moment Magnus grabbed her arm and began to twist the knife from her hand.

She felt the pain roil through her arm and her shoulder, and she gasped with it and tried to jerk away, but it was no good. He had twice her strength and he was quite prepared to use it.

She raised her other hand, striking at his chest, at his face, but he merely continued twisting her right wrist until she moaned, falling to her knees. He kept her down, still twisting, until with a sob of defeat the knife slipped from her numbed fingers and clattered to the ground. Lotti cried out and ran to her. It was the child who stilled Magnus' fury. He would have doubtless struck her, but he couldn't now, not with the little girl sobbing and trying to help her sister.

He stood over her, breathing deeply to regain control. He held the beautiful knife loosely on his palm, saying, "I traded this knife for several quite exquisite soapstone bowls. It is to be a present for my younger brother, Jon. I would have been most displeased had you managed to escape with it. I would have had to buy horses and come after you. But you gave me time, Zarabeth, time to go back to Olav's house and find a sobbing Toki with her husband. She said you had tried to kill her and she was demanding that Keith see the council and have you stoned, as befits a poisoning witch. But I told Keith that I would see to your punishment, and neither of them would ever have to fear you again. As you can imagine, that assurance did not please Toki. She wants your blood. She showed me the bruises on her throat where you had strangled her. She must have been most fond of Olav, for she has taken his murder sorely. And it is true, Zarabeth, I will see to your punishment. I have found you and you will go no farther. Now, get up, for I wish to return to the *Sea Wind*. I must decide what I am to do with you."

Her wrist throbbed and burned. She caught her breath and looked up at him. "Lotti," she said. "I won't leave Lotti here."

"You dare make demands of me? You dare toss your orders at my head? You are not my wife, you have nothing that binds me to you. What you are is my slave, nothing more."

"I won't leave Lotti," she repeated slowly, her mouth dry with fear and pain.

"By Odin's wounds, you beg for me to strike you!" Magnus realized he was yelling. He stopped himself, staring down at her, but in his mind he saw Toki's hate-filled face. She would surely harm the child now. He looked at the little girl, terrified and silent, standing next to her kneeling sister, her small hand on Zarabeth's shoulder. She looked up at him then, and he flinched at the fear on that small face. The child was innocent of any wrongdoing. He sighed, giving it up.

"Get up. It is time to return to my vessel. You have sorely tried me, Zarabeth, and wasted my time. As for Ragnar, I do believe his humiliation at a woman besting him could lead him to seek your death."

"I don't care."

"Ah, you would, if I chose to give you to Ragnar for punishment." He took pity on her then, for he had won and she was bowed, a pathetic scrap at his feet, defeated and crushed. He would not harm the child, so he ended it. "Come, the child goes with us."

Zarabeth looked up at him, uncertain, disbelieving. "Do you swear it?"

Irritated, Magnus said sharply, "I do not lie, not like you. I will not tell you again."

He made no move toward her. Zarabeth got to her feet. She held out her arms to Lotti, but Magnus forestalled her. "You are tired and will hold me back. Tell the child she need not fear me, and I will carry her."

Zarabeth leaned down and gently stroked Lotti's soft hair from her brow, saying softly, "Listen, sweeting, you needn't be afraid of Magnus. He is large, 'tis true, but he won't hurt you. Nay, don't pull away from me. I swear it to you. Let him carry you now, all right?"

Magnus said, impatient, "Can't the child understand you? Must you speak to her as if she spoke another language?"

Zarabeth ignored him. Finally Lotti nodded, and Zarabeth turned to Magnus. "She will let you carry her. Please, Magnus, she has done nothing to harm you. Do not hurt her."

"I am not a monster. I do not hurt children."

"Don't lie! I know what you Vikings do to anyone— even children—on your raids! You spit them on your swords, you fling them—"

"You will be silent now. I will not hurt her. Unlike you, Zarabeth, I do not lie."

She sighed, getting hold of herself. She believed him. At least Lotti would be with her. She had won, in a sense, if by any stretch being a slave could be called winning.

"If you had escaped York, where would you have gone?" He sounded pleasant as he walked beside her,

Lotti's head against his right shoulder, only mildly interested.

"I don't know. I thought perhaps to Wessex, to King Alfred's court. I could have served some rich lady there, sewing perhaps."

He snorted. "Your stupidity yet amazes me. You would not have survived a mile from York. There are outlaws, Zarabeth, and you are but a lone woman. Had you escaped, you would now likely be dead, raped until you bled your life away. But now you are safe again because you have a strong man to protect you. You will sew for me now, and do whatever tasks are assigned to you. You will learn quickly to obey. It will be good, for I grow tired of your ceaseless demands and complaints."

She said nothing, merely looked straight ahead. They passed people who knew her, and she was aware that they were talking of her, but she paid them no heed. She saw familiar buildings, familiar patches of gardens. "I will miss York."

"Aye," Magnus said, his voice laced with sarcasm, "doubtless it is a town of noble inhabitants. Like its people, its beauty is also astounding. You can smell them as well as see them." He waved toward a pile of refuse, whose odor was foul. "Listen, woman, these people would show you not a shred of kindness were it not for me protecting you."

She sighed. "You are right, I doubt not, but I don't really understand why no one believed me."

"I do not wish to hear your protestations of innocence again. There is my vessel, hurry, for we sail as soon as our feet are on board. I have no further wish to remain here."

The first man Zarabeth saw when they boarded the *Sea Wind* was Ragnar. His arm was raised to strike her. She tried to show no fear, but she was raw with it. She saw Magnus merely shake his head at the man.

Ragnar slowly lowered his arm, but his look didn't change. She said nothing, merely followed Magnus to the covered cargo hold. He drew back the otter skins and set Lotti on one of the roughly woven mats that covered the wooden floor. "Stay here."

Zarabeth sank down, drawing Lotti onto her lap. She was beyond tired, numb now, for she had failed yet won, for Lotti was safe, at least she was as safe as Zarabeth was. Would the child be treated as a slave when they reached Norway and Magnus' home? How were slaves in that foreign land treated? Were they beaten and given little food? Were they as pitiful as the creatures in the slave compound?

Fear curled powerfully through her belly.

She wished she could have bathed; her own stench was beginning to bother her. As for Lotti, the child was scratching her elbow and Zarabeth saw a sore there that badly needed cleansing. She ran her fingers through her tangled hair, pulling out twigs and clots of dirt and mud. She could only imagine how she looked. Well, it didn't matter. Magnus didn't care for anything save humiliating her. She wondered if he was cruel. She wondered if he would hurt her. She fell asleep and didn't stir the rest of the night.

At dawn the next day, the men of the *Sea Wind* cast off its ropes and left its moorings. She heard the sailors calling out to each other, heard Magnus tell the men to draw their oars. The huge square sail wouldn't be raised until they were free of York harbor.

The motion was smooth and rocking and brought Zarabeth to full awareness. She wished it was still night. She wanted only the darkness. It represented a sort of safety to her, a sort of protection.

When the mighty square sail caught the wind out-side the harbor, the vessel shot forward and the men cheered. She knew now they would pull the oars into the vessel and go about their other tasks. Her stomach growled. She turned to Lotti, took her small face between her hands, and said slowly, "Are you hungry, sweeting?"

The little girl frowned, and Zarabeth slowly repeated her question, miming eating. Lotti nodded vigorously and rubbed her stomach. Zarabeth patted her shoulder and said, more to herself than to her sister, "I will see if there is more of that stew Magnus fed me yesterday."

She rose and went to the otter pelts and drew them back. The men stopped speaking. Slowly, one by one, all twenty of them stared at her. She saw Magnus bending over, speaking to the man Horkel, who held the steering oar. He looked up then, aware of the sudden silence, and saw her. Magnus frowned at her and quickly made his way along the wooden plank that ran along the center of the vessel. He ducked to the side to miss the wind-filled sail. As he passed it, he turned to look up the twenty-foot-high mast with its long cross spar, then nodded, as if pleased.

"What do you want?" He had shouted even though he was near to her now. She strained to hear him over the thick whipping sound of the sail.

She didn't try to answer him until he was beside her. "Lotti is very hungry. Is there something for her to eat?"

Magnus had expected to hear something else from her, a plea for herself, perhaps. He should have realized, given her frenzy the day before, that her only concern would be for her little sister, for after all, she had risked her life to save the child. Wasn't she hungry as well, damn her? Wasn't there something for herself she wanted? Finally he said, "Get you back into the hold. I will have Horkel bring both of you something to eat."

Zarabeth nodded and turned, only to feel Magnus'
hand on her arm.

"Do not come out again. Even though you look
like a witch, my men at all times are woman-hungry,
particularly away from their homes. If you value your
woman's endowments, you will remain within." He
paused a moment, then added, a frown on his face,
"I will tie back the pelts so that there will be fresh air
within the hold, and light."

Zarabeth nodded again. Before she withdrew, she
looked out onto the sea. The wind whipped her hair
about her face, and she tasted the salty seawater on
her tongue. It was becoming cooler, and she wrapped
her arms about herself. Water slapped loudly against
the sides of the vessel. She could make out the distant
coastline. The men were still silent, watching, looking
at her. Were they judging her? Did they believe her
a murderess?

Not that it mattered. She went back into the cargo
hold. Before too much time had passed, Magnus himself came into the hold. Not Horkel. He was carrying
two wooden bowls filled with warm stew. He also had
bread, soft and fresh, wrapped in a coarse woolen rag.

"Do not expect food like this for very long. It will
take us five days to reach Hedeby, 'tis a large trading
town in Denmark. I have some trading to do there
before we sail north to Kaupang, up the Oslo Fjord."

He was being kind, Zarabeth thought, somewhat
confused. Was he coming to think that perhaps she
had been telling the truth? Was he coming to believe
that she hadn't lied about why she'd told him she
hadn't wanted him? His next words blighted her, leaving her feeling hopeless once more.

"You will cast no lures toward any of my men. They
would take what you offered them, but they would
give you nothing in return save their contempt. I have
their loyalty. You are naught but a slave, a female

slave, who has her uses, as I will use you this night. You want bathing, but no matter. Make yourself ready for me, Zarabeth, for I will come back when night has fallen and most of my men are asleep." Unfortunately, as the words left his mouth, Magnus realized that Lotti was staring up at him, her wooden spoon held in her hand. He'd forgotten the child. He felt a fool; worse, he felt like a man who had gone into battle without a weapon. He felt like a naked man caught in a snowdrift. He gave Zarabeth a look that bespoke retribution, turned on his heel, and left the hold.

Zarabeth would have laughed had she been able to, but she wasn't. She turned and mimed eating to Lotti. She was no longer hungry. The fresh sea wind came into the hold and she no longer felt ill from the stuffiness of the small space.

Time passes, Zarabeth thought, even though I lose track of the minutes and the hours, time still passes. And so it was. The night became another day that was hot and bright, the sun so harsh she wondered how the men could bear the hours under its searing heat. She played with Lotti, teaching her words, repeating them endlessly, speaking to her as she mimed ideas.

And she thought of Magnus, even when he wasn't in her line of vision. The *Sea Wind* was a good sixty feet long, and at her center she was at least fifteen feet wide. The men had stacked their oars in the high wooden Y-shaped holders and were lolling about, nothing for them to do. She heard them speaking, and they spoke freely, for perhaps they didn't care that she could hear them:

"I heard Tostig say that what Magnus would have paid for her in a brideprice, he paid instead in dane-geld to the son in payment for the man she poisoned."

"Aye, she killed the old man because she wanted

his wealth. A woman is a fool, she has no cunning. I could have succeeded—"

"Aye, but the old man wouldn't have wedded with you in the first place! You are ugly as a rutting boar and you have not what any man would want between your legs!"

There was laughter to that; then a man said, "She's pretty, aye, I'll give you that, but stupid she is, drawing Magnus in and then spitting on him. Why would she betray him? She'll pay, though, you'll see."

"Aye, when she sees Cyra . . . by Thor, that girl would make any man hard as a stone. She'll regret that she did."

"Forget not Ingunn, a hard taskmistress, that one, whose tongue feeds on contention, despite her angel's face. Life won't be pleasant for the slave."

And on and on it went, and Zarabeth wondered who Ingunn was. As for Cyra, Zarabeth remembered her well. She was also a slave, and she bedded with Magnus. That wouldn't touch her, Zarabeth thought. She didn't care what women crept into his bed, just as long as it wasn't her. She wouldn't be his slut.

When she turned to listen again, the men were wagering on when Magnus would bed her. She remembered being kissed by him, held against his chest, feeling his strength, his gentleness flowing into her. It was over now.

Time passed. She emerged only once daily from the cargo hold to empty the slops.

Two days out of Hedeby, Zarabeth awoke suddenly with the knowledge that something was very wrong. She jerked upright, shaking her head to clear away the sleep. Lotti was missing. She felt fear pound through her, and dashed to the entry of the cargo hold. She could only stare. Lotti was sitting on one of the men's bare thighs, a small monkey of a man with a thick black beard, whose name was Tostig. He was laughing and pointing out different seabirds to her. A seal played near the vessel, and Lotti was laughing, in her own way, and gesticulating wildly, and the other men had crowded around them. She was safe. Her bright ginger hair was blowing wildly around her face. Zarabeth stared in astonishment as one of the men came down on his haunches and began to braid her hair, so gentle his touch that Lotti scarce noticed. Another man produced a bit of leather to tie the braid. Lotti held out her hand to the man, and he laughed and patted her cheek and then his legs, and the man Tostig handed the little girl over to him.

It was unaccountable. Zarabeth couldn't take it in, this gentleness and kindness to a child. But so it was. She saw that Magnus was still down at the steering oar, lolling at his ease next to the helmsman. She turned back into the hold and sat down, leaning against a wool-wrapped box filled with soapstone bowls and pitchers and plates, bound, she supposed, for the trading market at Hedeby. She closed her eyes, wishing she could forget where she was and why she was here.

He came in so suddenly that she didn't have time to cry out, much less voice a protest. He filled the entry, the bright sun behind him, then pulled the pelts back down, and the small area was dim again.

"Lotti is fine and well-occupied with my men. I'm tired of waiting. I've come to take you, Zarabeth."

She didn't move, merely stared at him, disbelieving. "Why?"

He laughed. "I told you, I'm tired of waiting. You're my slave. If I want you, I'll take you whenever it pleases me."

She saw that he meant it. She scrambled back against the side of the vessel. "Please, no. It isn't right, it isn't—"

"It's what I want! I've paid dearly for you, Zarabeth!"

She was shaking her head wildly. "No, Magnus. I won't be your whore."

"You're a slave, and that is less than a whore. Also, since you are the only woman here, I must make do with you. I would ask you, though, how many men you've had before me."

She stared at him, remembering starkly the man who had professed to care for her, the man who had wanted to wed with her, the man who had held her close and kissed her tenderly and shocked her with his bold speaking. He was well and truly gone. In his place was this hard-faced man whose eyes were cold as the North Sea in the wintertime.

Feeling for him froze within her. She raised her face. "A dozen men," she said. "Aye, I have had more men than I can remember or count. Once Olav breached me, I could see no harm in it, for he was old and had little to offer me. Aye, at least a dozen various men, all different sizes they were, some hairy and dark, others like smooth polished wood." She shrugged then, smiling. "Since I am but a woman, counting comes with difficulty, but I do think it was at least twelve different ones."

She thought he would strike her. She saw the pulse pounding in his throat, saw the rage building in his eyes.

"Do not lie to me, Zarabeth, it angers me."

"Then do not ask me a fool's questions, you brainless knave!"

"Very well, then. I will tell you what to do. Pull up your gown. I wish to see your woman's endowments."

"No." The single word sounded strong and arrogant in the close cargo space, and Zarabeth wondered at it, for she was so afraid, she could feel the cramping in her belly.

She didn't have much time to consider what he would do. She had no time to react. He dropped to his knees beside her, grabbed her wrists in his hands, and pulled her forward. He made no move to kiss her, just pulled her tight against him, hauling her up to her knees. He said inches from her face, "You will do as I tell you. I will have no more of your defiance, no more of your stubborn pride, no more of your lies." He pushed her roughly onto her back and came down over her, pinning her down, her hands above her head.

He kissed her then, hard, forcing her lips to part. This was punishment and dominance and she wouldn't accept it. She began to struggle against him, heaving and arching her back, twisting to the side, but he was twice her size and had twice her strength. She felt him rear back, easing off her so that he was on his side, and he was looking down at her, at his hand that was jerking up the skirt of her gown.

"No!" She twisted her head toward him and bit his forearm. He made no sound, just sucked in his breath at the pain. In the next moment he grabbed both her wrists in one hand and jerked them again painfully over her head.

"No more fighting me," he said, and he was breathing hard and his voice was raw and she knew that he was going to take her, force her, as she knew some men hurt women. "Why do you care? I am just one more man to have you." She felt his member hard and pressing against her thigh and knew that he would do to her what Olav hadn't been able to.

"Magnus, please don't hurt me."

He laughed then, just laughed, and she felt humiliation fill her craw, for she had begged. She knew such hatred for him that had she been free, she would have sliced him with the knife at his belt.

He was smiling now, a cruel smile, and he looked

into her face as his hand smoothed over her breasts, downward to her belly, then further again to the hem of her gown. Slowly, his eyes never leaving her face, he began to pull the gown upward.

He saw the humiliation in her eyes, the pain of what he was doing to her, the immense anger that filled her, and it pleased him. He would break her, this woman who had rejected him to wed with an old man, this woman who had murdered to satisfy her greed.

His hand touched her inner thigh, and for an instant he closed his eyes over the intense feelings that coursed through him. He didn't want these feelings toward her, didn't expect them. Then he touched her soft woman's flesh and thought he would spill his seed.

He could bear no more. He knew his men were aware of what he was doing, knew they would hear her cry out when he thrust into her, but he didn't care. She was naught but a slave; her only purpose was to be what he wanted her to be.

He ripped her gown open, baring her to the waist, and rolled over on top of her, freeing himself. "Now," he said, his breathing harsh and raw and ugly. "Now. Hold still. Don't fight me now, Zarabeth, it will do you no good."

12

Zarabeth stared up at him, watching his eyes darken, his expression become more intent, color stain his cheeks. But he wasn't looking at her face, he was staring down at her naked belly, at the fiery red curls, as vivid and bright as the hair of her head. Strangely gentle, as if uncertain of himself, he lowered his hand and his fingers lightly skimmed through the curls to find her.

She couldn't believe he was touching her like this, couldn't accept it. She felt such shame, such fear, she thought she would choke on it. When his fingers slid between her legs, she cried, out, bucking wildly upward to dislodge his hand. But instead of defeating him, she felt his middle finger push slowly into her, widening her.

She cried out.

Magnus closed his eyes against the onslaught of feeling. It was just lust he felt, nothing more, just lust for a woman's body, any woman's body, but the heat of her and her smallness were overwhelming, and he knew his finger was hurting her, stretching her, for she was narrow and dry, her body fighting him. He pressed with difficulty further into her. She was crying now, twisting madly to get him away from her, but she couldn't move him, couldn't make him stop. She reared up suddenly, freeing one of her hands from his grasp, and struck him on the mouth as hard as she could. He simply thrust his finger further into her and

watched as she gasped with pain, her eyes going
blank, all movement frozen in that instant. Their eyes
met in that moment and he cleared away all expression and stared at her. He smiled at her as he shoved
his finger in more deeply. He pushed her back down,
holding her there with his palm splayed on her belly.
She was striking him, but he felt no pain, felt nothing
but the heat of her body, the softness of her, the
pain—no he wouldn't accept that, he wouldn't care
about that. What she felt mattered not to him.

By Odin, he couldn't believe her still a maid, yet
her passage was so narrow, so tight, he thought she
must be. He felt his member swell and harden; he was
in such need he knew he must come into her now or
he would spill his seed.

He withdrew his finger suddenly, wanting to retain
his control. He felt her flinch as he did so, but she
didn't quieten, but only increased her struggles against
him. He paid her no heed. He said nothing, merely
jerked her legs apart and rolled over on top of her,
pressing himself against her. He reared up then to free
himself from his loincloth, his hand trembling, his
body quivering with the pulsing need that was filling
him to overflowing. Suddenly, his hair was being
yanked off his head. He heard a shrill mewling sound
and he felt small fists pounding at his shoulders.

With an animal growl, fury blinding him, he jerked
about to fight off his attacker. It took him a moment
to realize that it was Lotti, trying to save her sister.

From his rape.

He didn't believe it was happening, but it was, and
he was both enraged and bewildered. He heard Horkel then, saying from without, "Nay, go not in there,
Tostig. Magnus will deal with the child. It is not our
business."

"Aye, but we should have stopped her! By Thor,
he will not be pleased about this."

He wasn't pleased; it was a vast understatement. Magnus wondered just what he was to do with a writhing woman beneath him, a sex that hurt him so that he thought he would die with it, and a small girl striking him with all her strength. He suddenly laughed, at himself, at the ridiculous situation. He gave it up; his need dwindled as the ashes on a summer hearth. He released Zarabeth and quickly rolled off her, coming up on his knees, quickly covering himself.

Zarabeth hadn't at first understood. Then she saw Lotti and realized that the child had thrown herself on Magnus. Lotti drew away from Magnus now, her eyes on her sister, tear streaks down her dirty cheeks. The child was terrified, but still she stood her ground between Zarabeth and Magnus, her mouth quivering, her small shoulders squared.

Zarabeth wanted to weep at the loyalty of her little sister. "Come, sweeting," she said quickly, scrambling to her knees and holding out her arms, " 'tis all right. I'm all right. Nay, don't weep, and don't be frightened. Magnus and I were just playing, aye, that's it, playing, wrestling the way boys do, but he wanted to show me some of the moves he knew, nothing more. Come and let me hug you."

She gathered the child to her, and soothing Lotti calmed her. She pressed the child's head to her shoulder and looked up at Magnus, who sat cross-legged not two feet from her. He was still breathing heavily, but had himself well in hand now. She watched a strange smile curve his lips as he said, "Aye, wrestling. Naught but a game, just as you told the child. Aye, but a game you will lose, Zarabeth, for I am your master in all things."

"You are an animal," she said clearly, and was surprised at the calm of her voice. " 'Tis no game to you, but a savage contest of might. You are the stronger, so you think you can take what you want from someone weaker. You disgust me." She looked away from him and continued stroking Lotti's back and whispering soft sounds to her.

His mouth tightened and he felt the familiar burning anger at her twist in his belly. But now wasn't the time. He waved his hand at the child. "What is wrong with her? She makes strange noises. Is she half-witted?"

"No, she is without hearing."

Magnus looked disbelieving. Suddenly he reared up on his knees and clapped his hands loudly at the back of Lotti's head. The little girl didn't move. He looked perplexed, then sat back again.

"Was she born this way?"

"Nay, Olav struck her when she was but two years old. She was unconscious for two days after, and when she awoke, she was without hearing." She paused, remembering her fear, her fury at Olav. "I wanted to kill him for what he'd done, for he didn't even care. She could have died and it wouldn't have touched him. To excuse what he did, he pretended she was a half-wit, and that is what he told others."

"You did get your revenge on Olav," he said, then immediately added, "She says your name, but it's in a slurred way."

"Aye, she could say several things before he hit her. And since she knows some sounds and some meanings of things, with patience, she can learn to speak more words."

"You should have told me this."

She stared at him, amazement, contempt, writ clear on her face. "Why? So that you could have planned your brutality with more craft? So that you would have but another weapon to use against me?"

"I would not use a child against any man."

"Aye, but I'm not a man, merely a woman."

"Nay, you're a slave first, and then a woman."

She looked down, not responding to him. What was the use? She patted Lotti and spoke quietly to her, pulling away so she could see the child's face. It was as if she no longer recognized that he was there. She'd simply retreated from him, withdrawn into herself. It enraged him.

"If the child cannot hear, how came she to enter in here?"

Zarabeth didn't bother to look up. "I do not know. I suppose that she saw you come in and pull the skins down. She is afraid of you. She sought only to protect me. I ask that you do not hurt her."

"I have told you before that I do not harm children."

"That is a lie. I know of Vikings such as you, and of your raids and the fighting madness that consumes all of you. You kill without reason and with no hesitation. King Alfred must continually fight you to keep his lands intact and his people from slaughter."

He was silent for a moment, for that was true. He shrugged then. "It is our way. Sometimes things happen that are not what I would wish. But it is the way such things are. Why do you feel pity for Alfred? He is naught to you, a chimera, a fable with no substance, spoken of by unhappy Saxons over their fires during winter nights. If Alfred were their king, he would abuse them endlessly. Guthrum is your king and their king and your dead husband's king. Your loyalty is to a Viking, not to the Saxon king."

She shrugged. "I hate all of you, truth be told, your senseless violence that leaves people dead or broken or slaves. All of you are savages, and I doubt not that the noble Alfred is just as savage as are you. You are right about that."

"Now you are the slave of a savage. I will hear no more of your plaints."

"I do not wish you to rape me."

"I don't particularly wish to force myself on you, but I will if you so foolishly continue to fight me. If you do, your pain will be but worse. I care not about your pain, but perhaps you will wish to think about it. I will take you, Zarabeth, make up your mind to it. What you want, what you feel now, make no difference to me. You are still a maid, are you not?" He did not wait for her to answer, merely spoke his thoughts aloud. "You were stretching around my fingers. Aye, no man has been inside you yet. So, you wed with an old man . . . perhaps you knew he couldn't take you and that you would not have to suffer him mauling you? Aye, or is it true that you began to poison him the very day you wedded him so you wouldn't have to suffer him in your bed? That he would not have the strength?"

"You speak with the voice of a mindless savage. Aye, it smacks of such truth, does it not? That I would prefer an old man to wed with rather than become your wife?" Her voice was weary and mocking and he wished he had simply kept quiet. "Aye, look at what I would have gotten had I not been so stupid . . . a strong man, so tender and gentle that he will rape an unwilling woman. All those wondrous words you spoke to me, they were lies, naught but a Viking's savage lies."

He rose suddenly to his feet, towering over her. "I did not lie! I would have loved you and guarded you with my life, I would have given you all that I was, all that I owned, but you chose that old man. Oh, aye, you murdered him, Zarabeth, of that I am certain. You see, I heard all the witnesses before you even came into King Guthrum's chamber. They all said the same thing, that you wanted the old man's wealth, that you knew you could control him, for he desired you and had even granted you all his earthly goods upon his death. Mock me no more."

He left the cargo area. She sat there still holding Lotti close, not moving now, frozen, wishing that somehow she could die but knowing that she couldn't, for there was Lotti, her brave little sister. She heard no man's laughter from without. Surely they would have guessed what had happened. She heard naught of anything. She held Lotti closer and rocked her back and forth. The child had saved her this time. And the next time? Magnus would never make such a mistake again. She knew too that he would have his way eventually. Again she was without choices.

Magnus would have killed any of the men if one had dared taunt him, if one had dared even look at him with a sly grin. He was frustrated and his body was tense, and his scalp was throbbing where Lotti had tried to yank out his hair. He strode down the center plank, then stopped and said to the silent men, "The child cannot hear. If you wish to play with her, you must be careful that no harm comes to her."

Tostig looked surprised. "Of course she cannot hear. Think you we are stupid?"

"Aye," Horkel said, "but the little one is not slow of learning. I taught her a word—'raven.' She can very nearly say it now."

"Aye, she's a sharp little tick," Ragnar said, albeit grudgingly. He wouldn't hold the child in disfavor because of her bitch of a sister. His head still hurt from the blow she'd struck him. "She counted all my fingers and toes."

"Then why did you let her—?" Magnus broke off, shaking his head. He said nothing more, but walked to the stern of the vessel and set himself to brooding.

By Odin, he had been a fool. He'd seen the child, but he hadn't realized she couldn't hear, yet his men had known very quickly. His blindness appalled him. He was the master of this vessel, and all its men looked to him, he was their leader, yet he hadn't even seen something so obvious as the child's lack of hearing.

"The child saved her sister," Horkel said to no man in particular, looking after Magnus and his stiff back. "But he will have her soon enough, I wager."

"Aye, but he won't harm the child to do it."

Lotti did not again leave Zarabeth.

That night it stormed and the sky was rent with lightning, slashing white bolts that left Zarabeth so terrified she could do naught but hold Lotti on her lap and, by soothing her, soothe herself. The vessel was sound, she knew, but it seemed to lurch up to crest the waves, only to career wildly into the deep churning troughs with sickening loud thuds. She could hear the water washing over the sides, knew the men were bailing out the bottom of the vessel as quickly as they could. She heard Magnus' voice shouting above the din. She heard the creaking of the mighty mast as the men took it down so it wouldn't be broken in the storm. Zarabeth felt strangely calm. She didn't understand her feelings toward Magnus, for they seemed to shift continually. But she knew deep inside herself that if they survived the storm, it would be his doing. In this, she trusted him.

Oddly, she went to sleep.

When Magnus entered the cargo area near morning, the storm almost spent, he very nearly smiled to see Zarabeth on her side, Lotti pressed against her, the both of them soundly sleeping. Without meaning to, he pulled a woolen blanket over them, for the early-morning air had become chilled with rain and wind. Zarabeth awoke suddenly and she stared up at Magnus. He said nothing, merely turned about and left the cargo space.

Late that afternoon the *Sea Wind* sailed into the harbor at Hedeby, a deep-cut inlet protected from the sea by wooden palisades built in a protective curve far

out into the water. There were tall earthen fortifications around the town, like a wide half-circle
ending at the water's edge. There were at least a
dozen Viking trading vessels pulled up onto the
land, for there was but one pier built out, and a
trading vessel was docked on each side of it. Smoke
rose from the number of huts that filled the inside
of the fortifications. Smells mingled, bringing a
heaviness to the air. There were wooden walkways
through the town, connecting all the buildings to
each other. And more people than Zarabeth had
imagined, many more than in York. And all of them
busy and talking and hurrying here and there on
their separate tasks.

She clasped Lotti safely to her as the men leapt out
into the water and dragged the *Sea Wind* out of the
water and safe onto the shore. She didn't have a long
time to wonder what Magnus intended. He called to
her then. "Carry Lotti in your arms to protect her.
Follow me."

Within a few moments her feet were on dry ground,
and Lotti was staring wide-eyed at the endless stream
of people. Men greeted Magnus and his men, and they
returned the greetings. But Magnus didn't stop. He
said curtly to Zarabeth, "Stay close. Hurry. I have
not time to waste on you."

She followed him, silent and staring as intently as
Lotti. She saw slaves hauling goods on their backs and
women carrying water in wooden pails from a central
well. There were stout merchants hawking their wares
before their shops. There was a runemaster carving
his special letters on a bronze cask, a smithy hammering at a sword. Magnus finally came to a halt
before a small wooden hut.

There was an old woman within, and she gave Zarabeth a toothless smile. "This is a bathing hut," Mag-

nus said. "You will wash yourself and Lotti. I will return soon. Go nowhere else."

She wondered where else she could possibly go, but said nothing. She nodded and followed the old woman inside the hut. It was hot with steam rising to the thatch ceiling. In the center of the single room was a huge wooden tub big enough for two people. It was circled with thick iron bands. The woman silently handed Zarabeth a square of soap and left her. At the doorway she turned and said, "Yer husband is fetching clothes from his vessel."

Her husband. She merely nodded. Quickly she bathed Lotti, scrubbing the child until she was trying to get away from Zarabeth's hands. She wrapped her in a big square of linen and set her on the woven mats that covered part of the floor. She took her face between her hands and said slowly, "Don't dirty yourself, sweeting. I will be quick."

When Zarabeth was in the tub, she closed her eyes at the pleasure of it and leaned her head back.

She awoke with a start, sensing something different. She opened her eyes to see Magnus standing over her, staring down at her, that intent expression on his face. She moved to cover her breasts, then realized that her hair, wet and thick and tangled, covered all of her.

"I brought clean clothing for both of you."

Then he turned and squatted down beside Lotti. She was staring at him, her eyes wary. He smiled and withdrew a lovely antler comb from his tunic. Slowly, with patience that left Zarabeth bemused, Magnus combed the tangles from the child's hair. Soon Lotti was leaning against him, and when he jerked too hard, she turned and pummeled his chest. Magnus laughed and told her to hold still, he was trying his best. Once her hair was long and untangled down her back, he rose. "You can braid her hair when you are through. I must go now."

Zarabeth simply stared at the doorway for long moments after he'd disappeared. She didn't understand him. Not at all.

By the time she had dressed and combed her own hair, it was late and her stomach was growling. There had been only a bit of dried salted meat to eat that morning. She took Lotti's hand and they walked to the entrance of the hut.

The activity hadn't slowed. There were so many people, pressing together, but there was laughter too, and she heard some singing from the distance. The old woman was nowhere to be seen. The sun was still hot overhead, and Zarabeth eased down on a woven mat at the doorway, drawing Lotti onto her lap.

She didn't immediately notice the powerfully built dark-haired man who was striding toward her. When she did, she saw that he was smiling and coming directly to her. She felt something in her respond with hunger at the kindness she saw in his smile.

She found herself smiling back at him. When he reached her, he said, "Good day to you, mistress. You and your daughter enjoy the sun?"

"Aye. And a nice bath." She waved toward the inside of the hut. "We were both very dirty."

"No longer," he said, and suddenly he was standing very close, towering over her. Zarabeth drew back and quickly stood, letting Lotti down to stand beside her, holding her close to her side.

"No," she said, still trying to smile, "no longer at all." There was no reason to fear this man. There were dozens of people about. He was being kind to her. "I have never been to Hedeby before. It is crowded, more so than York."

His smile didn't slip, but he ignored her words. "Is it true you came with Magnus Haraldsson, aboard the *Sea Wind*?"

She nodded, wary now, yet not understanding what it was he wanted.

"He is a fool." The man reached out his hand and lightly stroked a lock of her damp hair. She didn't move, merely drew back very slowly. He still smiled at her. "You're beautiful." He touched her arm then, and then jerked her toward him, dragging her off-balance. "He's a fool to leave you here unprotected. Ah, but you are beautiful." He touched her hair again, wrapping a thick tress around his fist. She saw the hunger in his eyes, recognized it for what it was. "I have never seen such a color. And your eyes—that green is beyond what a man dreams of. I would have you. Come with me now and I will save you from Magnus. He's a cruel man, all know of it, a savage who knows nothing of the needs of a sweet and gentle creature like you. He would hurt you, perhaps even kill you with his beatings. Come with me, quickly. I will care for you, treat you like a queen. Aye, quickly, come!"

"Go away. Leave me alone."

"Fear me not, for I would never harm such beauty as you hold. I have heard you're his slave. You would be a fool to stay with him. Come with me now."

Then, without warning, he leaned down, yanking on Zarabeth's hair so that she couldn't move without pain, and kissed her hard on the mouth.

Just as suddenly, Zarabeth heard an enraged cry. It was Magnus. In the next moment the man was whirled away from her and was staggering from the blow Magnus had given him.

Then Magnus was standing over the man, and he held a knife in his hand. "You dare to touch what is mine, you craven fool?"

The man held his jaw, then slowly rose. He shrugged, angered, for he had heard that Magnus was well-occupied. Well, no matter. There would always come another opportunity, another time. He said easily,

"The woman was there, and she was willing. She waved me over to her and spoke sweetly to me. Would you not take what was offered from such as she?"

Zarabeth was shaking her head, crying shrilly, "He is lying! He—"

"Shut your mouth!" Magnus turned back to the man, his eyes narrowed. "Get you from my sight, else I'll slit your miserable throat."

The man gave Zarabeth a melancholy smile and then took himself off. "He lied, Magnus," she said, frantic now. "He lied! He came over to us and he was nice, but then he grabbed me and wanted me to go with him. I told him to leave me alone, I swear it to you."

He interrupted her, his voice savage and cold. "Enough! By Odin, to think I actually believed I could trust you alone for even a moment! You damnable bitch! Come, I know what must be done to you."

He took her arm and dragged her down the center wooden walkway. Lotti, clutching to her skirt, ran beside her. Past a dozen huts he dragged her, to the blacksmith's. "Here," he said, and flung her inside.

Still she didn't realize what he meant to do. She backed away, pulling Lotti with her. "What do we here?"

"You are a slave. It is time you bore the mark of one."

Then she knew. "No, please, no, Magnus."

He ignored her and spoke to the smithy.

As the sun lowered for the night, Zarabeth walked beside Magnus back toward the *Sea Wind*. He carried Lotti.

Around her throat was a slave's iron collar.

She felt such humiliation, such hopelessness, she didn't want to go on. Were it not for Lotti, she believed that she would fight Magnus until he was forced to kill her. She walked several paces behind him, like a dog.

13

When the *Sea Wind* took the sharp wind off the Oslo Fjord and veered into the viksfjord that led to the Gravak Valley and the home of many of the Haraldsson family, Zarabeth heard the men cheer. She looked out of the cargo area, curious. The men were sitting back on their sea chests, their oars still as wind filled the huge red-and-white-striped sail. She met the gaze of Ragnar, the man she had struck to escape in York.

She wanted to shrink back at the barely veiled hostility in his eyes, but she forced herself to stand perfectly still.

"What want you, slave?" Ragnar asked, taking a step toward her. His eyes were on the slave collar around her neck.

"I wondered why the men were cheering."

"We near home. Another half-day is all, and then you will begin your life as a Viking's slave. You will not like it, and I shall be pleased at your misery. The slave collar becomes you. It fits you well."

"What goes here, Ragnar?"

Zarabeth marveled at the suspicion she heard in Magnus' voice. He distrusted Ragnar? Surely he knew the man despised her.

"Nothing, Magnus. Your slave here merely wished to know what the men were cheering about. I told her."

Ragnar turned away then and left them, whistling. She suddenly had the feeling that she was completely alone with Magnus, even though Lotti stood just beside her and his men were within feet of them, their voices a low rumble over the flapping sail.

"The men take their ease now. The wind will stay at our backs until we reach the valley."

"And your home? You called it Malek?"

"Aye." He fell silent and his look was on the collar that encircled her neck. It looked heavy, too heavy for a woman's slender throat. He hated it. Hated that he had done it. He turned away from her. "Stay in the cargo space. I want none of my men to succumb to your enticements."

Her craw was filled to overflowing and she gave him an utterly false smile, saying, "Enticements, Viking? How odd that sounds. Perhaps I am a sweetmeat?"

"Mayhap sweet between your thighs, but no place else."

She turned away, defeated by his distrust, but not for long, for she was too curious to hide herself in the cargo space. She sat in the opening with Lotti on her lap and watched the huge rising mountains on either side of the fjord, mountains jutting upward, their tops cloud-sheathed, covered with thick pine forests. How could one farm here, she wondered, when everything was so densely covered with trees? The water was so clear and so blue that it nearly hurt the eyes to look at it, particularly with the bright sun striking off it. The thick wadmal sail bulged and the men who held the ropes to control it struggled, their muscles clench-ing and twisting with the force it took to control the huge sail in the fast wind at their backs. The mast creaked with the pressure, and the man at the tiller was sweating and swearing loudly.

The air was cool and the sun hot overhead. Zara-beth couldn't imagine the land frozen with snow and

cold for five months of the year, not now, now with
all the vastness of the green and blue and the softness
of the air. She closed her eyes a moment. She should
have been coming here as Magnus' wife, not his slave,
but the collar around her neck, dragging on her every
moment of the day, told the endless truth.

She turned when Horkel said to her, "Do you know
about the midnight sun?"

When she shook her head, he continued, "It is high
summer, and here there is almost no night. The sun
still holds its course in the sky even when it is midnight. We call this time the season of the sun. Alas,
in the winter, the sun scarce ever shows itself, and its
season passes. You will become used to it, in time."

"It is very cold?"

"Aye, and the days are short and become shorter
still. But there are feasts and games and nights filled
with songs and drink and laughter."

Two hours later, the men began to shout and point.
Zarabeth looked toward the shore and saw a wooden
pier stretching out into the water. Beyond it was a
narrow beach covered with pebbles and driftwood. A
wide path wound its way upward from the beach to
a wide flat expanse of ground, cleared as far as the
eye could see. In the middle of the flat ground was a
circular wooden palisade some eight feet high. Beside
the palisade were fields filled with rye and barley and
wheat, shining gold and brown under the sun. She saw
men and women alike working in the fields. Would
she be doing that as well? The wide fields went to the
very edge of the tree line. Magnus had used every bit
of land available to him.

"This is my farmstead, Malek," Magnus said with
simple pride; then, just as suddenly, bitterness filled
him and he added, "It is your home now as well. But
you do not come to it as I had wished."

"It is beautiful," Zarabeth said, and meant it. He

did not respond. The next minutes were busy as the men lowered the sail and took down the heavy mast. Two men jumped from the vessel to the wooden dock and tied the heavy ropes around the thick wooden stakes. Others began to empty the cargo hold of its goods.

"Come," Magnus said. "The men will unload and then all will come together this night for a feast." He pointed upward to the people who were pouring out of the wide palisade gates, waving wildly.

Ingunn, daughter of Harald, and younger sister to Magnus, looked down at the woman who was walking beside her brother across the beach. It was the way the woman walked, the proud set of her shoulders, that told Ingunn the truth. He had brought home a wife. She felt her flesh chill. What would she become now? The woman was beautiful, aye, she could tell that even from this distance. That red hair of hers, so vivid and lush. She felt Cyra stiffen beside her and felt a moment of pity mixed with pleasure at the woman's comeuppance. No longer would Cyra dare to disobey her orders. No longer would she show her sly ways. No longer could Cyra use her, Ingunn, to gain her own way with her brother. But then again, they had shared an unlikely partnership and now it would be at an end.

Ingunn felt her hands clenching at her sides. She waited, dreading meeting this woman who was Magnus' new wife. Magnus' son, Egill, was standing beside her, his hand over his eyes, shading them from the harsh sun.

"There is a little girl beside the woman," he said, pointing a finger. "See, she's holding the girl's hand."

That gave Ingunn a start. Had he married a widow, then? She hadn't expected that.

"Her hair is strange," Egill said after another moment. "It's redder than any of the reds in Grandmother's tapestry. I hope she lets me touch it. I wonder what it feels like, hair like that."

Ingunn wished he would just be quiet. They grew closer. When Magnus disappeared from view, only to appear the next moment on the flat ground atop the hill, he smiled at her and Ingunn ran into his arms. He hugged her, then quickly set her aside, his eyes on his son.

"Egill," he said, and scooped the boy up high in his arms, then immediately set him down and buffeted his shoulder. He was a boy now, not a child. "I have missed you, boy. By Odin, you are larger than when I left you but a month ago. Have you been a good master in my absence?"

Egill nodded seriously, then turned in his father's firm grasp. "Who is the woman, Father? Is she your new wife? Is the little girl her daughter?"

"No, she isn't my wife. Now, away with you. You may go help the men bring up our new goods." Magnus didn't move until Egill had disappeared down the winding trail that led to the viksfjord.

He looked around deliberately. "Where is Cyra?"

"She is back there, waiting."

The red-haired woman came into sight then. She stopped some paces behind Magnus. Magnus called out, "Cyra, come hither!"

Ingunn stared. The red-haired woman made no movement; her expression didn't change. Ingunn turned to watch Cyra run to Magnus. Ingunn watched, stupefied, as he lifted Cyra from the ground and hugged her tight; then he bent her over his arm and kissed her long and deep and hard. "You are well?"

Cyra nodded happily. She touched her fingers to his lean tanned cheek. "Aye, I am well. I had believed perhaps you no longer wanted me, but 'tis no matter now."

It was at that moment that the wind quickened and

lifted Zarabeth's hair from her throat. Ingunn saw the iron slave collar around the woman's neck. None of Magnus' slaves wore slave collars.

None save this woman.

She blurted out, "This woman is your slave? She's not your wife?"

Magnus stiffened, then laughed, too loudly, too harshly. "Nay, I will wed with no woman. Aye, this is Zarabeth and she is my slave and will remain so. The little girl is her sister, Lotti. Take care, Ingunn, for she is without hearing."

A slave; she was naught but a slave! Ingunn stared at her. The woman's face was without color, but her expression was calm. Slowly Ingunn smiled. Ah, she would show the woman what a slave was for. She held no favor, as did Cyra. Aye, Magnus wouldn't intervene with this one. As for the little girl, she was hugging her sister's thigh, looking frightened, her oddly colored eyes—aye, they were of a golden hue—wide and wary. The child could not hear? She shook her head at the foolishness of it. A child like that shouldn't have been allowed to draw breath. She merely nodded to the woman and stepped back, waiting to take cues from her brother.

She watched him turn to the woman, Zarabeth, and say sharply, "Stand not there like a witless fool. Bring Lotti to the longhouse. 'Tis the large one there in the center of the cluster of buildings."

Zarabeth felt stunned at the sheer size of the farmstead as she walked through the gates of the palisade. It was like a small village enclosed behind its stout wooden walls. There were many wooden huts, some others of wattle and daub, all of them with thatched roofs. The longhouse looked like a great low wooden barn. There were few windows, narrow and covered with stretched animal hides. She saw the smoke rising from the hole in the great sloped roof. As she walked beside Magnus, he said, "Yon is the blacksmith's workshop. The smith's name is Rollo and he makes all our weapons, farm tools, and pots and pans. Next to the longhouse is the cow byre; the sheep are kept in the low hut next to it. The slaves' hut is over there." He paused, awaiting her reaction. She made none, but she did look at the mean stone hut for several moments. "Outside the gates of the palisade are the fields. We will harvest in some two months and prepare for the winter.

"There is the bathhouse, and next to it the privy. The covered hut behind it is for food storage." It was as if he were presenting his possessions for her approval, she thought vaguely, yet she would have naught to do with any of it save as a slave. She would have no pride in anything. She said evenly, "Your farmstead is of obvious value, Magnus. I compliment you on your achievements."

His jaw tightened. He looked down at her, but it was only the iron slave collar about her neck that he saw. Thick and ugly, and he knew that it must chafe her flesh. Make her flesh raw and ugly. But the man in Hedeby had claimed that she'd called to him, offered herself to him for his help . . . It had all made sense. Magnus shook his head. No more would he question this woman's motives. What was done was done, and that was all there was to it.

He turned and called out, "Ingunn, will you have a feast prepared by tonight?"

She hurried to his side, ignoring Zarabeth. "We have been preparing food and ale and mead for the past week, brother. All is ready. I have already sent a messenger to Father. I hope he and Mother and our brothers will come as well."

"And Orm?" Magnus gave her a sly smile.

He looked at her, surprised. Her eyes darkened and her jaw set itself in a stubborn line. She shook her head. "Father is displeased with him. Since you left, he has forbidden Orm to come near me. He becomes a foolish old man."

"Don't say that again. Our father has reasons for everything he does. We will speak of this more later." Magnus saw that Lotti was lagging behind, her small shoulders stooped with weariness, and leaned down to pick her up. She gave a startled laugh, an odd mewling sound, then wrapped her thin arms around his neck and yelled in a loud slurred voice that was perfectly clear, "Papa!"

Magnus looked down at his son, who was so jealous he was nearly red from ear to ear. "You are far too large for me to carry, Egill. You are nearly grown, not like this little girl here." He got no response from Egill, but continued easily, "Say hello to Lotti. She cannot hear you, so you must speak directly at her when she is looking at you and speak slowly so that she will understand."

"Her hair is ugly," Egill said. "Her face is ugly too."

Magnus eyed his son. "I had hoped you had become more a man than a jealous little boy. Taunts against little girls aren't worthy of men. I am disappointed in you."

"She called you Papa! You're *my* papa!"

"Aye, 'tis true, but blame her not."

Zarabeth said nothing. She well imagined that the little boy, who was the very image of his father, would not be pleased at the intrusion of a stranger.

She said to him, smiling, "You will grow up to be of your father's size, Egill. He will be very proud of you."

Egill looked at the woman with the very red hair and eyes so green they looked like wet water reeds. "I don't care what a slave thinks. You will hold your tongue, woman."

Zarabeth drew back, silent as a stone. The boy was right. She had no right to speak her mind, she had no rights, she had nothing at all. She held out her arms to Lotti, and her little sister immediately pulled away from Magnus. Zarabeth moved away from Magnus, holding herself away from the hurt.

She saw the slave Cyra immediately take her place. The woman was but a few years older than Zarabeth, and her hair was long to her hips and as black as a moonless night. Her eyes were a dark brown and her flesh a soft peach color. She was exquisitely beautiful and Zarabeth wondered from whence she had come. Ha, where she had been captured was more to the point. She was also a slave, but there was no collar around her throat. A slave prized for her work in the master's bed.

"I have worked with the flax," Cyra was saying to Magnus, pointing to a long rectangular field to their left. "I will make you fine trousers and shirts."

Cyra wore a gown of white, full-cut, belted at her narrow waist. The material was a fine wool, not harsh and coarsely woven. It was as fine a garment as Ingunn was wearing.

Zarabeth was tired and depressed. She wanted to be alone, away from Magnus, away from the dozens of talking people who lived and worked and spent their lives on this farmstead. She hated it.

She touched her fingertips to the cold iron of the collar and kept walking.

When Ingunn said loudly that Cyra would show Zarabeth to the slave hut, Magnus did not contradict her. He had no intention of allowing Zarabeth to remain there even one night, neither she nor Lotti, but he would handle the situation in private. It wouldn't hurt to peel away a bit more of her lamentable pride, that stiff aloofness of hers that infuriated him. Let her believe for a while that she would stay in that mean hut.

He paused a moment, though, when he heard Cyra say to Zarabeth, "I do not sleep in there. I sleep in the longhouse, with Magnus."

And Zarabeth said with sweet laughter, "I am pleased for you, Cyra. You will continue to bed the savage, and I will be free from his attention."

Blood pounded through him. He wished now that he had taken her that day, that he had ignored Lotti and just taken her and been done with it. Damn her, he wanted to hurt her. He was shaking as he walked into his longhouse. No, he could not have done that; he couldn't have taken her in front of the child, nor could he have abused Lotti in any way. But he would have her soon. There would be naught for her to do about it.

Did she really believe he would allow Lotti to sleep with the other slaves in that cold damp hut?

He watched Egill run to Horkel, who had followed him into the house.

Everything looked familiar; everything felt exactly the same, smelled the same. But it wasn't. Life had changed now, and no matter how he had thought to shape it according to his own whims, he knew in that instant that the future was no longer his to control.

Zarabeth was wearing one of her gowns, a soft pink wool with a white overtunic that she had worn in York. Then she had fastened it with two finely worked brooches at the shoulders. They were gone; she assumed that Toki had taken them. Now she'd knotted the ties of the overtunic at her shoulders. Her hair was combed and hung freely down her back. Ingunn had told her to serve the guests all the mead and ale they wished. She had merely nodded, half her attention on Lotti, who had come to a beginning under-

standing with several of the small children who played
freely throughout the longhouse. She didn't know who
the children were; it seemed not to matter. They were
all thrown together and there was always an adult who
chided them or played with them, or gently pushed
them out of the way.

Magnus' longhouse was rather like a low, wooden
barn. The floor was of beaten earth, so hard that
walking on it raised no dirt or dust. There were
smooth slabs of stone around the perimeter of the
room, set firmly up to the walls. The walls were made
of split tree trunks set side by side in a double layer,
standing upright. Zarabeth looked up to see that the
roof was supported by big wooden beams and sloped
sharply. At the close end of the long room were rows
of clean wooden tables where all the family and guests
were now sitting eating beef and mutton, venison and
wild boar. There were trays of peas and cabbage and
potatoes, and huge bowls of apples and pears and
peaches. Over the huge rectangular fire hearth, bounded
with thick stones that rose a good three feet high,
were two huge iron pots suspended by chains that
were hooked to the ceiling beams. One pot was filled
with veal stew, the other with a mixture of potatoes
and onions and garlic and beef. There were iron bars
over the bed of hot coals upon which thick slabs of
boar meat spit and sizzled. On a low table at the end
of the fire hearth stood at least six bowls filled with a
variety of herbs.

The men were drinking from carved cow horns. The
women drank from wooden cups, except for Magnus'
mother, who drank from a fine glass from the Rhineland. Zarabeth moved silently with the heavy wooden
pitcher that held sweet wine from France that Magnus
had traded for at Hedeby. She was very careful with
it, for she knew the wine was valuable. She walked
slowly toward the main table, where Magnus' father,

Earl Harald Erlingsson, sat in Magnus' own carved chair, his wife next to him. He was as tall as his son, so fair that his hair seemed white in the dim rushlight. He looked as hard and lean as a man of twenty. It was very likely, she thought, that Magnus would look like him in some years.

"Wench," Harald called out. "Bring me more of my son's wine!"

He had done it on purpose, she thought vaguely. He had seen her approaching with the wine, yet he had chosen to call attention to her presence. In that instant Magnus looked up at her. He frowned. It was hot in the longhouse and he saw the glistening perspiration on her forehead, the wet tendrils of hair that curled around her face. Her face was flushed from the heat and she looked more beautiful than he had ever seen her. He felt a clenching deep within him and quickly said to his older brother, Mattias, "I am sorry your babe died, but Glyda looks well again."

Mattias cast a worried eye toward his pale-faced girl-wife. "She is very young," he said. "She knows not how to carry a babe."

"What is there to know?" Magnus said, giving his brother a questioning look. "She is young, yea, that is true, but you get your seed in her and a child grows and is birthed. What else is there?"

"She was foolish whilst she carried the babe."

"How?"

"She wished always to take me into her, if you would know the truth, Magnus!"

Magnus stared at his brother and then a smile tugged at his mouth. "You complain because your wife likes to bed you?"

"The babe came early and was born dead."

Magnus shook his head. "You seek to blame where you should not. Stop it now, Mattias. Glyda is a sweet girl. She will bear you other children, healthy children." He shrugged, looking toward the gaggle of boys and girls who played in the corner, far away from the fire hearth, two of the women near them. Four of them were Mattias' children from his first marriage. "Besides, even if she does not bear you other children, what does it matter? You have cast your seed to the four corners of the Vestfold already."

"More wine?"

Mattias stilled his tongue to gaze upon Magnus' new slave. All his brother had said was that he had bought her in York. Mattias wanted to reach out his hand and touch her magnificent hair. The color was so unusual, so rich and deep, its redness incredible. "Aye, more wine," he said only. He turned to speak to his brother, when he stopped cold. There was hunger in Magnus' eyes, and something else . . . it was pain and anger and perhaps frustration. There was a mystery here. Mattias continued to study the woman after Magnus had waved her away. He heard his father call out to Magnus, "I wish to buy the wench from you, Magnus. How many silver pieces do you want for her?"

Magnus said easily, "You do not want her, Father, for with her she brings a little girl who is without hearing. A responsibility that I doubt would give you pleasure."

"Then why did you buy her if all this responsibility weighs so heavily on you?" It was his mother, Helgi, who asked the question. "The little girl with the ginger hair is hers?"

"Aye, her little sister." He waited until Zarabeth neared his younger brother, Jon, and said loudly, "I knew not the little girl was deformed until it was too late." He watched and was pleased to see Zarabeth react. He saw her hand shake; he saw her whirl about to face him, and she took a step toward him, stumbled on a child's feather-stuffed leather ball, and dropped the wine pitcher to the ground.

"Stupid wench!" Ingunn was on her feet in an instant and at Zarabeth's side. Before anyone knew what she was about, Ingunn struck her hard on the face. Zarabeth reeled back, coming perilously close to the fire hearth.

"Watch out!" Magnus leapt from his chair and ran for her, grabbing her arm as she flailed the empty air to regain her balance.

"Let her fall," Ingunn said in disgust. " 'Twould serve her right to have a burn or two, the clumsy slut! The wine, 'tis gone now, and not in our bellies as it should be. Nearly half a pitcher!"

Zarabeth was breathing hard. She tried to pull away from Magnus, but he didn't immediately release her. She looked up at him, fury in her pale face. "You lied, Magnus! 'Tis true you didn't know Lotti could not hear, but you had already agreed to bring her. You lied to your father!"

He shook her. Didn't she care that Ingunn had struck her hard? His sister's palm imprint was red and clear on her cheek. He could imagine that it still stung. He shook her again, angry at her for accepting his sister's attack. Then he drew himself up. With his actions, he was giving all his people and his family a great many bones to chew upon.

"Be more careful in the future," he said, his voice low and harsh. "I do not want you to harm yourself. I paid too much silver to have you."

He flung her arm away then and strode back to his table. His brother Mattias merely arched a thick blond brow at him. As for his father, Harald, he was laughing, huge gulping laughs that made Magnus flush. He wanted the interminable meal to be done with. He saw Cyra approaching him, her eyes narrowed, for she had witnessed what he had done, and he knew that he would have to speak to her soon. She was bearing a huge tray of baked beef smothered with cumin and juniper berries and mustard seeds and garlic. It smelled delicious, but Magnus had lost his appetite.

Cyra served him, her smile deep and warm. He looked away from her. His mother said, "Cyra, come here. I wish more meat."

The evening continued. Magnus presented his mother with a beautiful carved jewel box he had traded several soapstone bowls for in Hedeby. He gave it to his father's runemaster to carve his mother's name on the bottom of it. He gave his father a silver arm bracelet, thick and heavy and finely carved. Soon the singing began. Then Horkel, a master skald, began the story of a girl who managed to wed an old man only to poison him when he tried to bed her. Magnus tried to catch Horkel's eye. To his relief, Horkel neatly shifted the focus of the story and the girl ended up a slave in Miklagard, in an Arab's harem.

There were jests to be told then, but Magnus simply could not keep his mind on the revelry. He saw Zarabeth make her way to where Lotti was sitting alone, for the women had taken the other children and put them to bed. They hadn't touched Lotti. He felt anger burn in his gut but knew there was no logical reason for it.

Zarabeth picked up the drowsing child, only to look around. It was clear she did not know what to do.

Magnus rose and tried to make his way with great nonchalance toward her. "Zarabeth," he called out quietly. "Lotti will remain here in the longhouse. Let me show you where she will sleep."

Her relief was evident, but she only nodded. Magnus led her to the far end of the hall, where there were small chambers, partitioned off from each other on either side of the longhouse, leaving a narrow corridor in the middle. "In here," he said. Inside the small chamber was a single large box bed upon which lay four young children. They were sleeping soundly. "Here," he said, and neatly picked up one child after the other, pushing them more closely together. He lifted the woolen cover and held it silently until Lotti, smiling sleepily up at both of them, closed her eyes.

"Thank you," Zarabeth said, not looking at him.

"You would not be pleased if she slept in the slave hut and you slept here."

She looked up at him then, but remained mute.

"Aye, Zarabeth, you will sleep in my bed tonight, and any other night it pleases me to have you there."

14

"You have Cyra. She's beautiful and she wants you. Why would you want me?"

Suddenly, without warning, Magnus ran his fingers through his hair, standing it on end, and he cursed long and fluently. Then he had to laugh at himself. He'd clearly lost his head and forgotten the circumstances. He said aloud, "It is a feast night, and all will remain here until the morrow. My parents, aye, they will have my bed." He laughed again, shaking his head at himself.

"You will not make Lotti leave, will you?"

He heard the fear in her voice and it angered him more than he could ever have imagined. "Don't you care about yourself? Of course Lotti will remain where she is. Come, now, you have tasks to do. Tonight you will sleep wrapped in a blanket in the hall." He sighed again as if he were sorely put upon, and she had an odd urge to laugh.

Ingunn put Zarabeth to scrubbing wooden plates and bowls and iron pots and spoons, which she did willingly, for it kept her to herself and away from the men. When she heard a woman's voice, she didn't at first attend. The woman said again, "Your name is Zarabeth?"

Zarabeth looked up to see Helgi, Magnus' mother. Her face was flushed from the warmth of the hall and the wine she'd drunk. Zarabeth looked closely, but she saw no meanness in her fine blue eyes. Zarabeth remembered Magnus telling her about how his mother rocked and shook the huge butter churn. There had been love in his voice when he'd spoken of Helgi. She was a large woman, deep-bosomed, her hair silver, it was so light. She had a deep cleft in her chin, which she'd given to her son.

Zarabeth nodded.

"I have listened to Magnus' men telling all about how he saved you from a certain death, for you had murdered your husband."

"He saved me, that is true."

"The other is not true?"

Zarabeth shook her head wearily. "No, it isn't, but it matters not. He won't ever believe me." She shook back her damp hair and bared the slave collar. "I am nothing to him now. Nothing save a slave."

Helgi sucked in her breath. She hadn't seen the collar before, for the woman's hair was long and the neck of her gown high. Why had Magnus done such a thing to this woman? "Why did he save you?"

"I believe he wanted revenge."

"Mother! Leave her be. Don't listen to her. She doesn't ever speak the truth."

Helgi turned to her Magnus. "It isn't true that you bought her to gain revenge?"

"It matters not why I bought her! She is here, and here she will remain."

"Yes, that is true," Zarabeth said, her voice loud. "I have no choice, for so long as he holds my little sister, there is naught I can do."

Magnus forgot his mother was standing in front of him. Furious, he grabbed her wrist, jerking her close to him. "You will not say that again, damn you! I have told you that Lotti will never be a lever for me to use, for anyone to use. The child is under my protection."

"I do not believe you. You will threaten the child when you think it will bring me to heel."

Helgi watched the two of them and wondered what would happen. Never had she seen Magnus so lost to control. Of her three sons, he was the one who remained firmly in command of himself in any situation. He prided himself on his mastery of others and of himself. He was always calm, his voice easy and low. Whenever he felt strongly about something, his voice deepened even more, but he never, never bellowed in rage, as he was doing now. Now he was acting like his younger brother, Jon, who yelled and cursed and carped with frustration and irritation and didn't care if the whole farmstead knew of his feelings. It was a marvel to see this. Obviously Magnus cared deeply for the young woman with the wild nimbus of red hair around her face. He just didn't realize it yet. Or perhaps he did, and he was fighting it as hard as he was her. Helgi laid her fingers on her son's arm. "Release her, Magnus. You have never before abused a slave. You should not begin now."

"Aye, go to your Cyra!"

He smiled down at Zarabeth then, but it was not a smile his mother liked. "No, I shan't abuse you. And no, I shan't go to Cyra." He turned on his heel and went back to his father and brothers, who were singing loudly of King Harald Fairhair and how he had slain the rapacious Gorm of Denmark by strangling him with his long thick hair.

Time passed slowly. Zarabeth was so tired she felt light-headed. Yet there were always more bowls, more plates, more trays, more goblets. An endless stream. She saw from the corner of her eye that the other slaves were gone to their hut. But she was being punished. Many of the men were asleep, their heads on the tables, snoring loudly. The fire was banked, and no more smoke went upward to the hole in the roof.

Many guests were stretched out in neat rows, each wrapped in his blanket. Ingunn came over to her, yawning loudly. "You work slowly, slave. You will not close your eyes until you have completed this."

Zarabeth remembered Magnus' words. *Lotti is under my protection.* Very well, then. She would believe him in this. Her little sister wouldn't pay for anything she did. She smiled at Magnus' sister and said, "Nay, I think not, Ingunn. I am weary and will seek out my bed now, as all the other slaves have done."

Ingunn drew in her breath sharply. She hadn't expected this. Her anger flared. "You dare?"

"Aye, I dare." Zarabeth shrugged and turned away from the wooden tub filled with dirty dishes.

"I will flay the flesh from your back, you slut!"

Zarabeth saw the flash of unrestrained fury in the woman's eyes, but she paid her no heed. She walked quickly away, toward the large wooden doors on the longhouse. She shoved them open and went out into the night. But the strange thing was that it still wasn't night, not like night at home. This was the time of year when night didn't fall. It was well past midnight, yet the sky was still gray with dim light, as if it were late afternoon and rain was coming at any moment.

It was warm, with a mild breeze blowing up from the viksfjord. In the distance, across the water the mountains were shrouded in magnificent shadow and low clouds. She vaguely remembered the endless dipping and rolling green hills from her home in western Ireland, and that billowing mist that blew off the sea, always warm and always damp. Here it was dry and warm and so beautiful she wanted to weep with the irony of it all. But there was really no irony in it at all.

She lowered her face into her hands and sobbed.

She felt his large hands encircle her arms, felt him draw her back against his chest. The sobs wouldn't stop. She felt weak and out of control, and she supposed, vaguely, that she was, and she didn't care.

Slowly Magnus turned her to face him and drew her into his arms. He felt the force of her tears, felt the convulsive shudders go through her body.

"You're tired," he said after a long moment. "You are tired, and that is why you are crying."

She raised her face and looked up at him in the dim light. "Is that what you wish to believe, Magnus?"

He lowered his head then and kissed her. He tasted the salty wetness on her lips. It hurt him deeply, this pain of hers. He brought his hands up her back to hold her still, and his fingers closed around her throat. And stilled at the touch of the slave collar.

He'd had the smithy put it on her. He'd watched as the smithy placed the collar Magnus had selected around her throat. He'd watched her become paler and paler until her face had seemed washed of color. And when the collar was around her neck, he'd watched her eyes become blank and empty.

But it was her fault. She had enraged him, trying to seduce another man. He'd had no choice.

Slowly he pushed her away from him.

He didn't want to, but he looked down at her. Her cheeks glistened wet and her eyes still brimmed with unshed tears.

"Why did you betray me? Why?" He took a quick step back, away from her, appalled at his weakness, at the anguish in his voice. By Odin, that she could have brought him to this.

Zarabeth watched his face change, watched his eyes grow cold, watched him distance himself from her.

"I didn't betray you."

"Liar. Get inside the longhouse. You will sleep now, for there is much that will require your attention on the morrow."

He turned on his heel and left her, not returning

inside, but striding toward the gates of the palisade. She watched him speak to the guards, then pull up the thick wooden shaft that barred the gates.

She turned slowly and walked back into the long-house. There was no free place for her to sleep on the floor. Men snored loudly, as did some of the women. There were two couples who were caressing each other, but they were too sodden with drink to do much about it. Zarabeth stood irresolute for a moment, then made her way to the small chamber where Lotti and the children were sleeping. She lifted her sister and slipped into the bed. The other children obligingly shoved more closely together. Zarabeth was asleep within moments, Lotti snuggled close to her body.

Magnus believed she had left him. He searched every sleeping body in the large hall. She wasn't there. He looked in every chamber, his temper and his fear for her growing in equal measure. Finally, when he saw her asleep with the children, he thought he would collapse with the relief he felt. He shook his head at himself and took a blanket outside in the cool of the night. When sleep finally came, there was a woman in his mind, as real as the deep strokes of his heart, and she was taunting him, laughing at him, and when she turned, she had no face. She threw back her head, lifting her hair, and there was an iron collar around her neck.

It was late the following morning before all the men had left to return to their families. Magnus' brothers and parents remained until after the midday meal before taking their leave.

Zarabeth served them, silent and stiff, dark shadows beneath her eyes. Her gown was wrinkled and soiled from spilled food and her cleaning from the night before. Magnus wondered why she had not garbed herself in fresh clothing, why she hadn't washed herself in the bathhouse. Her hair was in a thick braid that hung between her shoulder blades. He noticed that every few moments her eyes searched out Lotti, who was playing with the other children. He saw his son watching the little girl, and there was meanness in Egill's clear blue eyes. He sighed. If only the boy would understand. He cursed softly, then turned to his brother Mattias, who said calmly as he chewed on a piece of warm bread, "You must deal with the woman. This cannot continue."

"It has only begun. What mean you?"

"You, Magnus, freely offer me your impertinent advice about my wife. To do you justice, I admit that I did allow Glyda to enjoy herself last night with my body. I felt her womb when I spilled my seed into her. Perhaps this time she will bear me a live child." Mattias paused a moment, staring toward Zarabeth. "I am not blind, nor am I particularly stupid. You watch this woman with her strange red hair like a hungry wolf who wants to devour her or strangle her. Then you gaze at her as though you would give your life to protect her. You can explain it to me, brother. Have you lost your wits and your manhood to this wench who poisoned her husband?"

"It is none of your concern."

"Father wished to know all of it, and so Horkel was bound to tell him what had happened. He says that you have acted with great honor."

"Horkel knows little of anything. He knows almost nothing, and yet he brays on and on."

"He knew that you wished to marry the wench and that she betrayed you."

"Enough, Mattias. I see Jon over there teasing one of my women. I will go best him with swords. He grows audacious as he gains his man years."

Mattias watched his brothers buffet each other on

the shoulder and proceed to insult each other with easy fluency. He watched them draw their swords and go into mock battle. Jon was built more slightly than his powerful brother, but he was faster, his movements agile. Both of them were laughing, mocking each other's skills. There would be no spilled blood, not today, not between these brothers. Men began to gather around them and shout advice.

"I would speak to Magnus about Orm," Harald said to his eldest son, Mattias. "I trust not the whelp. He will try to take Ingunn, I doubt it not."

"Ingunn would not go with him."

"Ha! I am not so certain of that. She mouths all the right words, Mattias, but she wants him. The girl is sullen and gives me evil looks. Her temper has always been uncertain; it becomes more uneven now that I have refused her Orm. And even if she obeyed me and rejected him, he would force her, and then I would have to kill him." Harald sighed deeply. "What if he gets her with child before I can kill him?"

Mattias laughed. "Father, you weave a tale with an ending that suits you not, even before the tale can come to its beginning! Magnus is here now. He will not allow Orm to come within the palisade gates."

Harald grunted, but was still frowning as he looked toward his daughter, Ingunn, who was talking to Zarabeth. She was angry, he could tell from even this distance. He hoped she would not strike the woman again. There would be trouble, though, he scented it in the air, just as he knew Orm would move on Malek to take Ingunn.

Ingunn was furious at the woman's insolence. Her hands trembled. "All you do is look at that foolish little girl! You will work, slave, else I will have you whipped!"

At that moment Egill, angry because Lotti had taken the thrown ball not intended for her, bellowed and threw himself upon the child. Lotti, not hearing him, had no warning, and Egill knocked her flat.

Zarabeth cried out and ran to the children. She lifted Egill and threw him off Lotti. When she turned the child over, she blinked in mute surprise. Lotti was grinning and pointing at Egill.

She shouted in her slurred yet perfectly recognizable way, "Egill! Fun!"

To Zarabeth's further astonishment, Lotti scrambled to her feet, shouting again, "Egill!" at the top of her lungs, and hurled herself at the boy. They went down together, arms and legs tangling, buffeting each other.

The children watched just for a brief moment; then they paired off and four different fights began.

Magnus, through sheer strength, pressed Jon's sword beside his face. "Do you cry 'Enough,' little brother?"

"Aye, but only until next time, Magnus!"

The men laughed and sheathed their swords. Then Magnus looked up to see all their audience turned away. And he saw the children wrestling, fighting, yelling, and his first thought was of Lotti. He felt a coldness in his belly. "Quickly!" he called to Jon, and ran toward the children.

To his surprise, there was Lotti, sitting astride Egill, her small hands fisted in his hair, yanking and laughing and bouncing up and down on him. As for his son, Egill was pulling at the little girl, trying to jerk her off him, but Lotti's legs were strong and she wasn't ready to give up her advantage. Magnus realized quickly that the boy was doing his best not to hurt her, and it pleased him. He saw soon enough that Egill was also trying not to laugh.

Magnus saw Zarabeth lean over and grasp Lotti beneath the arms and lift her. Zarabeth was laughing and kissing the child's dirty face. The sound was sweet and magical and it lighted up her face. He swallowed, turning away. It was the first time she had laughed since . . . No, he wouldn't remember that. It had all been a lie, all of it.

He wanted her. He bided his time all during the long day. He went hunting with his men, taking Egill with them. He watched her throughout the evening, working and serving, and always, she watched Lotti. He wanted to tell her that every adult in the house was aware of every child, but he didn't. She wouldn't believe him. The hours passed, and still he watched her. He had dismissed Cyra, had finally told Ingunn that Zarabeth had worked enough. He saw that his sister wasn't pleased at his interference, but she nodded, saying nothing. Still, he waited. He watched her pick up Lotti and carry her off to bed.

He waited another half-hour. Horkel began a song of Magnus' father, the hero in a sea battle of some twenty winters past, and how he had captured twenty slaves and several casks of gold and silver.

At last, when others were yawning, Magnus rose and bade his good-nights. It took him not long to realize that Zarabeth wasn't in the longhouse. He went to the slave hut. She wasn't there. He found her speaking to one of his guards who sat at his post atop the northern palisade. Magnus felt rage and jealousy flow through him until he realized with pain at his own weakness that the man was Hollvard, an old man, wizened, toothless, and with frailty in his muscles.

He walked quietly to them and stopped.

"Aye, mistress," Hollvard was saying in his slow precise way, "there be outlaws in the mountains, and so many places for them to hide. Aye, even a man with six other men must take care. 'Tis not always easy, this time or this land."

"Zarabeth," Magnus said, and placed his hand on her shoulder. He felt her stiffen, but she made no sound.

"Magnus, I was telling the mistress of our lands and customs."

"Aye, I heard you." He gave her a bitter look. "You were telling her it would be stupid for her to try to escape from Malek?"

"Nay, she didn't ask me about that. I was merely telling her of the dangers here."

"She asked you for a reason, Hollvard, doubt it not."

Hollvard shook his head, uncertain of his master's mood. Magnus said to Zarabeth, "Come now, 'tis time to go to bed." She looked up at him for the first time, raising her face for him to see her clearly, and he saw the fear there, the defiance, and it made his belly twist. He said, his voice steady and calm, "Do not look at me that way. Come."

And he took her hand, nodded good night to Hollvard, and led her toward the longhouse. The night was warm, touched with a sliver of moonlight.

He stopped and pulled her very slowly, very gently, to him. "Look at me, Zarabeth."

She looked up and he studied her features. Gently he touched his fingertip to her lips, to her jaw, up the bridge of her nose. He smoothed his fingertip over her brows. Then he leaned down and kissed her. Her lips were cold and set tightly together. He fancied he could taste her fear, but he refused to acknowledge it.

He only smiled. "Nay, sweeting. Part your lips for me. You did once, remember?"

He wasn't expecting it, and thus when she wrenched away from him, striking him with her fists, he didn't react quickly enough. She was running from him toward the gates in the palisade.

He started to yell at her, then thought better of it. He could just hear the men telling of how the female slave escaped him and he was calling after her like a fool.

He covered the ground quickly but she had managed to lift the wooden shaft and fling open the gates. She was through them before he could reach her. Hollvard was staring blank-faced after her. He'd done nothing to stop her. Magnus saw her ahead. She wasn't running down the path to the water, she had turned and was running toward the narrow paths through the barley field. He realized she wanted to make the pine forest. Then she could hide from him.

He caught her just as she reached the first line of trees.

He had no anger at her; indeed, if he had been able, he would have thanked her for coming here, for he fully intended to take her here, under the soft dim moonlight, in the shadow of the pine trees.

"I won't hurt you," he said, holding her tightly against him. She shook her head, but he grabbed her chin in his fingers and began kissing her. She jerked her face away, breathing hard, and he kissed her ear and her cheek. He grabbed her head and held it between his palms. "Now," he said. "Now."

He simply jerked her off the ground, and, cushioning the fall with his own body, came down on the soft ground beside her, her head on his arm. "Zarabeth, I won't hurt you. I am going to take you, and I don't wish you to fight me."

She looked up at him, looked into the face of the man she had loved, the man she now feared, and said very calmly, "Once you have taken me, will you return to Cyra and your other women? Will you leave me alone then?"

He could only stare at her, fury mixing with pain at her words.

"You do only wish to punish me, do you not? To make me submit to you, to prove you are the stronger,

to prove you are the master? Once you have done
that, you will be tired of it, will you not? You will no
longer care, and you will leave me alone?"

He said slowly, his voice clear as the night air,
"Even if I do not take you every night, you will sleep
beside me every night of my life and you will awaken
in the morning beside me."

"Why? I am nothing to you! You hate me, you
believe I lied to you, betrayed you. Why?"

He had no answer to that himself. He felt her
squirming beneath him and quickly held down her legs
with one of his.

He slowly began to pull apart the lacing over her
breasts. He didn't look away from her face even as he
parted the soft wool. His eyes flickered when his fingers touched her bare flesh, but still he looked at her
intently.

She felt his fingers, callused and hard, touching her
nipple, and she whimpered. "Do you not like that,
Zarabeth? You are so soft, so very soft."

His palms were rubbing back and forth from one
breast to the other, and still he watched her face,
watched her every expression. She couldn't make him
stop. All she could do was bear it. She withdrew into
herself. He saw it. "No, you will stay here, with me,
and you will feel me, Zarabeth, you will feel me
touching you and I will see your pleasure grow in your
eyes. You won't retreat from me, I won't allow it."

He leaned down then and kissed her. Her lips were
slightly parted and he forced them a bit more and
his tongue slipped into her mouth. He felt incredible
warmth surge through him. Warmth and tenderness,
and he didn't fight it. He couldn't fight it. He let it
flow through him and build and build. His need for
her was great, beyond anything he'd ever known, but
he would not savage her. He continued kissing her,
not demanding, just giving, wanting her to know that

he would go easily with her, and his hands kneaded and caressed her breasts.

She was holding herself perfectly still. Then his tongue thrust more deeply into her mouth and he felt her shudder, felt the heaving of her breast in his hand.

"Zarabeth," he said against her open lips. "Feel what I am doing to you." Everything in her froze in anticipation as his hand pulled apart the lacings and his palm was flat now on her belly, his fingertips touching her pelvic bone and massaging gently. Lower, she knew she wanted his fingers to go lower on her, it was there, those feelings, but she didn't really understand. To her utter humiliation, she moaned. She moaned from pleasure, but more from a need she did not understand but recognized to be there, deep inside her.

He raised his head and smiled down at her. His fingers remained still on her belly. "Again, Zarabeth." And his hand came down lightly over her woman's mound and his fingers found her.

She stared at him, and there was fear and excitement in her eyes, and growing anticipation, and he was pleased with himself and with her. Slowly, so very slowly this time, he began to caress her with his fingers. She didn't move. He saw the surprise, the embarrassment in her eyes, and said softly, "Nay, this is what a man does to give a woman pleasure. Tell me it pleases you, Zarabeth. Tell me."

She shook her head even as she whispered, "Aye, but it hurts as well . . . hurts . . ."

He lifted his fingers and felt her suck in her breath. He kissed her as he eased his middle finger inside her. By Odin, she was small, but her passage was moist now, for she was coming to her excitement. He thought to bring her to pleasure before coming into her, but he knew if he didn't come into her now, he would spill his seed. He hurt, and his sex was swelled and hard and ready. He gritted his teeth, but it didn't help.

He jerked up her gown and pressed her legs apart. Her eyes were no longer vague with growing excitement. There was only fear now, and he smiled, though it hurt him to do so. He positioned himself between her legs, then bent her knees. "Now, hold still. I won't hurt you." Slowly he guided himself into her. The heat from her body nearly sent him into oblivion, but he held on, held to control, and eased slowly, ever so slowly, into her. She was tight, her muscles squeezing him. He closed his eyes. He felt her fists pounding at his chest, his shoulders, but he didn't stop, couldn't stop.

She was crying. It wasn't supposed to be like this. She was lying there beneath him, letting him do as he wished with her. He was butting her maidenhead now, and the pain was building. He came over her, holding himself still, and gently kissed her cold lips. "Zarabeth, look at me."

She shook her head, her eyes tightly closed.

15

He didn't move, didn't allow himself to give in to the incredible desire that was prodding at him. He told himself again and again: She is just a woman who is a maid and I am her first man. That is the only pleasure there is from this mating. My possession of her. There can be nothing more.

"Look at me," he said again, his voice lower and rougher this time.

"No," she said, infinite pain in her voice.

And he said the words before he could stop himself. "Please, Zarabeth, I want you to look at me when I come fully into you."

Never in his life had he requested anything from a woman whose body belonged to him. He waited. Slowly she turned her face and opened her eyes.

She moved slightly under his weight, and Magnus groaned with the feelings it brought him.

He pushed forward just a bit and felt her tense. "That is your badge of maidenhood, a bit of skin that I will tear. Just a moment of pain, Zarabeth, then there will be no more."

"And then you will leave me?"

He smiled painfully, willfully misunderstanding her. "Aye, but I shall try to pleasure you before I do."

He grasped her wrists in his hands and pulled them above her head. He was stretched his full length on top of her, and he looked at her closely as he pushed slowly forward. He felt the skin stretch. He felt her trying to pull away from him, her flesh flinching and tightening around him, and he kissed her. "Slowly, sweeting," he said into her mouth. Then, suddenly, he reared back, and he looked into her eyes as he drove through her maidenhead and came to the mouth of her womb.

She cried out, unable to hold it in, and he covered her mouth with his. "No more," he said again and again. "Hold still and become used to me."

"It hurts," she said, and he felt the wet of her tears on his face. "I didn't think it would hurt like that."

"I'm sorry for it. I wish I could have spared you that." But there was no regret in his voice. On the contrary, his voice was filled to brimming with pride and satisfaction, and to Zarabeth's ears, filled with a man's triumph. She lay there silently, feeling him moving deep inside her. It was over now; he'd taken her; he'd won.

The pain was receding but she was still stretched to hold him. When he began to move, she felt the fullness of him, the slick hardness. It didn't matter, she told herself as he moved within her, it didn't matter. He had won, but she wouldn't let it matter. When he was done with her, he would be tired of her and leave her alone. Her maidenhead was gone now and he had been gentle with her, and for that she was grateful, she supposed. She was glad she hadn't fought him more than she had. It would have gained her naught but more pain. She felt nothing now save the stretching and fullness inside her and the revulsion for this man grunting over her, this man who was inside her body, who was doing to her precisely as he wished to do.

She listened to his breathing quicken, deepen. He moaned then, a raw deep sound, drawing back, and then he was pushing into her harder and harder still, and he was groaning wildly. Suddenly he froze over her, his head thrown back, and he gave a muted yell. She felt the wetness of him and knew that he had filled her with his man's seed.

He grew quiet. She accepted his weight, for she had no choice. She felt incredibly tired, yet oddly relieved that it was over and it hadn't been so horrible after all, this mating, this taking that men did of women's bodies. And he hadn't touched her, not really, not the part of her that was silently and wholly her.

He released her wrists and came up on his elbows to relieve her of his weight. He was still deep inside her, yet she didn't feel so full of him now.

"Did I hurt you again?"

"Aye." She saw too late that his additional sign of her innocence pleased him, and she wished she had lied.

"But you don't hurt now, do you?"

She shook her head, closing her eyes against the intentness of his gaze, wondering what was in his mind now.

"In a moment I will give you pleasure. I truly wish you hadn't had to suffer me before I could bring you to joy."

Her eyes flew open. He smiled down at her, enjoying her utterly bewildered expression, her disbelief at his words. He dipped his head down to kiss her.

"You will see."

Slowly he pulled himself out of her, feeling her flesh stretch more as he did so. But he didn't regret it, no, not ever would he regret taking her and knowing that he was the only man to come into her body. He came up to his knees between her spread thighs. There was blood on her thighs and on his member. He sat back on his heels and stared at her. In the dim night light he could see her clearly; her white thighs, widespread now, their flesh so soft to his touch that it made his breath hitch, and the vivid red curls that covered her. It drew him, that red hair of hers, and he touched her now, very lightly, just to see his long fingers on her and to know that she was watching him as he looked at her. She drew in her breath and he raised his head. Her breasts drew him now, flesh as white and soft as her belly and thighs. And he thought: She should be lying beneath me as my wife, not my slave. But she wasn't. He remembered that day when he had first seen her and he had known, actually *known*, that he would love her and only her and that she would be generous and warm and his. But she wasn't. He had been wrong in everything, except in the feelings that persisted for her deep inside him. He closed his mind; he would not deal with those myriad feelings, at least not now. He wanted to bring her to pleasure, he wanted to hear her cries when she burst into her climax. He had to have this final dominance over her.

He came down on his side to lie beside her. He looked down at her gown, bunched at her waist, at her belly, at her breasts, pale in the dim night light. He watched his hand caress her belly, watched his fingers find her through the red curls that covered her. When his fingers touched her, he looked into her eyes and saw the beginning of awareness there, of surprise, and of fear. Fear of him? Although he had no intention of hurting her, he supposed he could not blame her. He smiled at her even as his fingers found their rhythm. Her eyes widened with shock, with embarrassment, and she jerked away from him.

She curled up, her back to him, and he saw the shaking of her shoulders.

"Nay," he said. "Trust me, Zarabeth. Come, let me show you what it is to have a woman's pleasure."

She curled up more tightly and he felt near-pain in his loins at the sight of her buttocks and long white legs. He grasped her arm and pulled her onto her back again. "You will do as I tell you. You won't pull away again."

His words sent her over the edge. "You want to bring me pleasure, yet you play master to my slave with great enjoyment and ease. You want to dominate, Magnus, to subjugate, nothing more."

He ignored the bitterness in her voice, acknowledged that she spoke the truth, and shook his head. "Hold still. I won't tell you again." He laid his palm flat on her belly even as he gave her the order. His other hand went down her, finding her, and again his fingers delved deep and sure, and began a movement that was slow, then fast, so light, then deep as the very feelings in her soul. She closed her eyes against the humiliation of it. He was touching her and looking at her face, wanting to see her expression, knowing that she hated this probing of her body, this final seal of his victory over her.

Then, suddenly, there was an answering deep inside her and she froze, not at first understanding. He sensed it and quickly deepened the rhythm of his fingers. "You begin to respond," he said, and there was pleasure in his voice. He sounded proud of her, as if she were a dog performing tricks he told her to. Then, without warning, the answering changed, intensifying and fanning out as flames under a bellows, exploding into a pleasure so intense, so shattering, that she moaned with it and wanted to die because she had moaned. She was beyond humiliation now, for he was there watching and judging his efforts. She heard her own cries, soft and torn from her throat. The pleasure built inside her. She knew there was more, that there was something beyond the pressure and the fullness that was ever increasing now, and she knew too that she would be alone when it came to her. She never doubted that whatever it was would happen, for he was controlling her, not sharing with her. He was completely apart from her.

Magnus leaned over her, his warm breath on her cheek, encouraging her, telling her to lift her hips, to move against his fingers, to kiss him, yea, to kiss him and let her tongue touch his. And he watched her, watched her closely, and he saw when she could no longer control it, could no longer hold back from him or from herself. When her pleasure came, he kissed her deeply and took her cries into his mouth, deeper still, into his soul.

" 'Twas well done of you," he said when her breathing calmed a bit. "To have a woman cry out with pleasure makes a man feel quite proud of himself."

She felt desolate. She looked up at him, saying nothing, and saw the anger build in his eyes.

"You had no chance. Aye, you fought against it, Zarabeth, but you had no chance. Admit it now, you enjoyed yourself."

She shook her head. "It merely happened, that is all, nothing more."

His mouth was a grim line. "It will happen whenever I wish you to have those feelings. You won't ever pull away from me again, Zarabeth."

"What will you do?" she asked without interest.

"I don't know," he said, surprising himself at his immediate honesty with her.

She looked up at him for a very long time. Finally she whispered, "What do you want from me, Magnus?"

The slave collar glittered in the hazy light. He drew a deep breath. "Question me not further, woman. You are disobedient and insolent. Just don't press me, Zarabeth."

Again she said, "What do you want from me?"

"Come," he said abruptly as he rose. "What I want is to have you in my bed."

She stood slowly, starkly aware in that moment of

what had happened between them, for her body was sore and her legs were weak, and there was still a gentle pulsing deep inside her, a reminder of what he'd done to her, of what he'd made her feel. Aye, she felt a softness and a warmth, she couldn't deny it, yet at the same time she wished she could have lain there beside him whilst he had touched her and felt nothing, nothing save her hate for him, which wasn't hate and never had been, but now she felt raw and exposed and helpless and there must be hate for him, for he had brought her to it. She submitted silently as he straightened her clothing, then laced up the front of her gown. He smoothed the skirts on her legs and pushed back her tangled hair from her face. "You no longer look like a maid," he said, and grinned down at her.

"It matters not," she said, and shrugged. "I knew you would force me. I also knew that you could not really touch me, only my body. I expect that my body would react thus to any man's touch."

He had told her not to press him, but she had. She waited, watching the pulse in his throat, saw the tight lock he had on his jaw. His eyes were cold now as he stared down at her, and he seemed to be struggling with himself. Finally he merely took her hand and pulled her with him. He shortened his step to match hers. Neither said another word until they reached the palisade.

All was silent in the longhouse as he led her to his chamber. He still said nothing, just motioned her to remove her clothing. She turned away from him, refusing to let herself care, and slipped out of her clothes and under the wool blanket. He continued silent, merely stripped and came into the bed beside her. He drew her into his arms, ignoring how she stiffened against him. Magnus awoke toward morning and reached for her. She wasn't there. He was instantly awake. He roared out of bed, paused to gain control of himself, then walked quietly to the children's small chamber. She was there, sleeping soundly, Lotti wrapped against her.

He awoke her with hesitation, but quietly, so as not to awaken the children, and led her back to his bed. He jerked off the linen shift, but didn't stop to look at her. He wanted her too badly, both his anger and his desire blending together. He wanted to punish her and he wanted her to yell again when she reached the pleasure he granted her.

He began kissing her and didn't stop even when he came inside her and she moaned into his mouth, whether from the pain of his entry or from pleasure, he didn't know. Nor did he care at the moment. He rode her hard and quickly took his release. The chamber was dark as a cave, and for that he was thankful. He was afraid that if he saw her face he would hate himself. He knew he would see the emptiness in her eyes, the desolation that ground him down. And he knew, deep down he knew that her moan was from pain. He'd been rough, not preparing her.

He pulled away from her, and without a word, without pause, he came down on her and parted her legs to fit himself between them, and stroked her with his mouth. She fought him, outraged and frightened and disbelieving. But he wouldn't stop. When he felt the tension building in her, he loosened his hold. He smiled, for she no longer fought him. He tasted her and probed her with his tongue and caressed her with his mouth, and he could feel the building tension in her, and when the first cry broke from her mouth, he put his fingers over her and let her scream against them, muting the noise, giving her the freedom to yell her release.

He had won.

She was crying when he held her close to him to

sleep. "You are mine now," he said over and over as he stroked his hands up and down her back.

He took her to the bathhouse, where tubs were always full of hot water and the small room was filled with rising steam and so hot the sweat poured off. It was just past dawn and the sky was pink and pale gray with the coming of day. He said nothing, merely motioned for her to enter. He sat on a long wooden bench, leaned back at his ease with his arms folded over his chest, and told her to remove all her clothes.

It would never end, she thought, staring down at him. Slowly she shook her head.

"I have seen you naked. Why do you hesitate?"

She waved her hands around her. "There is light here and it shames me."

"As you will," he said, "but it matters not." He rose quickly, jerked off her linen shift. She realized he enjoyed her refusal and her struggles. She stopped fighting. She owned only one other shift. When she escaped him, she could not go naked.

When she was naked and sweating, he sat her down on a wooden bench and stepped away from her. He quickly stripped off his tunic, which was all he had put on when he'd pulled her from his bed. She looked at him, standing there before her, strong and tall and so finely made. It hurt her to look at him.

"Come here and bathe yourself. You smell of sex and of sweat." He gave her soap and a soft cloth. She scrubbed herself and it felt wonderful. "Straighten now and look at me." Before she understood what he would do, he had doused her with a bucket of cold water. She yelled with the shock. She wanted to hit him, but he was dousing himself with another bucket of cold water, shuddering and cursing, thoroughly enjoying it.

"Now, come here and sit down and feel the steam

envelop you. Then we will have more cold water. It is the Vikings' way. The Saxons stink from the day they're born. We do not.''

She sat there silent, her flesh heating in the small room, the steam rising above her head. When Magnus lay beside her on the long bench and put his head on her lap, she tried to move away, but the bench was narrow and he held her still, his arms now wrapping around her hips. He turned his face inward and began kissing her belly. When he pulled back and let his tongue touch her, she heaved him off her. He was laughing, actually laughing. He pulled her against him. Their bodies were slick with sweat and he pulled her close, then lifted her.

He sat on the bench with her and widened her thighs until she was pressed against him. He lifted her again and guided himself into her.

"Magnus!"

"Hold still. Ah, there. Now, move, do as you please.'' He folded his arms around her back and held her tightly. When she didn't move, he smiled, realizing she didn't know what to do. He clutched her buttocks in his large hands and lifted her nearly off him, then eased her back down his length again.

She gasped and locked her hands around his neck. He leaned closer and kissed her even as he worked her. He felt her excitement build, and because he himself was nearing his release, he quickly eased his fingers over her and felt her tighten and jerk against him.

Her body exploded into pleasure, and he kissed her hard, shoving into her until he could go no further, and he let himself go, heaving and gasping in the steaming hot air. He held her head against his shoulder and gently rubbed his hands up and down her back.

Her hair was wet and thick on her back, and he

lifted it to stroke her better. His fingers touched the slave collar and left it, scorched.

He eased her off him then and silently handed her the soap and wet cloth. She stood before him for a moment, utterly naked, her body flushed and weak and soft, and she hated herself and him and she was helpless against him. He saw it and accepted it and told himself he was pleased. He remained quiet, sitting on the bench, watching her bathe him from her body.

There was a small antechamber in the bathhouse. Someone had brought clean clothes for them. She closed her eyes. Someone had come in and seen them naked, perhaps seen him taking her and making her scream. Her fingers were clumsy on the fastenings of her gown.

He leaned down and picked up a clean dry cloth and wrapped it around her hair. He forced her face up with his fingers beneath her chin. She was scrubbed clean. He kissed her then and led her outside. The sun was bright overhead and the morning air cool. There were servants about, and slaves going through the gates in the palisade out into the fields. Why didn't they simply leave? she wondered. She would have, in an instant. Magnus halted her, pulling her toward him. He kissed her again, long and deep, in front of all his people.

"There," he said with deliberation. "Now there will be no more questions."

When Zarabeth came back into the longhouse, her hair was a damp mass down her back but she was gloriously clean and her face was shining. She tasted Magnus on her lips. She felt sore inside her body. She saw Lotti sitting with four other children next to Eldrid, Magnus' aunt. She was seated in front of the large loom weaving thread into cloth. She was as large as her sister, Helgi, Magnus' mother, but there were hard edges to her that softened only when the children came to her. She hadn't yet spoken a word to Zarabeth.

But Ingunn was free with her speech. "Magnus has finally finished with you, I see. I am surprised you can still walk. Did you have that many men in York?"

"Who knows?" Zarabeth said to Ingunn, and nodded to Cyra, who stood behind her, a distaff in her hands, holding it like a weapon.

"He always liked to have Cyra in the bathhouse. You do not bring him new amusements." Ingunn waited, but got no reaction at all from the woman. "I have already set your tasks. Get to work now."

Zarabeth only nodded. She cared not what she did—churning the butter or mixing the grain flour with water in a large wooden trough to make the bread dough. Her arms ached from kneading the dough. In York she'd never made so much bread at one time, nor had she ever in her life seen such a huge butter urn. Yet, basically, they were familiar tasks and she escaped while she worked. She thought of escape. She closed her eyes as she kneaded the dough, and he came into her mind. Magnus had touched her, no matter how hard she had tried to keep him from her. He had touched her, the deepest part of her, again and again. It wasn't just the pleasure he had brought to her, though that had made her lose herself in those precious moments, lose herself into a beginning she had not before known could be. She looked down to see that the dough was properly mixed. She supposed that it was; she had never seen so much of it. It took her another hour to shape all the dough into small loaves and ease them onto the long-handled paddles. She laid them carefully over the hot ashes of the fire. Sweat covered her forehead. Her arms quivered from fatigue. She thought fondly of the bathhouse and the dousing with cold water Magnus had given her. Then she thought of him taking Cyra there and doing the same things to her.

When she had finished, Ingunn was waiting with more duties for her. She sent her to the barley field with instructions to speak to Haki, who would tell her what to do. She went. The day was warm, but after the dim light of the longhouse and the close air, it felt wonderful to be outside. Haki was a bent old man with beautiful white teeth. He smiled when she came to him, and told her to go down the barley rows and pull out any weeds she saw and to wave her arms at any birds who dared to swoop down. She merely nodded and did as she was bidden. Her task was easy and mindless. Her stomach growled and she realized she had eaten nothing that day, for Magnus had dragged her to the bathhouse very early. She hoped there would be a meal soon. Heat poured down on her and through her. She was sweating freely and her back began to hurt from bending and straightening so many times. There were other slaves between the rows doing what she was doing. They were laughing and jesting with each other. She supposed she would become used to the work in time.

Time passed and the sun was in the western sky now. She was so hungry she felt faint with it. And thirsty, but Haki said nothing.

She wondered where Magnus was. She hadn't seen him since he had left her at the entrance to the longhouse that morning.

Finally Haki called to her to leave and return to the longhouse, for he had heard her stomach rumble. She tried to smile at him but could not quite manage it. When she came into the dim coolness of the longhouse, she immediately searched out Lotti. The little girl was listening intently to something Eldrid was saying. She noted the older woman was speaking slowly, pronouncing her words with great care, and she smiled. At least Lotti was not to be treated as she was. It took her another moment to realize that Eldrid was teaching Lotti about weaving. Other little girls were there, all listening. None of the male children were in the longhouse. She supposed they were with the men, learning woodworking, learning to fight, learning to make weapons.

She picked up a wooden bowl and scooped some hot porridge from the huge kettle suspended by a chain from a ceiling beam.

"I have not told you to eat," Ingunn said from behind her.

Zarabeth turned slowly to face Magnus' sister, and said calmly, "I have been working in the barley field. I have had nothing to eat since last night." She turned away from Ingunn. In the next instant the wooden bowl was slapped from her hold and she cried out when the hot porridge spattered on her hands and arms.

"Careless slut! Pick up the bowl and place it on the counter. I will have you beating the flax now, if you have the skill for it, and if you do not, you will remain at it until you have gained some!"

Zarabeth forced herself to take deep breaths to regain her calm. She wanted to murder Ingunn, and that would never do, but she could not let this continue. For whatever reason, the woman hated her. She said then, her voice low and calm, "I am hungry, Ingunn. I will beat your flax into threads when I have finished eating. No, I have not done it often, for in York there were others to do it. Now that I have explained, you will please leave me alone until I have eaten. You will wait with your orders until then."

Zarabeth bent down and picked up her wooden bowl. She heard a strange hissing sound behind her. She whirled about but wasn't quick enough. Ingunn brought the leather-thonged whip down across her shoulders. She felt pain sear through her and gasped.

She flung out her arms to grab the whip, but Ingunn was faster. She stepped back and struck again, so hard this time that Zarabeth fell against a huge cheese barrel and tripped. She was on her hands and knees now and the whip struck her full on the back, and she felt the wool of her gown split wide. She tried to fling herself on Ingunn, but the leather thongs struck her again, wrapping around her sides, the pain burning through her so that she gasped with it. It had to stop, but it didn't. Again and again the whip struck. She had to get up; she had to stop it. She shuddered with the effort to rise, and fell again to her knees.

She heard the women and children all talking, heard Cyra calling for Ingunn to kill the bitch. She heard Eldrid yelling at Ingunn to stop, but she didn't. She could hear Ingunn's deep, wild breathing. It only seemed to madden her more. Zarabeth's gown was shredded now, but she knew if she raised her head, Ingunn would strike her face and her chest. She felt blackness pulling at her and fought against it with all her strength. Then she heard Lotti, the strangled mewling sounds she made when she was distressed. Lotti was close now, and suddenly Zarabeth was screaming, "No, Ingunn, do not touch her! No!"

The beating stopped. Zarabeth raised her head, holding her shredded gown up to cover her breasts. Ingunn had grabbed Lotti and was shaking her hard. Then she was raising the whip to the child.

"No! You touch that child and I will kill you!"

Ingunn laughed. "She's naught but an idiot, your sister, and you are nothing but a slave!" She lifted the whip. Zarabeth jerked to her feet, only to fall forward.

"No!" she screamed. She realized it was only a whisper.

16

"By Thor's wounds! What are you doing? Ingunn! Stop it, woman!"

Magnus stood frozen, unable to believe what he was seeing. Ingunn was holding Lotti by the arm and had raised the whip. She was actually going to hit the child. He called her name again, but she didn't seem to hear him. She was panting, her breasts heaving, and she was focused entirely on the child. Magnus ran to her and grabbed her wrist just before the whip came down upon Lotti's back, wresting the whip from her hand.

She was white-faced, her eyes nearly black with uncontrolled fury. It shocked him, this viciousness in her. He threw the whip away, grabbed his sister's upper arms, and shook her hard. "What is the matter with you? Why would you strike a child? And with a whip! Answer me, damn you!"

Ingunn blinked at him, and he shook her again, but before she could answer, he heard Lotti making those raw mewling sounds and quickly turned to the child. She was running toward . . . He saw Zarabeth for the first time. She was on her knees, and was holding her gown up in front of her chest. Her hair was hanging down either side of her face, tangled and sweat-soaked. Her face was utterly without color.

He dropped Ingunn's arms.

He felt something in him twist and burn. He

204

watched Lotti throw her arms around Zarabeth's neck, saw Zarabeth's arms slowly come around the child's back.

Something was very wrong. He slowed himself. He reached Zarabeth but found that words wouldn't come to his tongue. He felt pain flow through him, raw and deep, for in that moment she fell to the side, taking Lotti with her, unconscious. He saw her back then, covered with purple welts from Ingunn's whip, saw splotches of blood where the whip had broken her flesh. Tendrils of hair stuck to her back. For a moment he was sickened with the shock of it; then black rage rushed through him like a wild fire. That he had brought her here for this.

He looked up to see his aunt. "Fetch hot water, Eldrid, quickly, and soap and clean cloths." Without another word, he lifted Zarabeth over his shoulder, careful not to touch her back. It was then that everyone seemed to become aware of him and of what had happened.

Ingunn yelled, "Leave her to the slaves! Let them take her to the slaves' hut. She is an insolent female, nothing but a slut whom you have already bedded! Why do you care? You brought her here to be a slave and your whore! She will be well enough this night for your rutting. She is nothing, Magnus, nothing!"

Cyra tried to catch his sleeve. "The woman insulted your sister, she yelled at her and called her horrible names and would not do as Ingunn told her to do and—"

Magnus shook her off, knowing that if he touched her, he would likely kill her. He carried Zarabeth into the dark chamber and laid her on her stomach. Slowly he pulled the red strands of hair from the welts on her back. He pulled her shredded gown to her hips. He heard a soft sobbing and turned to see Lotti, her small fist in her mouth, standing in the doorway, afraid to come closer.

"Come here, Lotti, and sit beside her. When she awakens . . ." He realized it would be difficult for her to understand. He left Zarabeth and went to the little girl. He lifted her, hugged her to him, smelling the sweet child-smell of her, then set her beside her sister on the bed.

He took her face between his hands and said slowly and calmly, "Stay beside her and smile at her when she awakens. All right?"

Lotti swallowed and slowly nodded. There was such fear contorting her features that Magnus wanted to yell with fury at it.

Instead, he gently lifted Zarabeth onto her side. There was but one welt that had snaked around her back and made a narrow red mark just below her breasts. He drew another deep breath and eased her back onto her stomach.

Eldrid came into the chamber. Behind her was a slave carrying a rushlight. She fastened it into the holder on the wall.

Magnus began washing Zarabeth's back. He didn't look at his aunt, merely said, "Tell me what happened."

"I am too old for this nonsense, nephew," Eldrid said. "I am teaching the little girl, just as you asked of me, but the sister, 'tis too much, Magnus. Ingunn hates her and wants her gone from here—that, or dead. What could I do? The child tried to help her sister, and Ingunn turned on her. What could I do?"

Magnus said nothing. He was washing the welts on her back. "Have you one of your herb remedies? She will have pain, and I would stop it if I could."

Eldrid shook her head. "Juice of the elderberry would do her good, but there isn't any. Only in the fall, perhaps in October. The woman is young, she will bear her pain as so many do, without your liking or disliking it."

He hated Eldrid in that moment, but he had no choice but to keep her here. She and Helgi, his mother, could not bear each other, so Eldrid had come to live with him some five years before. She had birthed no living sons to see to her well-being. She was sour and hard, except with children. Yet she had not protected Lotti. Ah, perhaps she had tried, but she was an old woman, depending on Ingunn as well as on him. And Ingunn had seemed as a berserker going into battle. He drew a deep breath and lightly patted a welt that had drawn blood just above her hips. He cursed then, soft and long, and looked up to see Lotti staring at him.

"Zarabeth," Lotti said, and lightly laid one small hand on her sister's shoulder.

Magnus said slowly, "She will be all right, Lotti. I promise you."

Zarabeth stirred some minutes later. She was lying on her stomach, and surely that was odd. In the next instant she realized that her back was on fire. Pain swamped her, and she hissed out her breath. She felt his hand on her arm, heard his voice next to her face. "Hold still. I can do nothing for your pain, I am sorry. Just hold still and breathe slowly and deeply."

And she did, for she really had no choice. She didn't open her eyes, but said, "Lotti. Is she all right? Ingunn was going to hit her, and I couldn't . . . couldn't stop her, I couldn't make my body move to stop her."

"I stopped Ingunn. Lotti is fine. She is sleeping now, next to you."

"Thank you."

"You won't be scarred."

She opened her eyes and stared at him. "I wanted to kill your sister, but I couldn't reach her. I saw her

raise that whip on Lotti and I heard her laugh, and
then . . ." She shuddered with the memory of it, and
Magnus, feeling furious and helpless and hating both
feelings, said, "Try to sleep now."

"I'm very hungry. That is what started it all. I was
so very hungry, and I simply wanted to eat some
porridge."

"I will fetch you something." He left her lying there
on her stomach, her face washed of color, even her
vivid red hair seeming faded and dimmed, hanging
damp and tangled beside her face.

He walked to the cooking counter of smooth wooden
planks that held wooden plates, knives, spoons, and
trays. He was aware of the painful silence in the longhouse. His men were staring at him, as were the
women. Only the children seemed unaffected, and he
heard them taunting each other, laughing, challenging.
He heard Egill yelling for a wager with another boy.

Ingunn was behind him, saying quickly, her voice
low and furious, "Do not believe her, Magnus. She
lies, I know it. She disobeyed me, refused to work.
What was I to do? She thinks that since she is your
whore, she need do nothing save watch the rest of us
work. Believe not her tales, Magnus! You already
know her for a liar, a murderess."

He turned slowly, a bowl in his hand. "Please put
some venison stew in the bowl, Ingunn."

Ingunn drew back. "For her? For that slut? I would
rather stick a knife in her black heart."

"Do as I tell you."

"No, damn you, I won't!"

"Then you will no longer be welcome in my house.
I am master here, and I will be obeyed in all things."

He hated using that kind of threat, but he saw no
other way. Ingunn took the bowl from him and turned
stiffly away. He watched her, thinking that he had
never before witnessed such unfairness in her, such

viciousness, then quickly rearranged his memory. Oh, yes, he had seen her drawn into jealousy before, and her fury had been uncontrolled. It had been over an arm bracelet another young girl had refused to give her. She was jealous of Zarabeth, and, fool that he was, he had taken all Zarabeth's weapons. He had made her a slave. He had placed her at Ingunn's mercy.

His sister returned with the bowl and handed it to him, saying nothing now.

He said very quietly, his eyes never leaving her face, "If you touch her again, I will take the whip to you and let you taste it on your back. If you ever put your hands on Lotti again, I will take the whip to you with even greater force. Do you understand me?"

"By Thor's hammer, she lied! I did nothing to her that she did not deserve. Just ask Cyra! She saw everything the slut did, ask her!"

"Do you understand me?"

"Why do you care? Did you not bed her? How many men had her before you? She bragged on how many men she'd had in York and how all she had to do to you was smile. Why do you still care?"

"Do you understand me?"

She realized in that moment that she no longer knew this man who stood in front of her, this man who didn't care about the truth or about her feelings, this man who was obviously against her now, who hated and scorned her, all because of that slave he'd brought to Malek to take her place. Nay, she no longer recognized this man who had been her defender when she'd been a little girl. He was now a stranger to her. She felt fury and defeat, and it took all her resolve to hold to her control. She said, "Aye, I understand."

"Good. Never forget, Ingunn, for I shan't." He left her then, aware that every man and woman in the hall was watching them and wondering. He had no intention of saying anything at all. He was appalled at his sister's loss of control, at the ferocity in her.

He fed Zarabeth until she was too weak to chew more. When she finally fell asleep, he picked Lotti up and took her into the children's chamber. He laid her down, smoothing the soft ginger-colored hair from her forehead.

"Sleep well," he said, and leaned down to kiss her cheek. "I will take care of your sister, I promise you."

Lotti smiled and closed her eyes. Magnus looked up to see his son sitting up on the far side of the bed. The boy looked infinitely miserable. Magnus walked to him and drew him onto his lap, even though he wasn't a child any longer. He spoke softly, so as not to awaken the other children. "Do not blame Lotti, Egill. She is only a little girl and she loves her sister. Would you not have tried to protect me had someone threatened me? From what I see, she is also fond of you. Do not hurt her, and do not treat her like your aunt Ingunn does."

The boy nodded. Magnus had no idea if his words would go to his son's heart. He hoped so.

When he returned to Zarabeth, she was asleep. He laid a soft white cloth over her back, gently eased her clothing off her, and got into bed next to her. He did not sleep for a very long time.

He fed her the next morning, bathed her back, and told her not to move. Zarabeth said nothing. She was stiff and her back ached, the muscles pulling and twisting, the flesh hot and blistering.

Magnus turned in the doorway, studying her pale face. "Do not worry about Lotti. Eldrid is looking after her."

"Thank you," she said, her voice dull.

She slept fitfully the rest of the morning. She could hear the activity clearly from the outer hall. She could hear Ingunn's voice, and she felt herself tensing with fury. She slept again, then awoke to a voice saying, "I see you are awake."

She felt fear despite herself. "Aye, I am awake, at least now I am."

"Do you intend to remain lying about for the rest of the day?"

Very slowly Zarabeth raised herself on her elbow. "You hurt me, Ingunn. My back pains me."

"Ha, I barely touched you, lying bitch! You carry on to impress Magnus, but he has guessed what you are about. Even though he has rutted you, he isn't stupid. His senses are returned now. You betrayed him before, lied to him, and now he knows what you really are. He has left, but were he still here, he would not protect you."

Zarabeth felt the blood pounding through her as her anger built, anger and fear that Ingunn had spoken the truth. "I did not betray him!"

"Keep to your lies, I care not. But you will cease your laziness and rise. There is much to be done and I cannot do it all. You take, yet return nothing. That is not the way of the Vikings, and you are but a worthless slave."

Zarabeth forced herself to sit up. She realized she was naked and pulled the woolen blanket to her chin.

Ingunn looked at her long and hard, the ungoverned hatred she felt toward this woman growing so that now it nearly choked her.

"Know the truth, slut. Magnus does not know what to do with you. He doesn't want you now, for he has had you and known not the pleasure he receives from Cyra, but you pretend to such pain that he cannot turn you out now. He wants to sell you, he told me but hours ago, but you are here crying and whining, so what can he do? I could tell him that all this is naught but an act, a sham, but I do not want to hurt him. You did quite enough of that, did you not? So now he has a worthless hag sleeping in his bed and gets nothing from her save what her skinny body offers to him. Just look at you—you are a witch, a bedraggled slut!"

The words pounded through her and Zarabeth wanted to shake her head to clear them away, she wanted to scream at Ingunn that it wasn't true, that she was lying, that Magnus didn't want to sell her, that . . .

"I will rise in a few minutes. Please leave, Ingunn, I must dress."

"And you wish to work now? Magnus will not allow me to whip you until you are well again. But he has left because he no longer wishes to see you. It pains him still, your betrayal of him. Do you tell me that you are willing to do what I bid you to do, without whining to Magnus?"

"Aye, I am willing." Aye, she thought then, she was also a fool, for she had let Ingunn weave her into a web of her own spinning with great ease. Her back throbbed and her head ached, but she refused to be a useless weight. She could not, she would not. Slowly she rose. At least her belly was full. Slowly she managed to pull open the lid of Magnus' chest. Her gowns lay there, where he had told her to put them. Slowly she pulled an old gown over her head, one that was frayed and too short for her now. Slowly she forced herself to walk into the hall.

Magnus steered his single-man boat cross-current to the northeastern side of the viksfjord. The water was calm, the air cool, the sun bright overhead, but he didn't particularly notice the beauty of the day. He was worried and he was angry, for once again he felt out of control of himself, a condition he should be getting used to, a condition that had begun when he had returned for Zarabeth.

When he reached his parents' farmstead, he waved to the guards, keeping his distance until he was recognized. This farmstead was twice the size of Malek, for there were at least one hundred people living and working here. The wheat and rye fields were bounded by high rock borders.

The farmstead village wasn't encircled with a wooden palisade, but rather came to the shoreline itself. There was a wall only at the rear of the farmstead, nearly against the line of pine trees so thick that it would take a very stealthy enemy to gain any surprise advantage.

He strode inside the huge longhouse and felt familiar memories flood him. He smelled the same smells as had the young boy, saw his mother's loom in its place where it had been as far back as he could remember. There was his mother, Helgi, in the middle of a score of chattering women and children, and she was smiling at him, coming quickly toward him, soon hugging him until his ribs ached, for she was strong as a man.

She was still smiling until she looked up at his beloved face. She touched her fingers to his cheek. "What is wrong, Magnus? Ah, no, you needn't answer that. It is the woman, isn't it? What has happened?"

Magnus laughed, a raw, ugly sound. "Is my face so open for all to see, then?"

"Only to a mother's sharp eye. Come and sit down." She called for mead, then followed her son to one of the long wooden benches.

He noticed a faint line of perspiration on her broad forehead. The hall was hot, overly so, and he frowned. "Come outside, Mother. You grow overheated in here."

Helgi smiled and nodded.

Outside, he took her arm and led her toward the shore. "Father is hunting?"

"Aye, the men must hunt enough for the winter. How go your stores?"

"I hunted with my men all day yesterday."

"I see."

He drew a deep breath. "Ingunn must be wedded. She cannot remain at Malek."

Helgi remained silent in her surprise.

He looked at his mother, and felt her love flow through him. Unquestioned love, he thought. There was nothing he could do, nothing he could ever say, that would change that. He gave it up without a whimper and told her what had happened.

". . . Zarabeth is now lying on my bed, on her belly, her back raw from Ingunn's whip. My house is a battlefield. Ingunn must go. She has changed, somehow. But perhaps you have already seen some of it. She loses control; she speaks rashly, without restraint. You must bring her here until Father finds a husband for her, since he has dismissed Orm's claim."

Helgi looked clearly at her son and nodded slowly. "Aye, I have seen it, but she is your sister. Why have Ingunn leave Malek? She is your sister, after all, and has seen to your household for five years now. Why not bring Zarabeth here? She will be a slave here for me. I will even buy her from you so that she would never be your responsibility again. That would bring you peace again, would it not?"

He stiffened and Helgi smiled into the distance, knowing this would be his reaction. "Very well, Magnus, you want the woman with you. You love her. Despite all she has done, you love her."

He said slowly, his brow furrowed, "I truly do not know if she poisoned her husband, Olav. I would have sworn that she could not have done it. There is a gentleness about her, you see, a caring that would make such a deed alien to her nature." He shrugged.

"But Olav's son and his wife . . . they swore and swore, and there were others as well."

"Possibly paid by the son. Did he not gain all the dead father's wealth once Zarabeth was removed?"

"Aye, 'tis true. The son, Keith, is weak, and his wife is a bitch. But I do not care now, not really. Even that man in Hedeby, the one she tried to entice into helping her escape, he—"

"What?"

He repeated himself. His mother looked thoughtful.

"I cannot imagine wanting to escape a known entity with one that is entirely unknown. You said the man was a coward and ran when he realized you were her master?"

He nodded.

"Then why would she want to entice him? Zarabeth is a fool? She did not realize he was a coward?"

"She is not a fool."

"Good. It seems to me, Magnus, that the man blamed her so you wouldn't kill him." Helgi smiled up at her son. "You will keep the woman with you. I will speak to your father this very evening about Ingunn. 'Tis a pity about Orm, but your father reviles him now and holds him in distrust. He would never consent to his having Ingunn."

"I had heard that he was set upon by outlaws."

"Nay, 'twas he who killed another man, a freeman, a man of worth. He wanted the man's silver and he took it. There is no doubt. If Orm's family were not so powerful, there would be retribution, but alas, there will not be any."

"Why not? Cannot the man's family bring it to light at the next meeting of the *thing*? Were there sufficient proof, the least the family could have would be dane-geld for a man's life." He laughed then, a bitter laugh. "I paid much for Olav's life, I can tell you. 'Twas nearly as much as I was prepared to pay for Zara-beth's brideprice."

He heard his mother draw in her breath and cursed his loose tongue, but it had always been so with his mother. He spoke freely with her and the habit was too strong to break just because he was beset.

"You knew I had planned to marry her, for Horkel told you, curse his eyes. But she refused me. I returned to take her and found that she was about to be killed for murdering Olav, her old husband."

"I wish to speak with the woman. May I, Magnus?"

He gave her a look that was so wary that she hugged him to her again. "You really cannot continue like this, you know. Ingunn is jealous of her and will con-tinue to be. Mayhap she would truly harm her. I would not trust her."

"She is a slave! There is no reason for Ingunn to hate her."

Helgi, ignoring his words, repeated what she had said: "Mayhap Ingunn would truly harm her. I would not trust her."

"I threatened Ingunn if she dared touch Zarabeth or Lotti again."

Helgi smiled at his simplicity. "Your life will con-tinue in unpleasantness until you have resolved every-thing. Ingunn will not ease her hatred of the woman. I will speak to you again after your father has come to a decision. Take care, Magnus, and strive to be fair."

He nodded and took his leave. An hour later he had returned to his own farmstead. He entered the longhouse and immediately made his way back to his chamber.

The small room was empty. He felt his belly twist, turned around, and bellowed, "Ingunn! Where is she?"

His sister was smiling and it was a smile that chilled

him to his bones. By Thor, he should have taken her with him back to his mother. "Where is she, Ingunn?"

She shrugged. "Why, she insisted on performing the tasks of a slave. I did not touch her. I did not force her or threaten her, ask anyone."

"Where is she?"

Again Ingunn shrugged. "She is with four other slaves at the marsh, digging up bog ore. You know how much we use, burning it with the charcoal in the ovens. Rollo whined for more, since he is making more farm implements for you. You know how hot his ovens must be to melt the iron."

He could only stare at her. Digging up chunks of bog ore! By Odin, it was a terrible job, dirty, back-breaking work that required great strength and endurance, and she, a woman, was doing it? His mother was right. Ingunn would never ease in her jealous hatred.

He turned and left the longhouse without another word. He strode from the palisade toward the clump of pine trees that bordered the marsh that lay a good hundred yards to the east of the farmstead.

Zarabeth wanted to die. She didn't want to cry or make a single sound. She just wanted to fall down and die. Her back burned so badly that she was beyond tears, beyond anything she had ever known. Her muscles were knotted and cramped. It didn't ease; it simply got worse and worse. Yet she dug with the hoe in the filthy black swamp until the blade hit the hard clumps, then she bent down to dig with her hands when she had uncovered the isolated lumps of bog ore. It had taken her several hours to be taught how to find the ore, and now that she knew, she had found a rhythm. But it was hard to keep going. So very hard. She had been a fool to let Ingunn taunt her into this. She had been a fool to allow herself to flaunt her pride. Pride! She had nothing but pain, and an iron collar about her neck that told all she was nothing to anyone. *Pride!*

A fool, naught but a fool, yet she kept digging, bending over and uncovering the bog ore from the slime, then pulling it loose, and finally lifting it out. She paused a moment, her breath hitching in pain that nearly bowed her to her knees, and in that instant she knew he was there, watching her.

She was filthy, her gown rent and wet and smelling of the bog ore and the filthy marsh water. Her bare feet and legs were black with filth.

Her hair had come loose from its braid. She breathed heavily and stood very still. She would not perform for him whilst he watched. She simply wouldn't do it. Was he here to taunt her? To order her to go faster? Was he here to tell her he would sell her? That he found her less than useless? He had taken her three times and hadn't found anything in her to his liking. Why should he keep her?

Magnus nodded to the other serfs, men all of them, bowed but stronger than most from years of back-breaking work. He reached her and raised her dirty face in the palms of his cupped hands. He looked down at her for a long moment.

Finally he said, "Drop the hoe."

She let it slip from her raw hands.

"Are you really so stupid as to be here?"

She stared up at him, mute.

He frowned. "Do you not understand me?"

"You want me to be here. You want to sell me because there is nothing more you want from me."

"We will speak of your strange fancies later. Come, now you will bathe and then I will tie you to my bed. You will remain there until I say that you may arise."

"I cannot," she said slowly, pulling away from him. She tried to straighten, but the pain ground through her back and she remained before him like a bent old woman. "I am naught but a slave, your slave. You cannot allow me to be shiftless and lazy."

"You're quite wrong. I can do anything I please with you. I suggest that you believe me and no other." He lifted her in his arms, felt her shudder from the pain in her back, but since there was nothing he could do about it, he merely tried to shift her so that she was cupped against his chest, his arm around her waist. "Hold on to me."

Ingunn said not a word when Magnus came into the longhouse calling for clean cloths. She said not a word when he later carried in Zarabeth, clean from the bathhouse and wrapped in those cloths, and disappeared with her into his chamber. She felt rage and impotence and knew that there was nothing she could do to stop this except to kill the woman.

She gave Cyra an assessing look and knew that she too would willingly stick a knife in the woman's ribs. What to do?

Then she knew. She trembled with her decision, yet knew that she would do it. She would not remain here. She would not remain to see this woman take her place. She smiled.

17

"Hold still. Do not flinch from me."
But it was difficult not to draw away, not to try to pull inside herself to avoid his hands on her. He was gentle, she knew, but it didn't matter. The pain was great and she felt weaker in spirit than she could ever remember.

Magnus rubbed in the cream his mother had sent, turning her back a sickly white. He had bathed her himself, from her filthy matted hair to her blackened feet.

She had suffered it without complaint. He gently combed her hair, pulling it away from her head and fanning it out to dry more quickly. He rose and looked down at her. He had pulled the blanket over her hips. He said to the back of her head, "Your pride is ridiculous, Zarabeth, if it leads you to commit such stupidity. I grow weary of rescuing you from the consequences of your arrogance."

"Then don't," she said.

He grinned down at her. Her voice was nasty and angry. It pleased him greatly. "But who else would rescue you?"

She ignored that, coming up on her elbows, twisting to see him. Color came into her cheeks, and his smile widened as she said, "I am not arrogant. 'Tis you who flaunt yourself before me and all your people, shouting at them that you are the master and will allow no other to gainsay you!"

"I do not have to flaunt. All know I am the master, and soon you will accept it as well."

She tried to strike him, but he merely grasped her wrists in one of his hands and pressed her back onto her stomach. "Don't be a fool. Lie still. If you will, you may continue your screaming, but content yourself for the time being with your words."

"I hate you."

"Nay, you don't hate me. When your back has healed, I will take you down under me and come inside you again. You liked that, Zarabeth, the way I moved over you, the way I touched you and filled you."

"Be quiet, Magnus!"

He gently caressed her cheek with his fingertip. "I have never before wanted a woman as much as I have wanted you. And I still want you, all the time I want you. Do you believe I shall ever tire of you?"

She pressed her face into the pillow. "You do not want me, you keep me in your bed only because you don't wish it known that you are cruel."

"By Thor's hammer, that is great nonsense that comes from your mouth. I want you in my bed now so that you will heal."

"I don't believe you."

He shook his head, knowing Ingunn had somehow convinced her that he no longer wanted her. He said only, "Nay, sweeting, all will be well soon. Believe me."

She turned to look at him again. Her face looked quiet and still as a statue's. "You will sell me, then?"

"Why do you believe I would sell you?"

"You won't sell me and keep Lotti here, will you? You wouldn't, would you, Magnus, no matter how much you hated me?"

He rose then, saying nothing more now, for she had managed, finally, to anger him. How could she believe he would do such a thing? He stood over her, his legs slightly spread, his arms at his sides, his hands fisted. "Who would buy you? Look at you—naught but a whining female who grows thin and loses her charms before she has even learned to use them on a man. The only reason a man would buy you would be the promise of what you would bring to his bed. You have willingness, Zarabeth, but little else as yet. Nay, I must keep you until you become skilled with your mouth and your hands, until you have learned to hold me inside you and drive me to madness with soft words and gentle caressing."

"I have no willingness, 'tis just that my body has no way to judge what you are! Nor will I become skilled, Magnus, I won't let you do that to me again."

"We will see. Hush now with your angry words. You must needs rest."

There was nothing more to say. She felt drained, empty of spirit and fight. She closed her eyes, pressing her face again into the pillow.

"My mother sent the cream for your back. It is of her own making. She used it on me and my brothers as far back as I can remember. It soothes and warms and leaches away the pain."

"How did your mother know her cream was needed?"

He was stymied, but only for a moment. "Why, we had no more, and it was just luck that brought one of her house slaves with another supply. Though, of course, I did hesitate to waste it on a slave."

"Wipe it off, then, I care not. I never asked for it or for anything else."

"No, you didn't, did you?" He leaned down suddenly and pulled the cover from her hips to her ankles. She cried out and tried to rear up. He held her down with his hand flat on her waist. "I want to look at you. I cannot take you now, 'twould be cruel and I would not much enjoy it for you would moan and groan and complain I was killing you."

Magnus knew he had to stop this. She had wounded his pride, but he was hurting her, and she had no recourse. He was become as vicious as Ingunn. He looked at her white buttocks, smooth and round, and he could feel them in his hands, and those long legs of hers, nicely shaped and sleek with muscle, and he could see her on her back, and he was deep inside her and her legs were wrapped around his flanks, drawing him deeper, and he was moaning and he never wanted to leave her, never, never . . .

He drew the blanket to her waist again. His hands were shaking. "I want you to rest now, Zarabeth. You will remain here until I tell you to rise. I will have one of the girls bring you food, and then you will sleep."

"I am not hungry."

He paused at the doorway. "As I said, you grow thin, and a man doesn't want to grind himself against a woman's bones. You will eat or I will force food down your skinny throat."

When Anna, the eleven-year-old niece of Rollo, the blacksmith, brought food to her, she found Zarabeth deeply asleep. She returned to Magnus.

"I did not wake her, Magnus."

"It is all right, Anna. Take the tray to Lotti and make certain she eats enough. If you wish to speak to her, you must remember to—"

"I know. I must look directly at her so she can see me speaking."

Magnus grinned and ruffled the girl's nearly white-blond hair. "You have a wise tongue, Anna."

The evening passed slowly. As much as he fought it, Magnus went several times to his chamber to see that Zarabeth was all right. She was sleeping soundly each time, but still he worried. Everyone noted his trips to and fro. He returned to hear the men discussing the killings on the Ingolfsson farmstead, a small property some two days to the south by boat. The Ingolfsson daughters had been raped, the younger boys killed outright. Haftor Ingolfsson had been gone hunting for winter stores with most of his men. He had returned to find carnage, his animals slaughtered, his slaves captured. There was outrage at what the outlaws had done, and word of the disaster had passed quickly. It was too bold, too daring. It was unexpected and frightening; no man liked the sound of it. No Viking would stand for it.

There would be a special meeting of the *thing* held in three days in Kaupang to determine the men responsible by the proof presented, and what was to be done.

Later in the evening, Magnus was sitting in his master's chair with its beautifully carved seat posts, thinking about what a mess his life had become, when he suddenly heard a child bellow, "Papa! Papa!"

He looked up to see Lotti running toward him, her thin arms outstretched, fear on her face, and again she shouted, clear as could be, "Papa! Papa!"

He caught her as she dived for him and pulled her close against his chest, pressing her head against his shoulder. She was sobbing, her body heaving and shuddering against him.

He spoke to her softly, his hand stroking up and down her back, then shook his head at himself. She couldn't hear anything he was saying. Slowly he pulled her away from his shoulder and sat her on his thighs. He pushed the tangled hair from her face. "What is wrong, Lotti?"

She was still weeping, but now her sobs were hiccups.

"Did you have a nightmare?"

She stared up at him, her eyes wide.

"Did you dream about monsters and evil beings?"

She nodded slowly, then said loudly, "Papa," and clutched him about the throat.

"A filthy little idiot—and you let her call you that! 'Tis disgusting!"

Magnus paid no heed to Ingunn.

Horkel said, "She spoke clearly, Magnus. She is learning very quickly here."

"I expect it is a word she spoke before she became without hearing. Zarabeth told me that Olav struck her head when she was two years old. She was not born without hearing."

He rocked the little girl in his arms, wishing fiercely in that moment that she had been born of his seed. She stiffened in his hold and he allowed her to lean back in the safe circle of his arms. "Zarabeth," Lotti said, and she was frowning, and there was that damned fear in her eyes again. He wished he could wipe it out for all time.

"Zarabeth will be fine. She's sleeping now, just as you should be, little sweeting."

Lotti raised her hand and lightly ran her fingertips over his lips. It tickled, and he grinned at her, trying to bite her fingers. She laughed, that harsh, mewling sound. It delighted him, that laugh of hers, and made him feel fiercely protective.

He hugged her to him again. She settled herself against his chest and was soon asleep.

Horkel looked at his friend for a long moment, then shook his head. " 'Tis no good," he said, and there was great sadness in his eyes and in his voice. " 'Tis no good at all."

Magnus knew what he meant, but he refused to accept it.

*   *   *

Zarabeth was sitting up on Magnus' box bed the next morning. He had gone before she awakened, but now she was hungry and needed to relieve herself. But she hesitated to go into the main hall. Ingunn would be there, and Cyra and all the others who had heard and seen and held her as naught but a murderess and a liar and a slave.

"Coward," she said to herself, and rose. She was stiff and it hurt to straighten her back. Ingunn was there, naturally, overseeing all the household chores as she sewed.

Lotti was with Eldrid, and the woman was showing her how to sew. Zarabeth had to lean down and hug her before the child noticed her. Lotti gave her a big grin and pointed to the stitches she had just made in a small gown.

" 'Tis lovely," Zarabeth said, and kissed her. But Lotti wasn't to be distracted, and turned back to Eldrid.

Ingunn said in a very neutral voice, "Aunt Eldrid is looking after her. It is Magnus' order. He is not here, but out hunting with the men. He said you were not to do anything."

Zarabeth wasn't aware that there was strain in her voice, but all the women and children in the longhouse who were listening heard it and felt the pain of it. "I would like to bathe."

Ingunn snorted. "I had heard stories that the people of the Danelaw were animals and smelled like the pigs they tended. Why wish you to bathe as often as a Viking?"

"I did not tend pigs. Perhaps that is why."

"Ah, is it because Magnus demands it? 'Tis true he likes his women to be sweet-smelling. You still think to hold him, don't you? Have you *looked* at Cyra, you stupid woman?"

"Aye."

"You are nothing compared to her! You are but a new diversion to him, nothing more, just a fresh woman's body to use and then discard. It is your coloring that fascinates him, but that is already passing. He already sees your hair as coarse and common. He will have Cyra again, you will see." Then, to Zarabeth's surprise, Ingunn turned a vicious eye to Lotti. What was happening here? She moved unconsciously nearer her sister.

It was Eldrid who spoke, her voice loud and clear and seemingly guileless. "Magnus loves the little girl. He gave her into my charge. Nothing will happen to her, I have vowed it to him."

"Ha! He merely feels pity for her, as he would for a wounded animal. See you to the little idiot, then. I care not!"

Zarabeth wanted to yell at Ingunn that her bile was foolishly wasted on Lotti. The child couldn't hear her, and thus the vicious words could not wound her. But they hurt Zarabeth deeply. She forced herself to turn away. She went to the bathhouse.

"Remove the gown. I wish to examine your back."

"Leave my gown alone. My back is fine. I have no need for you to strip me again."

He smiled at the fierceness in her voice. The pain had lessened and she was feeling stronger. She was hardy, Zarabeth was, and he suspected she could hold her own easily with Ingunn, if she weren't a slave. But she was; he had made her one.

He said with great patience, "Be quiet and remove the gown. I will rip it off you if you don't obey me, Zarabeth."

She didn't want to. It was daylight. The chamber was dim, as usual, but she knew he would look at her, and she couldn't bear it, she simply couldn't. He was a man and he had taken her, and, truth be told, he had given her a pleasure she had never expected could exist, but he didn't love her, he scorned her, and this assumption of his that she would do whatever it was he wanted was beyond what she could endure.

She turned and ran from the chamber. Her back was stiff and sore, but she had no more of his mother's healing cream, no more need for him to bathe her back.

"Zarabeth! Come back here!"

But she didn't. She turned to see him, only to run into the solid wall of Horkel's massive chest. His hands grasped her upper arms.

" 'Tis enough," he said, and merely held her as she struggled against his grip.

Magnus looked over her head and met his friend's eyes. "She might have run all the way to Kaupang. She has little sense and more pride than my father. However, hers isn't tempered with wisdom." He held out his hands, and Horkel turned her about and shoved her toward Magnus.

She kept her head down even as she stumbled against him.

Magnus sighed and dragged her back to his chamber. He didn't care that all his people were looking avidly, wondering what was between him and this slave. He didn't care what anyone thought.

He flung her onto the box bed. He sat down beside her, and calmly began unlacing the front of her gown. "I am glad you don't wear the overdress our Viking women wear. The shoulder brooches must be unfastened and the entire thing lifted over the woman's head. This is easier, faster. Ah, yes, your breasts. They please me, Zarabeth. Their size fits my hands."

She turned her face away from him, her eyes closed. She hadn't the strength to fight him. She would endure. The pleasure he had made her feel before was forgotten. Perhaps it hadn't even existed. Then suddenly he leaned down and gently began to suckle her nipple. Her eyes flew open and she cried out in embarrassment. She couldn't allow him to continue doing this to her, she couldn't. She tried to rear up, but he pressed his hand against her shoulder and pushed her back down.

"Hush," he said, his breath hot on her flesh. "Lie still and let me give you pleasure."

She shoved at his shoulders, at his head, her body twisting madly. "Nay, Magnus, please, don't shame me like this. All know that you have brought me here to your chamber, to your bed. Please do not shame me!"

He ignored her and suckled her other breast. He loved the taste of her flesh, her scent. He knew the moment she responded to him. There was an immediate softening of her body, a gentle lurching as she arched her back very slightly, but arch it she did, to press her breast closer and closer.

She moaned softly and he knew she hated the sound of that moan, for it had come from the very depths of her, from someplace inside her that should have stayed hidden and alone and untouched. But he was kneading her belly now with his hand, even as he was tugging and caressing her breast with his mouth. Then his fingers moved lower and she was suddenly holding her breath, expectant, flushed because of the throbbing there, nearly frantic at the ache that was centered there, and it was becoming more intense, more powerful, even as his fingers neared and came nearer still. When his fingertips touched her flesh, she cried out, shuddering with the force of it. He raised his head then and looked down into her face.

"I will bring you pleasure. Should you like that, Zarabeth?" He didn't expect her to reply. He smiled painfully as he watched his fingers touch her soft flesh again and find a rhythm to please her, and he knew quickly enough that soon she would be helpless against the onslaught of wild feelings that were coursing through her. He realized that Zarabeth didn't want to lie there passive beneath his searching fingers, she didn't want him to so completely control her, and so he encouraged her softly as she pressed upward, her hips lifting off the bed, and she felt his other hand beneath her buttocks, helping her, pressing her even harder against his fingers. "I will watch your face when your pleasure overcomes you," he said, and she would have given anything to keep that pleasure at bay, to fight him now, to swear that there was no such pleasure that she wanted, but she was helpless against it and she knew it, and finally she accepted it, she wanted it, she would die if it didn't come to her.

"Magnus," she whispered, pain and excitement blending in her voice. He shook with the force his name on her lips brought him. By Odin, he wanted her, wanted all of her. He didn't want her to fight him with her spirit, he wanted all that she was and would become in the years ahead.

He felt the tensing in her legs and the shudders that convulsed her entire body. He watched as her eyes widened and glazed with the strength of the passion that was building inside her. He watched as she could no longer hold that pleasure back. He watched her mouth when the cries, raw and deep, erupted from her throat, and he pushed her then, and pushed himself to give her all that he could, to make her realize that she belonged to him and to no other, to make her realize that she was no longer alone, locked inside herself, for he wouldn't allow it, and she belonged to him.

When it was over, when he was gently kneading her woman's flesh to soothe her rather than excite her, he said, "I want to look at you now, sweeting. I want to see if you can take me comfortably." She had no chance to protest, and no great hope of trying to

before he pressed her thighs open wide and parted
her with his fingers. She was still sore and he saw the
redness of her flesh and knew he shouldn't take her
again, not now. She needed another day, and then he
would have her, and she would enjoy his entry, she
would cry out with her acceptance of him.

He smiled a bit painfully. But it didn't matter. He
had given her pleasure, he had drawn her more inexorably to him, bound her to him, and now she would
not be able to so easily deny it.

He leaned down and lightly kissed the soft woman's
flesh. She quivered. "Nay, Zarabeth, I won't take you
now. You must needs have another day to accommodate yourself to me, for I was over enthusiastic my
first three times with you. But you will not forget the
pleasure I gave you. And when I take you tomorrow,
I will give you that same pleasure and you won't wish
to fight me ever again, Zarabeth. Do you understand?"

He saw that her eyes were closed. He saw the tears
trickling down her cheeks. He merely leaned down
and lightly kissed her mouth, tasting the salt of her
tears. "Are those tears of surrender to me, I wonder.
I will look later at your back." He covered her with
a blanket and left her.

But he didn't take her the following day, because
her woman's monthly flow had begun. He knew
because he had seen blood on the blanket. He said
nothing about it, not wanting to shame her, and he
guessed it would, for she was a private woman, unused
to sharing with another, particularly with him, a man.

He knew, of course, that she needed cloths, and he
saw to it that she had them. But he said nothing. Nor
did he touch her in any way. But he watched her to
see if she had any pain. If she did have cramping in
her belly, she gave no sign of it. If she wondered why

he didn't come near her or drag her to his bed, she gave no hint of it.

He sighed even as he left the longhouse for a long day of hunting. He had yet to hear from his father. Ingunn was more restrained now, at least in his presence. He had decided, though, that he could not trust her, thus he left one of his men there to simply watch over Zarabeth. She worked, but Ingunn did not try to force her to perform men's tasks, nor did she try to abuse her. As for Cyra, he had decided to give her to Horkel, for his friend fancied her.

Horkel had already had her as well. He had confessed it to Magnus, and to his immense relief, Magnus hadn't killed him.

Magnus had slapped him on the shoulder.

Soon Ingunn would wed, and Zarabeth would . . . His thinking came hard against a wall of his own building. Zarabeth was his slave. He'd sworn he wouldn't make her his wife, not after what she had done to him, to Olav.

He saw a buck in the distance, a shadowy form in the trees, frozen still as a stone, and slowly drew back his bow.

The late-afternoon sun was bright. Zarabeth had finished milking the two cows in the byre near the large storage hut. She held the wooden bar over her shoulders, the two filled pails hanging by chains down some three feet to maintain good balance. They didn't hurt her back overly, but she could not take more than small steps.

She looked up at the bright sun and beyond to the other side of the viksfjord at the high pine-covered mountains. It was beautiful, this country, beautiful beyond imagination. And so very warm, the air sweet with the fresh milk she carried. She didn't wish to return immediately to the longhouse, but she knew there was no choice. It wasn't wise to leave the milk out in the hot sun. It wasn't wise to inflame Ingunn.

She sighed and turned toward the longhouse. Then she heard a cry. Startled, she whirled about, for the sound was rough and garbled. It was Lotti. She didn't remove the wooden bar from her shoulders, merely speeded up. She came to the pile of logs used for burning in the longhouse and saw Egill holding Lotti down on the ground, jerking at her braids, pounding her head against the ground, all the while yelling at her. Zarabeth called out and began to run. The wooden bar and the full pails of milk splashed, and without hesitation she shrugged the bar off her shoulders, sending the pails splashing to the ground.

"Egill!" she screamed, running all the faster. "Stop it! Get off her!"

Lotti was kicking up at the boy's back and twisting wildly beneath him, but he was by far the larger and stronger and Zarabeth was terrified that he would truly hurt her.

"Egill! Stop it!"

He did not seem to hear her. She threw herself at the boy, locking her arms around his chest and lifting upward with all her strength. She heard Lotti's cries, felt the boy's resistance, and screamed at him yet again. She was cursing him, pulling and jerking at him, but he was holding on to Lotti's braids and wouldn't release them.

Suddenly she felt a man's hands on her, pulling her aside. She released her hold on the boy and fell sideways. She watched Magnus raise Egill's face in his palm and simply look at the boy. In the next moment, Egill was standing over Lotti, looking at his feet.

Zarabeth scrambled over to her little sister. "Are you all right, sweeting? Please, Lotti, please!" She frantically felt Lotti's arms and legs, smoothing her gown, cajoling her to open her eyes.

The little girl's eyes remained closed and there were dirt and tears on her face.

"You spilled all the milk, you worthless slut! You did it on purpose!"

It was Ingunn.

Suddenly it was simply too much. Much too much. Zarabeth lifted her sister to her shoulder, rose clumsily to her feet, turned on her heel, and simply walked away. She heard Magnus calling to her, but she ignored him. She heard Ingunn yelling, but she ignored her as well.

She kept walking, through the palisade gates, down the steep path that led to the viksfjord.

18

"Zarabeth! Stop!"

She heard him cursing behind her. She paid him no heed. He cursed more loudly now, more foully. She dismissed him and his curses and everything that was a part of him, that was a part of this alien land, a part of these alien people. All her attention was on the narrow steep path in front of her, at the end of which was the boat moored at the small dock. She'd never before rowed a boat, but it simply didn't matter; she would do it. She had no doubts about that.

"Zarabeth! Where are you going? Halt, now!"

She was running now, stumbling and careening wildly on the path, for his voice was closer, but she kept her balance, kept Lotti firmly against her body, pressing the child's face against her shoulder. She knew she wouldn't fall. She looked not at the path but beyond, at the boat. She was nearly there, she was nearly free.

"You'll fall! You'll hurt Lotti! Stop!"

Hurt Lotti! His son had tried to kill Lotti! She would hurt her? Her sister—the only person in the world who loved her and accepted her and believed in her? She closed out his words, for they distracted her. They had no meaning now. They were behind her, away from her, not a part of her. All she could see was that boat. All she felt was that burning need to be free.

She heard him close behind her now. She ran faster. She felt stones dig into her feet, but the pain was nothing. She felt a stitch in her side, but it didn't slow her. She smiled grimly and held Lotti tighter.

She looked only at that boat.

She ran onto the narrow dock, jerking the rope from its wooden post without slowing, and jumped into the boat. It rocked wildly, but she paid no heed. The boat would not tip over. She set Lotti down, saying nothing, for there was no time, and quickly eased herself down on the bench, grabbed the long wooden oars, and began to row.

Magnus ran full tilt onto the dock, his mouth filled with curses, his soul filled now with raw fear. Zarabeth was a good ten feet beyond him now. He saw that the sun was full in her face, saw her straining clumsily at the oars, but she was moving swiftly, for the current was fast. Each second took her further away from him.

He felt something inside him burst open, and suddenly he was wild, out of control, beyond himself. He felt like a berserker. He yelled, "No!" He gave a mighty cry and dived into the water. The shock of the cold water froze him for a moment, holding him under, but he merely waited until his body accommodated the chill, then kicked upward. His head cleared and he began to swim after the boat. The current was swirling, dangerous, but he was strong and he was determined, more determined than he had ever been in his life.

The viksfjord didn't flow smoothly east into the Oslo Fjord, but was cut off abruptly by a thick finger of land that jutted out into the water, cutting off the violent current, turning into swirling waters, shallow, dangerously shallow. He could tell that Zarabeth knew little to nothing about rowing a boat. Her movements were erratic at best, sending the boat in circles and sharp angles. It allowed him to draw closer. Her strength would soon be gone and he would then catch her.

He knew Zarabeth saw him. He realized too in that moment that she was somehow apart from what was happening, that she didn't really know what she was doing.

By Thor's hammer, he'd pushed her to this, and something inside her had simply given way. He was terrified. He saw Lotti swivel around on the narrow wooden bench. She saw him and began waving wildly at him, crying out, her sounds hoarse and ugly.

He swam faster, surprising himself with his power. He knew he would catch her when she reached the outjutting land, for she was still close to shore, too close, really, for in this area there were thick beds of water reeds. In that instant a current seized the boat, spinning it completely around, then tilting it wildly toward the land. He heard Lotti cry out and grab the side of the boat. He swam harder, yelling, "Hold on! I'm coming!" He wondered if Zarabeth had heard him, and if she had, if it mattered to her at all. If only there had been another boat, if only his men were here on the shore, if only . . .

Suddenly, without warning, he felt himself sucked down in the bed of water reeds, felt the waving arms tangle about his legs, pulling him inexorably downward. The water was shallow, more shallow than he'd imagined, not more than eight feet deep. He kicked free of them, only to feel himself now swimming into yet another thick bed of reeds, and they were around his legs, closing tightly and pulling him under, and this time he knew it wouldn't be so easy to escape.

He closed his eyes a moment, cursed his father's favorite curses, and pulled the knife from his belt. He drew a deep breath and forced his body to loosen, to let the reeds draw him under. Then he methodically began to slash himself free of them, but as each one fell away, there was another to take its place, and he was entwined as in a lover's arms, and wondered then if he would die.

He cut wildly through a good dozen of the reeds, enough this time to free himself, and pushed to the surface. He sucked in air and looked at the boat, still some fifteen feet ahead of him. To his horror, he saw that Lotti was teetering on the narrow board seat, shouting at him, waving her small arms toward him. He saw that she was afraid.

She was afraid for him.

He knew then, at that instant, what the child intended, and he yelled as loud as he could, "No, Lotti! Stay there! Zarabeth, hold her!"

But it was too late. The child screamed loud and long, "Papa! Papa!" and jumped into the water, flailing her arms toward him.

Magnus was tired, his arms numb and heavy, but the sight of Lotti jumping into the water to save him turned him into a madman. He swam harder than he ever had in his life. Vaguely he heard Zarabeth calling and shouting, saw her trying to maneuver the small boat around, saw her standing now, trying to find Lotti.

The water reeds, Magnus thought as he neared the spot where he remembered the child jumping. He dived under. The water was murky and the thin-armed reeds were thick, their constant motion spewing up sand and mud from the bottom of the viksfjord. He searched and searched until he thought his lungs would burst and his eyes burn closed.

He flew upward, clearing the surface, gulping in air. He was very close to Zarabeth now, the boat within short feet of him, idle now, stuck amongst the reeds.

He said nothing, merely sucked in air until his lungs felt near to bursting, and dived again. Nothing, and still nothing.

Again and again he dived. He couldn't find her. He came to the surface and saw that there were several of his men surrounding him, each of them taking turns at diving. The water had been so murky he hadn't seen them. If he hadn't seen a man, then a child could be so easily lost, so easily overlooked. He didn't know now exactly where she had jumped. It could have been further away or closer.

He found himself praying, offering anything—his very soul to Odin—if only Lotti would magically appear and be all right. If only she would surface and scream "Papa" at him.

He dived again.

He felt his arms being jerked up, and his head cleared the water. He fought until he realized that Horkel was holding one arm, Ragnar the other. He looked at them blankly.

"Hold, Magnus," Horkel said, but Magnus fought him, pulling both him and Ragnar beneath the water.

They released him and Magnus dived another time, and then once more after that, even though he knew there was no hope. The current wasn't strong here, for they were too close to the outjutting land and too close to shore and immersed in the water reeds. Lotti was only five years old. She had either been swept toward the Oslo Fjord around the outjutting land, or she'd been caught and buried in the water reeds.

He came to the surface, and the first person he saw was Zarabeth. She was in the water, one hand on the side of the boat, and she was calling, tears streaming down her face, calling and pleading for Lotti to come back to her.

Magnus couldn't bear it. He lifted his head to the heavens and cried out, a howling animal sound, savage and deep, so filled with anguish that his men froze at the pain of it.

Zarabeth heard that cry, saw the misery on his face,

and knew in that instant that Lotti was gone. Lotti was dead. She began shaking her head, screaming, "No! She isn't dead! She's there, somewhere! No!"

To Magnus' horror, she pushed away from the boat, struggling frantically as she continued to call for her sister. Magnus saw immediately that she couldn't swim. He caught up to her and grasped her arm, pulling her back to the boat. She fought him with amazing strength, until he realized, dimly, that he was exhausted.

Horkel caught her other arm, and together they got her back to the boat. Magnus pulled himself aboard, then took Zarabeth's arms and lifted her upright. But he couldn't bring her on board, she was fighting him too hard.

He leaned down and struck her jaw with his fist. She crumbled and he hauled her over the side.

Horkel said, "The men and I will try for a little while longer, we'll go out into a wider circle, but, Magnus, the current swirls about oddly here, and those damned water reeds can sap the strength of a grown man, and the child is so small—"

"Aye, I know it too well."

He wanted to dive again, but he knew that when Zarabeth regained consciousness she would leap over the side, and he would lose her too.

He fretted, feeling more helpless than he'd ever felt in his life, then hauled Zarabeth into his arms. She was cold, her body limp, her beautiful red hair matted and tangled across her face. He smoothed the hair back and cupped her face between her hands, saying, "They're trying, Zarabeth, they're trying. Ah, by Odin, I'm sorry, so very sorry." He raised his head then at a shout from one of the men. They'd found Lotti!

He felt excitement and hope; then it died. Tostig had brought up a log.

He knew that Lotti was dead. He even accepted it.

Too much time had passed. He knew it, but he found he simply couldn't accept it. The child had died trying to save him. She'd called him Papa and she'd jumped into the water because she thought he was drowning.

He couldn't bear it. He lowered his head against Zarabeth's forehead and cried.

Time lost meaning. He saw the men either swim to shore or climb into the boat. He saw Horkel take the oars. It seemed but a moment later that the boat was once again firmly tied to the Malek dock. Magnus carried Zarabeth up the narrow path that led to the palisade. The men were trailing behind, silent and grim, colder now even with the hot sun beating down on them, for they had lost.

Zarabeth stirred against his shoulder. He hugged her tighter to him, thinking she would struggle when she realized he was holding her. But she didn't struggle. He knew she was awake, but she didn't move.

"I'm sorry I struck you," he said, his eyes on the trail.

Her voice was a thin thread of sound. "Lotti?"

His throat was clogged with tears. He could only shake his head.

She tried to lurch out of his hold. She twisted and fought him until he stopped and set her down, holding her upper arms in his hands. He shook her. "Stop it! We could do no more. Do you understand me, Zarabeth? We could do no more!"

"No! You're lying! Please, Magnus, please! Let me go. I must find her or she'll be hurt, hurt . . ."

She was crying, tears streaming down her face, and she was twisting and flailing at him, until once again he struck her jaw and she fell forward against him.

"You had to do it, Magnus," Horkel said. "Do you want me to carry her now?"

Magnus merely shook his head and lifted her once again in his arms.

"You did all you could. All of us did. Once we realized what had happened, all of us were in the water searching for her. She died quickly, Magnus. With little pain. You must remember that."

He nodded. Tears thickened in his throat, and he kept his eyes on the trail in front of him.

He had never imagined such pain as this. It was inside him, deep and clawing and unremitting, and he knew that nothing could magically halt it. He remembered when he had been but ten years old and his little sister had died. But her death had not brought him anything like this pain.

He heard Horkel say gently beside him, "You knew, deep down you knew, Magnus, that the child couldn't have survived. By Thor, man, she couldn't hear!"

"What, then, Horkel? Better she die now than in two years? Three years?"

"I'm only saying that it was inevitable and no one's fault, not yours, not Zarabeth's. Not Egill's either."

Magnus knew Horkel was right, but it didn't ease a whit of the deadening pain.

There was an eager audience awaiting them inside the palisade, for everyone knew that something of import had happened. Even Ingunn was silent, wondering, waiting, and hopeful that the woman was dead. After all, Magnus was carrying her, and she was limp, her head lolling on his arm, and she was wet, so very wet, and deathly pale.

But the woman wasn't dead, and Ingunn felt impotent rage flow through her. The woman stirred. Ingunn stepped forward, blocking her brother's path, suddenly hopeful that Magnus had finally realized the worthlessness of the woman. She had dumped all the milk, hadn't she? And just for that little witless sister of hers.

"What happened to her? Did you strike her because of her insolence and disobedience?"

Magnus looked through his sister.

"What happened?"

"Be still, woman," Ragnar said. "The little girl drowned trying to save Magnus."

Ingunn's breath hissed through her teeth. One of them was dead, not the one she could have wished had drowned, but still . . . She shrugged. " 'Tis of no matter. The child could not have survived. 'Tis a wonder she lived so long. She could not hear. She—"

Magnus turned then, looking at his sister. Horkel had said nearly the same thing, but, by Thor, not with Ingunn's meanness and pleasure. His sister's words cut deep and raw. "You will be quiet, Ingunn. You will say nothing more, do you understand me?"

"But why do you care so? It was the woman's fault in any case. She was naught but—"

Magnus lost control. He handed Zarabeth to Horkel, stepped up to his sister, and backhanded her hard across the cheek. She screamed in pain and went down onto her side.

Magnus stepped to her and stared down at her. She was holding her cheek, and there was hatred and a goodly measure of fear in her eyes.

He thought again how odd it was that Horkel had said nearly the same words, yet from Ingunn he'd been unable to bear it, for the venom was deep and vicious in her voice. "You will soon be gone from my sight. I will send a message to our father this very day. He will remove you. I don't want to see you again." His words were terrifying because of the calmness with which he spoke. Ingunn didn't move; she was too afraid.

Cyra, no fool, stepped back, saying nothing.

Horkel had already carried Zarabeth into the long-

house. He laid her on Magnus' bed, then stood back
as his friend entered the small chamber.

Magnus merely nodded, and Horkel left them.

Zarabeth came back to awareness slowly, her mind
sluggish and vague. She felt very cold. She opened
her eyes, then lifted herself on her elbows. She saw
Magnus sitting on the bed beside her.

"What happened? Why is my hair wet? Ah, my jaw
hurts. Did you hit me?"

"Yes, I had to. I'm sorry."

She felt the wetness of her hair against her shoulders and back, felt the rough wool blanket against her
bare skin. She was naked save for dry cloths between
her legs. How could that be? Had he replaced the
cloths? She fell back, drawing the blanket to her
throat. Magnus was still sitting there, looking at her,
saying nothing.

She frowned and fought to remember and to grasp
what had happened, and then she knew, all and
everything.

"Where's Lotti?"

His face tightened.

"Where's Lotti?"

"She's dead."

She reared up, dropping the blanket, uncaring, and
grabbed his tunic in her hands. She shook him,
slammed her fists against his chest. "Where is she?"

But she knew; deep down, she knew.

Magnus held her wrists and pressed her back down.
The cover was at her waist, her breasts heaving
deeply. "I'm sorry, Zarabeth," he said, and his voice
was harsh with his tears, but she didn't hear him,
wouldn't accept his pain.

But she knew it was true. She moistened her lips
with her tongue. "She drowned?"

"Aye. The current isn't all that strong in that partic-

ular place, but it's erratic. There are thick water reeds
that can hold a grown man under. We couldn't find
her. She was so very small, you see."

She turned her face away. Magnus felt her stiffen,
even though she didn't seem to move at all. She stiffened and she went away from him and he couldn't
bear it.

"Zarabeth, don't."

She made no response.

Then suddenly she turned her head to face him. She
simply stared at him; then she began laughing. It was
an ugly sound, raw and harsh, and she was gasping
out the words through her laughter. "She tried to save
you! She thought you were drowning! That little girl
thought only to save *you*! By all the gods, 'twas madness! Why didn't you drown? Why? I hate you! You
killed her, you wanted her dead, you—"

Pain ripped through him. He rose unsteadily to his
feet. Her laughing stopped. Her face was pale, her
eyes dark and vague. Then she closed her eyes and
turned her face away from him. Defeated, he pulled
the blanket over her, then turned on his heel and left
the chamber.

Horkel awaited him outside. He waved at the closed
door. "The woman is all right?"

"No."

Magnus started at the sudden burst of loud weeping.
It was piercing and heartbroken. He started forward.
Had Ingunn finally forgotten her hatred of Zarabeth?
To his astonishment, it was his aunt Eldrid, and she'd
covered her face with her hands and was screaming
tears and fury, rocking back and forth on the wooden
bench.

When she saw him, she got control of herself.

He walked to her, lifted her from the bench, and
folded his arms around her scrawny back.

She wept until she had no more tears.

Magnus released her then and eased her into his own chair. "Rest," he said. "I'm sorry, but we did all we could to find her."

He turned then to Ragnar. "Please go to my father and tell him what has happened. Tell him . . ." Magnus paused a moment as if wishing he could leave the words unspoken. "Tell him that he must come for Ingunn, and soon."

Ragnar left. Ingunn resumed her duties, her face hard, her eyes red from weeping, all feeling frozen within her, all feeling save a festering hatred. Magnus saw the imprint of his hand against her cheek but felt no guilt about it. She ignored him completely.

The day dragged into evening. He couldn't seem to rouse himself. All his people were scattered into small groups, speaking quietly. The children were strangely silent. Even the animals kept themselves from underfoot.

Magnus went to his chamber and silently moved to his bed. Zarabeth appeared to be asleep. He sighed deeply, removed his clothes, and eased in beside her. It was then he knew she was awake. He decided to say nothing. She was lying quietly. He knew she couldn't bear for him to come near her again, to force her to recognize that his own grief was bowing him to his knees, for in her mind he should have no grief. Lotti should have been nothing to him. He was, after all, a Viking, a man without conscience, a man who had no compunction about slaughtering, a man who cared naught about any other person but members of his family. She hated him. Lotti would be alive were it not for him.

Were it not for him, Lotti would be with Keith and Toki in York. Were it not for him, King Guthrum would have seen her killed.

She closed her eyes. There was simply too much to cloud her reasoning, too much pain and uncertainty to see through the emptiness and find answers within herself. She wanted to fall asleep and never awaken. Lotti was dead. All her focus seemed stripped away from her. Her reason for existing, for drawing breath, was gone.

No one realized that Egill was missing until very late that night.

It was Horkel who shook Magnus awake, drawing him from a terrifying dream that had no monsters, only a vast emptiness that drained his very soul.

He jerked up, shaking his head.

"Magnus, quickly, Egill is missing!"

Magnus could only stare at him in the dim light. "My son is missing," he repeated as he frowned over the words. He hadn't thought of his son, not once. He felt anew a wash of fear, and was held motionless by it.

It was too much.

"Come, you must hurry. No one has seen the boy since we returned with Zarabeth this afternoon. I fear he feels he is to blame for Lotti's death."

Magnus threw back the covers, his heart pounding so loudly he thought it would burst from his chest. Over and over he was thinking: Not Egill, not my son too, no, it would be too much. Not even the gods could demand that much.

He left Zarabeth, not knowing whether she had heard or not. It wasn't important. He had to find his son.

By dawn every man, woman, child, and slave had searched within miles of Malek. There was no sign of Egill.

The boy had vanished.

When Harald and Helgi arrived with Mattias and Jon and a half-dozen men, Magnus was so weary and so deadened he could barely speak. His father drew near, stared at his son, and without a word drew him against his chest.

Magnus had forgotten that he had sent Ragnar to
them. He leaned against his father, and it came to
him suddenly that he was the larger of the two, that
somehow his father had shrunk physically. Strange
that it was so and that he would notice it now. Harald
was his father and Magnus felt his strength flow into
him. He didn't weep. He was beyond tears now,
nearly beyond feeling.

He stood back then and said calmly, "I do not know
what to do now, Father. I am glad you are here.
Mother, please come inside. Ingunn will—" He broke
off and his face hardened, his hands fisted at his sides.

"You have come to remove her, I trust?"

Helgi stepped forward and lightly laid her hand on
his bare forearm. "We will take her back with us, but
now, Magnus, now let us go inside."

Mattias simply hugged his brother briefly, releasing
him with no words spoken. Jon merely looked at Magnus, his brow furrowed, then shook his head.

Magnus agreed. It was too much, far too much.

His family's presence was a blessing. It gave him
and all his people something new to focus on. He saw
Ingunn run into Helgi's arms and begin sobbing as if
her heart would break. He turned away from the
scene, saying to his father, "Wish you some ale?"

"Aye, I would like that."

Helgi listened to Ingunn and her endless stream of
complaints without comment until she knew she could
not allow it to continue. She set her away and said
sharply, "Hush now, daughter, I grow weary of your
grievances, for they show me the depths of your selfishness. You have grown mean, Ingunn, and are filled
only with your own importance. Get you to work now,
for your brothers are hungry. I will speak to you of
your future later."

It was Helgi who took a tray of porridge and fresh
warm bread to Zarabeth. She was surprised to see the

young woman clothed, sitting on the edge of Magnus'
bed. She was, however, just sitting there, staring
straight ahead, making no movement, making no sound.

"Zarabeth, heed me. Do you remember me? I am
Helgi, Magnus' mother."

Zarabeth looked at her without interest. "Is it true
that Egill is missing?"

"Aye, 'tis true."

"Both of them. Egill and Lotti, both of them gone.
It is too much, Helgi."

But there was no expression on Zarabeth's face.
Her words could have concerned the porridge that
steamed from the wooden bowl.

"Come and eat, Zarabeth. I brought you a tray only
because I believed you would still be abed. But you
are dressed. Come, now."

Zarabeth simply looked at her. "Must I?"

"Aye."

Zarabeth shrugged and rose. Her red hair was thick
and wild down her back, dry now, cascading over her
shoulder to cover her breast. She looked like a pagan,
Helgi thought, her coloring richer than the most vivid
threads on a tapestry. But her green eyes, a green rich
and deep, were dull and vague.

Zarabeth followed Helgi from the chamber and into
the main hall. When she saw Magnus seated beside
his father, she stopped abruptly.

"I cannot," she said. "I cannot."

Magnus sensed her, nay, *felt* her before he saw her.
It was odd, this effect she'd had on him since the first
moment he ever saw her. By Thor, it seemed decades
upon decades ago, yet it was just moments, just a few
weeks of time in the past. He stared at her and silently
willed her to look at him. She did.

Then slowly she raised her hand to her throat. He
watched as she fingered the iron collar around her
neck, the slave collar he'd had the blacksmith fasten

on her. Then, just as suddenly, she went wild. She began pulling at the collar, jerking at it as if it were choking her, as if she were strangling. She tugged and yanked, saying nothing, making no sound at all. She was like a madwoman. All eyes were turning toward her, talk ceasing. Magnus rose quickly and strode to her.

He grabbed her wrists, pulling her arms down, holding her. He saw how she'd torn the flesh of her throat with her own fingernails, and he saw the scratches that now trickled blood, and he yelled, "Stop it!"

She looked straight ahead, at his throat, strong and brown and unfettered, and said, "I would kill you if I could."

He felt anger then, cleansing anger, and shook her until her head jerked back on her neck. "The same way I saw to it that your life was saved? The same way I brought both you and Lotti out of York? You are not being fair, Zarabeth."

"I care not. There is nothing now."

Magnus closed his eyes and loosened his hold on her. She jerked free and made a soft keening sound, her fingers pulling and jerking again at the collar. He grabbed her arms once again and drew her very close. He stared down at her pale face, into the depths of her vague, wild eyes. Then he said, "Enough! Come with me. Now."

He dragged her from the longhouse.

His father raised a thick blond brow at his wife. She merely shook her head, turning when Ingunn said, "He'll kill her now. Finally he realizes that she has ruined everything. She killed Egill, she—"

Harald roared, "Shut your mouth, Ingunn!"

Eldrid began to weep again, soft dragging sobs.

Helgi, for the first time in seven years, walked to her sister and put her arms around her.

19

Zarabeth was beyond thought. She struck his arms, his chest, fought him with all her strength, dug her bare heels into the packed earth, but it did no good. It didn't even slow him. He had twice her strength and he was determined. On what, she didn't know. She simply fought him. She felt as if he were pulling her arm from its socket, but she was silent, only fought him and fought him. Even as Magnus left the longhouse, he was shouting, "Rollo! Rollo!"

He was going to kill her now, she knew it. He was fetching a weapon from the blacksmith and he would kill her with it. She would die here in this alien land by the hand of a man who had once sworn to love her, a man who had wanted her to be his wife before . . .

Suddenly Zarabeth didn't want to die. Even though Lotti was dead, the only other person in her life who had truly needed her, depended upon her, loved her without reservation, Zarabeth realized she didn't want to die too. She didn't want to become nothingness, she didn't want to lose what she was, not yet, and she yelled, so panicked her voice shook, "No, Magnus, don't kill me! I won't let you kill me! I don't want to die now!"

She redoubled her efforts to free herself, for the words, once spoken aloud, became real, as real as her coming death itself, as real as the blow that would strike her down. She changed tactics and suddenly threw herself at him, her hands fisted, nearly knocking him off-balance, her fists pounding at his head. She screamed at him again and again, beyond herself, "No, you can't kill me! I don't want to die!"

Magnus stopped cold. He felt her fists hitting him, felt the pain from her blows, but it was as nothing. Her words . . . He simply stared down at her. He clasped her wrists in his hands, still saying nothing. Finally Zarabeth stopped as well, panting, so terrified she could do naught now but look up at him helplessly.

"You think I would kill you," he said slowly, his eyes roving over her face, studying her, and there was so much pain in his voice that it even burst through her fear and she felt it as a part of herself. But it wasn't part of her and she was fooling herself. He would kill her, kill her . . . She couldn't believe him.

"Aye! Why would you drag me out here and yell for Rollo if not to kill me?"

Again he simply looked at her. Then he raised his hand, and she flinched, preparing herself for the blow that would surely come now, but he only laid his palm against her cheek, cupping it gently, and said, "I won't kill you. If you died, a part of me would die as well. No, Zarabeth, I won't kill you. Ever, I swear it."

She slowly nodded. She believed him, knew that he was speaking the truth. She realized suddenly that she had always believed him. He had gone to a good deal of trouble to save her life in York. Why would he take it now? She stopped her struggles. She had been a madwoman, beyond thought, beyond reason. She had been beyond him. She shuddered and stilled. He took her hand and led her into the blacksmith's hut. She hadn't been here before, and upon entering the hut, the heat from the circular stone furnace hit her face with such force that she fell back.

"Come, you'll get used to it."

Rollo was a dark man with a thick black beard and a cast in one of his black eyes, making it look a pale gray. His legs were too short, but his upper body was more muscular than Magnus', his arms like tree trunks. He was on his knees before the furnace, pumping a huge leather bellows to heat it more. He looked up at Magnus, said nothing, then looked at Zarabeth. He rose slowly, handing a sword to Magnus.

" 'Tis yours, sound as it was the day I fashioned it two years ago. We go again to search for Egill?"

Magnus accepted the sword, saying, "Ragnar leads twelve men now in the search. Soon I will go out again. But first, I want you to remove the collar from her neck."

Rollo said nothing. He started to push away Zarabeth's hair, but Magnus forestalled him. He gathered her hair in his hand and pulled it upward, baring her neck. Rollo touched the collar, saw the seam in it, and nodded.

"You will hold yourself very still, mistress, else you might lose your pretty head."

Zarabeth's heart was pounding. He was freeing her. She stared up at him, not understanding why but accepting it. She wanted to weep. He was freeing her.

"Kneel here. Magnus, keep all that hair free from her head. The red of it would blind me."

It was over quickly. She didn't flinch when the heavy iron hammer came down on the collar, once, twice, and on the third time it flew apart. She remained on her knees, her neck positioned on a block, her eyes closed, and when she heard the iron collar fall to the ground, she whispered, "I feel so light." Magnus helped her to rise. She rubbed her fingers over her throat. The skin was abraded and red, but it didn't matter. She wanted to feel her neck the way it had been before.

She listened to Magnus thank Rollo, listened to the men discuss Egill's disappearance.

"We leave for another search soon, Rollo," Magnus said again at parting, and took Zarabeth's hand. He led her back to the longhouse.

He held her hand tightly, as if afraid she would break away from him. He said, not looking down at her, "You will wed with me now. I have rings for us, made by a jeweler in York, when you said you would wed me before."

Zarabeth was dumbfounded. He'd had her slave collar removed, and now this? "Wed with you? But you hate me, you believe me a murderess, that I betrayed you. Lotti is dead, Egill is missing, and you wish to wed with me?"

"Aye, we will be done quickly enough."

"But why? No one wishes you to. I bring you nothing!"

"It didn't matter before to me and it doesn't matter now. You could be wearing only your hair and it wouldn't matter to me. Will you exchange your pledge of faith with me?"

"But why, Magnus? Why?"

He drew a deep breath, but still he did not look at her. His hold on her hand tightened more and she flinched in pain. He had no answer, and only repeated, "You will wed with me now. Any questions you have will wait. My son is somewhere out there and I must be after him again soon."

She said nothing more. She wondered if he believed his son to be dead, dead like Lotti. Both of the children? How could he bear it?

"Will you, Zarabeth?"

She nodded slowly, saying nothing. It was inevitable, her bonding with this man. She'd accepted so long ago. She couldn't deny him now.

She tried not to react when Magnus told his family

of his decision. She simply closed her eyes at their collective looks of astonishment, Cyra's white face, and Ingunn's look of hatred. She wondered dully, standing there in their midst without a word to say, if she would spend the rest of her life dependent upon another, all decisions affecting her to be made by someone else. Then she shrugged. It did not matter, none of it, for Lotti was dead, after all, and even though Zarabeth would continue to live, continue to eat and breathe, the joy in it would be gone and would remain gone.

Soon, so soon she couldn't quite grasp it, she and Magnus were standing facing each other and he was holding her right hand, saying, "Before these witnesses and before our gods, I pledge my lifelong faith to you, Zarabeth. You will be my wife until death claims my body, and I swear to protect you with my sword and with my body, and we will live together in peace and you will share in all that I possess and all that I will ever possess."

He shoved a beautiful gold ring onto her middle finger.

He leaned forward and said quietly, "You will say the same words to me, Zarabeth."

"But I am a Christian, Magnus. There is no priest here. How can these words between us make us one?"

He smiled then, and merely repeated, "Say the words. You are in my land now and there are no Christian gods here that we recognize in our souls."

"I pledge my faith to you, Magnus."

"You do well. Continue."

Her voice strengthened. "I will live with you in peace and I will give you all that is mine to give. I will protect you with my life."

"And your loyalty, Zarabeth? Do you pledge me your loyalty?"

"I pledge you my loyalty and my fidelity."

"Will you give me constancy? I wonder. Now slide the ring on my finger."

She did, and he leaned forward, grasping her upper arms, and kissed her forehead. "Your words pleased me. Would you truly protect me with your life? Would you honestly give me your loyalty? Above all others?" When she merely ducked her head, he released her, turned, and looked at his father, then at Mattias and Jon, and finally at his mother. "You are our witnesses. Is there anyone who is displeased with this joining?"

There was no word spoken.

"Good. Zarabeth, attend me now. You will remain here with my mother and you will prepare food. We will search now for my son. I know not how long we will be gone this time."

She grabbed for him, turning him about, pulling at the cloth of his tunic. "But I would go too, Magnus! 'Twas not Egill's fault, and he must have blamed himself and run away. Please, let me help you search for him. You must!"

The pain was momentarily banked in his eyes. He even managed a smile at her. He stroked her vivid hair as he said, "Nay, you will not. Obey me, Zarabeth." He turned to Helgi. "Keep her safe, Mother, and keep her within the palisade walls."

He was gone, his brothers and father following him out of the longhouse, the rest of the men hurrying after them.

Helgi hugged her new daughter-in-law. "Worry not, Zarabeth, they will find the boy."

"He ran away because he felt guilty." Zarabeth drew a deep breath. "He shouldn't die because Lotti did."

"Magnus will find his son. Your generosity toward the boy pleases me, as it pleased him, but you must understand that Magnus wants you kept safe above all else."

Zarabeth realized she was wringing her hands, saying yet again, "But Egill wasn't responsible, he wasn't, Helgi. If only I could find him and speak to him."

"Well, you cannot. You will remain here, as your husband wishes, and that is that."

Ingunn came to stand by her mother, but all her attention was on the woman who'd taken everything from her. The woman she'd known would take everything from her the moment she'd seen her walking up the path behind Magnus, wearing that damned slave collar, her red hair vibrant beneath the bright sun. Aye, she'd known then. Magnus was naught but a fool. She said, ostensibly to Helgi, "I wish to leave Malek now. I do not ever want to come to this farmstead again. My brother was blind to what she is, and now he has pledged himself to this whore, this murderess, and his son is probably dead, and all because of her and her idiot sister."

The fragile hold Zarabeth had on herself snapped. She snarled like an animal, deep in her throat, and leapt upon Ingunn, her hands wrapping around her throat. "You venomous bitch! I would cut out your tongue if I could. You are mean and vicious, and it should be you out there, not Egill, not that poor little boy!"

Zarabeth felt another's hands pulling at her wrists, not a man's hands, but a woman's hands imbued with incredible strength, and she heard Helgi saying softly, over and over, "Enough, Zarabeth. Leave her be. Leave her be. That's right. Come away now."

Zarabeth's fingers fell away from Ingunn's throat. She was trembling with the aftermath of her rage. She saw Ingunn grabbing her throat, massaging it, and there was such hatred in her eyes that Zarabeth couldn't bear to look at her.

Helgi looked from one to the other. "There will be no more insults or baiting, Ingunn. You have no reason to hate Zarabeth. Your brother has chosen her for his wife. You knew he would take a wife and you would no longer have that position here. Why have you chosen such a path? Ah, but 'twas a false life anyway, and not fair to you or to your brother. It is done and over with. You will accept it. You will go about your work and you will keep your foul words behind your teeth."

"But—"

"Enough! We will find you a husband, one who is honorable, and you will forget Orm. Nay, I will hear nothing more about him! It is even said that it was he and his men who killed the men at the Ingolfsson farmstead and raped the Ingolfsson women. Would you still care to have such as he? He has proved himself an animal."

"It isn't true! Orm wouldn't do such things, he wouldn't! It is a lie made up by men like my father who are jealous of him!"

Helgi continued, ignoring Ingunn, "It is time for you to become wife and mother, Ingunn. You will forget Orm. I will say no more about it."

Zarabeth saw the daughter bow to her mother's command. She felt the rage flow out of her, leaving her limp and shaking.

Helgi led her to one of the wooden benches and pressed her down. Helgi studied her closely. "You truly do not blame Egill for Lotti's death?"

Zarabeth shook her head. "He is a little boy. He was jealous of Lotti, for Magnus gave her a lot of his attention. I was wrong to believe he was truly hurting her, but something inside me simply—"

"I know," Helgi said. She patted her daughter-in-law's shoulder. "Why do you not go bathe now? It will make you feel better."

But I was the one to blame, Zarabeth wanted to

say. I was the one who carried her away, who put her in that boat. I am the one who killed her.

But she said nothing, for to say the words aloud would brand them forever in her soul, and she knew she wasn't strong enough to suffer it.

When she was clean again, her hair brushed and braided, her gown fresh and unwrinkled, she found she couldn't move, didn't want to move. She stood there, seeing her little sister lying tangled in those water reeds, her hair floating out from her small head, and Lotti was so still, so still . . .

She didn't realize she was crying until she tasted the salt from her tears. She turned quickly and ran into the longhouse, ran to Magnus' chamber. She sat on the edge of the bed and cried. No one came to bother her.

She hadn't realized there could be so many tears. They choked her, made her throat raw, burned her eyes. She whispered, "Lotti, I'm so sorry. My God forgive me, I failed you."

The men didn't return until nearly midnight. There was still the dim half-light of summer, giving the surrounding countryside an eerie glow that never failed to surprise Zarabeth. She was standing outside the palisade, looking over the water, knowing deep inside her that Lotti was there, gone from her forever. If only she could imagine her resting, at peace, sleeping, her small hands tucked beneath her cheek.

She rubbed her bare arms, for the night breeze had cooled and there was dampness in the air.

She saw the men in a long single line climbing up toward her. They hadn't found Egill. She looked at Magnus, her new husband, and he looked defeated and exhausted. She felt pain twist deep within her. The two children, both gone, one because of the other and both because of her.

The tears started again.

Magnus saw her, standing there so quietly, looking toward him, her face wet with her crying. He merely shook his head and walked to her. He said nothing, merely looked down at her. He touched his fingertip to her wet cheek. Slowly he drew her into his arms and pressed her head against his shoulder.

"We did not find him, nor did we find any trace of him. He could still be alive."

Zarabeth raised her face. "Then Lotti could also still be alive."

Magnus realized the fallacy of his words, but they were all that had sustained him. They were all that kept his grief at bay.

He heard himself say, "Yes, that is true." But he knew it wasn't true. Lotti had drowned, her body either washed out by the current to the Oslo Fjord or still there, close by, strangled and trapped in the thick water reeds. Just as his son was dead. He didn't know where he was, that was all. Why had the boy disappeared? Had he run away because he feared he would be blamed for Lotti's death? Where could he be? The possibilities tortured him, for there were animals to kill a small child, animals to haul his body away and eat him. And there were men, outlaws, who would torture a child, and perhaps demand ransom for him, and then there could be . . . It went on and on and Magnus knew he must stop it.

He pulled back from his wife.

"We are together now as we should have been from the beginning. Whatever has happened cannot be changed. We must face what is and endure it."

"It is difficult, Magnus."

"Aye, I know." He touched his fingertips to her cheeks, dry now, then glided them over her brows and her eyelids.

"I could not stop my crying."

The men straggled around them, going into the

longhouse to eat, others simply going in to fall into
an exhausted sleep.

"Now that I am back, I will hold you when you
cry."

But who will hold you, she wondered, for no one
sees you cry.

Magnus' family remained two more days, the men
searching for hours at a time for Egill. No one said
anything about giving up the search, but there was no
sign of the boy. It was as if he had vanished.

Within the longhouse, Helgi went about teaching
Zarabeth those household tasks she'd had no opportunity to learn in York. She was brusque, always matter-
of-fact, but never unfair or impatient.

"In York, your family was small and those things
you didn't have, you could buy or obtain in trade. But
here, Zarabeth, you must know how to do everything,
for the traveling merchants who visit come rarely and
you cannot depend upon them. Now, to dye cloth . . .
See this lovely soft reddish brown? It comes from the
madder plant. Ferns and these small onions make a
lighter brown. And this beautiful golden color, we
make it from this lichen. You are Irish, Zarabeth, so
you must have heard of the saffron dye made from
bulbs of autumn crocus."

Zarabeth concentrated, for there was no choice, and
she learned, despite the hollowness deep inside her,
the constant gnawing of guilt and pain.

Helgi taught her to cure fish. She held up a trout
that she had just cleaned and gutted. "We will smoke-
dry it and then salt it. When there is a fierce storm
and fishing is impossible, then you will have a good
reserve of dried fish and thus won't go hungry. You
see here, Zarabeth, you hold the fish open by these
wooden skewers, and we hang them up by these tiny
wooden rods passed through the heads."

Helgi taught her to comb flax fibers, making them

fine and soft and free of all tangles. Zarabeth knew
how to spin her thread on spindles, but Helgi knew
ways of twisting the fibers more tightly together so
that the thread was stronger and more enduring.

Ingunn did nothing more than her mother instructed
her to do. She watched, and there was no more fury
on her face, just blankness and a strange kind of
stillness. It was the stark absence of feeling rather than
the bouts of rage that bothered Zarabeth.

Cyra had decided that she would take Horkel, and
announced it to Zarabeth. She seemed to have forgotten that she herself was a slave, for after all, Zarabeth
had also been a slave, yet now she was mistress of the
farmstead. As for Horkel, he ignored Cyra whenever
he saw her during the day, but each night he grabbed
her hand and pulled her from the longhouse. In the
morning she was smiling and looking well-pleased with
herself. Magnus said nothing, and his silence was in
itself agreement with whatever Horkel wished.

Cyra did what Zarabeth bade her do, without complaint, as did the other servants and slaves.

Life went on, continuing with such an air of normalcy, with such obliviousness of what had happened,
that Zarabeth realized with the force of someone striking her that she could not be a part of it. It was
beyond her to pretend that everything was normal and
the same as it had been before. She watched all the
men and women, listened to them speak and laugh
and argue. She couldn't bear it. She was plunged into
such a depression that she simply withdrew into herself. She worked and she oversaw all the cooking and
cleaning and planting, for it was her responsibility.
But she remained apart from it. Still, she realized that
the different tasks, the plain hard work, the monoto-
nous chores, did grant her something—they dulled her
mind.

Aunt Eldrid continued with her weaving; it was all

that she did, and she did it well. She played with the children, instructing the girls, but there were harsh lines bracketing her mouth now and her eyes were bleak. Helgi avoided her sister, and Zarabeth wondered at it, as would someone who was vaguely curious, nothing more.

She worked until she was so tired she wasn't even hungry. Magnus said nothing to her about it. When she fell into bed, he merely took her into his arms and held her. As for Magnus, life had never seemed so completely out of his control, nor had he ever experienced such endless pain as he did now. His son, his little boy who was only eight years old, was gone from him. His features remained impassive with the knowledge of it, but deep inside, he wondered if he would survive it. And as he lay in bed during the long hours of the half-twilight night, he tried to fill his mind with memories.

He hadn't spent many summers at home, for the sea and trading had blossomed early and passionate in his blood. Indeed, this was the first summer in five years he had been here, hunting, helping in the fields, for like Zarabeth, he found that the harder he worked, the easier the time passed. And he knew he couldn't leave her, not yet. As he lay there in his bed, Zarabeth's gentle breath warm against his heart, he shifted from memories to his brother, Jon. He wondered where Jon was traveling to this summer. He had taken his boat, *Black Raven*, and his twenty men, young and brave and eager, all of them, and had left just the week before. Magnus wondered if he would be raiding near Kiev, for he enjoyed the savages of those strange regions, particularly did he enjoy fighting them and killing them and taking slaves and earning more and more gold and silver through his trading skill when he sold them to the Arabs and to the wealthy men who lived in the golden city of Miklagard.

Magnus wished he was there now, with Jon, with the wind on his face and a fight to consider. He wished he had never met Zarabeth, never become ensnared with Lotti's loving nature, never allowed himself to go back for her. But it had happened, and as he had told Zarabeth, nothing could change what had happened. But acceptance remained hard, for both Lotti and his son were dead. Dead and gone from him. But he couldn't accept it. It held on to his mind, eating at him.

Zarabeth stirred, moaning softly, and he tightened his hold on her and kissed her temple. His wife.

On the morning of the third day, his parents packed their chests and prepared to leave.

"I have taught Zarabeth much," Helgi told her son. "She is a bright girl, and willing. You have chosen well, Magnus." She paused a moment, stroking her long fingers over her son's soft white tunic. "But she is so hurt and raw. She tries to hide it, but it is hard for her. I watch her sometimes and I can tell that she has gone away, deep inside herself, where the pain lessens. As for you, Magnus, it isn't as hard for you to hide what you feel, but your pain goes as deep as hers. You are more withdrawn than she is. The two of you together can heal each other, if you will but allow it. I don't suppose you have yet told her that you care for her?"

He shook his head. "I do not care for her," he said, and his voice was firm and strong and the lie was so evident to his mother that she had to duck her head away to hide her incredulous smile. "It is true. I had no choice. I was responsible for all that happened. It was my duty to fix what could be fixed. I could not allow Lotti's sister to continue as a slave."

Helgi continued as if he hadn't spoken. "Zarabeth is also a girl who has not known much affection, at least since her mother died. Thus, she lavished all her love upon the child. If you would let her, she would confer all that love on you. Can you imagine such love?"

"She should give me her love, and she will. She is my wife. She owes me her loyalty. She pledged it to me, you will remember."

"You always were a stubborn boy," Helgi remarked with some amusement. "But, my son, facts have a way of coming to look one in the face. Do not keep your eyes closed for too long a time, Magnus." Helgi kissed him, found Zarabeth standing alone at the end of the hall, and hugged her close, saying, "Don't forget that woad dyeing is very unpleasant in its process and in its smell, for 'tis such nasty stuff. But once you have bathed the cloth two times—forget not, Zarabeth, two times—then the beautiful blue will appear and you will think that it was worth it. It is, also, a very handsome color on Magnus. It matches the vivid blue of his eyes."

"Two times," Zarabeth said, and gave her mother-in-law a small smile.

Helgi blinked. It was the first time she had seen Zarabeth even attempt a smile. It transformed her face. She said a brief silent prayer and turned to her husband.

Ingunn left with her parents. Before she left, she said to Zarabeth, "I will find a way, you whore. Oh, aye, I will find a way."

Zarabeth stared at her but said nothing. Ingunn was leaving. She wouldn't have to deal with her again.

Even though fifty people lived and worked at the Malek farmstead, without Magnus' parents and brother and their retainers, it seemed quiet, too quiet. Zarabeth found herself going every morning, after Magnus and his men had left to hunt, to the sacred place. It was a temple set inside a small circular wooden fence at the back of the farmstead. She didn't know the rituals of the Viking religion, and no one bothered to tell her if what she did was right or not. Actually, she treated the small wooden temple as she would a Christian church. She knelt inside and prayed.

It brought her a measure of peace. She wished she could ask Magnus about it, but she didn't. He was distant, seldom within her hearing and sight, and very quiet even when he was there. There was not much laughter now at Malek.

He offered her comfort and she recognized it in his silence, in the gentleness of his hand when he touched her shoulder. It was as if he knew when the black despair overcame her.

He didn't touch her save to offer support and consolation. She was grateful, but she had no words to express that gratitude. She existed, and endured.

She had been his wife for nearly two weeks when Magnus realized suddenly one morning, just looking at her, that lust once again was swelling his member. He wanted her. He watched her reach up to pull down an iron pot from a hook. The movement drew her gown tightly across her breasts. He looked and felt the familiar swelling of his member.

He drew a deep breath and slowly rose from his chair.

20

Zarabeth turned at his approach. Without thought, without conscious decision, she smiled at him.

Magnus came to a dead halt. Her smile warmed him to his heart, and he found that he was smiling back at her. Then, as he watched her, it seemed that she realized that she was smiling, realized that it was wrong of her to smile, for Lotti and Egill were dead, and the smile fell away, leaving that damnable blankness in her expression.

He shook his head and came to her then where she was stirring porridge in the huge iron pot. He leaned down, lifted the thick braid off her neck, and kissed her. Her flesh was moist with the heat from the fire and sweet with the scent that was hers. The slave collar was gone. Her flesh was soft and smooth again. She tried to draw away, for there were many in the longhouse, and she hated to think that they were looking and seeing Magnus kiss her. Nor did she want him to touch her. It made her want to shrink inside herself, to pull the coldness deeper and keep it close.

"Don't move," he said against her throat, and kissed her again, his mouth firm and smooth.

She stopped her stirring, and her hand fell away from the long-handled spoon.

She waited; she suffered him. He stopped then, and he pressed his forehead against hers. Then he raised his head and simply looked down at her. It was as if he were trying to make a decision, trying to figure something out. She said nothing, merely waited.

"You are my wife," he said, and kissed her mouth. "Don't forget that, Zarabeth." He kissed her again, lightly, gently, not trying to part her lips, then released her. She started back, her face pale, her hands in front of her as if to ward him off. He said nothing.

That evening when Magnus and his men returned with a freshly killed wild boar, he went immediately to the bathhouse, as was his wont. When he came into the longhouse, he strode to her as if she were the only person in the room, and took her in his arms. He kissed her in front of all his people, and if he was aware that she was stiff and unresponsive, he made no sign of it. Again she suffered him, not moving. He hugged her, kissed her eyebrows, her nose, her jaw. When he released her, he looked grave, but still he said nothing.

Whilst they ate veal stew, scooping up the thick gravy with fresh warm bread, Magnus turned to her and said, "What did you do today?"

She stared at him. Such a mundane inquiry. It shook her, this realization that life continued with no pauses in its allotment of minutes and hours, no differences to show that death had come. She was silent for many moments.

"The meal is good. You prepared it well."

"Thank you, your aunt Eldrid helped me with the herbs. I . . . I have done the mending today. There were several of your tunics that were in need of my needle. There was blood on another one from one of your kills. Your mother showed me how to remove bloodstains."

He smiled at her and took another bite of veal stew.

"I also had Haki make a figure stuffed with grass and straw and stick him on a wooden pole to frighten away the birds. They would eat all our apples if I hadn't done something. Perhaps it will also be useful in the barley fields. I had heard about it from a traveling merchant in York. The farmers in King Alfred's Wessex use them."

In the past, one of the servants would remain in the orchard banging on a brass plate to keep the birds away. Now that servant could be used elsewhere, if her straw figure worked. "It is a good idea, and we will see if the birds agree. I am very fond of apples. Will you make apple jelly this fall for the winter?"

She nodded.

"Is all in readiness for Horkel and Cyra?"

"Aye, very nearly. Aunt Eldrid is making more of her special beer."

Since Eldrid's beer was actually from his mother's own recipe, Magnus merely nodded.

"What did you do today?"

"I killed a wild boar." He paused a moment, scooping up peas with his spoon. "I set several of the women to preparing the meat."

When she would speak, he added, "I knew you had no experience in it. There will be time. You need no more to do right now."

It was kind of him, she knew. She sighed and took a sip of milk. After the meal she directed the women to their duties and listened absently to the men speak of the day's hunt.

She heard Ragnar, a man who still held her in dislike, say suddenly, fury in his voice, "It is Orm—even his father knows it, and has rejected him. It seems he failed to kill everyone on the Ingolfsson farmstead. One of the women survived. She will speak against him at the meeting of the *thing*. He will be banished, if he isn't killed first by one of the Ingolfsson men, and all that he owns will be forfeit for the lives he has taken."

The man Ingunn had wanted to wed, Zarabeth thought. Orm Ottarsson, the man she still swore was innocent. Zarabeth tried to stir up a bit of pity for Magnus' sister, for this man was worthy of no one, but she could find none.

The other men added their thoughts and opinions—there were many, for they had drunk much beer—until one of them, a slender fellow named Hakon, who seemed to wear a perpetual frown, said, "Magnus, you agree, do you not? You will go to the *thing*, won't you?"

"Aye," Magnus said after some moments. "I suppose I must go. My father has asked it of me."

Ragnar made a rude noise. "He scarce hears you, Hakon, for his mind is on her."

Magnus didn't allow his anger to show. He smiled and rose. "What you say is true, Ragnar. She is beautiful and she is gentle, and she is my wife."

Zarabeth was sitting near the far wall, sewing a tunic for Magnus, when suddenly he was there, standing over her.

"It is time to retire. Come."

She nodded, set aside the fine soft blue woolen material, and rose. She followed him to his chamber, not pausing until she was in the room itself. She remembered then his kiss of the morning and stilled.

The room was cast in the dim light of the summer half-night.

"Zarabeth? Come to me now."

She didn't want to. She wanted no reminders that she was flesh and blood, that feelings coursed through her, that she had felt deep passion at one time, a time when she had been whole, a time when she had wanted all of him, all of those unknown emotions. She wanted to live, that was true, she wanted to continue, and to feel life, but this losing of oneself in another . . . no, she didn't want him to touch her and come inside her.

"Zarabeth, I will not tell you again."

She knew there was no choice. She took off her gown but left on her shift. It came nearly to her knees.

She lay on her back, staring up into the darkness. Magnus said nothing, merely propped himself on his elbow and leaned over her. "I would take you now, Zarabeth. It is time. We have need of each other. Let me give you comfort and pleasure."

She didn't move. She felt Magnus' mouth touch first her cheek and then her mouth. He was gentle, his tongue lightly probing against her closed lips.

Magnus realized very quickly that she had locked herself away from him. It infuriated him even as he understood it. He kissed her harder, forcing her now, furious that she would be cold as a stone when he was so hot, his mouth burning, his member throbbing with need against her thigh. Why was she doing this to him? He was her husband.

He touched her breast lightly, with just his fingertips, and was further enraged because she still wore her shift. He wanted to rip it off her, but he didn't.

He was surprised at the calm of his voice when he said, "Take off the shift, Zarabeth. There is never to be anything between us at night."

When she didn't immediately obey him, he forced her upright and began to work the shift up over her hips. She yielded to him then, and soon he had pulled the shift over her head and tossed it to the floor. "Now," he said.

She lay on her back, cold and alone, nurturing the emptiness inside her, focusing on it. She was fully aware of his warm hands on her body, of his mouth touching her breast. When his fingers found her and began a gentle rhythm, she felt a burgeoning awareness in that emptiness, a beckoning in the deepest part of her, and she tried to jerk away from him. These feelings weren't right, she didn't deserve them.

He held her down, his fingers splayed on her belly. "I know there is passion inside you, for I have tasted it and felt it and taken it into me. Why do you punish me with your coldness? Why do you punish yourself?"

"I cannot," she whispered against his shoulder, her fisted hands against his chest. "Please, no, Magnus, please."

He gave an animal growl and came over her, pressing her legs apart and settling himself between them. He kissed her again, teasing her, using all his skill to make her respond, but she was locked against him. He hated it and he hated her in that moment, and with a growl of fury he reared back, lifted her hips in his hands, and came into her. She wasn't ready for him and he felt her pain and the stretching of her woman's flesh. But he didn't stop until he touched her womb. He looked down at her and saw in the dim light that her eyes were tightly closed. "Damn you," he said, "open your eyes!" He began to move. Soon her flesh eased and dampened and he knew he couldn't hold back much longer. She was so cold and still beneath him, so very apart from him. His body pulsed with an anger that grew and grew, and with it, his endless need for her, a need that he now accepted. Though he wanted to curse her and dominate her and force her to accept him with a passion to match his own, he knew this time he had failed.

He concentrated on his own passion, on the swollen need, and on the release when it came. He arched his back and cried out, and in that instant he forgot all but this moment of pleasure, this instant of sheer feeling that blotted out the damnable pain. He rolled off her and away onto his back. He said nothing for many moments, not until his heart slowed and he knew he was again in control.

"If you cry, I will surely beat you."

She had stuffed her fist into her mouth. She turned on her side, away from him.

He knew she was crying, could feel her trembling, but he also knew that she was trying to keep silent, and thus he ignored it. "I will take you every night, Zarabeth, every single night, until you come back to me. I will not accept this. You must allow me to come back to you."

She felt the wetness of him on her thighs. She nurtured the pain he had inflicted deep inside her, for it gave her more reason to stay within herself, within her own emptiness.

Magnus slept finally. When the dreams came, they were bright and vivid and filled with a fierce sense of truth. He saw his son, he actually saw Egill, and the boy was ragged and dirty, but he was alive. He saw a man strike him and he felt the blow as it landed on the boy's shoulder. He cried out in rage.

"Magnus, wake up! Wake up, you've had a nightmare!"

He was trembling, his flesh damp and cold. He jerked upright. He shook his head to clear the visions away. He whispered, even as he clutched Zarabeth to his chest, "I saw him, I saw Egill, and he is alive, I am certain of it. I saw a man strike him. By God, I saw it, Zarabeth, and it was clear and it was real."

Zarabeth finally made out his features in the dim light of dawn. A dream, and he believed it true? She had heard of such things. Seers had visions. He was trembling, and she pressed herself more closely against him, giving him what comfort she could, without thought, without decision. She recognized only that he needed her.

Magnus drew a deep breath. He was here, in bed, Zarabeth against him. But the dream had been so solid. He eased away from her and rose. He left the longhouse, naked, and walked to the temple.

He remained there until the sun was bright in the morning sky. There had been no answers and he was left tortured by what he had seen.

Horkel and Cyra married that day and left Malek to return to the small farmstead Magnus had allotted to Horkel in return for his service. Many of Magnus' men itched to be off trading, for the summer was full upon them and it wasn't right that they remain here doing the work of the slaves and the women. They wanted to make their fortunes.

But Magnus didn't want to leave Zarabeth. The next evening Ragnar drank more than was wise and said loudly, "We become weak and fitful as women here! We waste the long hours of summer when we could be making ourselves rich and richer yet. What say you, Magnus? A quick raid to the south, at the mouth of the Seine. We sail in and take what we want from those rich villages on the coast. We'll be home before September comes and be richer than we are now."

Magnus didn't respond. He was thinking back to his dream. He hadn't told any of his men about it, not even Horkel or Tostig, but it preyed on him endlessly.

"Aye," said Hakon. "Or we could go trading to Birka. We have many soapstone bowls of fine quality."

Ragnar drank more. He got no response from Magnus and it enraged him. He walked to where Zarabeth was sitting with three other women, shelling peas. "Aye, tell him to go, mistress, for 'tis because of you that he stays. Perhaps he fears you will flee him. He can bring you back gold and silver and Rollo can melt it down and give you all the jewels you could desire. Isn't that what you want? By Odin, answer me! We all know that you give him nothing!"

Zarabeth raised weary eyes to the man who still disliked her simply because she'd bested him so long ago. "I want nothing, Ragnar."

"You certainly don't want Magnus. Aye, I hear his cry of release, for I am still awake here, thinking, but I hear nothing from you, mistress, not a sound, not even the slightest moan, and before . . . ah, before, when he first took you, we all heard your cries, those mewling sounds you made to draw him in. All a lie, for you are cold and a murderess and you felt naught for him. You used him, used me, and I trusted you, fool that I was, as did he."

Suddenly Magnus was there and he was gripping Ragnar's shoulder, gripping tighter and tighter until the man cried out at the fierce pain.

"You dare," Magnus said, pulling Ragnar to within inches of his face. "She is my wife and you insult her as if she were a common slave."

"She is a murderess and was a common slave until she enslaved you!"

Magnus struck him, and Ragnar went down like a stone.

The other men were on their feet in an instant, crowding around, speaking all at the same time. Magnus stood over Ragnar and thought as he rubbed his knuckles: You were my friend, despite your hot blood and your quick rages, but now . . . He shook his head. Now there was naught but strife. Nothing made sense anymore. Nothing.

Aunt Eldrid said in a sour voice from behind them, "I would that all of you seek your beds! 'Tis unsavory in its lateness. You disturb me, all of you drunken louts!"

He took her, quickly this time, silently, for he was upset by Ragnar's words, and savagery still pounded thick in his blood. When he had finished, he pulled away from her. He ignored the harsh pull of her flesh, knowing he had hurt her again, but not wanting to recognize the pain or that he had caused it.

Zarabeth lay there feeling the wet of his seed on her thighs, feeling the soreness deep inside her, thinking of the anger and violence between Magnus and Ragnar. She knew they were friends. She didn't want them to be enemies, not because of her. She said, "I was told that you were never here in the summer months, that you were off trading and did not return until the early fall. I will not run away if that is why you remain now, Magnus, I swear it to you."

"I know you would not, Zarabeth. After all, where would you go? Back to York? Back to Keith and Toki? Perhaps to be taken and executed for your crime? No, I am certain you wouldn't leave Malek. I am a fool, but my foolishness does know some boundaries."

"No, I wouldn't leave. But, Magnus, I will be all right if you choose to go trading."

He felt his belly churn in anger and frustration, and it spilled over into his voice, despite his efforts. "Cease the show of virtue and nobility, Zarabeth, for it is a lie that will gain you nothing. You want me to leave so that you will not have to endure my touching you!"

When she didn't respond, Magnus turned quickly, coming over her, grabbing her arms, and pulling her upright. "Isn't it the truth? Admit it, Zarabeth, admit that you loathe and despise me. You would probably kill me if you could but have a chance to escape with your life."

He shook her again, and her head snapped back. "Answer me, Zarabeth!"

"I have never killed anyone in my life!"

He heard fury in her voice and it goaded him further, this anger of hers, for it gave him purchase for his own anger, unlike her show of emptiness that left him floundering and weak and gentled until he was no longer a man.

"Ah, haven't you? You did not murder Olav? You did not sneak poison into his food from the day you wedded him? Tell me true, Zarabeth, did you kill him because the thought of him taking you sickened you? And he would have had the right, for he was your husband. Or did you kill him for his worldly goods?"

"I didn't hurt him! I cared for him even when he was vilely ill! It was Toki, by my Christian God, I swear it to you! She poisoned him. She and Keith came by everything that was Olav's, not I."

He released her and pushed her back. He was on his knees beside her, his hands on his thighs.

"So there is still some passion in you if one prods you enough."

She lay there staring up at him, her mind sick with her anger and with herself. "You did that on purpose?"

He shrugged. "I know not, nor does it matter now."

"Leave, then, Magnus. You have it right. I do not want you to touch me. It sickens me."

He wanted to strike her. It was powerful, the feeling of violence in him. Instead, he flattened his hand over her belly. "I wonder if a babe grows inside you yet." She pulled at his wrist, trying to dislodge his hand. He took her hand and wrapped her fingers around his swelled member.

She sucked in her breath. Her entire body stilled. He felt her fingers tighten and he groaned at the pleasure of it, all the while wondering what was in her mind, hoping that some part of her was responding to him.

"No," she whispered.

"Aye," he said, breathing hard now. He took her hand from his sex, clasped both her wrists in one of his hands, and jerked them over her head. "I would take you again, Zarabeth, because I am your husband and it pleases me to do so." His fingers were between

her thighs and sliding into her. She was still wet with
him, and stretched, and his fingers probed and worked
deeper into her.

She bucked her hips, and he laughed, deeply, fully.
Then he released her hands suddenly and pulled her
up to her knees. He lifted her then, widening her legs
about his flanks, and came up into her even as he held
her tightly against his chest. He found her mouth and
probed deep with his tongue even as he worked deep
inside her body.

He moaned, jerking as his release hit him, so
quickly, nearly without warning, and he crushed her
to him. He quieted finally, but he continued to kiss
her shoulder, her throat, savoring the taste of her, the
heat of her flesh, in his mind removing the evidence
of the iron collar he'd forced her to wear. He rubbed
his chest against her breasts, felt his heart pound anew
at the feelings it brought to him. He knew he loved
her, he accepted it now, praying that all the pain in
their lives would ease with the passage of time, praying that the time would come when she would forgive
him and forgive herself for being alive when Lotti was
dead.

She was limp against him, her cheek pressed against
his shoulder.

He felt her tears hot against his skin. He hugged
her legs to his flanks and gently lowered her onto her
back. He was still deep inside her, deeper now as he
pushed forward. He balanced himself on his elbows
above her. "Why do you cry? I didn't hurt you, not
this time, for you were still wet with me. Why,
Zarabeth?"

She looked up at him. "It is too much, Magnus,
and I cannot bear it."

"And if I tell you I understand you, will you consent
to believe me?"

She felt the force of his words pushing at the emptiness with which she'd filled herself. It frightened her. "I would that you would leave. Vikings kill and raid in the summer months. You have not had your fill of it."

He went hard into her now, her words filling him, pulsing through him, heating his blood and his anger. Harder and harder he drove into her, until he again found his release. When he rolled off her, he said, "I will take my men and leave after the meeting of the *thing*. Wear your grief like a badge of pride, Zarabeth, flaunt it, and let all know that you suffer, that you grieve endlessly, and that all those around you must respect this, else you will turn on them. And when you weep with your self-pity, I would that you choke on it."

21

Magnus and three of his men left four days later for the meeting of the *thing*, held near Kaupang in a valley belonging to King Harald Fairhair. They were riding, not going by the *Sea Wind*, for she was being repaired, her steering oar being replaced. Zarabeth saw him mount his stallion, Thorgell, a huge beast bred by Magnus' father. The slave holding the reins abruptly dropped them at Magnus' nod and Thorgell pranced to the side, then reared onto his hind legs. Magnus laughed and patted the great beast's neck even as he clamped his thighs around the stallion's belly. He looked magnificent in his thigh-length tunic of lavender wool over trousers of dark brown wool. Cross-gartered brown leather boots came to his knees. A wide leather belt studded with silver and gold was around his waist. His blond hair shone in the morning sunlight, and in that bright light his features were so clean and pure that it hurt Zarabeth to look at him.

She turned away, tired and depressed and already lonely, which was stupid, because she had wanted him to go, wanted more than anything to be left alone with her grief and with her emptiness.

He called out her name. She turned to see him riding toward her. In the next moment he had leaned down and pulled her up and was holding her against him. Thorgell danced to the side, and Magnus only

laughed. He kissed her hard and released her. She
stared after him until he was gone from her sight
around the outjutting point of land.

She worked, and worked harder still, hoping to so
exhaust herself that she would sleep at night. More
often than not, she lay there staring up at the beamed
roof into that muted half-light of the summer nights
and wished for blankness.

On the third day, she came out of the longhouse at
the shout from a slave. It was Helgi, accompanied by
six men, and she was clearly upset.

"Ingunn is gone!"

Zarabeth stared at her, and she said again, "Ingunn
is gone!"

"Come inside, Helgi."

Helgi saw her sister, Eldrid, and turned quickly
away, her hand on Zarabeth's sleeve. "Sometime during last night, she ran away, that, or she was kidnapped. Have you seen her, Zarabeth? Have you
heard anything?"

"Nay, nothing. Why would she leave her home?"

"Orm Ottarsson!" Helgi's broad handsome face,
flushed from her exertions, was now flushed with
anger. "I knew she was lying when she assured her
father she would obey him, I knew it because I know
her. She wanted Orm and she refused to believe that
he was an outlaw, a man without honor! By Thor,
he'll shame her and our family."

"Where is your husband?" Zarabeth struck her
hand to her forehead. "Oh, he is at the *thing*, as is
Magnus."

"Certainly Harald is at the *thing*! Ingunn waited,
she isn't a fool, though I would like to beat the girl
until she weeps at my feet! Ah, Zarabeth, then you
have neither heard nor seen anything of her?"

Zarabeth shook her head. "I'm sorry, Helgi. Here,
drink some ale, it is newly brewed and cool."

Zarabeth saw Helgi glance over at her sister once again, then immediately turn away. "Would you care to remain here, Helgi? We can send a messenger to your husband and to Magnus. He told me it was but a day's ride away."

"You're a good girl, Zarabeth." Helgi sighed, the harsh color leaving her face. "Nay, I will return home. Perhaps the stupid girl has come back, though I doubt it. I suppose what's done is done." She rose, again sighing deeply. As if it had just occurred to her, she smiled and said, "You are all right, Zarabeth?"

Zarabeth nodded, stiffening without conscious thought, awaiting the words she knew would come, and Helgi said, her voice cool and emotionless, "Time lessens the pain, you will see."

Zarabeth looked into the older woman's eyes— Magnus' light blue eyes—and said what was in her heart: "Nay, I don't believe that it will. There is too much of it, you see, and I am not strong enough to allow it to lessen."

Helgi recognized that honesty. "There has been too much change for you in too short a time, too much pain, too much uncertainty. It has nothing to do with your strength or your weakness, Zarabeth. But I will tell you this, daughter, you will carry your pain and your grief until you rid yourself of your guilt. You cannot really begin to be my son's wife until you deal with this. Now, tell me, how does Magnus deal with Egill's loss?"

"He dreamed he saw Egill alive, but in some sort of captivity."

Helgi touched the amulet she wore around her throat. "Perhaps," she said. "Perhaps."

After Helgi and her men had left, Aunt Eldrid came to where Zarabeth stood, looking off into the distance at nothing in particular, and said, "It is odd—this tale about Ingunn, I mean. Ingunn isn't stupid. At least she wasn't stupid until you came, then she became a vindictive creature I scarce recognized. Normally, Ingunn always acts for a reason. No, my dear sister doesn't know her daughter as well as she believes she does. Aye, it is odd."

She would say nothing more, even when Zarabeth questioned her closely. Sour old woman, she thought, and went about preparing some turnips to roast beside the herring just caught in the viksfjord.

The next day, it rained, a thick cold rain that gave a hint of the harshness of winter. Zarabeth shivered, wondering about those cold, dark months that would surely come. What would life be like then? She watched the heavy dark clouds billow over the mountains. The waters of the viksfjord churned and heaved. She wondered what Magnus was doing, what he was feeling. It surprised her that she wondered about him.

Zarabeth found herself hoping that he was warm and protected from the rain. A wifely thought, she realized. A very wifely thought. By the Viking gods, she was a fool.

Late that afternoon the rain stopped and the sun came out. Everyone breathed a sigh of pleasure and poured out of the longhouse. No one cared about the large pools of mud that pockmarked the ground both inside and outside the palisade. The slaves went into the fields, women washed clothing in huge wooden tubs beside the bathhouse, and the children wrestled and shouted and fought and did the tasks assigned to them. Rollo's hammer rang out loud and solid from the smithy's hut. Eldrid spun the fine flax into stout threads.

The air of normalcy had returned. All was as it should be again, except that it wasn't. Suddenly, as before, Zarabeth couldn't bear it, this everyday laughter, the common jests and talk that surrounded her. She walked through the palisade gates and down to the shore. No one said anything. She walked to the water's edge. The water still swirled, its color darkened from the churning. She looked at the boat, the one she had taken, the one from which Lotti had jumped—jumped to save Magnus—and she felt herself folding inward. It was a strange sensation, one that allowed her to feel exactly what she was doing. Head down, she began to walk up the shore, not caring where she was going. She simply wanted to be alone for a while. Suddenly she heard a dog bark and looked up. There, in front of her, stood a young man, tall, as well-formed as Magnus, his hair a rich wheat color, his complexion fair, his eyes a startling silver blue. He held a sword loosely in his hand and he was merely standing there staring at her.

"Your hair," he said at last. "I have never before seen such a color, though my men have told me of it. Red as blood, they said."

Her hair! What nonsense was this? She looked at his sword. She looked behind him but could see no one else. He appeared to be alone. Surely there was no reason for her to be afraid of him, at least not yet.

"Who are you?"

He smiled, revealing very white teeth. He was a handsome man, she thought dispassionately, still eyeing that sword. She wondered if people above, within the palisade, could see them, and if so, what they would do.

"I have waited for you, and the wait had become tedious. I would have attacked Malek earlier, but I didn't really want to. I wanted only you, and now it appears that the gods have delivered you up to me. I doubted mine own eyes when I saw you leave the safety of the palisade."

"I doubt your Viking gods have anything to do with my being here. Who are you? Why would you want me?"

"I do not like a woman's tongue to be shrill, nor do I like demanding questions." He took a step toward her, and Zarabeth took a step back. She eyed the distance up the incline to the palisade gate, wondering if she could outrun him.

He said, "You cannot. You are but a woman, and thus you could never outrace me. Now, I would look more closely at you. I won't hurt you. Hold still."

He walked to her, the sword still held in his right hand. He stopped in front of her and, to her surprise, lifted her long braid in his hand, pulling it forward. With quick, nearly angry motions, he pulled it apart. He ran his fingers through her hair, then gathered a thick tress around his hand and rubbed it against his cheek. "I hate the braid. You must leave your hair free and loose. The feel is as rich and vibrant as the color. Ah, and the smell. Lavender? You are very foreign, just as Ingunn said. The green color of your eyes is also unusual. I have never seen a green so pure and deep, like the greenest moss deep in a forest where little sunlight filters through. I wonder, is the rest of you different as well?" He grinned then and chuckled. "Of course, Ingunn would never admit that you were beautiful. She hates you, you see."

And then she knew. Ah, yes, she knew. "You are Orm Ottarsson, aren't you?"

He was still grinning at her. "Ah, so you still have your wits about you. My fame has preceded me. Aye, I am Orm Ottarsson and you are Zarabeth, wife of Magnus."

"Why are you here? It isn't safe for you to be here. Even now your deeds are being discussed at the *thing*."

"I have come to take you away from here, away from Magnus Haraldsson. I have long wished to do him in, and Ingunn has no tender feelings for you. She has begged me to avenge her. She wants you

dead, truth be told, but she would never admit to that.
What she so prettily begs me to do is to sell you to
some Arab in Miklagard and thus turn a tidy profit."
He touched his fingertips to her jaw. "I do not believe
you would make a good slave, though I doubt not I
would get much gold for you. Are there still marks
from the slave collar Magnus put on you? No, I see
that they are gone. You must have angered him
greatly for him to humiliate you thus."

"Yes," she said. "But I meant not to anger him.
'Twas not my fault."

"It matters not now. He forgave you and wedded
you. At first I did not credit it, for Magnus is such a
proud man, unbending as an oak. When we were
boys, he could be more stubborn, more inflexible,
than any of us. I remember seeing him pale with fear
when a wild boar turned on him, but he swallowed
his vomit and made his stand, and he killed the beast.
Aye, a proud man, Magnus." He was looking at her
again, and rubbed her hair between his fingers.
"Ingunn is as proud as her brother. She can be merci-
less as well. I have always admired that in her."

"Ingunn has no reason to hate me. I did nothing to
her."

He shrugged, saying, "She is a passionate creature
whose heart is easily bruised, whose mind is easily
twisted. She saw you as a threat, saw you as the
woman who would usurp her, and thus set out to
destroy you. She wasn't wise in her methods, though,
for Magnus cares for you above all others, including
that little whore of his, Cyra, but Ingunn didn't fully
realize that until it was too late—for her."

"She has told you all these things? You kidnapped
Ingunn from her home?"

He laughed then, shaking his head. "Helgi wants to
believe that, I doubt not, but she is no fool and she

knows that Ingunn came to me freely. I had but to send her a message and she flew to me."

"Magnus, his father, and many others are at the meeting of all free men and they are considering evidence of your deceit and trickery. You should leave Norway, Orm. I have heard it said that many of your countrymen sail to the west, to lands discovered and settled by the Vikings."

He nodded, smiling at her as though he were her friend, a guest, not a man standing before her with a sword in his hand. "You are right, of course. There is little for me here now." He looked bemused. "How odd that one of the Ingolfsson females lived and is right now telling of my rape of her. I had thought her well dead with all the rest of them. There was much gold and silver there—the man who told me was right about that. I have more than enough now." He looked up at the strong palisade that protected Magnus' farmstead. Then he looked out over the viksfjord to the mountains beyond.

"But this is my home and it pains me to be forced away. Aye, I have wealth now, but no land."

"No one forced you to kill and rob and rape."

He looked at her then, and there was no longer a smile on his face. "I do not discuss my deeds with women. You have no understanding of what forces drive a man."

"I understand Magnus, and he is more a man than any I have ever known." The moment the words were gone from her mouth, she froze, understanding flooding into her. Magnus was kind and fiercely loyal and he had truly wanted her to become his wife. He had loved Lotti and mourned the child's death. And to lose his own son on the very same day . . . She felt small and petty and stingy. She had given him no comfort, provided him no understanding. She had wallowed in self-pity, ignoring him and his pain, selfishly shutting him away from her. She closed her eyes a moment, wishing that she could shut out all that she had done, all that she had said and thought, for now she understood—oh, yes, she well understood—that she had lied to herself and to him.

"Did Magnus take your maidenhead?"

She drew back, her eyes still clouded with her thoughts, and then his words came cleanly into her. Again she looked up that winding path, and saw herself running and running. She saw him catch her. What would happen then? She didn't see that.

"Answer me, woman! Was it Magnus who took your virginity, or another man, that first man who wedded you?"

" 'Twas Magnus."

"Ingunn reviles you, calls you whore and slut, but I doubted it. She calls you these names even as she screams out the pleasure I give her. It is strange, but she is, still, only a woman and there is no sense to her actions." He paused and looked upward toward the palisade. "You are right. Soon someone will notice that you are gone and perhaps even see me here speaking to you. We will leave now, Zarabeth."

She turned and ran.

The meeting of the *thing* had continued now for three days. Harald was the chieftain who directed that the evidence against Orm be brought forward. But it was the Ingolfsson daughter, a girl named Minin, who was only twelve years old, who brought the meeting to a near-hysterical climax. Orm had raped her and then thrown her against some rocks, believing her dead. She had lain without consciousness for three days. She spoke in a quavering child's voice, and each man there saw his own child in her stead; each man knew such fury he choked on it.

Orm was proclaimed outlaw. He would have to

leave Norway, if he wasn't killed first, for the Ingolfsson men wanted his blood.

Magnus sat across from his father and his brother Mattias that evening. It was warm and still bathed in the summer-evening half-light.

"I would go home," Magnus said.

Mattias grinned at him. "Your blood is heated, Magnus, and you would have your bride consume you."

Magnus said nothing. He was seeing Zarabeth on her back beneath him, her eyes closed, her arms at her sides, her hands fisted, as he took her. That last night before he'd left to come to the *thing*, he had taken her yet again, as he had told her he would, and when he was done, he saw the tears seeping from her closed lids down her cheeks. She had made no sound. The tears had merely continued. By Thor, he hated it, hated her and himself as well.

"Nay, I would just leave here," Magnus said. "My men wish to go on a-raiding, Ragnar tells me, just a small raid, he explains, to relieve the men of their boredom and fatten their caskets and relieve some fat English monks and their monastery of their gold and ornaments." He sighed. "Perhaps we should go. Either a raid or we could hunt down Orm and take all the gold he's stolen."

Mattias said absently, "Toke Ingolfsson will kill Orm, and it is his right." He looked at his father, who was rubbing a knotted muscle in his shoulder. "I agree with Magnus. Bring all this to a close on the morrow and let's go home. I have my own bride to keep happy."

Harald grunted, then winced as Magnus began to massage the knotted muscles in his shoulder. "Glyda isn't a bride, she's a wife, and only Freya knows why she cares more for you than you will ever deserve. You're a rutting stoat and the poor girl must constantly suffer your pawing and your—"

Mattias laughed and buffeted his father's other

shoulder. "Me? A rutting stoat? Glyda is the one, Father, who pats the side of our bed and gives me those long-eyed looks."

Magnus listened with half an ear to their jests. He missed Zarabeth and he worried about her. He didn't want it to be true, but it was. Other men joined them, and Magnus moved away, wanting to be alone. He had felt wounded since the day Lotti and Egill had died, wounded inwardly, where none could see. He strode to the edge of the giant encampment and looked back at the myriad tents and cook fires spewing smoke into the air. He turned to stare at the snow-covered mountains in the distance. He had dreamed again of his son, and Egill appeared the same way he had in the first dream—alive but ragged and dirty. It ate at him, this damnable dream, for he was a straightforward man and this dream, or whatever it was, disturbed him profoundly. No, his son was dead, just as was Lotti. He had to accept it, for if he didn't, how could he expect Zarabeth to?

He wanted to return to Malek.

He had to see her again.

Orm caught her in half a dozen steps. He grabbed her around the waist and hauled her off her feet, back against him, and he held her there, laughing, pressing his face against the back of her head. Then, without warning, he whirled her about and slapped her.

Not hard, just enough to sting her flesh and make an imprint of his hand on her cheek. Just hard enough so that she would fear him. "A taste of punishment," he said, his face very close to hers. He was studying her expression, looking closely, hoping to see tears in her eyes. There were none, and he was tempted to hit her again, but he didn't. It was enough for now. "You gave me no choice but to strike you. Don't be foolish again, Zarabeth, else I will have to give you more than a simple taste of pain."

But she couldn't help herself. She slammed her fist into his belly, then began to struggle against him, tried to rip his face with her fingernails, and finally he grunted in disgust and slammed his fist to her jaw. She slumped against him, unconscious. As he lifted her over his shoulder, he looked upward to see if any in the farmstead was looking. He saw no one.

He carried his sword in his right hand and held his left to her buttocks to hold her steady over his shoulder.

When he reached the pine forest some fifty yards up the shoreline, one of his men emerged.

"By Odin, look at that hair—'tis magic, that color. Let me touch it."

"Nay," Orm said. "Let us away from here. If we are quick about it, we will be back to our camp by this evening."

"She is gone," Eldrid said again.

Magnus was shaking his head. No, it couldn't be true.

"Two days ago. She simply disappeared. It was after a storm and she left the palisade and none saw her again. I am too frail for this, Magnus. The girl is flighty and wounded. Leave her be. Aye, perhaps she will return on her own."

Magnus wanted to strike the old woman. He turned on his heel and went to Hollvard, the old man who had guarded the palisade gates of Malek for two decades.

"Aye, Magnus, I watched her leave, her head bent, deep into her thoughts, I remembered thinking. It had rained so hard that all of us were annoyed with each other, all of us just wanted to be outside, and so it

was that she left the palisade and walked down the
path to the water."

"She had nothing with her?"

Hollvard shook his head.

"Then someone took her away by force."

"Aye, perhaps."

He heard the doubt in the old man's voice. Hollvard
believed, as did all the rest of his people, that she had
killed herself or simply walked away into the woods,
there to be killed by wild animals. Magnus didn't
believe it for a minute. Zarabeth was a fighter. She
would not destroy herself.

He called all his men together, and another search
began. None of them said a thing, merely searched as
they had for Egill. It was Ragnar who found a ragged
piece of her gown on a bush some twenty yards into
the pine forest.

Magnus studied the piece of cloth and the bush.
"She was being carried," he said at last, standing.
"Over a man's shoulder, a man nearly of my height.
She was taken from Malek." He wanted to yell with
the relief he felt at their discovery, but it was quickly
quelled.

She had been taken. By whom? Was she still alive?

Eines, a small man who was a superb tracker, came
forward. "This way, Magnus. There are still prints,
vague, but enough for me. Thank Odin that it hasn't
rained since that day."

Eines, Magnus thought, falling into step behind
him, had no shortage of conceit. He prayed the man
was right and not bragging to hear himself speak.
They came upon the camp late in the day. It had been
abandoned, Eines stated, some two days before.

"What do we do now, Magnus?"

He turned to Ragnar. "We arm ourselves and prepare for stealth and cunning. I know who took her
and I will have the bastard's blood."

22

Zarabeth felt a stinging slap on her cheek, then a dash of cold water in her face. She sputtered with the shock of it and opened her eyes.

Ingunn was kneeling beside her, an empty wooden cup in her hands. "So, you're not dead. Orm was worried that he had struck you too hard. But I told him that I would wake you quickly enough."

Zarabeth said nothing. Ingunn sat back on her heels, her eyes narrowing suddenly as Orm strode over to them. He came down on his haunches, leaned over, and took Zarabeth's face between his hands. He studied the bruise on her jaw. His touch was gentle as he traced the now-yellowing flesh.

"I hadn't meant to strike you so very hard. You have been unconscious for a very long time." Then he grinned at her. "You won't ever fight me again, though, will you?" Again he touched her jaw. Not so gently this time.

Pain shot through the side of her face, but she didn't make a sound. She looked at the man who had taken her from Malek. "Where are we?"

He smiled widely, but it wasn't a pleasant smile. She braced herself for another blow, but he didn't touch her. "I told you before that I dislike shrill questioning, particularly from women."

"I am not shrill. I am merely questioning."

"She makes a mockery of me, but I'll forgive her

imprudence this time." Orm grinned at Ingunn, whose
face was tight. He said to Zarabeth, "Not far from
Malek. No, not far at all. Now that you are awake,
you will make yourself useful. We must be gone soon.
Ingunn, see that she obeys you."

Orm touched his fingers to Zarabeth's hair, his gaze
so intent it frightened her. He then rose, hands on his
hips, to look down at her. "Be about your tasks now."

"Get up."

There was venom in Ingunn's voice, and triumph as
well. Zarabeth got to her feet, the movement sending
waves of pain into her jaw. She rubbed it gently, then
opened and closed her mouth several times. Her jaw
wasn't broken, thank her Christian God and the Viking gods as well.

"You will get no sympathy from me, Zarabeth, so
don't try your stupid tricks." Ingunn stepped closer.
"I told you I would pay you back for what you have
done to me. I told you I would make you regret what
you did, and here you are. Now, you will carry these
things." She threw several bound bundles at her. Zarabeth picked them up. They were heavy. Orm called
out then, and she shifted the bundles in her arms.

There were only two of them walking, an older
woman and she. Orm and his two men and Ingunn all
rode. She wondered who the woman was, but she kept
her head down and away from Zarabeth, as if she
were afraid of her. Whoever she was, the woman
appeared to be a captured slave, just as she herself
was. Unconsciously Zarabeth touched her fingers to
her throat where the iron slave collar had once encircled her. She closed her eyes a moment and pictured
Magnus in her mind. He would find her. He would
come for her. If he still cared at all about her.

Unless all the people at Malek convinced him that
she had fled or that she had killed herself. She remembered that last night with Magnus. He had taken her

and she had chanted over and over to herself that she hated what he was doing to her, hated him for forcing himself on her like that night after night, and the tears had come and she'd known he was looking at her, seeing her tears but hearing no sounds from her, and he'd pushed deeper then, and deeper still, as if to prove that what she felt, what she did, meant nothing to him. Then he had left the next morning and she had looked away from him even after he had kissed her in front of his men and ridden away from her laughing.

With two of them walking, the pace was slow. Finally Orm called a halt. He called to one of the two men, Kol, and ordered him to take the other woman up on his horse. Orm took Zarabeth on his horse, in front of him.

Ingunn rode close. "Let her have my horse, Orm. I will ride with you. This isn't right, having a slave treated so finely."

"I would think having her ride a horse singly, without one of us holding her, would be treating her more finely."

Ingunn chewed her lower lip, searching wildly for something to say that would change his mind. She saw that Zarabeth was markedly silent. She watched as Zarabeth accepted Orm's hand, watched the muscles in his arm bunch as he lifted her up in front of him. He then held her against his chest, his arms around her, holding the horse's reins in front of her. Ingunn felt great fury, a greater sickness in her belly. She wished she had a dagger; she would surely stick it in the woman's ribs.

"Ingunn!"

She swallowed her anger and eased her mare beside his stallion. "Aye?"

"Tell me more about this slave with her strange hair and strange name. You called her a slut and a whore and said she had bewitched your brother. Why is this?"

"My brother wished to wed with her, but she betrayed him. She sent him away and wedded with an old man who was richer than Magnus. Then she poisoned him slowly. She is not to be trusted. She is a witch, with many tricks."

"I trust no one, man or woman, so I am safe. As for her tricks, well, do you believe me a fool, Ingunn?"

She looked at him stupidly for a moment, then saw that his eyes had darkened, the blue irises blazing nearly black. Quickly, for she was suddenly afraid of him, she shook her head.

"Say it," he said.

"Nay, you are not a fool, Orm."

"Good. You please me when you are obedient, Ingunn." His eyes lightened, and the wildness was gone from them as suddenly as it had come. Ingunn remembered the brief speech she'd had with him before he'd gone to take Zarabeth. She had said, her voice trembling, "Perhaps I am a fool." The instant the words were out of her mouth, she had hated herself for speaking them.

"What mean you?"

"I came to you because I believed you loved me. I left my parents' farmstead to come to you."

"And now you change your woman's mind? You *are* foolish, Ingunn. You will be my wife, doubt it not."

Now she said, "What will you do with her?"

"I have yet to decide."

Ingunn had nothing more to say. In her mind's eye, she had seen Zarabeth, that wild red hair loose and full down her back, and felt the familiar rancor boil in her belly. She would still have her revenge. Orm was a man, and she mustn't forget a man's weaknesses. Magnus had succumbed to this woman and turned on her, his own sister, very quickly.

Orm was speaking again, but it wasn't to her. It was to Zarabeth. "Does your jaw still pain you?"

"Nay."

"Excellent. You seem a strong woman, and that pleases me. Now, tell me, what do you think Magnus will do when he returns to Malek and finds you gone?"

"He will come after me and he will kill you."

It was Ingunn who laughed at that. "Ha! All will tell him that you fled from him, or that you jumped into the viksfjord like that little idiot sister of yours."

Zarabeth twisted about to look at Ingunn, her face twisted with pain and rage. "I told you never to speak of Lotti like that."

"And what will you do about it, you slut?"

Zarabeth tried to fling herself off the horse at Ingunn. Orm was taken by surprise and nearly missed grabbing her in time. She was flushed and breathing hard with fury, he realized, not with fear. "Hold still, else I will strike you again!"

"My little sister is—"

"Was, Zarabeth, *was*! She's dead!"

"As dead as Egill! Do you mock him, Ingunn?"

Ingunn hissed breath out. "Say you nothing about Egill. He was a fine boy, he was Magnus' heir, not a pathetic little slave with no blood ties to him, to any of us—"

Again Zarabeth tried to pull free of Orm and fling herself upon Ingunn. Orm held her. He watched, his expression mocking, as Ingunn pulled her mare some distance away.

"A slave shouldn't have such passions," he said, his breath warm against Zarabeth's cheek, and he wrapped a thick tress of her hair round and round his hand until he was pulling her head back against his chest. "Now, you will be silent. We have some way to go yet before we make camp."

Ingunn kept her distance.

Orm called a halt for the night when they reached a small copse of pine trees hidden from view near the base of a snow-covered mountain. "In another day or so we will reach the Oslo Fjord and my vessel, the *Wild Tern.*"

Zarabeth was desperate to know where he intended to sail, but she kept her mouth shut. She realized, dispassionately, that she was afraid of him and that she had to tread warily around him. She couldn't begin to imagine what he would do, how he would react, from one moment to the next. She was told to gather firewood. The man Kol stayed with her, doing nothing himself, merely watching her. He was dark, his face pockmarked, and he was so silent, even when he moved, that she found herself continually looking over her shoulder to see where he was. He didn't try to touch her, merely watched her with that silent look of his until she wanted to scream.

She didn't realize how hungry she was until Orm handed her a charred piece of roasted rabbit. It was delicious, even the black burned flakes. She wanted more.

He held a piece just out of her reach. "What will you give me for another piece?"

His voice was soft and teasing, not at all the voice of a vicious killer. He stood over her, his legs parted, and he waved the piece of rabbit in her face.

"I have nothing to give you."

"Perhaps not," he said, and to her surprise, he handed her the other piece. Her stomach settled and she felt waves of tiredness hit her then. She was asleep within minutes.

Orm stood over her. She'd quietly fallen to her side,

her legs drawn up, and her cheek was pillowed on her palm.

He picked up a blanket and covered her with it. He looked up to see Ingunn staring at him.

"Come, Ingunn," he said, and rose, stretching out his hand to her.

Her cheeks flushed, for he'd spoken in a normal tone of voice, and both Kol and Bein looked up. Both of them knew what he intended. She felt shame at his blatant use of her body, and she was not yet his wife. Still, what else could she do? She had come to him, trusting him, and if she stopped trusting him, why, she would have nothing.

She rose, pretending to adjust the skirt of her gown, pretending that they were going for a walk, perhaps to discuss their future together.

She heard one of the men snigger. It was Bein, and she hated him for the way he looked at her and the way he spit when he looked away.

"How would you like me to take you, Ingunn?"

"They are listening! Say not such things!"

Orm laughed, and in sight of his two men, in the sight of the other woman, who was a pathetic creature, he pulled her against him and kissed her soundly. Then he pushed her back, still holding her with one arm, and let his fingers trail over her throat downward until his palms were brushing across her breasts.

She cried out in mortification, and he laughed, releasing her. She ran from the camp, knowing that he would follow, knowing that he would not even lower her to a soft blanket, but push her against a tree and jerk up her gown. It was how he punished her. He had done it several times now when he thought her unwomanly in her speech to him.

He pushed her against a tree this time as well, and she was crying silently during the long minutes when he was grunting against her. When he was finished with her, she pulled down her gown and wished she was dead. "You must bathe, Ingunn, your sweet woman's scent is gone. I like my smell on you, but not the sweat of the horse."

She nodded, walking away from him, saying nothing, for there was nothing more to say.

She fell asleep finally, only to awaken when he pressed against her back. "Hush," he said, and kissed her ear. "Forgive me, Ingunn. I hurt you and it angers me that I did so. I will make it up to you now."

She felt his hand under her gown, moving upward, and she wanted to pull away from him, wanted to scream at him to leave her alone, but then he was touching her and she closed her eyes and let the pleasure build within her. She whimpered softly, her fist against her mouth when her release came, and she heard him laugh softly against her ear.

"There," he said. "Now you won't give me your wounded looks. You are pleased, are you not? I want you to thank me, Ingunn."

She whispered her thanks to him. He laughed again and left her.

The following morning, Ingunn kicked Zarabeth in the ribs. "A slave doesn't sleep whilst her mistress works. Get up and collect more firewood. Be quick about it, Zarabeth."

She did as she was told, her companion the same one as the evening before. Kol looked sullen this morning, his pockmarked face even uglier today. Still, he remained silent, making no move toward her, watching her.

Orm let the two women slaves walk for three hours before calling a brief halt. He brought Zarabeth up on his stallion in front of him again. Ingunn said nothing. He called out to her, "The woman needs to bathe. There are no men's smells on her, but the scent of horse is strong. We will halt at the small lake that lies just east."

Kol said, "But that is away from the fjord, Orm! Do you not wish to be gone from here? All of us are outlaws now. The *thing* will have come to no other conclusion, not with that silly little girl speaking against us." Kol turned on Ingunn. "Aye, 'twas *her* proud father who called them all against us, we all know it well!"

"There are none to follow us as of yet. Fret not, Kol, for I am your leader and I do not make mistakes."

The man spit on the ground near Ingunn's mare. "You brought her, did you not? You plan to wed with her!"

Orm's eyes narrowed. Then, to Zarabeth's astonishment, he laughed. "Listen, both of you. Aye, Bein, I see the same doubts in your ugly face. Aye, I have Harald's daughter here because with her in our midst, he would dare not attack us. Have none of you any wits? She is a superb hostage!"

Ingunn gasped aloud. "Nay, you lie! I came to you because I did not believe you had done those things—"

"Ah, but I did, Ingunn."

His voice was very soft, terrifyingly so. Ingunn turned white, her eyes dilated. Zarabeth felt a lurch of pity for her, and an increasing fear of Orm.

Then Orm laughed again. "I am no monster, Ingunn. I did nothing at all. I was but testing you. Kol heard from an old man that one of the Ingolfsson daughters said it was us. She lied. All of you, attend me now. This beautiful woman, Ingunn, daughter of Harald—I will wed her, for I love her dearly, and all of us will leave this cold land and make our way to the west. We will settle in the Danelaw. We will buy lands there with all the gold and silver we have gained in our trading."

Bein and Kol spoke low to each other. Zarabeth felt confounded. He was slippery, his tongue agile, and she was afraid of him. Color had returned to Ingunn's cheeks, and now she was smiling, under Orm's spell again.

I must escape, Zarabeth thought over and over as the afternoon hours passed. I must escape. Orm would kill, then laugh and deny it even as the blood dried on his hands.

That evening when they stopped to make camp, Zarabeth was once again sent out for firewood, Kol her companion. He grunted at her, pointing to the branches that lay on the ground. He wasn't going to help, merely watch her.

Finally she said, knowing the time had come, "I must be by myself for a moment . . . just for a moment."

He looked at her, no expression whatsoever on his face. "I will watch," he said, and crossed his arms over his chest.

She discarded several ideas in the space of a moment. Finally, she merely shrugged, looked past him, her eyes widening. When he whirled around, she picked up the skirt of her gown and ran as fast as she could into the pine forest, ducking behind a thick pine at the last moment. There was no crashing of under- growth, for Kol was silent as an animal. She felt terror creeping over her. Where was he?

Suddenly she heard him yell, "Woman, wait! You come here, do you hear me?" He paused and she held her breath, for he was but feet away. "Orm will be mightily displeased with you. He will punish you! His punishments aren't pleasant. He could break your jaw this time. Come here, now!"

He was closer, moving silently. She fancied she

could hear his breathing. She closed her eyes, pressing closer against the tree bark. He was saying again, "You won't escape me, woman. Come now, and I won't be angry with you."

She didn't move. But she was ready, and suddenly he was there, coming around the tree, his movements stealthy, his step silent. He saw her and jerked back, but not in time. She heaved a rock as hard as she could in his belly. He howled, falling forward, and when he did, Zarabeth lifted that same rock again and struck him on the head. He went down without another sound. Now you are silent, she thought.

She was free. It was exhilarating. For a moment she couldn't believe it. She stood over Kol, panting, holding that blessed rock. She had seen the rock and had seen herself hitting him with it, but the fact that she had actually succeeded left her momentarily dumbfounded. Quickly she knelt beside him and took his knife. Then she was running through the forest, knowing even as she ducked branches that the trees were fast thinning. In a very few minutes she would come out into a long narrow meadow. She would be in full view of Orm and Bein. Ah, but the trees on the other side of the meadow were so near, not far at all. She could make it, if only she could run fast enough.

Magnus dismounted and stretched. He patted Thorgell's neck, then leaned down with Eines to check the tracks.

"We're close, Magnus."

Magnus grunted.

"Two of the horses are carrying two people. I'd say a man and a woman on each of the horses."

Magnus saw in his mind's eye Orm carrying Zarabeth in front of him. Who was the other woman? Ingunn?

"This other horse carries only a woman."

Ingunn, he thought. It had to be. Who was the
other woman?

"So," he said, "we have three men and three women."

"Aye, 'tis so."

Magnus rose and looked toward the horizon. "He
travels to the Oslo Fjord. I wager he has a vessel
there, waiting for him, and I wager it is finely provis-
ioned. Then he plans to leave Norway."

Ragnar came up to him. "How old are the tracks?"

Eines turned his head away.

But Magnus knew. "They will make the fjord and
their vessel before we can catch up with them."

"Did she go with him willingly?"

Magnus turned to Ragnar then, saying in a low
voice, "I know that you dislike her. But your reason
is a paltry one, Ragnar. She took advantage of you,
aye, that wasn't well done of her, for you had come
to pity her and mayhap even trust her a little, but
attend me. She was terrified for Lotti. She could think
only of saving her little sister. Rid yourself of your
dislike of her, else I must rid myself of a man I have
held as a brother for many years."

Ragnar's face was frozen.

"Would you not have done the same thing were
your sister in danger? You would have killed, would
you not, without thought? She did not want to hurt
you, only escape you."

"She is a woman."

Magnus laughed at that. "Aye, she is, and she is
my wife now. Make your peace with her."

"I do not believe we will find her so that I can make
peace, Magnus." He turned now and placed both
hands on his friend's shoulders. "You said it yourself:
Orm will reach his vessel before we can catch up to
him."

Magnus shrugged him off. "Let us ride."

But he knew that they should turn back and finish

the repairs on the *Sea Wind*'s steering oar. But something made him kick Thorgell in the sides. He would
ride to the edge of the fjord before he gave it up.

The horses were blowing hard when finally Magnus
called a halt. There were six of them, all tough men,
all seasoned warriors, armed and ready to fight. By
Thor, he wanted Orm. He wanted to kill him. He
cared not that Ingolfsson had a prior claim. Orm had
taken Zarabeth.

He raised his eyes to the darkened sky. Thick gray
clouds floated past the half-moon. It was quiet, so
very quiet, and his thoughts were screams inside his
head. His son, Lotti, and now Zarabeth. Had he
sinned so grievously? Which gods had he so offended?
No, he wouldn't believe that Zarabeth was dead. He
wouldn't believe that Orm would reach his vessel first.

Zarabeth didn't look back. She focused on the line
of pine trees across the meadow. She ran until the
stitch in her side was so bad she was holding her arms
around herself. But she didn't stop. It was a twisted
dead branch that tripped her, and she went flying.
The grass was tall here, and it softened her fall.

She lay on her face, not moving, feeling the roiling
pain through her chest as she tried to breathe. Then
she heard the pounding of horses' hooves. Closer and
closer. She pressed her cheek to the grass, and the
pounding was louder and the earth was shaking
beneath her face.

"By Thor, she is hurt!"

It was Orm. She lurched up and tried to run, but
she stumbled again, and would have fallen except Orm
leaned off his horse and jerked her up around the
waist. He held her against his side until he had ridden
out of the tall grass. He set her down then. He didn't
move, merely looked down at her.

"Why did you try to escape me, Zarabeth? I told

you that you should not try. Now I have no choice. I will have to punish you."

She raised her head then. His face was as calm as his voice, but his eyes had darkened. They were glittering in the bright sunlight, and there was a wildness in them that stilled her tongue. She stood there saying nothing.

"Answer me, Zarabeth."

"I want to go home. I want to return to Magnus."

He laughed. "When we reach York I will have another slave collar put about your white neck. Come here."

He carried her back to camp. His arms around her were gentle. He said nothing. She was afraid to face him. She feared she would see the madness in his eyes.

A fire was burning sluggishly. The smell of roasting pheasant was strong. Kol was sitting there on a log, holding his head in his hands. He looked up at her and she knew he would kill her if he had the chance. Ingunn was pale with rage. The other woman, Zarabeth realized now, had been beaten. She was bent, her eyes reddened from crying. She was in obvious pain.

"You found her," Ingunn said, her voice flat.

"Aye, certainly. She is a woman and she was on foot. What would you have me do to punish her, Ingunn? A slave attempting to escape. It's a severe crime."

"Let her work until she falls over."

"That is not enough," Orm said. "Look at poor Kol. She brought him low, and his head will pound for days to come. Nay, her punishment must be something she will not soon forget."

"Flog her, then, I care not."

"Her flesh is so very white. I dislike the thought of marking her. Did you beat her, Ingunn?"

"Aye, I did."

"Did you mark her?"

"I don't know, for Magnus tended her."

"There are other things I should prefer doing to her."

Ingunn nodded toward the other woman. "Like the things you did to her?"

Zarabeth realized then that the other slave, that older woman who was thin and bent, her hair straggling down her back, had not been beaten. Orm had savaged her. He had raped her.

"Nay, Ingunn, I should do different things to Zarabeth. I shouldn't want her to cry as much as that hag did."

Kol spoke up then. "We must leave, Orm. There is no time to punish the woman now. Magnus Haraldsson will come for her, I know, for I know his reputation."

Bein said, grinning, "I would like to punish her as well, Orm."

"You shan't take her, Orm! We will leave!" Ingunn was on her feet, shouting.

Suddenly Orm turned and backhanded her, sending her sprawling dangerously close to the fire. She cried out, scrambling away from the heat.

Orm merely rubbed his palms together. He was smiling, and again there was that glittering in his eyes, darkening them, but his expression was calm and his voice was even genial. "Do not tell me what I will or will not do again, Ingunn. Next time it will not go so easily with you. Now, I am hungry. Feed me and feed our poor slave here. After all her efforts, she must be in need of Bein's pheasant."

23

Zarabeth hated the dim half-light. It was nearing midnight, and yet that strange spongy light kept the night darkness at bay. She knew that regardless of darkness or light, Orm would come soon and he would rape her. He had watched her, saying nothing, merely sat cross-legged beside the fire, watching her. And Ingunn had watched him. As for Kol, he had vomited earlier, and now he slept. Bein had simply dragged the other woman to her feet and pulled her into the trees.

When they had come back, Bein shoved her to the ground and threw a blanket at her.

Zarabeth wondered if the woman was all right. She had never said a word, never acknowledged anyone else's presence, merely done as she had been told, her head bowed, her shoulders bent. She had no front teeth and her upper lip had sagged in, making her look older than she probably was. Zarabeth had no idea where she had been captured. Her gown was ragged, her feet bare, her hair tangled and matted to her head. Zarabeth wanted to go to her, but to her astonishment, some minutes later the woman was sound asleep, snoring. Zarabeth sat with her back against a pine tree. She waited. Orm had fed her, but not enough, and he had known it wasn't enough. He was toying with her. Her stomach rumbled and cramped with hunger. She needed to relieve herself, and finally, in desperation, she said softly, "Ingunn, I must go into the forest for a moment."

Ingunn looked away from her. Orm said, "I will take you, Zarabeth."

"Nay, leave her be! I will go with her!"

Orm grinned at Ingunn. "If she wishes it badly enough, she can kill you, then she will have to deal only with me. Do you want that, Ingunn?"

"I want us to leave this place. I want us to go to the Danelaw and buy slaves and land and build a longhouse that surpasses my father's. I want us to be wedded, Orm."

"All that? You must know that I have already been to the Danelaw and purchased land. Good farmland near the Thurlow River."

Ingunn was obviously surprised. "You already sailed to the Danelaw?"

Bein said, "Aye, and we traded furs and hides and some sea ivory from walrus tusks. We even sold some slaves and—"

"Enough, Bein. Now, Ingunn, when we reach the Danelaw, we will buy more slaves. We already have two, and they are both fine, do you not agree?"

"Take the one over there for your men's lust, but leave Zarabeth here. Let her go. She will survive or she will die. I care not what happens to her now. Let us go, Orm, and be free of this land and of my father."

"But you wanted me to avenge you. You begged me to sell this woman, for she had deceived Magnus and thwarted you. Your woman's words confuse me."

Ingunn got to her feet. "I will take her into the forest now. I too must have some privacy."

He shrugged, not moving when they left him.

"He will rape me, Ingunn. You know he will. Do you want him to do that?"

"I won't listen to you. Hurry now or he will come."

"You're afraid of him. There is something wrong with him, Ingunn, surely you see it."

"Hurry!"

But he was there soon enough, watching as the two women straightened their gowns.

"It is time for Zarabeth's punishment. Should you like to watch, Ingunn?"

"You will beat her?"

He shook his head. He was smiling, that strange calm smile. His eyes glittered in the dim midnight light.

"What will you do to her?"

"I will have Kol take her. Is that sufficient punishment?"

"Kol is ill from the blow she gave him."

"Ah, then Bein."

"He cannot. He raped the other slave. He is old and has not sufficient powers."

"Then I am the only one left. She really must be punished. Go back to the camp, Ingunn. I will bring Zarabeth back when I am done with her."

Magnus knew they were close, but not close enough. Already Orm and his party would be boarding his vessel. Perhaps they were pulling on the oars this very minute. Perhaps they were already sailing due south to Hedeby. He closed his eyes against the pain of losing her. So much loss. Too much. Where would Orm take her? Magnus knew he hadn't protected her as he had pledged to when he made his vow to her.

"By Thor, I don't believe it!"

Magnus turned at Eines's shout.

"Come here, Magnus, look! They're close, very close, not more than three hours ahead of us. Look at these tracks! Is the man a fool?"

"Aye," Ragnar said. "A stupid fool. Does he not

care that someone could be following him? Does he think you a coward? Has he lost all his wits?"

Magnus felt fierce purpose fill him.

Ragnar said quietly behind him, "Ingunn is with them."

"Aye, I know. Our horses are blown. Let them rest, but no longer than an hour."

They were all exhausted, their muscles cramped and stiff, but not one of them complained. They hunkered down and ate dried beef and hard flat bread.

"What will you do with Ingunn?" Ragnar asked as he chewed the tough beef.

"I will give her back to my father. It will be up to him to decide what is to be done with her."

Ragnar looked at him, and his voice was firm and strong. "I will take her, Magnus, if your father agrees to it. I will beat her, doubt it not, if she behaves churlishly. I can control her."

Magnus smiled at his friend. "I believe you are the one who has lost his wits, Ragnar."

Zarabeth faced Orm from a distance of six feet. Her gown was tattered and filthy. Her hair was matted and tangled down her back. She felt exposed and more afraid than she ever had in her life. Ingunn was walking away, her head lowered.

"Ingunn, no! Do not leave!"

She paused but did not turn back.

"I am not an ill-looking brute, Zarabeth. Why do you not want me?"

She looked at him then and saw the honest puzzlement on his face. She very nearly laughed. His eyes were calm as his voice. There was no madness in him yet. Still, he terrified her. He unbuckled the wide leather belt at his waist, all the while watching her.

"If you rape me I will kill you."

He smiled. "You are a woman. You speak nonsense, yet I do not like to be threatened by you, Zarabeth. If you don't wish to feel my belt against your back, keep your tongue in your mouth." He raised the wide belt with the sword still deep in its scabbard.

She kept her eyes on his face and repeated, "If you rape me I will kill you. You will have to kill me first to protect yourself, for I swear it to my Christian God and to your Viking gods as well."

He was on her before she could move. He slapped her hard. She staggered against a tree, lurched forward, and slumped down to her knees. He stood over her, looking down at her, rubbing his hands together.

She pushed her hair from her face. Her breathing was harsh; her cheek felt raw. She should simply let him take her. She shouldn't struggle against him. She should endure.

But something deep inside her rebelled. She didn't want to be passive; she didn't want to submit. She didn't want to force herself to endure, to silently suffer whatever he would mete out to her.

She raised her face then and said, "If I do not kill you, Magnus will."

He raised his hand again, fisted it, then very slowly lowered it back to his side.

"I am as brave as Magnus but far more daring, as you know yourself. I am as strong as Magnus. As boys one of us would always win in wrestling and weight lifting. But he took one path, doing what his father demanded of him, wedding with that silly girl his family had selected for him, taking his grandfather's homestead, Malek, becoming naught but a farmer and a trader, whereas I . . . I wanted to . . ." He frowned as if waiting for the words to come into his mind. He was silent for many moments; then he shrugged. "I have known more women than Magnus. I would pleasure you more than he does. You come from the Danelaw. I will return you there, to your home, and

you will live well with me and not know any want.
There is no reason for you to fight me."

"There is every reason. Magnus is my husband. He
is kind and loyal and he loves me."

"He has deceived you, you stupid bitch. And those
are words one would say of one's father. They are not
the words a woman should say of a man who gave her
passion. Kind? He is weak and looks not to himself
to take what he wants. Loyal? Aye, Magnus is loyal,
for his brothers would kill him were he not. He is part
of them, not a man separate." He saw that his words
were having no effect. It infuriated him, but still he
smiled, saying easily, "Like me, Magnus enjoys a variety of women. He will not hesitate to take them in
front of your nose, be you wife or no. Did he not take
Cyra with you there, watching? Did he not mock you
with her presence?"

"I thought you said you knew more women than
Magnus."

His mouth tightened with irritation. "Of course I
do, 'tis just that Magnus will take whatever female
lives at his farmstead. He never ventures away for a
woman as I have done."

She whispered, "Ingunn . . . do you not plan to wed
her? Do you not plan to keep me as your slave?"

He laughed and rubbed his knuckles over the thick
reddish-blond stubble. His look was cunning. "If you
come to me willingly, I could make Ingunn your
slave." He leaned down then and began to wrap a
thick tress of her hair around his hand. "I would breed
a babe off you with hair this color. A man who would
command men, a man strong and powerful, a man
who would rule all of Norway, all of England, a man
who would make King Alfred's sons look like puking
infants."

"I would kill any child of yours."

She had pushed him too far. His eyes glittered dark

and wild. She knew it, but still she wasn't fast enough. He grabbed her arms and pulled her to her feet. He did not strike her again, merely ripped the front of her gown to her waist. She was wearing a shift beneath it, and he ripped it as well, baring her breasts.

His belt lay on the ground, the sword in its scabbard still hooked over the leather. She didn't struggle yet, knowing instinctively that if she did, he would strike her again, and perhaps this time she would lose consciousness. She had to be alert, she had to act when she found the chance. She was stiff in his arms, but nothing more. His breathing was ragged and deep, and within moments her clothing was in rags around her bare feet.

"By Thor, you are more than I expected." His hands were rough on her breasts as his mouth came over hers.

His hands pressed against her belly, and he was trying to wedge her legs apart. With a growl of frustration he pulled back and began to yank and pull at his tunic. When he was naked to the waist, he pulled her against him, moving his chest against her breasts, and he was groaning.

He released her for a moment to jerk off his trousers and rip off the cross-garters from his soft leather boots.

Zarabeth leapt for his sword. She had it in her hands, was trying to jerk it from its scabbard, when he was on her, his hands wrapped around her hair, and he was pulling her inexorably backward, and she was crying with the pain and with the bitter taste of failure.

He jerked the sword from her hand and threw it some feet away. He was naked now, over her, and suddenly he threw himself between her legs. He was smiling down at her and his eyes were filled with triumph.

He reared up to position himself. She lurched up, her fists pounding into his face. Her nails scored his cheeks and she felt the flesh tear away, felt his blood well over her fingers. He roared with anger and pain. His hands were around her throat and his fingers were squeezing hard and harder still and she felt pain in her chest, building and building, and she knew she would die now. He was cursing her and there was madness in him and now the madness was him.

Suddenly his hands fell away from her throat and air surged into her lungs. She coughed frantically, sucking in air.

"Hurry, Zarabeth!"

It was Ingunn. She stood over an unconscious Orm, his sword in her hand. She had struck him hard from behind with the sword handle.

"Is he dead?" Her voice ripped out, a curious croak, and the pain of it made her shake.

"No, no. We must hurry."

Zarabeth pushed him off her and jumped to her feet. "I'm naked," she said, staring down at herself dumbly.

"Here!"

Zarabeth caught Orm's tunic. She pulled it over her head. It came to her knees. It smelled of him.

"Horses, Ingunn. We must get the horses, else we won't have a chance!"

"Nay, Kol is awake, as is Bein, and the horses are kept close, you know that. We will go on foot. We can hide. Hurry, else he will awaken and catch us!"

Zarabeth wanted to kill him. She stood uncertain for a moment, then quickly gathered together the leather cross-garters he'd ripped from his shoes and tied his hands behind his back. Then she tied his ankles.

"Hurry!"

She stood over him for a moment, staring down at him. "He is mad, Ingunn."

"I care not, come along! He will kill me as well as you if he catches us."

Ingunn grabbed the leather belt and shoved the sword back into its scabbard. Then she stared at it as if it were a snake to bite her. Zarabeth grabbed it and wrapped the belt around her waist and cinched it. It hung low on her hips, but it held there.

She had no shoes, but it didn't matter. She ran, Ingunn at her side. They were deep in the forest before they halted, each holding her side.

"A moment," Zarabeth said. "A moment, Ingunn."

Zarabeth leaned against a tree, the pain sharp in her side, air ripping painfully through her throat, and she felt light-headed. Her stomach cramped from hunger. She raised her head to see Ingunn on her knees, her head lowered.

"Why did you save me?"

Ingunn sucked in great gulps of air.

Zarabeth waited. She could hear her own breathing, sharp in her ears, and Ingunn's as well, both harsh and ugly in the stillness of the forest.

"Why, Ingunn?"

"I came to realize that he had changed. I had refused to believe my father when he told me of the things Orm had done. You see, I thought I *knew* him, and I loved him." She shrugged. "Whenever I met him he made me believe in him, even though I began to guess that something had happened to him. I don't know what it was. But he used to be so . . . happy and gentle in his ways, at least toward women. He changed, Zarabeth." She rose then and looked back the way they had come.

"He will come after us any moment now. To kill me. To kill you as well, after he has raped you. If you want to live, we must hurry now."

Zarabeth staggered forward. It was dark now, finally, and they were running across a narrow strip of swampland that gave into another thin forest of pines, then stopped at the edge of the viksfjord.

"Faster," Ingunn said from behind her. "He will find us, by all the gods, I know it."

"Nay, we will beat him." She prayed as she ran, prayed to her Christian God, to each of the Viking gods in turn. The pain in her side was unbearable, but she merely ran hunched over, holding herself, her breathing hoarse, her throat burning.

They stumbled in the boggy ground, falling several times, helping each other up, only to run and stumble again.

When they heard the horses coming they both slammed to the ground, uncaring of the mud and wet. Zarabeth's hands were filled with swamp mud. Her face was pressed into the wet earth. She thought of the last time she'd lain on the ground, waiting helplessly for Orm to come capture her. And he had come, and he would come again. The sword was heavy, dragging down at her side. She wasn't helpless this time.

The horses were coming closer. There was no long grass in this boggy swamp to hide them, only short marshy reeds, and Zarabeth knew that at any moment Orm would see them.

"I won't wait this time, damn him!" She jumped to her feet, pulling the sword free from its scabbard as she tried to keep her balance in the muddy earth.

"Zarabeth! You fool, lie down, quickly!"

"Nay! He won't take me back again. Not this time! This time I will fight him."

Magnus was keeping Thorgell to a steady pace. He didn't want to kill his prized animal. The moon was bright overhead, the meadow was narrow and long. They were close, he could feel it. Suddenly he saw an apparition rise from the floor of the meadow. He felt a tremor of sheer terror choke in his throat. The vision, or whatever it was, was waving a sword like a demented thing. It was a woman—demon or flesh?

The stallion didn't falter even though his fist tightened on the reins. He heard Eines cursing, heard Ragnar's breath draw in sharply, heard the other men muttering.

"What is it?"

Then he recognized his wife, her flying hair, streaking down her back, thick and tangled. She was wearing a man's tunic and a wide loose belt that hung low on her hips.

She was challenging him, sword raised above her head, legs apart, her body ready.

Zarabeth brought the sword down in front of her and held it there with both hands. She waited, her heart pounding, beyond fear. It wasn't Orm. It was Magnus. A sob caught in her throat. She dropped the sword and began running toward him, the filthy swamp mud sucking at her feet, all the pain in her body forgotten.

"By all the gods!" Ragnar yelled, and kicked his horse's sides. "I'll kill it!"

"Nay, Ragnar! 'Tis my wife!" Magnus kicked Thorgell into a gallop. He rode to her, leaned down, and scooped her up with one arm. He was laughing, deep and freely, and he was holding her tightly against him and her arms were around his neck.

He pulled Thorgell to a halt. He looked at his wife, filthy, smiling, her eyes bright with relief. "You would have held me off with your sword? Right there in the middle of a swamp?"

"Aye. I was very angry, you see."

"I see," he said, and leaned down to kiss her. "You are also very filthy."

"Magnus," she said into his mouth, and tightened her hold around his neck. He grunted and pulled her across his lap. Thorgell pranced to the side, not liking her weight or the swamp smell of her.

"Ingunn is out there hiding."

Magnus called his sister's name. She rose and stood silently under the moonlight.

"Ragnar, take her up with you."

"We must hurry," Zarabeth said, panic flaring suddenly. "Orm must be conscious by now. He will be coming after us."

"Good."

She heard the pleasure in his voice, the anticipation. There was nothing for it. He was a man and a warrior and he wanted his enemy.

She said as calmly as an old campaigner, "There are six of you. There are only three of them. They have one woman who is a slave."

Magnus wanted to find Orm immediately. He wanted to kill him slowly and he wanted to do it himself.

She smiled at him, her fingertips touching his mouth. "Thank you for coming after me. I would like you to catch him, Magnus. He is like a dangerous animal. He must be stopped."

"I am worried for you."

"I have his sword. I am a dangerous woman. Let us go."

He kissed her again, squeezed her against him until she squeaked, and click-clicked Thorgell forward. He shouted for his men to follow.

They rode back from across the meadow, slowing down to get through the dense pine forest.

"So close," Magnus said against Zarabeth's temple. "I feared he would be gone with you. He has a vessel near, does he not?"

"Aye. I don't know why he waited. He veered inland, then came back north to the viksfjord. Perhaps he wanted you to come. Perhaps he wanted to face you and fight you."

"Did he hurt you?"

"He did not rape me. He would have, but Ingunn struck him down. I tied him with his cross-garters and then we ran."

He hugged her. "You did well, as did my sister."

When they neared the camp, they rode single file. Then Magnus called for a halt. They dismounted and he bade Zarabeth wait there with the horses. She watched him silently make his way to the edge of the trees.

She felt sick to her stomach. Ingunn came to stand beside her.

There was a shout. "He's gone! The bastard is gone! The miserable coward."

The women looked at each other, then ran forward.

Eines was on his knees examining the fire and the ground around it. "I don't think he tried to catch the mistress at all, Magnus. I think he came back here— see, his prints show that he isn't steady on his feet— I think he simply decided it was too dangerous and they all left."

All but one. They found the woman slave naked and dead beside a tree, strangled.

It was then that Ragnar found a series of rough finger drawings made in the sand on the far side of the fire. There was a small boy with a rope around his neck and he was being led by a man. The man was smiling and holding pieces of gold in his free hand.

"Egill," Magnus said. "It is my son. Somehow he managed to capture Egill."

"Your dream," Zarabeth said, her hand on his forearm.

"Aye, he's a slave, but he's alive. By Thor, where did Orm take him?"

Ingunn came forward and went to her knees to study the drawings. "He said nothing to me about capturing Egill, nothing at all." There was shock in her voice.

"But we know where Egill is," Zarabeth said with a smile. "He's in the Danelaw."

24

It was just past dawn, the sky a soft pink with folds of pale gray. The air was cool and still; the creatures in the forest were silent. Zarabeth lay against Magnus, her head on his shoulder. She listened to his even breathing, her palm flat on his chest, against his heart. In a day and a half they would be back at Malek. Back to her home.

She burrowed closer and his arm tightened about her back, an unconscious gesture to keep her safe and close.

He had come after her. He had wasted no time, given no thought to the possibility that she could have fled from him or even leapt to her death off a cliff into the viksfjord. She came up to her elbow then and looked at his face. There was a slight smile on his lips, she was certain of it, and without thought she leaned down and kissed him lightly on the mouth. She kissed him again, then once more.

He opened his eyes slowly, even though she knew he'd come instantly awake at her touch, for that was how he was.

"It's early, Zarabeth. I have need of rest. You have worn me to the bone chasing you to the edge of the earth. However, I don't wish to discourage you. You may kiss me again."

She did, saying between the light, nipping kisses, "You came after me."

He went still and she stopped kissing him and looked down into his face as he said somberly, "Did you believe for one instant that I would not?"

"No, not for an instant. I don't think Ingunn doubted it either. She was always trying to get Orm to hurry, but he didn't. He is quite mad."

"Aye, perhaps now, but when we were boys . . ." His voice trailed off and he said abruptly, "Your stomach is making so much noise I cannot go back to sleep."

"I have been hungry since Orm captured me."

He frowned then. "Why have you not said anything?"

"I did not think of it until just a moment ago. No, Magnus, don't move yet. I won't starve until the sun hits its zenith, I promise you." She sighed. "Ah, 'tis good to be clean again even though the viksfjord water nearly froze my eyebrows from my face." She kissed him again, remembering the bathing both of them had done in the viksfjord the evening before.

"When I have returned you to Malek and Ingunn to my father's farmstead, I will take my men and sail to the Danelaw."

She said nothing for several moments. She was still propped up on her elbow, over him, and she leaned down again and kissed him once more. He came up to kiss her back this time, but she pressed him down. "I am trying to think," she said. "You mustn't distract me."

"That is nice for a man to hear. You are certain that now I could distract you?"

She looked worried and he felt a leap of anger at her. She had come running to him the evening before, hurling herself upon him, trusting him completely. But now she was behind that wall of hers, that cursed barrier that he had sworn to breach. But he held his tongue. She had bathed with him, seeming to enjoy it, but had fallen asleep before he could show her how much he had missed her. And now she had kissed him, willingly, so many times he couldn't believe it, and she was lying easily against him. He saw her look over to where Ingunn lay wrapped in a blanket, sleeping soundly, her white-blond hair spread about her head.

"Ingunn saved me, she truly did."

"I don't wish to speak of my sister. How is your throat?"

"Do I still sound like a frog?"

"You sound like a wet cloth slapping at an open wound."

"That is a disgusting image, Magnus. Was your first wife silly?"

"Silly? Dalla?" He looked at her, his eyebrow cocked upward.

"Your parents arranged for you to wed with her? Was she silly?"

He shook his head. "Orm told you these things?"

"Aye."

"The truth was that Orm wanted her himself, but her parents believed me to be the better man for her."

"Was she silly?"

He laughed then and pulled her down against him, squeezing her. "Aye, she was silly and she laughed as openly and freely as a child and she loved to dance in the moonlight, even when the ground was covered knee-deep with snow."

She was silent, trying to picture such a creature. She said on a sigh, "I do not remember the last time I laughed openly."

He couldn't either.

"I have never danced in the snow."

"Mayhap you could also be silly every now and then—occasionally giggle and poke your fingers in my ribs."

"Aye, mayhap."

"Either kiss me again or let me sleep, Zarabeth."

"If I kiss you, will you force me?"

Anger roiled inside him. "You have already kissed me more times than I can count. But they weren't really a woman's deep kisses. Kiss me again, as a woman ought, and you will see."

She leaned down and pressed her mouth lightly to his. Her lips were dry and firm. He lay very quietly, not returning her kiss, letting her take what she wanted, letting her invade him, then withdraw, only to return again when she found no aggression in him. His sex swelled and throbbed but he didn't move. When would she realize that she belonged with him? When would she stop fighting herself and him?

She raised her head and stared down at him. Her look was brooding. Finally she said slowly, "I had forgotten the taste of you." He thought he would spill his seed at her words, just simple words, yet they shook him to his very core. She kissed him again, then shimmied down to press against his side and lay her cheek back on his shoulder.

"The next time you kiss me, Zarabeth, I will kiss you back and I will caress you and come inside you."

He felt her tremble at his words. "Mayhap in the future you will feel silly and laugh when we are making love. It doesn't have to be such a devoutly serious business."

She didn't know, and such a notion seemed strange to her. It seemed a very serious business.

The men were stirring. Magnus gave her another squeeze, then eased away from her. He rose and stretched, naked and lean and powerful in the soft morning light. He looked down at her and was pleased to see the candid interest in her eyes. She was staring at him quite openly. "I will fetch you one of my tunics to wear."

He smiled when she strapped Orm's wide leather belt around her hips, but he said nothing. He guessed wearing the sword made her feel she was in control. The sword banged against her leg whenever she took a step. Her legs were long and bare, as were her feet. He watched her try to untangle her hair with her fingers. He could have told her that she looked wild and beautiful, as savage as a warrior goddess. Then she rubbed her bottom and the image was swiftly gone. He laughed. He made certain she ate her fill before they left camp.

The day was hot, the sky clear. They rode near to the shore, the trees to their left, for there was no tracking to be done now and it was a quicker way back to Malek by this route. Magnus carried Zarabeth in front of him. She leaned her head back against his shoulder and dozed. She felt safe; she felt at peace. It was a strange feeling and she was loath to let it go. She fell deeply asleep with the scent of him in her nostrils, the gentle sway of the stallion beneath her, his arms holding her steady.

Ragnar's stallion came even with Thorgell. Magnus turned to see his sister regarding him solemnly. She said, "I want to know what you will tell our father."

"Mother already came to Malek, frantic to know if anyone had seen you. Now all know that you escaped our father's farmstead to meet him, Ingunn. What would you have me say? All know that you sacrificed your honor to him."

"I saved your wife's life."

"You did, but not because you care one whit about her, so do not pretend that you do. You hated to see Orm take another woman. You feared that he would want her and not you. Isn't that right?"

Ingunn was silent, but Ragnar said, "You speak harshly, Magnus."

"Ragnar, you speak blindly. Look well at her, speak

long with her, and listen to the feeling behind her words before you decide to take her."

Ingunn's eyes widened. "What do you mean? Take me? What is this, Magnus?"

Magnus stared between Thorgell's ears. "Ragnar wants you for a wife."

Ingunn seemed to swell up even as she sat there. "I don't want him! He is a lout and a boor and I have seen him fondle any female who chances to walk by him. He is no more faithful than a flea."

Magnus turned the full force of his anger on her and she drew back from the harshness of his expression, the coldness of his voice. "You are a fine one to accuse another of faithlessness. You who gave yourself to Orm. You want to reproach Ragnar? He is a man, not a maid whose virginity represents the value she places on herself."

"Did your precious Zarabeth come to you a virgin? She was wedded to an old man and he—"

"Hold your tongue, Ingunn, or I will grant Ragnar full permission to beat you now. We are speaking of you and why you call Ragnar a boor and a lout. Why?"

Ingunn rallied, for she had known Magnus all her life. His anger was swift to come and equally swift to dissipate. He was her brother, after all. "He treats me badly. He has always been rude toward me, always smirking at me."

"You sound like a sullen spoiled child. You deserve to be treated badly."

"He won't listen to me. He doesn't care how much I have suffered."

"He shows wisdom. As for your suffering, you brought any suffering you have endured upon yourself. You twist things, Ingunn, and you refuse to see your own hand in your woes. Your tongue is tangled about itself."

"Ragnar cares naught for me. He wants only to be allied with our family. He is vain and ambitious."

"I don't understand how he could care for you, but I shan't doubt his word. I believe he shows a lack of good judgment, but it is his patience to be tested if he takes you, not mine, thank Odin. As for our family, why, I cannot imagine a man who would not wish to be allied with us."

"I won't have him! Father won't make me take him. He cannot, it is not our way."

"You will do as you are bidden this time, for you have grievously wounded our family. I will encourage our father to hand you over to Ragnar. I gave you no schooling at all, more fool I, but Ragnar will bring you to submission. He will teach you to temper your damnable tongue."

Suddenly Ragnar was laughing, and both brother and sister looked at him with expressions so close it made him laugh all the harder. He went on laughing, more loudly, more deeply. Zarabeth stirred, came fully awake.

"What is it, Magnus?"

He frowned at the hoarseness of her voice, but she didn't need any more anger, even though it was directed toward another. He leaned down and kissed her ear. "It is Ragnar. He fancies that he will beat Ingunn until she falls faint with love for him."

"I cannot truly imagine that happening, Magnus."

"I won't have him!" Ingunn shrieked.

Ragnar stopped laughing. He released his horse's reins, grabbed Ingunn about the waist, and turned her to face him. "Listen to me, you silly woman. Whom will you have if not me?"

Ingunn slapped him hard. He wasn't expecting the blow and thus wasn't prepared. Both of them nearly fell from his horse's back. He thrashed until he regained his balance. He said nothing, merely stared at her. Ingunn tried to pull away. Then Ragnar smiled. He lifted her from the saddle and with one quick motion brought her over his thighs. He smacked her buttocks until she was squirming and screaming at him. He was laughing again, and his stallion was dancing wildly to the side. Ragnar paid no heed. With each smack he gave a dictum. "Ingunn, you will not gainsay me. You will obey me. You will sweeten your tongue. You will not flail me with it, but rather kiss me whenever I wish it. You will show me only winsome smiles. No more barbs will fly from your mouth."

Magnus urged Thorgell forward. Zarabeth buried her face in his tunic. It astounded her how life could rebound in such wide sweeps, from terror to laughter to indignation to insults. Ingunn was still yelling and Ragnar was still smacking her and laughing and telling her what she would do. Magnus was warm against her and she knew that she would come back into life and share in its pain and its laughter. She knew she could not much longer seek only to slip away from life and watch it from afar, remaining untouched and isolated.

They rode in silence for some time, distancing themselves from the others. Occasionally they heard Ingunn's sharp voice and more of Ragnar's laughter, as well as loudly shouted comments from the men.

Magnus drew to a halt beside a small clear lake, loosening Thorgell's reins so his stallion could drink. "Are you thirsty, Zarabeth?"

She was. They dismounted and she came down to her knees at the water's edge, cupped her hands, and scooped up the cold water. It tasted wonderful in her raw throat.

"Better?"

"Aye," she said, and rose, the sword clanging against her thigh.

Magnus stood looking over the viksfjord. "Egill is alive. I find it strange that I, a man of little imagination, dreamed he was alive, dreamed that he was also sold into slavery. Orm has much to answer for.''

"I am going with you."

He turned abruptly on his heel to face her. She was standing there clothed only in his tunic, that ridiculous man's belt hanging at her hips, the sword in its scabbard coming nearly to her foot. He smiled. "No."

She paid him no heed. The only sign she gave that she had heard him was that her chin went up. He went to her and took her hand in his, drawing her against his side. "I will keep you safe this time. You will remain with my parents until I return."

"Remain like a prisoner or a child with your parents? I have been a coward, Magnus, but no more. I must return with you to York. That is where we go, is it not?"

He shrugged.

"I know where Orm bought his land."

"Where?"

"I will not tell you until you promise you will take me with you."

"You will not force me into this, Zarabeth. I will simply ask Ingunn."

Zarabeth lied swiftly and cleanly. "She doesn't know. Orm told only me."

"I will ask her anyway. Come, we have a long way to ride yet before we can stop for the night."

Zarabeth gave a wistful look at the clear blue water. "Another bathing would be nice."

"Perhaps this evening," he said. He leaned down and kissed her. "If you are nice to me, perhaps I will bathe you myself this time."

He kissed her again, then tugged her to Thorgell, who was chewing on the thick water grass.

Their return to Malek in the early afternoon was a joyous occasion. Magnus allowed Ingunn to remain the night. She would be taken, by Ragnar, on the

morrow back to her parents' farmstead. She was silent
and sullen and Zarabeth wondered if the woman
would ever change, if she would ever forget her own
grievances long enough to be pleasant, long enough
to let others enjoy themselves.

Zarabeth fell back quickly into a familiar pattern.
A bountiful meal was prepared, fresh beer brought
out, cold and biting from the nets lowered in the viksfjord. The women served platters of broiled deer and
wild boar steaks. There were boiled peas and baked
cabbage with onions and potatoes braised in the burning embers. Zarabeth ate with the women, speaking
together of domestic matters while Magnus and the
men drank beer and discussed their voyage to the
Danelaw. They were leaving in three days. There was
fitting-up of the *Sea Wind* to be done, supplies to be
gathered and stowed, and the steering oar had yet to
be finished. Zarabeth said nothing more to Magnus.
She would go with him to the Danelaw. She simply
wasn't yet certain how she would manage it.

Zarabeth fell asleep curled up on the mistress's
chair, a tunic with needle and thread in her lap. Magnus stood over her, glancing at the material she was
sewing. It looked to be a tunic for him, and he was
inordinately pleased. The material was soft pale blue
linen. Her stitches were small and perfect. He loved
her so much at that moment, he wanted to shout with
it. He carefully removed the sewing materials from
her lap, then lifted her in his arms and carried her to
their bedchamber. He didn't light the lamp. It was
dark as a pit, since the single narrow window was
covered tightly.

He undressed her and himself.

He wanted to see her but decided lighting the lamp
would wake her. He sighed and covered both of them.
She was exhausted and he himself was feeling weary.
He fell asleep, his member heavy, his thoughts of his

wife, seeing her in her man's tunic, Orm's sword belt strapped around her hips. "It is now my sword," she'd informed him when he'd asked her if she wanted him to take it. "I won it fairly and I shall keep it."

He slept deeply until the voice came, soft and insistent in his ear.

"Do you remember the things you said to me in York, Magnus? You were arrogant and brash and daring and I found you vastly pleasing. You made me laugh and you shocked me and I wanted you so very much. You told me how you treated Cyra and I believed you mad. You said, so very seriously, that you wouldn't hurt me, even if I wished you to. You were so solemn, as if conferring a great favor on me. I thought you unbelievable and bold and wonderful. I still do."

"I also promised to please you, Zarabeth, but until now, I haven't much succeeded."

"Aye, you did promise, but I do not think it all your fault. You wanted me to come back to life and you could think of no other way to force me to." She wasn't in the least surprised that he was awake. "I have done much thinking, Magnus. It is time for me to leave—"

He sucked in his breath, fully awake now, instantly enraged with her. He lurched up, taking her with him. "I will never let you leave—"

"—or it is time for me to be your wife."

"Ah," he said, and she was surprised when a deep shudder went through him. He pulled her tight and they were naked and pressed against each other. He kissed her nose, her jaw, her eyes, smoothing her eyebrows with his fingertips, pushing her hair from her face, and saying, "I won't ever force you again. I could no longer bear it were you to lie beneath me crying, your hands fisted at your sides while I came inside you. I will no longer abide that, Zarabeth."

"Then I think you should lie on your back and I
will come over you."

She'd surprised him yet again. "Soon. I want to feel
all of you against me now." He moved over her, on
his elbows, his back slightly arched, his sex rubbing
against her, but not yet entering.

He leaned down to kiss her as he moved over her
breasts. This time it was different. She opened to him,
rubbing her hands up and down his back, down over
his buttocks, and she shivered at the feel of him, the
smoothness and warmth of his flesh, the depth and
contour of the muscles in his back. She moved her
legs, loving the heaviness of his thighs over hers, the
crinkling of his hair against her.

He felt her opening, the end of her resistance to
him. He lay still on her then, kissing her deeply, his
hands fisting in her hair, his sex pushing against her.
"Open your legs, Zarabeth," he said into her mouth.
When she eased them apart, he came up on his knees
between them and looked down at her.

He cursed, for he wanted to see all of her clearly.
He leaned forward and splayed his fingers, his hands
covering her breasts, kneading them now, then coming
downward to encircle her waist, lower still to rest on
her belly, then banding around her to take her buttocks. He lifted her to his mouth. As much as he
wanted her, he refused to take any chances that she
wouldn't gain her woman's pleasure. He brought her
to his mouth, and when his warm lips touched her,
she cried out. He smiled as he caressed her with his
mouth, and when she was thrashing beneath him,
panting, he stopped a moment and whispered to her,
"I want you to scream for me now, Zarabeth. I want
to feel your shuddering, feel your legs stiffen, feel you
opening and yielding to me." He lowered her then
and eased his middle finger into her. "I want to feel
you convulse around my finger." He began caressing

her again, and his finger was moving deeply inside her, and she screamed, arching upward, her eyes wild and savage.

Her hands gripped his shoulders, her fingers digging into his flesh, and she screamed again, and at the moment of her scream, other screams and cries came to him . . . but no, they were within him, those screams, deep inside him, and he wanted her desperately.

Zarabeth quieted but the screams continued, more loudly now, and Magnus heard his name yelled out. He trembled to come into her now, but another yell pierced through him. He shook his head, trying to get a hold on himself, trying to understand.

"Magnus!" It was Tostig's voice, and he yelled again, this time flinging open the bedchamber door.

"By Thor, Magnus! We're being attacked!"

25

Magnus leapt from the bed, grabbed his trousers, and tugged them on as he said, "Quickly, Zarabeth, dress yourself, then wait in here until I see what is happening."

He was gone and Zarabeth heard the shouts and screams. Then she smelled smoke. The longhouse was on fire.

She was dressed in a moment and running into the main hall. The smoke was growing heavy, for the roof was afire. The thick beams still held, but for how long?

"Zarabeth! Quickly, get everyone out of here. Save what you can!"

She didn't think, didn't allow herself to slow. She gave orders, calmed where she could, moved quickly, not thinking, trying not to breathe in the ever-thickening smoke. Men, women, and children, all were carrying out their belongings and a chair or a chest or cooking implements. Two women were carrying out the huge upright loom, all the shuttles they could carry, and Eldrid's distaff.

Eldrid! Where was she?

Zarabeth ran back into the bedchambers. All were empty. Save for one. Eldrid lay on her side on the dirt floor and she was unconscious, overcome by the smoke. Zarabeth grabbed her beneath the arms and dragged her out into the main hall. Thank the gods

one of the men was there. She shouted to him and he
lifted the old woman over his shoulder as if she were
naught but a bag of cabbages. Zarabeth grabbed the
rest of the cooking pots, directed the others to carry
whatever they could hold. Clothes and blankets were
dragged along the dirt floor, outside to safety. The
smoke was thick now, and her still-raw throat burned
and she was coughing, her eyes watering. Magnus was
there beside her then, and he grabbed her arm.
"Come, it is unsafe now."

"Your chair!"

One of the men shouted that he would fetch it.

She saw Magnus' tunic on her own chair and she
wrenched free of him, stumbling, as she ran to fetch
it.

Magnus wanted to beat her, but when he saw the
smile on her smoke-blackened face when she held up
the tunic, he could only shake his head.

They were all outside now, all their people gathered
around to watch the longhouse explode into flames.
Their faces were blank with disbelief. It wasn't possible, yet it was happening and they were watching it
happen. The other huts surrounding the longhouse
were made of stone, but their thatch roofs were
quickly aflame. The heat grew stronger and stronger.

Zarabeth was looking around, trying to count heads,
to see that everyone was safe. Eldrid was coughing,
sucking in the fresh air. At least she was alive. She
saw then old Hollvard, the gatekeeper, and he was
lying huddled on his side, an arrow sticking obscenely
out of his back. Two other men, both guards, lay near,
both dead.

What had happened hit her full force at that
moment. She turned to her husband, waiting for him
to finish giving instructions. Then he turned on his
heel and she grabbed his sleeve.

"Hollvard," she gasped, "someone killed him, Magnus! And two others as well."

"Aye. Stay here. We are bringing up more water from the viksfjord. It won't help much, but maybe we can save the food-store hut and the bathouse."

He was gone from her, and Zarabeth stood there feeling helpless and deadened. Hollvard, killed! But who? That old man who had always been kind to her, from the very first, even when she had worn the slave collar.

Then she knew. She felt such rage that she shook with it. Slowly, with no show of outward feeling, she made her way through their people, studying every face, speaking a soothing word here, a word of encouragement there.

Ingunn wasn't there. But Zarabeth had known she wouldn't be.

It was when she found Ragnar, near to one of the storage huts, a sword thrust through his shoulder, that she raised her voice and cried out in shock and rage.

She fell to her knees beside him. He was still alive, but the blood was flowing freely from the wound high on his left shoulder. She ran to the well, grabbing Magnus' new tunic from the ground as she went. One of the men had filled his bucket, and she quickly dipped the soft wool into the water, wringing it out as she ran. When she reached Ragnar, she cleaned the wound as best she could and pressed the tunic against it to stop the bleeding.

She wasn't aware that she was crying until Magnus gently laid his hand on her shoulder and said quietly, "Come, Zarabeth, let the men carry Ragnar into the open, where there is less smoke."

An hour later, Malek's people were still huddled in small groups near the barley fields, staring at the smoldering ruins of the longhouse and the roofless huts surrounding it. The palisade walls were standing in places, straight and upright and untouched. Just a few feet away there was naught but smoldering timber left.

Five people were dead. Ragnar was still alive and Eldrid was attending him.

The animals were safe and the fields were untouched, but the destruction within the once-secure compound was nearly complete. Zarabeth looked over at her husband. He was speaking quietly to one of the slaves, a young man whose eyes were still red and tearing from all the smoke. She watched Magnus speak to many more of the people, then saw him pull away and walk off toward the pine forest at the back of the palisade. He stopped and turned, and she saw such naked rage in his face that she drew back.

He stood there for many minutes looking at his once-flourishing farmstead. It was gone now, years of work and tending. But it was but stones and lumber, she wanted to tell him. They had saved nearly all the things from within the longhouse, including his chest. She would help him. They would rebuild. They still had their crops, their lives, their belongings. They still had each other.

Zarabeth looked away, unable to bear it. It was past dawn now, and soon everyone would be hungry. She had several men collect stones to stack around a small fire pit. Then she had long stakes hammered into the ground, deep notches cut into the tops. Then the men lowered a cross-stake carefully into the carved notches. Chains were wrapped around the top stake. Now Zarabeth could hang pots from the chains. She kept busy, kept toiling so that she wouldn't have time to think.

Ragnar was still alive, but all of them knew it would be a close thing. Eldrid stayed with him, wiping his face with wet cloths, feeding him water, waiting for Helgi to come with her store of medicines.

It was in early afternoon that Magnus' parents

arrived, bringing no more than a half-dozen people with them. Mattias and Glyda hadn't come. It was soon obvious why. They had had to leave their farmstead well-guarded, Mattias in charge. They would take no chances that Orm would attack while they were gone. Indeed, all wondered if that was his plan.

Zarabeth listened to Magnus and his father speaking; rather, his father was yelling and tugging at his hair.

"By Thor, that a daughter of mine could betray us thus! How could she do it? Does Orm have such an unnatural hold over her?" His question wasn't meant to be answered. He fell into mumbling curses and shaking his head.

Helgi said in a low voice to Zarabeth, "No one suspected? You sensed nothing?"

Zarabeth remained thoughtful and silent, saying finally, "Nay. She was quiet when we returned. She stayed by herself for the most part. She did nothing to gainsay me. She made no snide remarks. Ragnar kept after her, teasing her, ordering her about, but she didn't seem to mind it. Now, of course, when I think back, she was too quiet, as if she were biding her time, waiting."

"But why?" Helgi struck her palm against her thigh and winced from her own blow. "If she wanted to remain with him, escape Norway with him, she didn't have to save you! She did not have to pretend to strike him and flee with you."

"I was certain that she struck him hard, Helgi. Now I don't know. But she seemed overwrought when he pretended to want me and not her. He taunted her with it. I had believed she'd struck him more to punish him than to save me, to pay him back for humiliating her. But it mattered not, at least then."

"But why plan this diversion—and that is what it was—and return to Malek? Why?"

"I will tell you why, Mother." It was Magnus and he was standing over his mother, his shoulders squared, his face hard as stone. "Orm probably decided that Zarabeth would be too much trouble. She would never come to him willingly. He would have had to kill her, and he wanted revenge against me more than he wanted her or her death. He also wanted more wealth before he left Norway. He must have followed us back closely. I didn't really wonder why he hadn't stayed and fought me, for he had only two men to my five. He may be mad, but he isn't a fool. It wasn't ever his plan to stand and fight. He must have somehow gotten to Ingunn—that, or it was all a sham and planned to happen just as it did.

"Why else did he continue to divert from the direct route to the fjord and his vessel? I don't know. Zarabeth told me that Ingunn continually pressed him to hurry, that I would come. There are many questions and no answers as yet. But I do know that all my jewels are gone. All my gold and silver ornaments and coins are gone. They were kept in a cask behind a hollowed-out log near the front of the longhouse. All Ingunn had to do was wait until there was panic from the fire, then calmly retrieve the cask. Why, had anyone asked her what she was about, she could have simply said she was saving the cask for me."

"But you could have been killed!" Helgi turned away, her shame and rage palpable.

"And Orm was waiting outside the palisade for her to bring him the jewels and coins. He killed Hollvard and is responsible for five other deaths as well."

His mother still looked stunned and ill, and Magnus hugged her to him. "I suppose we are lucky that Orm didn't try to take Zarabeth again. Perhaps he waited after the fire was blazing to see if she would separate herself from me. But she didn't. The bastard was out there, Father, watching all the destruction he had

brought about. Ingunn must be punished for this. I
am sorry, but she is no longer my sister. She is as
much my enemy as is Orm. At least my vessel is
intact. There were a dozen men working on the *Sea
Wind*, and thus Orm couldn't take her or destroy her.
I vow his death before the summer is over."

Zarabeth felt weighed down with his hatred, with
his vow, with the stolid endurance he practiced. He
worked harder than she did, cleaning away the burned
timber, looking to salvage, looking to repair.

At the end of a very long day, as they sat about the
outdoor cook fire, all warm with the blankets Helgi
had brought, Zarabeth thought she had never been so
weary in her life. She could think of nothing to say.
She lay on her side, her head on Magnus' thighs, listening to him speaking to his father and the men,
slaves and freeman alike.

She felt the strength of him beneath her cheek and
remembered what he had done to her so few hours
before. He had given her a woman's pleasure and it
had made her wild with feeling, torn her away from
any barriers she might have erected against him. But
when she had screamed with her pleasure, there had
been other screams as well . . . She shuddered. Magnus gently stroked her arm, now listening to his father.

"A father should not have to bear this," Harald was
saying. "How many men will you take to the Danelaw, Magnus?"

"I cannot go after them yet. First we must rebuild.
All must be secure before winter comes, else it will
all be for naught."

"Mattias and I will be here to help you with many
of our men."

"Thank you, Father."

Zarabeth awoke, wincing at the hard ground beneath, yet wonderfully warm from Magnus' body

curved around hers. His hand was cupping her breast, her head resting on his upper arm. She nestled closer and he kissed her ear, whispering, "Nay, don't do that, for I cannot take you now."

She smiled and turned to face him, snuggling against him. "What will happen, Magnus?"

"We will rebuild. I promise that you will know no want, come this winter, Zarabeth."

"All I want this winter is to have you with me."

He felt himself swelling with pleasure at her words. He hugged her tightly to him, his arms enclosing her closely. "When the snow is higher than your head, you will want more than my warmth."

"Perhaps. I also pray that we will have Egill returned to us as well. Magnus, I am so sorry. If I had not come here, if Ingunn had not hated me so much—"

"I doubt it would have made any difference to her," he said sharply. "Bleat not, Zarabeth, for I won't allow you to carry any guilt for this."

"I pray you will cease likening me to a goat, Magnus."

"A ewe, sweeting." He kissed her mouth and hugged her tightly against him. "I want you very much. You can feel that, for I am obvious in my feelings. But I will make it up to you, Zarabeth, and to myself as well."

Their people were beginning to stir and Magnus roused himself, coming up onto his elbow. He looked toward the burned-out longhouse, and rage seared through him again. His grandfather had built the longhouse and had seen that it was Magnus' upon his death. Now it was gone. Still, it was only timber and waddle and daub and thick beams and thatch. Unlike a life, all the buildings could be replaced.

Magnus said aloud to Zarabeth, "I pray that Ragnar will live."

Ragnar worsened that day despite the poultice Helgi prepared for his wound. His body burned and he spoke of strange things, of memories from long ago, Magnus said. Zarabeth remained at his side, bathing him with a cool wet cloth, praying hard. By the following evening, he was still and Helgi was saying, "He sleeps. I think he will live."

Zarabeth rose, so relieved she could shout. Just as suddenly, she felt the ground tilting upward, felt herself swaying as if pushed by unseen hands. She felt light-headed. She collapsed where she stood.

As darkness closed over her mind, she heard Magnus shout. She wished she could speak to him, but there was only blackness now, shrouding her mind, and she succumbed to it.

"It must be exhaustion," Harald said, looking down at his daughter-in-law, held in his son's arms. Magnus was sitting in his master's chair, which was in splendid isolation, Zarabeth in his lap.

"Aye, I should not have let her work so hard, not after her ordeal at Orm's hands."

"Nonsense," said Helgi. "Zarabeth is no frail little female. That is not it at all."

"What is it, then, woman?"

Helgi smiled at her husband's intolerant tone. "You cannot bear not to know everything, can you, Harald?" she remarked as she patted Zarabeth's forehead with a wet cloth. "You men must always have the last word, the last right word about everything. Well, this time you don't."

"Woman, I swear I will discipline you if you do not mind your tongue!"

Had Magnus not been so worried, he would have laughed. The thought of his father raising his hand to his wife was ludicrous. Helgi was smiling, knowing her husband as well as did Magnus.

"So what is wrong with the girl?" Harald finally asked. "Since you are the all-wise witch."

"She is carrying Magnus' babe."

Magnus nearly dropped Zarabeth. He stared at his mother. "She is with child?"

"Aye, I imagine so. When she awakens I will question her. There are very simple signs, you know, my son."

He sat there clutching his unconscious wife to his chest, thinking back, trying to remember when last she had suffered her woman's bleeding. It was not too long before. It was when Lotti had drowned and Egill had disappeared. He stared up at his mother, who was smirking toward her husband.

He said slowly, "I am afraid."

Helgi forgot her game with her husband. She knelt down beside Magnus' chair and gently began smoothing Zarabeth's thick hair from her face. The hair was soft and so very rich. She marveled at the color. Zarabeth's brows were darker, a rich brownish-red, and her lashes were thick and the same shade as her brows. Her cheekbones were well-sculptured, her skin smooth and very white. Helgi thought of a little girl who would somehow look like her son and Zarabeth also, and shook her head at herself. "Why? She is not like Dalla, Magnus. You have known her well. Is not her belly wide, her bones well-spaced? Her hips are not narrow."

"I don't know. When I have looked at her, I had no thought of childbearing in my mind."

His father laughed. "I can understand that. Married to this old woman here, though, it is difficult for me to remember such things."

"Ha! There is more gray in your hair, old man, than in mine!"

Magnus looked toward the smoldering remains of his home, his mother's laughter in his ears. No matter what seemed to happen in life, no matter how hateful, how sad, how awful things got, there always seemed to be something left, someone there, that made him want to continue. He lowered his head to Zarabeth's forehead. He had seen her, decided he had wanted her, and given her wishes little or no thought at all. He had always been confident, so sure of himself and what he was. He had given her a large dose of what it was he wished to have, never doubting that he would have her. If she had purposely betrayed him, well, he had deserved it. As for his own behavior, he knew all he had brought her was unhappiness and pain and humiliation.

Now his child grew in her womb. It was terrifying, and yet, at the same time, he felt incredible joy. He felt the wet of his tears on his face.

When Zarabeth awoke, it was to see her husband's face close to hers, and he was staring at her intently. "What happened to me? I don't understand. I'm lying on you and—"

"You fainted."

It was odd, but she was lying in her husband's lap. Slowly she raised her hand and touched her fingers to his cheek. "Are these tears?"

"Aye."

"But why? I was merely tired, mayhap overtired. Nothing more." She grinned a bit unsteadily. "My life of late has been a bit exciting and just a bit unpredictable."

He dipped his head down and kissed her lightly on her closed mouth. "Have you ever fainted before, Zarabeth?"

She shook her head. "I am not subject to such nonsense, Magnus."

"That is what my mother said."

"Why were you crying? Is there something wrong with me? . . . Oh, no, is Ragnar all right?"

"He is fine. Do you have wide hips?"

"If you will let me rise, I will try to crane my head about and look."

"Hold still." He pulled her a bit higher over his left arm. His right hand went to her belly and he gently splayed his fingers over her. Her hipbones were beyond his reach. "That is good, I suppose. I will tell my mother of my discovery and see what she thinks."

She tried to push his hand away. "Magnus, there are people everywhere! Someone will see!"

"I am your husband. Let them look."

"Let me up now. I feel fine, and it is silly for me to be sitting on you in this ridiculous chair when there is naught about but . . ." She had pulled herself abruptly upright as she had spoken. She stared at him, and suddenly her face was as white as her belly. "Oh," she said, and fell back against his arm. Suddenly there was fear in her eyes. "What is wrong with me? I thought I would faint again, and I felt so dizzy . . ."

"You carry my babe."

". . . and light-headed. I felt light-headed before, but I believed I was merely hungry, that I was afraid of Orm and what would happen, merely . . . *What?*"

He grinned at her. "Nay, don't move, I don't want you to faint again. It scared all the wickedness out of me. That's right, just hold still. You carry my babe."

She stared up at him, unable to grasp the reality of it. No, no, reality was Lotti drowning, reality was Egill disappearing, reality was lying on the ground naked with Orm over her . . . "I am with child? You are certain?"

"Aye."

His eyes blazed with pleasure, the blue so vivid, so startling, that she couldn't look away, nor did she want to.

"I have never had a child before."

She sounded lost and afraid and strangely bereft, and he didn't know which emotion to address first.

"Except Lotti. She was my child."

Now he knew where to begin. "Zarabeth, we are not going to replace Lotti. She was special and she will always remain in our hearts and in our memories. Nothing can change what she was to us." He drew a deep breath. "I cannot claim for certain that Egill is alive. It would be foolish of me to assume that I will find him and bring him back safely with me. If he, like Lotti, is dead, then both of the children will remain in our hearts. This child . . . we will pray that he reaches manhood and that he knows the health and happiness his parents will know."

She leaned her cheek against his chest and he held her there, his face against the top of her head.

"What will happen?" she asked, her voice muffled against his tunic.

Magnus opened his mouth to speak, when there came a furious roar from behind him. He slewed about in his chair, clutching Zarabeth to him, to see Ragnar trying to rise, Eldrid attempting to hold him down. He was yelling and cursing, his arms flailing about. He struck Eldrid away and staggered to his feet, weaving where he stood.

26

Zarabeth couldn't bear Ragnar's pain. If she could have held Ingunn's throat between her hands, she surely would have squeezed the life out of her. Ragnar was shuddering with pain and with the knowledge of what Ingunn had done to him, to Magnus, to Malek.

"Orm struck me himself," he said over and over, even as he tried to pull free of Magnus. "She watched. She stood near him and watched. She told him that I had beaten her. *Beaten* her, Magnus!" Ragnar stopped, sucking in air, his face gray with pain, clammy with sweat, trying to get free and get hold of himself at the same time. "Then she told him not to kill me, she told him that I deserved to feel pain for what I had done to her. I deserved to look the fool."

Eldrid was trying to soothe him, clucking at him, and he knocked away her hand.

"Lie down, Ragnar," Magnus said. He didn't wait for his friend to respond. He simply picked him up and laid him flat on his back. "Now, you will stay there. What was your intent? To go after Orm now, this minute? Control your rage or use it to heal yourself. We will all go soon enough, and you will be with us. Nay, Ragnar, keep your fury under your tongue for the moment, and obey Eldrid. She doesn't want to see you underground. Nor do I."

Magnus, satisfied that his friend would hold his peace, turned back to his wife. "How do you feel?"

In truth she felt weak and dizzy, and her stomach was pitching. "I'm all right," she said instead, and tried for a sickly smile. Magnus merely shook his head at her, looked back at Ragnar, then lifted her in his arms. "The both of you will rest. I fear, though, that Ragnar will regain his bloom before you do. Nay, hush, Zarabeth. I want you happy and well."

And that, she thought, settling down on a pile of blankets, her back propped against a tree, was that. She was asleep within minutes.

It was the oddest thing, Zarabeth thought later. The slave hut hadn't been touched by the flames. It was the only building left intact. More men arrived from Harald's farmstead, and rebuilding began. It was a slow process, for the old wood still smoldered, and several times men turning up stumps were burned when embers flamed up.

The sound of falling trees became a familiar one. The raw wood smelled sweet and soft. They could use only oak, and since there were few oak trees, treks to find them took time. Everything took time.

Helgi remained, helping Zarabeth oversee the cooking and the washing and all the other myriad chores. The men erected thatched huts, for Magnus knew it would rain and he wanted to protect Zarabeth.

Whilst the rebuilding went on, Magnus went quietly about refitting the *Sea Wind* and finishing repairs. Anger burned in his gut, and it grew each time he viewed the devastation of his home. His grandfather had selected the name Malek for his farmstead, but none knew where the name had come from, even his father. In truth, no one cared now, not even Magnus. Malek belonged to him, and it would remain his.

On the fourth day after the fire, Haftor Ingolfsson arrived, two of his sons with him.

They viewed the destroyed farmstead and stayed to help. They wanted to know if Magnus knew the

whereabouts of Orm. Magnus denied any knowledge.
He lied smoothly, and Zarabeth kept her thoughts to
herself. The Ingolfssons were huge men, fair-haired,
well-knit, and fierce. Their anger at Orm was great.
They wanted to find him badly.

"Why did you not tell them the truth?" Zarabeth
asked Magnus one night when they lay side by side
under the stars. The night was warm, so there was no
need to retreat under the thatched hut roof.

"I want him myself."

She accepted that. She sighed and pressed closer.
She felt a soft pulsing in her belly. Magnus had not
made love to her since that night of the attack and
the fire.

"I also want you."

She smiled and moved closer, pleasure filling her at
his words.

"But I'm afraid that I will hurt you."

She came up over him, her face but inches from
his. She bit the end of his nose and grinned. "What
happens to a man if he does not relieve himself?"

"Choose another way of saying it, Zarabeth."

"Very well. If you do not spend your man's passion,
what happens?"

"I become a bent old relic, my belly swells, my hair
turns white, and my teeth rot out."

Her laughter rang out, free and joyous. He stilled,
satisfaction filling him at the sweet sound.

"Oh, Magnus, all that? Is that a white hair I see?"
She was laughing, tugging at his blond hair, pulling at
it, looking closely. "No, not a single white strand.
Now, show me your teeth."

He obligingly opened his mouth and she studied his
white teeth, then kissed him. "I won't let you up to
see if you are yet bending. Ah, husband, we must
ensure that you do not become this old relic of a

man." She ran her hand over his flat belly. "Ah, no swelling here as yet."

"Nay, 'tis you who will do the belly-swelling."

He kissed her, knowing that surely some of their people were close by, not yet asleep, yet he didn't care. He whispered in her ear, "If I take you, will you scream when your pleasure comes? Tell me truly, Zarabeth, shall I have to place my hand over your mouth?"

"Aye," she said, and giggled. "It is your own fault, so cast not the blame on me when it is you who make me howl like a demented wolf."

He shifted, gently shoving her flat on her back. He was over her now, looking down at her laughing face. "I believe the only way that I am to save myself from baiting and taunting by my men is to proceed thus. Nay, say nothing. I am your husband and I will do things the way I wish to."

He kissed her until he felt the yielding deep within her, the acceptance of him not only as her husband but also as a man. He ignored the restless twisting of her body beneath him, holding her still beneath him until she punched him in the arm.

"All right," he said, and kissed her again, only this time he caressed her breast with his hand, kneading her gently. "You're larger," he said between kisses. "Tell me if I hurt you."

He didn't, and she wanted him. But he refused to allow her to touch him, to go beyond the pace he himself had set.

Finally, when she tried to bite his tongue, he laughed, his voice deep and warm in her mouth, and eased his fingers up beneath her gown to caress her woman's flesh.

When he began to rhythmically caress her, she had no way to control herself, for the feelings were compelling, too full, quickly becoming uncontrollable. He encouraged her as she keened softly, deep in her throat.

"You are doing well, Zarabeth. It delights me, this pleasure in you."

And when she stiffened and arched taut as a bow, he deepened the pressure and took her cries into his mouth.

He relished each of the small quivers that followed her release. Gently he eased her onto her side away from him and came into her. He nibbled on her ear and she tried to twist about so she could kiss him some more, but he wouldn't allow it. "Hold still," he said. "Let me come deeper . . . aye, that's it. Let me take you . . ."

Zarabeth pushed back hard against him and he groaned. He gripped her hips in his large hands, controlling the depth of his thrusts until it was too much for him and he buried his face in her hair, and she felt his moans to her very soul. This, she thought, was what was real. This was sharing and knowing and pleasing and being pleased. It was trust and belonging and it was wonderful.

It was Tostig who found it and brought it to Zarabeth. She was sewing, one of the few occupations the women deemed suitable for her. The day was hot and the sounds of building and men's laughter and cursing filled the air. She looked up at him and smiled. "Aye, Tostig, how go you?"

"I am fine, mistress, 'tis just that . . ." He stopped and stuck out the piece of cloth nearly a foot in length. It was a jagged strip of wool dyed a soft blue, faded now to almost gray from exposure to the elements.

She raised her face. "What is it? Where did you find it?"

"In amongst some leaves at the base of a pine tree,

just over there, on the outjutting land. We must have overlooked it when we were first searching for Egill."

Zarabeth felt her heart thud, loud, slow strokes. Her fingers clutched the wool. She flew to her feet, yelling, "Magnus! Magnus!"

Tostig caught her arm. "It is the little girl's, isn't it, mistress?"

She looked at him, her eyes wild and vague. "Aye, it must be . . . Magnus!"

He heard her scream his name and bounded forward. He saw her standing beside Tostig, and she looked white and ill and she was weaving where she stood.

"Zarabeth!"

She whirled about at his voice, picked up her skirt, and ran toward him, shouting, "It is her, Magnus, it is!"

She drew up, weaving, and just as suddenly she turned utterly white and fell. Tostig tried to catch her, but he was off-balance and she bore him to the ground with her.

When she awoke, she was lying in her husband's lap, and he was sitting in his chair, now set beneath a pine tree. "It is, Magnus, it is hers, I know it! It wasn't in the water, it was on the land, at the base of a pine tree—"

"Mayhap, but you mustn't—"

"Did Tostig not tell you where he found it? It wasn't anywhere near the water. Lotti didn't drown!"

"You are certain the wool strip is from the gown Lotti was wearing that day?"

He saw that she wasn't completely certain. She was breathing hard, still too weak to sit up. He held her closer. "Easy, now, easy."

"I think so. Eldrid would know. If it is Lotti's, she made it for her."

"Did she not make gowns for the other little girls using the same wool?"

She had, and Zarabeth was forced to nod.

"We will see. Bring her here."

Eldrid did know. None of the wool used in the gowns was exactly the same. She looked at the strip of wool, clapped her hands to her face, and shrieked.

Zarabeth looked up at Magnus' grim face. "Where is she? In the Danelaw with Egill? Orm took them both, didn't he? Do you think Orm saved her? Do you think he was watching and pulled her from the water? Or perhaps Egill saved her and Orm captured both of them over there, on the outjutting land, out of the sight of you or your men. But why did he leave that rude drawing showing Egill, and nothing to show Lotti? Why?"

York, Capital of the Danelaw
One of King Guthrum's Manor Houses

The Viking children amused her, the boy so protective of the little girl, yet proud and stolid, both of them. It was rare that they spoke, and when one of them did, it was usually the boy, Egill. The little girl spoke only the boy's name. That single word seemed to convey a wealth of meaning to him, all depending on the tone and lilt of her voice. They made quaint signs to each other, their own private language, and Cecilia thought it clever. If they spoke of her, well, she was beautiful, gentle and kind to them, so their opinion of her could not be bad.

Guthrum had presented them to her on her twentieth birthday, smiling as he had said, "For my beautiful Cecilia, two children to do your bidding as I do, only they are small and won't intrude whilst they carry out your wishes."

She had expected jewels and had pouted for two days until she realized that her uncle and lover, also the king of the Danelaw, had provided her with a very efficient means of communicating with him whenever she wished to see him. No one paid attention to a little boy or to a little girl, particularly to slaves. One or the other would carry a token of affection or a message to the king's chambers if need be, and no one thought about it, even Guthrum's wife, that jealous bitch, Sigurd.

Cecilia sighed. She was bored. Guthrum should have already arrived, but he hadn't yet come. He was likely closeted with his men, laughing and crowing at the news of more lightning raids into King Alfred's Wessex. That, or he was likely immersed in strategies for Alfred's final defeat, for the Saxon king had forced a treaty on him some years before and also forced him to mouth prayers to the Christian God. Aye, when need be, Guthrum could be as pious as one of Alfred's bishops.

Cecilia picked up a honeyed almond and ate just a part of it. She smiled. It was just like Guthrum. He always was fond of nibbling at the edges of the English kingdom, always rubbing his age-spotted hands together at the huge revenues coming into his coffers.

Of course, he always denied any knowledge of raids into King Alfred's lands when angry messages arrived from Alfred. He would shake his head, look mournful, and feign distress and send the messenger on his way, his palm filled with silver coin.

Cecilia looked again at the children. She frowned this time. 'Twas a very handsome Viking named Orm Ottarsson who had presented Guthrum with the boy and girl, along with more silver coins than Cecilia could count, in return for removing a Saxon family from rich farmlands on the River Thurlow, lands he wanted for himself. She'd seen the man, and found herself impressed with his arrogance and his sleekness. She thought herself a clever woman to his clever man, and thus tried to seek him out. But he had left York to return to Norway. It was depressing, but Cecilia knew that he would return, and when he did, why, then she would see.

Cecilia rose and walked into the small walled garden outside her bedchamber. The stone walls were eight feet high with roses climbing over the top, covered with red and white blossoms. There was a small fountain in the center of the garden, surrounded by an old Roman mosaic, rectangular in shape. It was still intact, showing strange seaweed-draped creatures rising from the sea, mating with the fierce Celts. Egill and Lotti were there, and he was speaking to her, using his hands as he spoke, as if to give emphasis to his words. She drew closer to listen.

"Say it again, Lotti. Come on, say it."

Lotti made some slurred sounds, but Cecilia understood. The little girl had said "good morning." What was going on here?

"Good morning to you," Cecilia said gaily as she walked toward the children. The boy paled and took a protective step closer to the little girl.

They were both garbed in white wool tunics that were lightly belted with soft blue pleated leather at the waist. The tunics were sleeveless and came to their knees. The garments told others that they were slaves, but the soft, excellent quality of the wool also indicated that their master or mistress was of a generous nature. The children were fine-looking, and that pleased Cecilia. The little girl's hair was a rich ginger color and her eyes were an odd golden hue. She showed promise of great beauty when she became older, but that didn't bother Cecilia. She didn't like to be surrounded with ugliness, even in little girl slaves.

"Lotti," Cecilia said to the child, "go pick me a red rose and be quick about it. The king will be here soon and I wish to wear it in my hair." She patted her thick brown hair as she spoke.

Lotti darted a glance toward Egill, and he moved his hands quickly and easily, pointing to the rosebush.

Cecilia didn't notice. She was studying a scratch on the back of her hand, wondering where it had come from.

Egill waited, hoping that Lotti would pluck a red one and not a white one. They hadn't yet made up signs for colors. He waited, tense and stiff, watching her.

She broke off a red rose and he felt a flood of relief. He had no idea what would happen if the woman realized Lotti couldn't hear and spoke only very little. Lotti handed Cecilia the rose and Cecilia gave her an absent pat on the head, as one would a dog that had performed well.

Egill felt naught but contempt for the woman and her ridiculous vanity. About King Guthrum, he didn't know what to think. The man was older than Egill's grandfather, yet he tried to pretend to youth, tried to caress and pinch Cecilia as if he were her lover and a young man of passion. And Cecilia played the game with him. Egill had first thought to tell the king who he was, but then he'd heard Guthrum tell one of his council, a man who leered at Cecilia behind the king's back, that he was pleased the children were Viking get. He would see for himself if Viking children would become as dangerous as their sires in captivity. Egill had realized then that they knew they were his own countrymen. He didn't care. He was amused.

He wondered if perhaps the king knew his father. As yet he hadn't sensed a right time to approach him. Guthrum had an uncertain temper. Egill wasn't stupid. He had no intention of angering this man who held the power of life and death over him and Lotti.

Egill brooded. He thought of Orm Ottarsson, who

had taken him and Lotti even as they had lain sodden and gasping on the shore of the outjutting point, trying to suck life into their bodies. Egill had seen Lotti facedown in the shallow water and dragged her out, tearing the binding water reeds from her. He'd nearly drowned himself, but he wouldn't have cared if the little girl had died. He had pounded her chest and her back and finally she'd begun to breathe again, wretching. And then he'd looked up and there was Orm Ottarsson staring down at them, smiling. For a moment Egill thought he would return them to his father. He'd wrapped them up in warm blankets and had taken them away. When Egill had asked Orm what he intended, the man had struck him hard and laughed. He had given them as a bribe to the king. And that was another problem. Surely then the king would believe Orm's word and not that of a boy who was also a slave. Egill didn't know what to do.

He missed his father; he saw him in dreams, tall and fierce, his eyes going remote and sad when he looked inward, thinking of his only son. Egill knew his father must believe him dead, for he'd considered all the possibilities, seeing in his mind's eye how his father and his men would have searched for him, and, not finding him, would conclude that he had died somehow with Lotti or been killed and dragged away by wild animals.

He saw that Lotti had fallen to her knees and was raptly studying the Roman mosaic. She found it fascinating, her small fingers tracing over each of the brightly colored figures. Cecilia, having placed the rose in her hair, was now looking about for something to do. Egill thought her a useless creature. Even Cyra, who had been his father's mistress, hadn't been useless, not completely.

"Egill."

Lotti was excited by one of the tiles. Egill gave her

a tolerant smile and walked to her, dropping to his knees beside her.

The tiles showed a very handsome man wearing nothing but a strange white pleated cloth wrapped around his waist and held with a wide leather belt. He wore a golden helmet on his head. He was large, muscular, and looked to be very sure of himself. He was standing at the bow of a boat, men bent over oars behind him, and he had his sword drawn and was looking toward the horizon.

The handsome man looked like his father.

Egill made a sound in his throat and Lotti quickly swiveled around and placed her hand on his arm.

She was smiling and nodding. In the next tile the man was ashore, his sword still pointed at an unseen enemy, and he was ready to strike. In the final tile, there was the enemy, a monster cloaked in thick dark smoke, writhing and hissing. The handsome man severed the monster's neck with his sword.

"Father will save us," Egill whispered. "It is a portent." He heard footsteps and turned quickly. It wasn't Cecilia; it was King Guthrum, and Egill felt both fear and hope build inside him. The king looked to be in a temperate mood today. Egill looked at the battle-scarred king, his face seamed and leathery from a life spent in the sun, his shoulders bent slightly forward, his thick ebony hair threaded with gray, as was his short beard. His clothing was rich with golden thread.

Lotti was very silent, her eyes on the king. Her hand slipped into Egill's. They waited, watchful and wary.

King Guthrum nodded to them, not really paying them any heed. He was speaking to another man, one who was garbed like a soldier. Guthrum called out suddenly, "Bring us Rhenish wine, boy."

Egill didn't want to leave. He wanted to listen to

the men. He turned quickly to Lotti and made signs for her to watch the men and try to understand what they were saying; then he walked quickly away toward the antechamber where he would find one of Cecilia's house servants.

The king's soldier, Aslak, was saying in a fierce voice, "I tell you we must cease these silly woman's taunts, sire. We must gather in force and attack Alfred. The damned Saxons run hither and yon, without direction. The treaty with King Alfred means nothing. You have said so many times."

The king was stroking his beard. "Aye, 'tis true. What is it you want to do, Aslak?"

"I would lead men to Chippenham itself, to the very gates of the king's house. We would travel swiftly and stealthily, and that would give us the surprise. We would take all the gold and coin we can carry. Alfred must be shown that a Viking bows to no man, particularly to a Saxon. It is time to strike the death blow."

Guthrum liked the sound of those arrogant words, for he had himself spoken similar ones many times, but he wasn't a fool, even though the words did stir his blood. Aye, but his blood was thinner now, much thinner. "Leave me to think about it, Aslak. 'Tis a risk we would take. Alfred isn't like the other petty little lordlings. Nay, he is a man and a fighter. Let me think about it."

"Someday, sire, we will hold all of England. Do you not want to be the man to lay the final claim? The man to hold all in the palm of his hand?"

The king laughed as he looked down at his gnarled hands. "Ah, Egill, you bring the wine."

Aslak said abruptly, "The boy looks familiar. His features touch a chord in my memory."

Guthrum agreed. "Aye, the boy looks familiar to me as well." He crooked his finger. "Egill, come here, lad. Have you a father still living?"

Egill didn't know what to say. The moment had finally come, and he stood stupid and stiff as a rune marker. Did the king hold Orm in high regard? It would seem that he did from what Egill had observed going on between the two men. The king thought he looked familiar. Did he know Magnus Haraldsson? Did he hold him in favor? Would Orm see that he and Lotti were killed if he spoke the truth? Egill looked toward Lotti. By Thor, she was his responsibility, and if she were harmed, he would never forgive himself. He had nearly lost her once. He wouldn't lose her again, ever. He shook his head even as he said, "Nay, sire, my father is dead."

King Guthrum had already turned away. Egill's words had fallen on departed ears. Egill sighed silently, wondering if he were a fool.

Both men drank their wine from finely wrought glass goblets. Guthrum said after a moment, "You take your notion of a surprise attack on Chippenham itself from me, Aslak. Aye, and that pleases me. We did it before and brought them bloody death. Why not again? They've had time to replenish all their goods and ready new plunder for us. Let me ponder this."

"Wait not too long, sire."

"Nay, I shan't. Ah, here is Cecilia."

Aslak grunted even as he stared at her with such ferocious lust that even Egill recognized it for what it was.

Egill looked at Lotti, hopeful that she hadn't recognized anything. She was smiling at him and he moved toward her. Suddenly, without warning, one of the king's stewards appeared. Behind him waited a young woman with white-blond hair, a young woman who was Ingunn, his aunt, his father's sister.

Lotti saw her and made a frightened moan.

27

The morning was bright; the North Sea waters were calm and smooth. The thick wadmal sail flattened, then puffed out with a loud snap in the erratic westerly breeze. Zarabeth brushed her hair from her face and shaded her eyes against the glare and the slick droplets of salt water. She fancied she could see York in the far distance, but as they drew nearer, it was in truth a cloud bank, gray and billowing thick and deep, stretching across the horizon. The *Sea Wind* moved smoothly forward, closer and closer to York, trailed by seabirds hopeful for food scraps.

A gull swooped down onto the railing, ruffled its feathers, and squawked loudly, but Zarabeth paid it no attention. She was seeing Ragnar standing at the head of all Malek's people, their line stretching from the long wooden dock up the winding narrow trail to the gates of the palisade itself. She could nearly smell the raw new lumber, sweet and moist, in the morning air. All Malek's people were waving at them, shouting advice and good wishes. Ragnar stood silent, nearly whole again, his left arm still in a loose sling, having accepted the protection of Malek in Magnus' absence. It was Eldrid who would oversee the work in the longhouse, though she'd carped and complained that she was too old, too weak, for such responsibility, to which Magnus had said, "Nonsense, Aunt. You are wise and just. Rule my home and be in readiness for our return."

They were going to find Egill and Lotti, alive and healthy, Zarabeth was certain of it. As for her stubborn, overly protective husband, Magnus would accustom himself to her presence. He would stop scowling at her and ignoring her. He had agreed, finally, to her accompanying him, for in the end she'd given him no choice.

She had looked him straight in the eye on that final evening before he had announced departure and sworn that she would leave Malek in his absence and find her way to York on her own.

He'd ranted and cursed and thrown two wooden bowls, stomped around the palisade grounds, even threatened to lock her up. Finally he'd tried to enlist his mother's help, for she'd been visiting during those last days, but she, to his utter astonishment, had taken Zarabeth's side. "It is her right," Helgi had said, lightly stroking her callused palm over her son's cheek. "Understand, my son. Lotti is her sister and she must see the child and touch her and bring her home herself. It wouldn't be right for you to deny her this. She is a Viking woman now, Magnus."

He'd been left with nothing to say, though angry words and commands and threats had choked in his throat, and finally he'd bellowed, "But she's with child!" to which both women merely frowned at him with tolerant scorn.

Now they had nearly reached their journey's end. Only another half-day, she'd heard Tostig say. Perhaps a day, depending on the wind and its constancy. Zarabeth felt Magnus beside her; then after a brief moment his arms went around her and he pulled her back against his chest.

"Soon," he said, and hugged her more tightly against him. "Are you feeling well?"

"I feel wonderful."

"I've decided to stop ignoring you. It does no good except to make me lonely and gain me condemning looks from the men. I'm tired of pretending you're not with me, Zarabeth. It does me no good, after all."

She turned and smiled at him. "Nay, it doesn't, and I'm glad you want to see me again. I've missed you, husband, missed the touch of your fingers on my lips, and, aye, the fullness of you inside me."

Magnus leaned down and lightly kissed her mouth. When he straightened, he studied her face intently. "Listen to me, Zarabeth. Despite all we think we know, despite all we want and expect, we cannot be certain if either Egill or Lotti is alive. Orm could have lied. He is a master when it comes to amusing himself at another's expense. Aye, tormenting others ranks very high with him. We must be prepared to face whatever comes, but we will face it together."

"They're alive."

"Even with the dream, I know it would be foolish of me to claim it for a fact."

"They're alive."

He merely hugged her again, but said nothing more. He was nearly as certain as she was that Egill and Lotti lived, but he feared to say the words, feared somehow that fate would turn against him were he to pretend to that knowledge.

Ingunn stood before Egill in the corner of the garden, uncertain what to do. The king's mistress, his niece Cecilia, had shrugged and left them alone. "I do not understand you," Ingunn said, so irritated with him that she wanted to strike him. "I have come here to save you, and you refuse to leave this pathetic little girl!"

"Where is Orm Ottarsson? Does he know you are here? Does he know what you're about?"

Ingunn eyed her nephew. The boy had changed. His voice sounded just like Magnus'—sharp and imperious, as if he were used to giving orders and she, as a woman, was to obey them. She was angry. She was saving him—by Thor, she'd sold her most valued brooch to get the coin—and yet he was acting like she wasn't to be trusted, and she was of his flesh! "It isn't important," she said. "You will come with me now and I will see that you go home to Malek."

"It is important," Egill said. "Orm Ottarsson stole both Lotti and me. We were barely alive. I feared Lotti would die at any moment, for there was so much water in her chest and she couldn't stop vomiting it up. But he didn't care, not until he realized how he could use us. He brought us here to York and used us as a bribe to the king for the farmland he wanted. He was pleased with what he had done. If you bring me back to him, he will be very angry."

"Nay, he won't. Besides, you won't see him."

"He hates my father. I heard him talking about how he would see my father pay for all his pride and his arrogance, that he would make him regret that he had married my mother. He bragged how he would steal Zarabeth as well, and use her as he wished. He boasted he could plant a babe in her womb and then he would return her to my father. He hates all of us except for you. I don't understand that."

"What Orm feels for your father has nothing to do with me. He loves me. I am soon to be his wife. There's nothing more for you to understand. Come now, we must leave. I have a vessel waiting for you."

Egill planted his legs wide apart, his fists on his hips. He smiled at his aunt. "I have already told you, I won't go anywhere without Lotti. Buy her as well and we will both leave here."

"That cursed idiot child! She is naught but a pathetic scrap, a worthless slave. You didn't like her, you never liked her! She stole your father's affections. She can't do anything save make those awful mewling noises. You will come with me now, Egill. Forget her."

She grabbed his arm, but the boy merely stared at her, not moving. She shook him, but he held his place. He'd gotten stronger. He was no longer a little boy. Her breath hissed out when she saw the scorn in his eyes, his father's eyes, and they were cold and unforgiving.

"You betrayed my father, didn't you? You probably betrayed Zarabeth as well. You tormented her and abused her with that whip, and she had never done anything to hurt you. Is she here? Did Orm capture her as he vowed to do?"

Ingunn stepped away from him. "No, you stupid boy! That bitch is safe as can be at Malek. Malek is now hers! She is wedded to your father! How do you like that—she is now your *mother*! By all the gods, she won!" Ingunn rubbed her palm over her forehead. "I was a witless fool to come here, risking my own life to save you. You ungrateful whelp, if he knew I was here, he would kill me!"

"At least I am not a traitor. If I had to die, I would not go to my death with shame or guilt heavy on my soul."

"You little prig!" She slapped him hard. Egill's head snapped back on his neck, but he held his place. He made no move against her. He planted his feet more firmly. He stared at her with contempt.

"Damn you, you're free. I paid the king a lot of silver for you. It matters not to me whether you leave or not. I have tried to do my duty by you." She whirled about, only to pause and turn slowly to face him once more. "Listen to me, boy. You know nothing, do you understand me? I was your father's steward, his helpmeet, the one he could depend upon to take care of Malek. It was my farmstead as much as it was his! I was more than a wife could be, for I am flesh of his flesh. I oversaw everything at Malek, even his women, and yet he threw me away for that filthy whore. Ah, and there is that whore's sister, that squalid little idiot! See how she cowers behind you, just as her slut sister cowered behind Magnus, telling him lies about me! Aye, and complaining that I had hurt her, mistreated her. All lies, everything she said was a lie. Stay with her sister, Egill, I care not!" She took an unmeasured step toward Lotti, her hand raised.

"Don't," Egill said. "Don't touch her, Aunt, or I will make you pay for it. I am no longer a child. My father would want me to protect one who is weaker than I. Lotti is not only in my care, she is also mine."

Ingunn stared at the boy. He meant it. He would very likely attack her, she who had cared for him after Dalla had died, she who had treated him like her own child. Suddenly it was too much. Tears came to her eyes and she sobbed. She turned on her heel and left the manor house, only to stop abruptly, unable to go on, though she wanted to. By Thor, would it never end? She paused yet again, furious with the boy, but she knew what she had to do, aye, she knew. She had no choice.

King Guthrum rubbed his fingers over the richly carved oak post of his chair and stared at Magnus Haraldsson. He'd agreed immediately to see the man. He liked him and trusted him, as far as he'd trust any man, and he was infinitely curious as to what he wanted.

"So," he said slowly, his eyes on his fingers tracing over the elaborate carvings, "the boy is your get. I thought he looked familiar, as did Aslak. Aye, he has the look of you. His aunt bought him back from me and took him away. 'Twas yesterday she came. I assume he is gone now."

"And a little girl? Her name is Lotti."

"Aye, I recall the little one. The woman didn't want her, though even my dear Cecilia knew she and the boy were inseparable. It is almost as if they acted as one. I assume she is still with my, er, niece Cecilia."

Guthrum heard Zarabeth's sharp intake of breath and turned to her.

"I recognize you now. You are the woman Magnus saved some months ago, the woman we believed had poisoned Olav the Vain. It is odd, aye, very odd indeed."

"What do you mean, sire? And no, I did not poison my husband."

"Aye, all know now that you were innocent of his murder. It was Toki, wife of Keith, Olav's son, who killed him. She is dead now." He rubbed his hands together, obviously pleased at the solution.

Magnus stared hard at the king, wondering at the vagaries of fate. If he hadn't returned, Zarabeth would have been put to death for the crime and everyone would have been pleased and relieved, certain that justice had been meted out. Now Toki had been shown guilty and she was dead. By the gods, it was more than a man could explain to himself.

Zarabeth echoed some of his thoughts, her voice disbelieving. "Dead? Toki has confessed to what she did?"

King Guthrum shook his head. "Nay, 'twas her husband who told the council that it was she and not you who had killed his father. He said she confessed it to him when she was drunk. He beat her to death for it."

Zarabeth moved closer to Magnus. He felt the quiver of her flesh, the withdrawal of her being from the coldness of the king's announcement.

"Aye, Keith said she was a vicious shrew, filled with envy and malice. He said she deserved to die by his hand, for as her husband he was in part responsible for the evil of her act." Guthrum nodded wisely, his countenance certain and benign. "I agreed with him, as did the York council. He prospers now and is gaining stature. He looks more like his father by the day. He begins to strut about wearing silver and gold armlets and many rings, and he wears only the finest clothes. He has taken a new wife, a lovely girl of fourteen who will bear him many sons. He has given me several gifts."

Fate, Magnus thought again. Its workings eluded him, as they did all men. He took Zarabeth's hand and squeezed her fingers as the king continued, his look one of a ruler endeavoring to be just. "I had forgot that Olav the Vain had said you were to receive all that he owned were he to die. Since you were innocent of his death, you should be recompensed."

"Aye, I believe it just, sire," she said. She looked up at her husband and smiled. "I should like back the coin Magnus paid to Keith in danegeld for his father's death."

"It will be done."

"Sire, we wish to fetch my son and Zarabeth's sister. If my sister, Ingunn, took the boy away, then I must also know where to find Orm Ottarsson, for she is with him."

The king said nothing for many moments. Then finally he said, "If the little girl is still with my niece, why, I will give her to you, for Ingunn Haraldsson paid me much for the boy. Go, then, Orm Ottarsson lives by the River Thurlow, on the north side. He has named his farmstead Skelder, and it is three hectares in size. He is a good subject, a man who will bring me strength and coin."

The king gave Magnus a deliberate stare, but Magnus merely nodded and smiled. His voice was bland. "Orm has always been good at many things, sire. My wife and I thank you for your kindness and your generosity. We will remain loyal to you, as always."

Magnus stared at his huge countryman, the master of the vessel *Water Path*. Grim Audunsson was rough and crude and the strongest man Magnus had ever wrestled with. He'd lost to him three times to date. Grim was also wily and greedy, and blessed, in his view, with little conscience. Magnus watched him spit and shake his shaggy golden head. They stood on the dock at the harbor, beside the *Water Path*, the smell of fish strong in their nostrils, the harbor wind sharp in their faces.

"Aye, Orm was here and he was as mad as the white death. He didn't try to hide it from me. He used to hide his anger years ago, or perhaps he didn't have it when he was younger, but he doesn't bother to hide anything now. A berserker, Magnus, that's what he seems now. His eyes were black with excitement, his hands fisting and twisting, ready to kill anything he could catch. I can easily see him clothed in naught but a bearskin, whipping himself into a frenzy before he kills without fear, without conscience. He is not an easy man now, Magnus. Nay, he is more dangerous than a berserker, for his rages come on viciously with a simple taunt, a smile, even a jest. Aye, he is as unpredictable as a Frenchman's moods, and he would speak so calmly whilst he cut your throat. Aye, I gave him the woman and the children. What else could I do?" Grim shook his head and spit into the water. "I wonder if he'd kill the woman. He looked ready to, I'll tell you."

"The woman is my sister, Ingunn. The children are mine. Orm took them all, stole them from me, and set fire to my farmstead."

Grim shrugged, but his eyes narrowed. "I am sorry, but again, what could I have done?"

"You could have killed him yourself. You are the strongest man I know." He looked at the flexing muscles in Grim's arms. "Does age sap you, Grim?"

Grim gave him a huge smile, showing a large gap between his front teeth. "I could have snapped his neck with my hand, 'tis true. But he paid me, Magnus, paid me ten silver pieces. The woman had already given me silver pieces to take the boy back to Malek, so I am now rich enough to buy my wife a new brooch. She's a lively little creature. I stole her from a village in the Rhineland. She ran from me but I caught her about the waist and flung her over my shoulder. I married her six weeks ago. She has fine black hair, such a color as I've never before seen, and the blackest eyes you can imagine, and that sweet woman's nest between her thighs, well . . . I was thinking about that jeweler on Coppergate, Old Gunliek is his name. What do you think, Magnus?"

"I think I should kill you."

Grim laughed, an uncertain laugh but one that conveyed the message that he could laugh and escape punishment. Magnus knew that Grim had tightened his body, had prepared himself for action. He wasn't a fool. Whatever Grim was, he would remain. It wasn't up to Magnus to make him sorry. He felt Zarabeth's hand lightly touch his back. He drew upon what little control he had left. Brawling with Grim Audunsson would gain him naught, Zarabeth was right about that. Besides, Magnus thought, his lips twisting, he just might end up with his face smashed or a broken arm, which wouldn't do him any good at all. He could imagine Zarabeth's reaction to that.

"Did Orm tell you he was returning to his farmstead?"

"Aye. He said he had preparations to make at

Skelder. He said he was expecting a visitor and he wanted to ensure his visitor had a proper welcome."

Magnus nodded, then turned to leave. He said over his shoulder, "I shouldn't use old Gunliek. He cheats on the gold weights. Go to Ingolf on Micklegate."

He led Zarabeth from the harbor.

"Orm knows we are here. He knows you will come."

"Aye, he knows." He hugged her close. "We must move carefully now, Zarabeth. Everything depends on how we proceed now."

"If only Ingunn had left Egill and Lotti alone! If only she hadn't interfered! We would have them with us now, safe and sound."

"It would seem my sister at last realized what she had done. She was trying to save them, even Lotti. And herself, it would seem." He looked at his wife straight and said, "All that you say is true. However, we still wouldn't have Orm. And I will have him, Zarabeth."

Ingunn couldn't move. She'd tried, two times now she'd tried to move, but the pain had been so great she'd nearly lost consciousness again. She lay huddled on the earthen floor, the cold seeping through the thin material of her gown, her bruised flesh rippling with agony, her cheek pressed into the dirt. She knew several ribs were broken, as well as her left arm. She was thankful she couldn't see her face, for he'd struck her with his fist repeatedly. She'd tasted blood and her own tears on her mouth.

And Egill had tried to protect her. By Thor, he was just like his father.

She whimpered softly. Everything she had done had been wrong. She was weak and spiteful and blind, and now she would die alone, locked away in this filthy hut, and Egill would die as well. Or Orm would sell him again as a slave, both him and Lotti.

Ah, Lotti. She'd seen how much the boy loved the little girl, how he had shielded her, shared everything with her, his impressions, his thoughts, no matter how private, no matter how frank. At times Ingunn had thought them nearly as one, so closely attuned to each other were they. And she'd seen herself then, suddenly and without warning, seen herself hating the child because she was of Zarabeth's flesh and she'd hated Zarabeth and had wanted to hurt anything that was part of her. And that was why she'd gone back into the manor house and taken both children to Grim's vessel. She'd had to make amends. She'd had to do something right, something to redeem herself.

Orm had been there, waiting for her. She realized she hadn't really been surprised that he had been there, standing on the dock, his legs spread, staring at her, his eyes cold and black and dead. She couldn't even shudder with the memory of it without the pain roiling through her, making bile come into her throat, choking her. He hadn't touched her until they'd returned to the Thurlow River and Skelder, the name he'd given to his new farmstead, the one he'd stolen from the Saxon family, with King Guthrum's blessing.

Failure tasted vile. She tried again to rise, but when she tried to balance herself on her elbow, her arm collapsed and she fell hard again to the packed earth.

She couldn't die. She couldn't leave Egill in Orm's power. Slowly, very slowly, she moved her left arm.

Inside the longhouse, Orm brooded, his chin balanced on his palm. The house was filling with rancid smoke, for the hole in the roof was nearly clogged. Saxon pigs! They'd accepted this fault, not even considering fixing it? There was no bathhouse either, and he'd put the slaves to work immediately to building one. He turned his head to look at the boy and the little girl. They sat together in a corner, the boy speaking softly to the girl. There were others surrounding them, but the pair seemed oblivious of them.

Magnus' get! Ah, it tasted good, this victory over his enemy. He'd been a fool to sell the children to Guthrum. The man had treated them too finely, not showing them what it was to be a slave, another's property, alive at another's whim. He thought briefly of Cecilia, the king's mistress, and smiled. She would enjoy a young man in her bed. Perhaps he would oblige her. He'd found her silly and charming, and her body wasn't displeasing to him. Nor did he now have to concern himself with Ingunn, the faithless bitch.

"Egill! Come here!"

The men and women in the longhouse went silent for a moment with the sound of his voice. The boy was still, raising his eyes. He stared across the room at Orm. Slowly he rose, patting Lotti's shoulder, trying to silently calm her, for her eyes were large and frightened.

"Now, or you'll taste the whip!"

The men and women looked furtively at the boy. They resumed their duties, afraid for the new master to see them doing nothing.

Egill stopped in front of Orm, standing straight and silent, waiting.

Orm wondered if he should simply beat the boy to death. Instead he said, "I have decided to sell you to the Saxons in King Alfred's Wessex. What do you think of that?"

"Will you send Lotti home to Malek?"

Orm laughed. "Perhaps I will."

Egill felt a leap of hope, then a squeezing of a fist around his heart. Orm was mad. Nothing he said could be believed. He would kill Lotti before he would ever free her.

He still saw Orm beating Ingunn, his fists hammering her face. The man was without mercy, without conscience.

"Aye, but then again, perhaps I won't. Your father should come soon, boy. Then we will see. Don't look so surprised. I left him messages. He isn't stupid. He will know and he will follow. And that strip of material from the little girl's gown. Aye, I left that for Zarabeth so she would know. I wish I could have seen her face. She has a very expressive face, one that gives away all her feelings and thoughts. I do wonder if she cried with hope.

"I have wanted Magnus for a very long time now. For a very long time I've wanted to kill him slowly, wanted to hear him scream with pain, beg me to release him from his pathetic life, just like that bitch sister of his did. I wonder if she still clings to life. Perhaps I should go and see. If she does, perhaps she needs another lesson in obedience."

"Why do you hate my father? He has never done anything to you. Surely it isn't because my grandfather judged him to be the better husband for my mother."

Orm raised his arm, then slowly lowered it again. The boy wasn't being impertinent. Orm pondered the question, his brow furrowing. "Did I say I hated Magnus? Nay, I merely want to kill him because of what he is, how he thinks, how he behaves. He has annoyed me for a long time now, this just and proud sire of yours, boy. As for your mother, Dalla, she was silly and vain, but I had selected her. It wasn't right that I not have her. It wasn't right that Magnus be the one to win. I don't like defeat, boy. I won't accept it."

Egill remained silent now. Orm Ottarsson was a frightening man. There was no way to reason with him that Egill could see. No, the only thing to do was to escape. He had to warn his father. He had to save

Lotti. He felt very old for his eight years, and very small. But he had to try.

Orm rose then, towering over Egill. The boy didn't back away or cower. He would bring the boy to heel, but not now. There was time for him to do just as he wished.

"I believe I will see if your aunt still whines and clings to life."

28

Ingunn knew he was coming. Any moment now he would appear in the doorway of the hut and he would look inside, his eyes accustoming themselves to the darkness, and then he would see her. He would grin, for she wouldn't be able to hide her pain from him. She wouldn't be able to get away from him, and he would know it and enjoy it.

He would hit her again and he would laugh, that or he would remain serenely silent, his eyes flat and calm, and he would continue to strike her until she was dead. Then he would leave her, there in the dark chill storage hut with its damp earthen floor, and he would kill the children.

Ingunn dragged herself to the rough wooden door. Slowly, gasping with the pain that each move brought her, she pulled herself up. She was panting, trying to keep the black dizziness at bay. In her hand she held a heavy farm tool, a long piece of wood, indented at the top so a man could grasp it firmly. The base was a curving iron hook for digging up rocks and turning hard soil. To grip it tightly brought shuddering pain. She didn't know how she would raise it and strike him with it, but she would, she had to. She didn't want to die.

Orm strode from the longhouse, keeping to the narrow rutted path that led to various huts that sur-

377

rounded the main structure. It was muddy from a rain from the early morning, strengthening the smell of manure and rotted flesh. He looked at the piles littering the ground. Damned pig Saxons! He had yet to clear away all their filth.

The night was still and black, with but a sliver of moon in the sky. The land was flat before it sloped gently to the banks of the Thurlow River just a hundred yards beyond. How different this alien land was from Norway, with its midnight dim light that cast shadows and hinted of mysteries, and faded slowly, finally, into warm darkness. It was too gentle, too soft, this land, but he would accustom himself to it, as would his men. All the slaves he now owned would accustom themselves to him, their new master. He'd had to flay the back of one surly fellow, a Saxon, who had spit at the ground at his feet. He was probably dead from his wounds by now.

Orm smiled. Soon Magnus should come. He was ready for him. His men were hiding along the paths to the farmstead, ready to send him word when Magnus and his men approached. Orm whistled, slapping his arms, for it was cool now. He looked down at his hands and frowned. He'd broken the flesh over his knuckles from striking Ingunn. His fingers hurt to flex them. He should have finished the job he'd started. He would finish it now. She'd betrayed him; she was of no use to him now.

He pulled the crossbar from the narrow wooden door and shoved the door inward. He stared into the darkness, adjusting his eyes. He saw nothing but the vague outlines of farm tools. He was quick of reflex, but not quick enough. He heard her breathing, heard a whoosh of air, and just as he turned, he felt pain sear through his head. Then he felt nothing.

Ingunn watched him fall to the ground. He was unconscious, not dead, curse the fates. She raised the tool to strike him again, this time with the curved iron hook, but her broken arm wouldn't stand for it. She watched helplessly as the tool slipped from her fingers. She realized her leg was broken and she stumbled, flailing her good arm frantically, then fell to her knees beside Orm. She lurched onto her side and lay there, breathing hard, trying not to lose consciousness.

It was as she lay there, next to the man who had betrayed her, that she knew what she would do. She pulled herself toward the open doorway. Just a little bit further . . . She could do it.

Orm groaned.

She closed her eyes and prayed to Freya, her goddess. A spurt of strength shot through her. She grabbed at the door grip and pulled herself to her feet.

Orm was shaking his head now. He was trying to sit up.

Quickly she heaved herself outside. She slammed the door and leaned against it, a bent old hag wearing torn rags, her right arm hanging uselessly at her side, weaving about drunkenly on one good leg. She could barely draw a breath for the pain in her chest. She knew she had to lift the crossbar into place. If she didn't, he would burst through the door and it would be over. Freya, she prayed, her lips moving, saying the name over and over. Help me.

She lifted the heavy crossbar and set it into its iron slots. She'd done it. She couldn't quite believe she'd done it. Now she needed a torch. She had no idea where Orm had placed his men. Some were surely in the longhouse, guarding Egill and Lotti. Others were doubtless spread about waiting for Magnus. There were at least a dozen small fires dotted around the longhouse, men gathered about them.

All she needed was a torch. Slowly she staggered forward, her left arm around her ribs.

A man appeared suddenly through the smoky haze of a campfire. "Hold! Who are you? What goes on here?"

Ingunn felt all strength and hope slip away from her. She saw the man, one of Orm's bullies, striding toward her. Then the man stopped suddenly, like an animal who had heard a strange sound and must place it.

Ingunn heard it then. It was Orm, shouting and banging on the hut. The man ignored her and raced toward the hut.

No, she thought, oh, no. She'd been so close, so very close. She felt tears burn her eyes. She picked up a broken branch from an elm tree and stumbled forward. No one was at the campfire; it had been only the one man. Ingunn pressed the branch into the glowing embers and watched it burst into flame, for the leaves were long dead and dry. She carried the torch forward, not slowly, not weaving, but straight and tall, marching like a soldier toward the hut. The man was there and he was heaving at the crossbar.

It didn't move.

Ingunn came up behind him and set the blazing torch to the back of his head and his tunic. He whirled around, staring at her as if she were a vision from hell itself. Then he smelled the acrid odor, realizing then that he was on fire. He screamed and ran, slapping at his head.

Ingunn heard Orm yell, "Open the door quickly, you fool! I must get the woman. By the gods, she'll pay for this! Open the door! It's just a simple block of wood! Pull it out!"

Her smile deepened. "Orm . . ."

There was dead silence.

Then his voice came, calm and soothing. "Let me out, Ingunn. You shouldn't have hit me, sweeting. I believe you cracked my head. I was coming to release you, coming to bring you to the longhouse and tend to your wounds myself. I didn't want to hurt you so badly, but I had to punish you for what you'd done. But no more now, Ingunn, no more, ever again. You will be my wife and I will love you and protect you."

"Will you truly, Orm?"

"Aye."

She heard the confidence in his voice and smiled more widely. "You would marry me tomorrow?"

"Aye, open the door now, sweeting."

"Soon, Orm, but first, you must be chilled, for the night air is crisp. It will be fall soon and then snows will come, but you won't be here then."

"Ingunn, what mean you? Come, don't speak such nonsense. Open the door, else, I'll—"

"You will what, Orm?" She set the torch to the wooden walls, but they didn't catch fire easily. She raised her arm, moaning softly with the pain of it, and touched the flame to the thatch roof. It caught immediately, and sprang up, bright orange, the heat intense, the smoke billowing upward.

She knew the instant Orm realized what she'd done. There was panic in his voice. And fear. He shouted, "Open the door, you stupid woman! By Thor, I'll make you pay for this, you bitch, I'll—"

She interrupted him gently, but firmly, her voice chiding him as if he were a heedless child. "Be not so impatient, my love. In a little while, Orm, I'll release you, but first I want to warm you. I want you to feel the same warmth you intended for Magnus and Zarabeth and all of Malek's people when you set the torches to the longhouse. I shouldn't have believed you, I shouldn't have forgiven you for burning Malek, but I did. I accepted your word that it was an accident, something you hadn't intended, something one of your men had done. I knew, of course, that you lied, but I didn't want to admit it to myself. If I had, I would have had to admit that I was a fool and naught but your dupe and a traitor to my own family.

"Do you feel the warmth yet, Orm? The thatch is burning nicely now. Soon, my love, soon now you will be so warm you will yell with it."

Ah, yes, he knew now what she had done. She smiled as she listened to him yelling and cursing her, listened as he tore at the door and the walls of the hut. She listened as he struck the door and the walls with the tool with which she'd struck him. She wondered vaguely if he could possibly free himself. She didn't think so. She moved back from the hut, for the flames were jumping outward now, and the heat was bright and intense. She saw the hut shudder, heard the low rumbling of the beams that supported the thatch on the roof.

She heard him scream as the roof crashed inward. Then there was madness.

Egill stood next to his father, his hand on his arm. He was content with the simple touch, knowing now that all was well. Lotti was on Zarabeth's lap, sleeping soundly, her fingers stuffed into her mouth.

"Ingunn is alive, but I don't know if she will regain her mind."

Magnus nodded at Tostig's words. Tostig was exhausted. He moved to a scarred wooden bench and sat down, leaning his elbows on the table. They'd killed those of Orm's men who elected to fight. They'd simply released the others, who had thrown down their axes and swords. He looked down at the wooden table and saw layers of grease and bits of old food ground into the wood, rancid and rotten. The Saxons lived like animals.

Magnus' sister was lying in a small back room, a torn and bruised woman with dull and empty eyes, her body as broken as her mind. He had hoped to see her die for all she had done. Now he wasn't so certain. He shuddered, thinking of Orm Ottarsson's death. When they'd come to the hut, Ingunn had been kneeling in front of it, the strange firelight casting madness itself onto her bruised face. She was speaking to Orm, saying soft love words, telling him that she would never leave him. They'd stood there even as his screaming had stopped.

Ingunn had looked up at Magnus and said, "Orm knew you would come. He enjoyed taunting you, 'twas a game that pleased him mightily. I am glad you're here." She had fallen silent. She'd said nothing more.

Zarabeth leaned over and kissed Lotti's forehead. Then she looked up and smiled at Egill. "You saved her. Thank the gods you were there to pull her from the water, to press the water from her body. You saved her and then you protected her with your own life. I give you all the thanks in my heart. You are a brave boy, Egill."

"She needs me," Egill said. "She grows more certain of herself with each passing day, but she still needs me. She says many things, now, Zarabeth. I feared that she would give up when Orm caught us with Aunt Ingunn at the harbor, but she didn't. She told me that we would be all right. She patted my hand. I was proud of her."

Magnus could only marvel at the man-words coming from his son's mouth. The changes the past months had brought stunned him. He supposed he had expected to find Egill just as he'd been the day he disappeared. But he hadn't. He'd found a boy who was strong and responsible and caring. Magnus rose, grabbed Egill beneath the arms, and lifted him high. Then he lowered him and hugged him until Egill protested that his ribs were crushed. Magnus eased his hold and whispered against his son's cheek, "By Thor,

I have missed you. I will guard you more carefully in the future."

Zarabeth laughed, then immediately sobered. She was looking puzzled. "How did she tell you, Egill, that you would be all right? I don't understand."

Egill showed her, speaking the words slowly, accompanying them by swift hand gestures.

Lotti stirred in Zarabeth's arms, straightened, and yawned. She smiled sleepily, then said, her voice imperious, "Egill! Come here!"

The boy grinned at his father. "She becomes more the female by the day, Father."

Magnus watched his son walk to Lotti. He watched him lightly stroke his palm over the child's face. He heard him speak softly and distinctly to her, watched him make the quick hand and finger gestures. Then, to his surprise, Lotti nodded and eased back into Zarabeth's arms. She was asleep within moments.

"Zarabeth is your mother now, Egill."

"I know. It is good."

"She carries my babe."

The boy was silent for many moments. Zarabeth realized she was holding her breath. Then he said, "That is good too. Lotti and I both want more brothers and sisters. I'm tired now, Father. We will remain here for the rest of the night?"

"Aye. Tomorrow we will return to York."

Zarabeth said with great relish, "And then we will all go home to Malek."

"Aye," Egill said. "That's what Lotti wants too."